TO KILL A COPPER KING

**Center Point
Large Print**

Also by Stan Lynde
and available from Center Point Large Print:

Marshal of Medicine Lodge
Summer Snow
Vendetta Canyon

TO KILL A COPPER KING

A Merlin Fanshaw Western Mystery

STAN LYNDE

CENTER POINT PUBLISHING
THORNDIKE, MAINE

This Center Point Large Print edition
is published in the year 2011 by arrangement with
Kleinworks Agency.

The text of this Large Print edition is unabridged.
In other aspects, this book may vary
from the original edition.
Printed in the United States of America
on permanent paper.
Set in 16-point Times New Roman type.

ISBN: 978-1-60285-990-6

Library of Congress Cataloging-in-Publication Data

Lynde, Stan, 1931–
To kill a copper king : a Merlin Fanshaw western mystery / Stan Lynde.
p. cm.
ISBN 978-1-60285-990-6 (library binding : alk. paper)
1. Fanshaw, Merlin (Fictitious character)—Fiction. 2. Montana—Fiction.
3. Large type books. I. Title.
PS3562.Y439T6 2011
813'.54—dc22

2010049313

To the people of Butte
who make it still
the richest hill

HELENA, MONTANA TERRITORY— APRIL 1888

The tall man entered the church warily, like an animal fearing a trap. He was dressed in the manner of a Victorian gentleman in frock coat, embroidered vest, silken cravat, and unpressed woolen trousers. He wore a top hat, and carried a walking stick. Closing the door behind him, he paused. He did not dip his fingers in the holy water fount. He did not remove his hat.

Before him, on each side of the carpeted aisle, straight-backed pews fell away in ordered rows, terminating at the raised floor of the chancel. A sanctuary lamp illuminated the altar. Nearby, votive candles guttered in red glass beneath a raised statue of the Blessed Mother. Silent and empty, the room seemed to slumber in the dim light.

The man held his breath, the better to listen. He heard nothing. Breathing again, he took a careful step.

Odors, faint and evocative, reached his nostrils. Oiled wood. Waxen candles. Incense. Slowly, he made his way to the front of the nave and turned left, to the Mary side and the pulpit. He did not genuflect as he passed the altar.

7

A small, enclosed booth constructed of richly carved wood stood against the church's north wall. The man approached the structure and opened its door. Entering the compartment, he knelt and clasped his hands before him. Darkness was nearly total. Turning his face toward the latticed grill that separated him from the adjacent compartment, he spoke.

"Charon? Are you . . . Charon?"

"Yes," came the reply. The voice was cynical, mocking. "Bless you, my son."

"I'm new to this," said the tall man. "What do I do now?"

"You brought the money?" The voice was matter-of-fact, casual.

"The tall man swallowed. "Five thousand, in bank notes. I understand that is your fee."

"No," said the voice. "My fee is ten thousand. Half now, the rest when the job is done."

"That is not acceptable. My employer won't pay . . ."

The voice turned hard. "Don't waste my time. Your employer is one of the richest men in the territory. He is accustomed to the best. That is why you sent for me."

The tall man's fingers trembled as he took the envelope from the inside pocket of his coat. "All right," he said. Sliding back the grill, he passed the packet through the opening. "There's five thousand here."

"And five thousand more after," the voice replied. *"I want to hear you say it."*

"Yes, yes. The other five when the job is done."

"Good. Tell me again, so there are no misunderstandings. What is the job?"

"You . . . you are to kill a man. In Butte City."

"Oh? And what man is that?"

"You are to kill . . . Marcus Daly!"

ONE

LAST CHANCE GULCH

When I caught up with Bobby Lee Duckworth back in May of 1888 he was holed up in a wolfer's cabin east of Fort Benton, and he was ragged as a scarecrow and poor as Job's turkey. I knocked on the cabin door and stepped to one side, just in case. "Who's there?" asked a voice from within.

"Merlin Fanshaw, U.S. deputy marshal," I replied. "I'm takin' you in, Bobby Lee."

Bobby Lee opened the cabin's door a crack. His eyes were sad as a basset hound's. "Yes," he sniffed. "I expect you are."

He swung the door open wide, and I stepped inside.

Bobby Lee handed me his rusted old cap and ball revolver, butt first. If the weapon had ever been cleaned a man couldn't tell.

"That horse I stole ran off and left me afoot,"

Bobby Lee complained. "I ran out of grub a week ago. I was livin' on prairie dogs and rabbits until I shot up all my powder and ball. Then I tried catchin' frogs, but I fell into the durned Missouri and the current carried off one of my boots. I ain't been havin' a real good time here, deputy."

"Well, you know what they say, Bobby Lee. Crime does not pay."

"It sure as hell don't seem to," he agreed.

The trip to Great Falls took two days, Bobby Lee and me taking turns riding my buckskin and walking. Truth is I wound up doing more walking than Bobby Lee, but then I had two boots and he had only one. By the time I turned him in at the Cascade County Jail I was glad to get shut of my hard-luck prisoner.

"How much time you reckon the judge will give me?" Bobby Lee asked.

"Sheriff tells me that horse you stole made it back to its owner. I don't expect you'll get much more than thirty days."

"Do me a favor, deputy. Tell the judge I'm a hard case. Maybe he'll give me *sixty* days. I'm partial to the food here at the jailhouse."

"Tell you what," I said. "I'll just say you're incorrigible, and let the chips fall where they may."

Back in the sheriff's office, I signed the paperwork that transferred Bobby Lee's custody to the county. "Get the poor devil some shoes," I said. "He lost one of his boots in the Big Muddy."

The sheriff shrugged. "The way of the transgressor is hard," he said. "I don't expect he'll be walkin' much for a while anyway."

Reaching inside one of the pigeon holes in his roll-top desk, the sheriff withdrew a folded sheet of paper. "Telegram came for you yesterday," he said. "It's from your boss, over in Helena."

I unfolded the telegram and read it. The message was brief. "Meet me soonest my office. Take the train."

My boss, Chance Ridgeway, was U.S. marshal for the territory. I knew he maintained an office at the Goodkind Block at Helena, but I had never had reason to visit him there. Truth is I'd never been to Helena at all, although I had heard a good deal about it.

Helena was a town in a hurry. Born in July of 1864 when prospectors struck gold at Last Chance Gulch, Helena and I had something in common. We were both twenty-four years old in that year of 1888. The town had grown from a rough mining camp to a city of commercial buildings and mansions, and the capital of Montana Territory. Now, some fifteen thousand souls made their home there, including fifty millionaires. The town had come a long way since 1864.

For most of her early years, Helena was served by freight teams and stagecoaches out of Fort

Benton over the Mullan Road. Then, in 1883, the Northern Pacific Railroad reached the city, followed in 1887 by the Montana Central. "Take the train," Ridgeway's telegram had read. I left my horse and saddle at a Great Falls stable, treated myself to a shave and haircut at the barber's, and bought a ticket for Helena.

I was waiting with my valise on the platform when the train pulled in. I heard the long wail of a steam whistle, and then a 2-6-0 Mogul locomotive rolled in, pulling a baggage car and three passenger cars. The big engine braked to a stop, its brass bell clanging and the smoke from its stack billowing up into the clear afternoon sky.

Back beyond the tender and baggage car, the conductor swung down and set out his iron step. Passengers descended and hurried away with their bags. Outbound travelers clambered aboard to take their place. I followed them, greeting the conductor with a grin. "Good day for a train ride," I said.

"It's *always* a good day to ride *my* train," he replied.

Once on board, I made my way through the cars until I entered the day coach behind the baggage car. I chose a seat by a window, stowed my saddlebags and valise in the overhead rack, and sat down. Only four other people occupied the car. A young couple sat together near the front of the coach, with eyes only for each other. I figured them for newlyweds on their wedding trip.

For just a moment, seeing the young couple reminded me of my longtime lady friend, Pandora Pretty Hawk, and I felt a pang of regret. Pandora and I had known each other since our first days at school, and I came to believe we would someday be married. Now Pandora was married, all right, but not to me. She grew tired of waiting and worrying during my long absences, and married another. She was now Mrs. Johnny Peters of Dry Creek, Montana, and was happy, by all accounts. I reckon Johnny was happy, too. Well, I thought, two out of three isn't bad.

Back at the rear of the car, a whiskey drummer sat alone, his sample case on the seat beside him. And facing me, just across the aisle, a hard-eyed cardsharp in a business suit played solitaire atop his Gladstone bag, cheating nobody but himself for a change.

I smiled. Chance Ridgeway, my boss, would say *any* man who cheats at cards also cheats himself. Ridgeway had no tolerance for evildoers. He once told a frightened young pickpocket, "I am in the *justice* business, son. You must look *elsewhere* for pity."

I looked at the cardsharp. His eyes were a peculiar greenish shade, and when they met mine, he quickly looked away. As I watched, he played the jack of hearts on the queen of diamonds and went on to run the game. He smiled, apparently pleased with himself. I thought about telling him of his mistake until I realized two things. First, playing the red jack on the red queen was *deliberate* on his part. And second, whether or not the man cheated at solitaire was none of my business. I looked out the window and thought about the ways in which we all deceive ourselves.

Couplings jerked. The train pulled out of the station, wheels clicking faster on the rails as the engine built up steam. Minutes later, we swung around the falls of the river and headed south. The door to the coach opened, letting in the noise and the rush of our passage. The conductor stepped inside. Closing the door, he made his way through the car like a sailor walking a swaying deck. "Tickets, please," he said. "Have your tickets ready!"

When he reached my seat, I handed him my ticket. He punched it and stuck it in a slot next to the window. "How long 'til Helena, Captain?" I asked. The conductor consulted his watch. "Four hours, give or take," he said, "I expect we'll get there on the advertised."

We raced across a broad plain. Mountain ranges to the east and southwest rose cool in the distance. The train dropped into a rocky defile, cars swaying as we followed a twisting course along the river. On the hilltops, rock formations thrust up from the crests like the bones of some ancient monster. The defile narrowed, became a canyon. We swept through thick stands of fir and spruce. Willows grew tender green along the banks.

Sudden darkness marked our entry into a tunnel, followed by blinking sunlight as we passed out again into brightness. The canyon deepened, narrowed. Off to our right, a fast-flowing stream rested briefly in quiet pools and dashed away again.

I was enjoying the scenery, but it seemed I was the only one. Now the cardsharp was dealing poker hands atop his suitcase, calculating odds with pencil and paper. The whiskey drummer sat slumped in his seat, sound asleep. And the newlyweds still appeared to have no interest in anything but each other, which was a good thing, I suppose.

The sun was low in the sky by the time we left the canyon. The train dashed through rolling hills and broke out into a broad and sunlit valley. In the distance, the city of Helena lay nestled in a narrow gulch against the flank of a mountain and spilled out into the valley itself. Again, I heard the single, long wail of the train's whistle, and the squeal of brakes as wheels locked against the rails. A second later, the conductor made it official. "Helena!" he said. "Next stop, Helena!"

When I stepped off the train, I saw that the city was still more than a mile away. The sun sank behind the mountains, and lights began to appear in the windows of houses and commercial buildings. Delivery men off-loaded freight from the baggage car, and passengers from the train were greeted and escorted to waiting carriages. I looked around, thinking Ridgeway might have come to meet me, but he had not.

I turned back to the conductor. "Say, pardner," I said. "I'm new to Helena. How does a man find the Goodkind Block?"

The conductor pointed. "Take the streetcar, cowboy," he said. "The Goodkind Block is downtown, corner of Sixth and Main."

I looked where he was pointing. A buff-colored trolley, drawn by a chestnut team, waited beside the station. People were already climbing aboard.

"Much obliged," I said, turning toward the trolley. Over in the city, still more lights appeared. "The town sure seems to be lit up this evenin'."

"*Electric* lights," said the conductor. "First town in the territory to have 'em. Just turn a switch, and banish the darkness. Modern times have come to Montana."

"They sure have," I said. I turned and stepped up into the trolley, as if I used street cars and electric lights all the time. I looked confident, or hoped I did, but it was all a bluff. The truth is I was nervous as a blind cat at a dog show.

• • •

The trip downtown was a real eye-opener. Buildings of brick and stone raised four and five stories high. Streetcar tracks ran along brick-paved streets. Power poles cluttered the view, some holding as many as fourteen crossbars. Top buggies and surreys shared the boulevards with beer wagons and drays. Men in dress suits and women in silks strolled together under the streetlights. Music drifted out of saloons and dance halls, drawing laborers and sporting men inside.

I got off the trolley at Bridge Street and walked over to Sixth and Main. With one last look at the bright lights and the crowds, I opened the front door of the Goodkind Block and stepped inside. In the building's foyer, a sign at the foot of a long staircase read: U.S. MARSHAL—ONE FLIGHT UP. I took a deep breath and climbed the stairs.

Opening a door at the second-floor landing, I entered a large room furnished with desks, chairs, and file cabinets. Near the door, a fair-haired youth sat behind an oak desk. He looked up from his paperwork and smiled. "Yes?" he said. "Can I help you?"

"I sure hope so, pardner. I'm Merlin Fanshaw. Marshal Ridgeway sent for me."

The young man pushed his chair back and stood up. "Yes," he said. "You'd be the deputy from Dry Creek. I'll let the marshal know you're here."

Across the room, Ridgeway appeared in the doorway of a private office. "No need, Stebbins," he said. "I've been expectin' deputy Fanshaw. Come on in, Merlin!"

I thanked Stebbins with a nod and walked over to Ridgeway. He was smiling, and so was I. It was good to see him again.

Ridgeway never seemed to change. Now in his sixties, the old lawman was lean as a whip, and gangly as a sand hill crane. His hair and handlebar moustache were snow white, and his ice-blue eyes were clear as a boy's. He shook my hand when I entered his office and showed me to a chair.

I looked around. The marshal's office looked much as it had in Silver City. Papers, ledgers, and law books cluttered his desk. His old brass library lamp still lit his work space, although I noticed it had been converted to electricity. Chest-high filing cabinets filled the space behind his swivel chair, and a Regulator clock and a map of the Territory occupied the wall above them.

A furled American flag stood against the north wall, beside a framed portrait of Honest Abe. A second framed portrait, of the current president, Grover Cleveland, hung beside it. Navajo rugs gave color to the dark oiled wood of the floor, and a coat rack held the marshal's coat and hat.

There was an object on the south wall I hadn't seen before. It was a small wooden box with a bell on top and a black cylinder dangling from a hook beneath it. Modern times had come to Montana, all right. The marshal's new office boasted a telephone.

"It's good to see you, son," Ridgeway said. "How did you find our fair city?"

I grinned. "Nothin' to it, Chief. I just rode the train and got off when the conductor hollered 'Helena.'"

Ridgeway chuckled. "Yes," he said, "That would be one way to find it, I suppose. I guess what I'm asking is what do you *think* of the city?"

"Biggest town I ever saw. Tall buildings, streetcars, electric lights. Big doin's for a country boy."

"Yes," Ridgeway said. "As you see, I've got me a telephone now. I can speak into a mouthpiece and send my voice halfway across the nation on a wire. The West is changin', and so is keepin' the law.

"The hell raisers and the killers can't just shoot up a bank, jump on a horse, and ride off into the badlands like they used to. Nowadays, lawmen have the telegraph, the telephone, and photographs of the outlaws. It's gettin' harder all the time for a culprit to hide.

"But progress works both ways. Lawbreakers are not only adapting to the law's new tools, they're learnin' how to use 'em to commit crimes. It's a game of cat and mouse. The cat gets a new tool to catch mice, and the mice use it to bamboozle the cat."

"Keeps life interesting," I observed.

"It does that," said Ridgeway.

Ridgeway fell silent. *Now,* I thought. *Now, he'll tell me why he sent for me.*

I was wrong.

The marshal smiled. "I don't expect you've had supper," he said. "Why don't we go out to a chophouse and put on the feed bag?"

"Suits me right down to the ground," I said. "As you may recall, I never pass up a chance to eat."

Ridgeway put on the high-crowned Stetson that was his trademark, and shrugged into his overcoat. "Yes," he said. "I do recall that about you."

Outside on the street, traffic seemed to have slowed some. People were still out and about, men and women strolling along the boulevard, but it seemed to me they were fewer than before. Some of the shops were still open at that hour, all brightly lit by the new electric lights. "Can't get used to those lights," Ridgeway said. "They brighten the world, but they seem harsh to me. Maybe I'm gettin' old, but I believe I prefer gaslight, or an oil lamp."

The marshal led the way up the block to the end of the street and turned the corner. A cozy restaurant invited us inside. Soft light glowed in a large front window, and a name was painted on the glass in gold leaf and black paint: ZIMMERMAN'S. Ridgeway opened the door, and we went inside.

Round tables, covered by white cloths, filled the room. Most were occupied by couples and groups of four and more, but there were a few vacant tables near the front of the restaurant. Ridgeway took off his overcoat and hat and hung them on a coat tree near the door. I followed his lead and hung my hat next to his.

A plump, red-faced man wearing a chef's jacket and apron came out from behind a counter, beaming as he approached Ridgeway. "*Herr* Ridgeway!" he said. "*Guten abend!* Velcome to Zimmerman's!"

"Evenin', Karl," said Ridgeway. "We need a quiet table and a good supper. Can you handle that for us?"

The man called Karl nodded, but confusion was in his eyes. "*Hendl?* You vant chicken?"

"No," Ridgeway said. "No chicken. I asked if you could *handle* our *needs*."

Karl laughed. "*Ach . . . handle!* Ja, ja! I can *handle* you—Komm mit me, *bitte!*"

Guiding us to a table near the window, Karl was still chuckling as he seated us. "My English is not so very good," he said. "In Bavaria, 'hendl' means 'chicken'!"

Ridgeway smiled. "Your English is a heap better

than my German," he said. "Tell you what, Karl—bring us two orders of Wiener schnitzel and some beer. When you see us slowin' down, fetch us some strudel and coffee. Other than that, pay us no mind. We've got talkin' to do."

"Wie man hört," Karl said. "I understand. *Soon* comes der schnitzel."

Karl was back in seconds with two schooners of beer. He set them before us, nodded slightly, and disappeared in the direction of the kitchen.

Ridgeway lifted his stein and said, "Here's how."

"How," I said, and we drank.

Now, I thought. *Now he'll tell me why he sent for me.*

This time, I was right.

TWO

A MISSING WITNESS

Ridgeway drank deeply and then carefully set his beer stein back upon the table. Wiping foam from his moustache, he favored me with a thoughtful look. For a moment, the marshal was silent, as if corralling his thoughts. Then he said, "Tell me, son. How much do you know about Butte City?"

It was my turn to round up my thoughts. "A mining camp, now a city, just across the mountains from here," I said. "Started out back in the sixties with a gold strike. Gold began to play out in the seventies, and the camp nearly went belly up. Then a miner discovered the hill was rich in silver. He developed his claim, built some smelters, and the town boomed again, this time as a silver camp."

"That's right," Ridgeway said, "but that wasn't the end of it. Six years ago, an Irish miner named Marcus Daly bought a silver mine at Butte Hill called the Anaconda. As he began to develop the property, he reached the three-hundred-foot level and the silver ore suddenly played out!

"Well, that was the *bad* news. The *good* news is the ore was rich in *copper!*

"At the time, very few hard-rock miners knew anything about copper. Most believed only gold and silver were worth goin' after. The camp had no copper smelters, no miners to work a copper mine. Such copper as the country needed was already produced by native mines back in Michigan.

"I don't know for sure, but it may be that Daly took a look at the future and saw a huge, growing market for copper. Up until 1880, folks thought electricity was a passing fancy, but that notion was about to change. Back east, Edison patented his incandescent lamp and a passel of other electrical applications. All across the nation, cities and homes required copper wire. Telegraph and telephone lines needed it, too—miles and miles of it.

"Daly played his cards close to his vest. He bought up other claims on Butte Hill, and before long he controlled all that part of the mountain he figured had value. Then he brought in armies of miners, built himself a copper smelter and a town named Anaconda—named after his mine—just twenty-six miles away. At the present time, the miners are minin', the smelters are smeltin', and Marcus Daly is well on his way to bein' one of the richest men in America."

I was growing impatient with Ridgeway's history lesson. The copper bonanza in Butte and the men who helped bring it to pass were common knowledge in every town in Montana. I figured I was up on the subject, even if I didn't know every detail.

I cleared my throat. "I already know who Marcus Daly is," I said. "Leastways, I've heard about him. I understand Daly and another high roller—banker, mine owner, and merchant name of W. A. Clark—have had a major falling out. They used to be friends, but now they're rivals and full-bore enemies. Like the Good Book says: 'War is in their hearts.' "

At that point, Karl came out of the kitchen carrying a tray. He marched up to our table and placed a steaming plate of Wiener schnitzel before each of us as if he was performing a magic trick.

"*Sie bitte*, chentlemen," said he, "specialty of *der haus!*"

Ridgeway stared at the meal in feigned awe. "Mighty fine-lookin' vittles," he observed.

"Best-lookin' Wiener schnitzel I ever saw," I said. My compliment was faint praise. It was also the *first* Wiener schnitzel I ever saw.

Weiner schnitzel, it turned out, was veal, breaded and fried. Gravy and green peas shared the plate, together with buttered German noodles. As soon as it cooled off enough to eat, I dug in and commenced to put it away. Ridgeway did the same.

"All right," I said. "So there's a mountain of copper over at Butte City, and Marcus Daly and W. A. Clark are fightin' over it. What does all that have to do with us?"

Ridgeway pushed his empty plate away and leaned back in his chair. "Nothin,' maybe," he said, "and *somethin',* maybe. Marcus Daly's name came up recently in a curious kind of way.

"In Helena, the biggest landowner on Wood Street is a woman name of Josephine Hensley, although she's better known as Chicago Joe. She runs dancehalls, saloons, and a vaudeville house called The Coliseum.

"Far as I know, *this* Coliseum don't have gladiators or hold chariot races, and I don't recall hearin' about anyone feedin' Methodists to the lions, but the goin's-on at Chicago Joe's are pritnear as depraved as they were over to ancient Rome.

"Josephine has a stable of good-lookin' harlots she brought in from her old stompin' grounds in Chicago. The young ladies dance, sing, and frolic in the dancehalls, and Joe receives a commission on dances and drinks. The girls are free to make other business arrangements on their own."

"Which keeps Chicago Joe on the right side of the law," I said. "More or less."

Ridgeway nodded. "More or less. Sometimes she tells the local lawmen when a particularly notorious burglar is in the area, or when some enterprisin' safecracker hits town. Josephine don't mention any names, so she is able to walk a fine line between her clientele and the police."

"Sounds like Chicago Joe has a good business plan."

The marshal frowned. "So far," he admitted. "However, I expect she will one day get careless and step a little too far over the line. When that day comes I intend to see that the full weight of the law falls upon her like a cat on a dickey bird."

Again, Karl interrupted Ridgeway's monologue. He brought coffee and two orders of apple strudel, and picked up our dinner plates and eating tools. "Eppel strudel for the chentlemens," he announced. Then he left the bill and hurried off to attend his other customers.

Ridgeway resumed his story. "I happened to be

in the Coliseum last week," he said. Suddenly, he seemed to realize how this confession might sound. He flashed a hard glance at me. "I was there to make sure there was no law-breakin' goin' on," he said.

"Anyway, while I was there, Josephine told me a sort of strange story. Seems one of her regular customers, a gent name of Digby O'Dhoul, is sexton over at St. Elmo's Church. You know, he digs graves, stokes the furnace, rings the bell on Sundays—that sort of thing.

"Well, accordin' to Josephine, O'Dhoul is a good man, but he has this little drinkin' problem. Also, from time to time, he gets a hankerin' for female companionship. When that happens, he gen'rally goes down to Wood Street to get his needs met.

"Last week he shows up as usual, but he's nervous as a bridegroom. Josephine asks him why, and he tells her. O'Dhoul says he was takin' a nap at the church one evenin' when a stranger walks in. O'Dhoul watches the man make his way over to the confessional and step inside.

"What O'Dhoul hears next brings him out of his nap and wide awake. He hears the stranger talkin' to a man, but the man he's talkin' to isn't the priest. Instead, O'Dhoul says, he hears the stranger hire a man to commit *murder!*

"When Josephine hears this story she's dubious to say the least. O'Dhoul has been known to see and hear all manner of things while in the grip of *delirium tremens*. Josephine asks him if he's sure heard what he heard. O'Dhoul says hell yes he's sure. He says his *liver* may be in bad shape, but there's nothin' wrong with his ears."

"That is quite a tale," I said.

"There's more. O'Dhoul says he heard the stranger call the killer 'Kar-on' or 'Cha-ron' or somethin' like that. Paid him five thousand dollars in bank notes for the murder and agreed to pay five thousand more when the job is done." Ridgeway shook his head. "All that money," he said, "just to kill a man."

The marshal took a sip of his coffee and carefully placed the cup back in its saucer. Then he said, "To tell the truth, I didn't take the story all that serious. I thanked Josephine for tellin' me and went back to my office. But I couldn't stop thinkin' about it. Ten thousand dollars truly *is* a heap of cash just to pay for a killin'. I figured the victim must be a mighty important person.

"The assassin would have to be world class, too. I decided to give my new telephone a try. I called the Pinkerton Agency back in Chicago. Talked to an old friend of yours—Abigail Bannister. You remember Abigail, don't you, son?"

"Oh, yeah," I said. "I remember Abby. What about her?"

"Well," said Ridgeway, "as you may recall, Abigail is a detective for the agency. She told me there *is* a contract killer who goes by the name 'Charon.'

"She said this hired assassin takes his name from Greek myth, from Charon, the Ferryman of Hades. According to the myth, Charon is the boatman who takes newly departed souls across a river that separates the living from the dead.

"Abby went on to say this modern-day Charon is deadly as a sack of cobras and merciless as a blizzard. Nobody, she said, has a description of him."

I sat straighter in my chair. The hair on the back of my neck stood up. Ridgeway had my full attention.

"Are you sayin' you believe O'Dhoul's story?" I asked.

"No," Ridgeway said, "but I don't know enough *not* to believe it. Accordin' to O'Dhoul, the last thing he heard the stranger say was the name of the potential victim."

Ridgeway paused, for dramatic effect, I figured. I was determined to wait him out, but my curiosity got the better of me. "All right," I said. "What *was* the name?"

Ridgeway's ice-blue eyes locked onto mine. "Marcus Daly," he said.

My coffee was cold. The apple strudel lay untouched on my plate. No longer interested in food, I thought about the implications of Ridgeway's story. Digby O'Dhoul was an unlikely witness. His account of a stranger hiring an assassin inside a Helena church was a wild one. O'Dhoul was a booze fighter, according to Ridgeway. There was less than one chance in ten thousand his tale might be true. But if by some chance it *was* true, a killer was stalking one of the wealthiest and most important men in Montana.

"All right, Chief," I said. "What do you want me to do?"

"I want you to find O'Dhoul. Josephine says he hasn't been in her place since the night he told his story. Chief Sims of the city police department says O'Dhoul usually winds up in the drunk tank on a fairly regular basis, but he hasn't turned up there in weeks. And he hasn't been back at St. Elmo's. When I asked the priest where he thought his sexton might be, the good father just rolled his eyes and said, 'Heaven only knows.' Which might be true, but it ain't especially helpful."

Ridgeway paused. "There is one possible lead, but it's a thin one," he said. "When I talked to Josephine, she said one of her soiled doves is a particular favorite of O'Dhoul's. Might be worth talkin' to her. Her *nom de mattress* is Bucktooth Betty."

"*Bucktooth Betty?* Did you say Bucktooth Betty?"

"I did. Do you *know* the woman?"

"Well, no . . . that is, sort of. I did know a sporting woman of that name. Six years ago, at

Rampage. That was the year you and me met, Chief."

"I remember. You were runnin' with George Stark-weather's gang. I persuaded you to change sides."

That wasn't exactly how it happened, but I didn't feel like arguing the matter right then. "Yes, sir. Anyway, this Bucktooth Betty was one of Slippery Mayfair's whores. Good-natured girl, she was. Looked sort of like a blue-eyed beaver, with those big front teeth and all."

"Sounds like you knew her pretty well."

"Some, I guess. I didn't know her in the *biblical* sense, you understand."

Ridgeway's face was without expression. "Of course not," he said.

The marshal stood up from the table. "I expect she'll be workin' tonight," he said. "Why don't you look her up tomorrow? Find out if she has any idea where O'Dhoul might be. Most of Josephine's girls stay at the Grand, over on Bridge Street. I expect your friend Betty does, too."

"She's not really my *friend,* Chief. But yes, sir, I'll do that. I'll call on her in the mornin'."

Ridgeway paid the bill, and we stepped outside. Stars glittered above the quiet street, their brightness dimmed by the street lamps. A cold wind sighed out of the canyon and laid a chill on the evening. "There's an extra bunk up at the office," Ridgeway said. "You can sleep there tonight, if you've a mind to."

31

"Much obliged, Chief," I said. "I believe I will. I'll get an early start tomorrow."

"Not too early," Ridgeway said. "Them painted cats sleep late, I'm told."

The Grand, on Bridge Street, was a square, three-story brick structure in the very heart of Helena's Tenderloin District. When I approached its front door the next morning, the building seemed to slumber in the sunlight like a drunkard sleeping off a jag. The street was deserted, with only a discarded whiskey bottle and a couple of cigar butts on the sidewalk to hint at the previous night's debauchery.

I rang the doorbell and waited. Minutes seemed to pass, and then I heard the slow shuffle of feet from inside. The door opened a crack, and then wider. A frizzy-haired slattern in a silk wrapper appeared in the doorway, frowning at the brightness.

"Come back later," she said. "We're closed."

I tipped my hat and smiled. "I'm Merlin Fanshaw, Miss. I'm a deputy U.S. marshal, here on the law's business, not yours."

The girl's lips formed a sullen pout. Her frown deepened. "Wha'ja want?" she asked.

"I'm lookin' for a lady called Bucktooth Betty." Remembering Ridgeway's gibes, I bit my tongue. "I'm . . . an old friend of hers."

The doorkeeper stared at me through half-closed

eyes. She looked at my badge. Seconds passed. Finally, she swung the door open wide and stepped back. "I guess ya better come in then," she said.

I entered a dimly lit foyer. The smell of cheap perfume thickened the air. "Ain't no *ladies* here," the girl said, "but we got a Betty, all right. She's in the kitchen, with the others. Follow me."

We passed from the foyer into a hallway. I heard female voices, laughter. I caught the smell of coffee, and of frying bacon. Then we turned a corner and I found myself surrounded by a whole durned *blare* of strumpets!

A passel of half-naked women lounged around a big table, smoking cigarettes and drinking coffee, clipping their toenails and putting up their hair. Visions of flimsy wrappers and bare flesh flashed before me; arms and ankles and bosoms and knees, faces and lips and eyes seemed to fill the room. As for the women, they didn't seem at all startled by my sudden appearance. *I* was the one who was skittish.

Bucktooth Betty came to my rescue. "Merlin!" she squealed. "Merlin Fanshaw!"

Betty was on me like a family dog at a homecoming. She exploded out of that nest of chippies and flung her arms around me like I was her long-lost sweetheart. Before I could fend her off, Betty planted a bucktoothed kiss somewhere near my left ear and stepped back to hold me at arm's length. Her little blue eyes were shining, and she looked so sweet and comical I nearly laughed out loud. "Well, hello, Betty," I said. "You haven't changed a bit!"

It was a lie, of course. Six years had passed since I'd seen her, and Bucktooth Betty showed definite signs of wear and tear. But then maybe *I* did, too.

"Well, look at you," she said, touching my badge. "More handsome than ever, and a peace officer, too! It's good to see you, Merlin."

"You, too, Betty. I heard you were workin' for Chicago Joe."

"Yes," she said. "I have come up in the world some since Rampage."

She smiled a sly smile and lowered her eyes. "What can I do for you, darlin'?" she asked. "We ain't receivin' customers yet, but if you want to . . ."

"No," I said, faster and louder than I meant to. "I'm here on legal business. Is there somewhere we can talk?"

Betty's face assumed a serious expression. "Sure," she said. "Let's go into the parlor."

Taking me by the hand, Betty led me into a spacious room just off the hallway, furnished with overstuffed chairs and divans in the Turkish style. An upright piano stood against one wall and a faded oriental carpet covered the floor. The room smelled faintly of whiskey, cigar smoke, and that heavy perfume so favored by the girls of the night. I chose an upholstered rocker near the room's only window and sat down. Betty took a seat on the footstool, facing me, and adopted a wistful look.

"I'm lookin' for a feller," I began. "I'm told you might be able to help me find him."

Betty's expression didn't change, but her voice took on a cautious tone. "Why, who might *that* be, darlin'?"

"Feller name of Digby O'Dhoul," I said. "I understand you're a particular favorite of his."

Betty's eyes narrowed. "My stars," she said carefully. "Has Digby committed a crime? Is he wanted by the law?"

"No," I said, "nothing like that. But I think he may be in danger because of something he saw . . . something he heard."

Betty looked away, out the window. "Digby ain't a troublesome man," she said. "Truth is, he's nice . . . gentle, and sort o' sweet."

"It sure would be a shame to let somethin' bad happen to a feller like that."

For a long moment, Betty was silent. She continued to gaze out the window, as if looking for help in making her decision. Finally, she turned back to me.

"Well," she said. "He does have family over in Butte City . . . a brother name of 'Scrapper,' and a sister, as well. Digby goes over and visits them sometimes."

"You don't know what *part* of town they live in, do you?"

"He mentioned something once about an area called the 'Cabbage Patch,' but I really don't know. If you go there, look up a hack driver called Fat Jack Jones. Jack knows everybody."

I stood up. Taking Betty's hand, I helped her to her feet. "I'm much obliged to you, Betty," I said. "You've done the right thing."

She wanted to believe me, but worry was plain on her face. Her blue eyes were wide as they looked into mine. "*Have* I, Merlin?" she asked. "Have I *really?*"

Marshal Ridgeway was waiting for me in his office when I returned. "I talked to Bucktooth Betty," I said. "She says O'Dhoul has a brother and a sister in Butte City that he visits sometimes. Maybe we should check her story out."

The marshal looked thoughtful. "You believe she's tellin' the truth?"

"I do, Chief. I told her O'Dhoul could be in mortal danger if we don't find him."

Ridgeway's eyes narrowed. "That's a fact. If there *is* a hired killer out there and if he learns that O'Dhoul is talkin' about him . . ."

"Yeah," I said. "O'Dhoul could be headed for no more breakfast forever."

The marshal leaned back in his chair. "All right," he said. "Why don't you go over to Butte

36

City and see if you can locate the man? Ask him about what he heard and saw that night at St. Elmo's."

"Sure, Chief. Do we have a description of him?"

Ridgeway rummaged through the papers atop his desk and produced a small photograph, mounted on cardboard. "Better than that, son," he said. "The priest at St. Elmo's gave me this."

I took the photo from Ridgeway. A balding man with haunted eyes looked out at me from the picture. Even in the portrait, he looked nervous.

"Priest says the photograph was taken maybe two years ago," Ridgeway said. "O'Dhoul is about thirty-five years old. Stands five foot six. Has brown hair, going to gray. Eyes are blue. No scars or marks. Oh, and he's left handed."

I tucked the photo away in the pocket of my shirt. "This will help," I said, "but even if I find him, he may not want to talk. Sounds like his encounters with the law haven't been all that pleasant. They seem to have mainly involved the paddy wagon and drunk tank."

"That's true," Ridgeway said, "but he's runnin' scared now. He might welcome the law's protection. And a sympathetic ear."

Ridgeway got to his feet. He walked to the window and raised the shade. Sunlight flooded the office and painted the buildings outside. Above the sheltering mountains, the sky was clear. For a long moment, the marshal said nothing. Then he turned from the window and sat down again behind his desk. His face was troubled.

"Watch yourself over there," he said. "According to Abby, nobody knows what that hired killer looks like. If he decides *you* are a threat, you ain't likely to see him comin'."

I hope I sounded braver than I felt. "Quit tryin' to cheer me up," I said.

THREE

THE RICHEST HILL ON EARTH

Before he left the office for the day Ridgeway loaned me a book entitled *Copper Mines of the World* and suggested I settle in and learn something about the subject. I struggled with the book for most of the afternoon, but I have to confess my efforts to educate myself were mostly in vain.

I fell asleep twice, but I refused to give in. Each time I dozed off I shook myself awake to wrestle with the book again. Then, just before suppertime the words went blurry on me and I threw in the towel. The following may give you some idea of what I was up against:

"The copper minerals of the Butte ores consist chiefly of chalcocite (copper glance), bornite (peacock copper), enargite (sulpharsenide of copper), and cupriferous pyrite. Corellite (cupric

38

sulphide) occurs in considerable amount at two mines, but forms an insignificant percentage of the total output."

And then there was this passage, which, to put it in technical terms, was to me as clear as mud (wet soil): "The actual fault fissures are marked by attrition clay containing rock and mineral fragments. When indurated by infiltrating solutions, this resembles the quartz porphyry. As the interfault material contains workable ore bodies, stoping is sometimes continuous from one vein across to another."

Oh, I'll just *bet* it is, I thought.

I went out to supper at a hash house on the gulch that evening and then came back to the office and turned in early. I tried to read a chapter from the mining book but once again found its content more stupefying than edifying. Before I was able to struggle through a single page I dropped off into a sound and dreamless sleep.

I was awake well before sunup the next day. I buckled on my .44, packed my valise, and made myself a breakfast of beef jerky and warmed-over coffee. Descending the stairs, I stepped out into the morning. The streets were empty, brightened only by the circles of light beneath the street lamps. I caught the trolley at Bridge Street and set out for the Northern Pacific depot with other early risers.

Behind us, the city came awake. Delivery wagons and carts rumbled along the narrow streets. Lights flickered on in the windows of businesses and homes. Above the mountaintops, darkness left the sky as coming daylight erased the stars. Over the driver's shoulder, I watched the horses plod steadily toward the depot, striking occasional sparks with their shod hooves. Then we reached the station, the driver drew rein, and I joined the passengers who were taking the train to Butte City.

Families with children, tradesmen and merchants, big-shouldered working men and hungry-eyed drifters all crowded the platform and boarded the train. Once inside, I claimed a window seat and stowed my valise. People continued to file in, taking their places in the coach. I watched them as they passed, thinking I might see a familiar face. But I didn't find one.

The sun exploded above the eastern horizon, painting the hilltops and mountains with light. I looked out my window toward the rear of the train and saw the trainman signal the conductor that the doors of the cars were all closed. The conductor nodded, waved to the engine driver, and stepped up into our day coach. "Tickets, ladies and gentlemen," he said. "Have your tickets ready, please." The couplings tightened with a jerk, steam blasted into the sunlight, and the train began to move. I took out my pa's silver watch and checked the time. We would be in Butte City by noon.

For the first hour we rolled west across the valley toward a massive mountain range. The grade grew steeper, leaving the valley behind and below us as we climbed steadily upward. A short time later the train entered a long tunnel and passed through to the western side of the divide.

Coming out into sunlight, I saw that snow-capped peaks surrounded us; we were racing through timbered valleys and sunlit parks. I grew up around mountains. I've traveled their trails and canyons on horseback and on foot, but it seemed to me then there was no finer way to see mountains than through the window of a fast-moving train.

I thought again of Digby O'Dhoul. Fishing his photograph out of my shirt pocket, I studied it by the light that poured through the car's window. Thirty-five years old, Ridgeway said. The man looked fifty-five. His face was pale and sallow. Thin strands of hair lay lank upon his balding pate. Sunken eyes pleaded with the camera. His mouth, thin-lipped and tense, turned down at its corners. O'Dhoul seemed a timid man. He was also a drinker. Seeing his photograph, I'd have known that without being told.

O'Dhoul's face was nothing like my pa's face,

and yet memories of Pa came quickly at the sight. Pa's hair was thick, shaggy and wild. Pa's skin was brown from the sun. Pa was quick with a smile, and reckless as a Cheyenne dog soldier. Care *free,* you might say, but you'd be wrong. Pa had cares aplenty. Like O'Dhoul, Pa chose whiskey as his master, and whiskey used him hard. But whiskey held up its end of the deal; it killed Pa's pain of missing my mother. It killed the hurtful memories that wouldn't let him be. And in the end, it killed *him* when he got drunk and rode the crazy black stud he was breaking off a rimrock.

I was his son and heir. Pa left me an old Colt's revolver, a rusty Sharps rifle, his spurs, his silver watch, and his Texas saddle. He also left me memories both good and bad and considerable pain. Like the story about the rich feller who died. A stranger asks how much the man left, and the lawyer says, "All of it." Well, Pa left 'all of it' to me, but there wasn't a whole helluva lot.

I returned O'Dhoul's photograph to my pocket. Somewhere up ahead I would find the man. I would listen to his story, and maybe I would calm his fears. I was a lawman, and I cared as much about justice as anyone, but I was not Chance Ridgeway. I figured sympathy *was* my department.

The train swept through wooded slopes and open parks, past aspen groves and pine forests, and raced along a rushing stream. Mountains rose blue in the distance. Smoke from the engine drifted past the windows and cast a shadow alongside the tracks. Behind me, the conductor's voice announced our progress: "Garrison! Next stop, Garrison!"

Airbrakes locked. The train slowed, halted. A farmer and his wife got to their feet, bundles and baggage in hand, and hurried up the aisle. Through the window, Garrison was a scatter of buildings, rough hewn and temporary. Our stop was brief. Within five minutes, we were on our way again.

Croplands and hay meadows came into view. Houses and barns huddled beneath cottonwood trees along stream banks. Cattle grazed in the fields. Beside my seat, the conductor stopped, bent low, and looked out my window. "That's the Deer Lodge Valley," he said, "home of the town of Deer Lodge, and the Territorial Prison. Ever been there?"

"No," I said, "but I helped send a few bad men that way."

The conductor gave me a second look. Beneath my open coat my deputy's badge winked sunlight. "Peace officer," the conductor said. "I *thought* you had the look. No offense, deputy. Just making conversation."

"No offense taken," I said. "My first time in this part of the territory. Appears to be good livestock country."

"It is that. Conrad Kohrs ran upwards of fifty thousand cattle out of his Deer Lodge ranch, but the winter of eighty-six and seven hit him hard."

"Him and a good many others. Is Deer Lodge the biggest town in the valley?"

"It was," the conductor said, "until Daly established the town of Anaconda and built his smelter. I hear there are five thousand people living there now."

"Must be good money in copper if a man can just up and build his own town."

"You haven't seen the half of it," the conductor said. "If Daly, Clark, and the other tycoons keep on the way they have been, they're liable to rebuild *Montana*."

"Nice talking to you," the conductor said. Turning away, he started up the aisle. "Butte!" he called out, "Next stop, Butte City!"

I wasn't ready for the sight, or smells, of Butte City. Stepping down from the train, my first impression was that the city was ugly as sin. Buildings of every shape and size staggered up a rocky slope crowned by steel head frames that straddled the mine shafts. Dusty, rutted roads and rickety sidewalks wound uphill to the mines. Smoke and fire poured from smokestacks at the mills, and miners' cabins shared the slope with the gray-green tailings of the mine dumps. My eyes burned; my mouth tasted like burnt matches.

There were no trees or shrubs anywhere. What little grass there was seemed stunted and dying.

People crowded the train station. Arriving passengers were met by hackney drivers and rigs from the hotels. Freight handlers off-loaded boxes and packages. Recalling Bucktooth Betty's advice, I asked a teamster where I might find the hack driver named Fat Jack Jones.

The teamster shifted the cud of tobacco to his cheek and spat a brown stream into the street. "He's been here and gone," he said. "Took some folks uptown. But he'll be back directly."

"What does he look like?"

"Fat Jack? Well, he ain't fat, for one thing. He's lanky and lean like Abe Lincoln, with chin whiskers like Uncle Sam. Wears a buffalo coat and a black top hat. You can't miss him—ain't *nobody* looks like Fat Jack."

"Much obliged," I said, but the teamster was already walking back to his wagon. I leaned back against the depot wall and waited.

The teamster's description served me well. When Fat Jack Jones came back to the station I really *couldn't* miss him. He came driving a four-passenger rockaway behind a matched team of bay geldings, and he was smoking a cigar. I met him at the curb. "Mr. Jones?" I inquired.

"*Mister* Jones was my *daddy,*" he said. "I'm Jack Jones. Where to, sir?"

I grinned. "*Sir* was *my* daddy. I'm Merlin

Fanshaw, U.S. deputy marshal." Handing him my valise, I climbed up and took a seat beside him.

"Tell you what, Jack," I said. "I'm a stranger here in Butte, and I need someone to show me around. After that, I'll need a good hotel, and the answers to a few questions. I'm no high roller, but it's worth ten dollars to me."

"A sawbuck makes you a high roller in my book," the coachman said. "Show me."

I handed him a ten spot. "You just bought the grand tour," he said. "Hang on."

Fat Jack rattled the reins and started the team uphill. "First and foremost, there are the mines, more than three hundred of 'em, and the stamp mills and smelters out on the flat, all goin' full blast day and night. See them head frames up on the ridge?" he asked. "Miners call 'em gallows frames, or *gallus* frames. Each one serves a mine shaft. That sound you hear is the cables runnin' against the sheaves as the hoists bring up skips full of ore and dump 'em in the bins. The same hoists send the miners down, and—with any luck—bring 'em up again.

"It was Marcus Daly himself who first called this place 'The Richest Hill on Earth' and by God that's what she is. Butte is the greatest minin' camp in the world!"

Jack took a drag on his cigar and blew tobacco smoke out into the sulfurous air. "There are miners here from everywhere," he said, "from

Ireland and Wales, from Finland and Italy and Germany and France. There are old timers from the California lodes, hard-rock miners from Colorado and Nevada, and men from the free-copper pits of Michigan. There are Bohunks and Serbs, and Norskis and Swedes. They tend to settle near the mines where they work, and when it comes to socializin' they mostly stick with their own."

Fat Jack turned the team onto a wide street that curved up toward the mines. The way was steep, and the horses leaned into their collars with a will.

"Butte City ain't one town, but many," Jack continued. "Neighborhoods like Meaderville, Walkerville, Dublin Gulch, and Centerville are all settlements that make up the camp.

"W. A. Clark hires mostly miners from Cornwall, England—'Cousin Jacks' they're called. Cousin Jacks are specialists when it comes to sinkin' mine shafts. Many of the Cornishmen work in the Never Sweat Mine over in Centerville, below Dublin Gulch.

"Now some folks think Dublin Gulch got its name because miners from Dublin, Ireland, live there, and I suppose some of 'em do. But that ain't how it got its name. Teamsters started callin' it *Doublin'* Gulch because in the wintertime they have to double up the teams in order to pull the ore wagons up the grade.

"Italian miners tend to congregate at

47

Meaderville. Irish miners live near the Anaconda and Mountain Con mines, and wherever else Marcus Daly has interests."

Wagons, buggies, and drays filled the street. Men crowded the sidewalk, many entering and leaving saloons and bars along the way. Several of them seemed to know Fat Jack. They waved to him as we approached, and some called him by name.

I guess the wind shifted about then, because the smell of sulfur suddenly grew stronger. Smoke thickened, and a yellow-brown haze made it hard to see more than twenty feet ahead. I covered my nose and mouth with my kerchief, but it didn't seem to help much. Jack, on the other hand, must have grown used to it. He fired up a new cigar and puffed away until the tip was cherry red.

"We're on Main Street right now," Jack said, "comin' up on Park. This is the hub of the city. The streetcar terminal is here, and this is the junction where the east, west, north, and south parts of Butte begin."

"I see a lot of men on the streets," I said. "Are most of 'em single?"

Jack nodded. "Aye. There's some of 'em married, but most are not. Only a few have wives to bless their hearth and home; for the rest, there are the girls of the line."

He waved his hand vaguely toward the south. "Nearly every building on East Galena Street between Main and Wyoming is occupied by sporting women. How many horizontal workers practice their trade in this town is anybody's guess, but I'd say somewhere between sixty and eighty."

Jack grinned. "Of course, I haven't *counted* all of 'em yet."

For the next two hours Fat Jack showed me the city. I saw business buildings of brick and stone, miners' shacks and modest homes. Jack drove me past the new courthouse, and Marcus Daly's thirty-two-room house up the hill just behind it. We passed City Hall and the post office, churches and dance halls, and W. A. Clark's new mansion, still under construction.

The city's business district was paved with a variety of materials. Streets and byways were surfaced with cobblestones and bricks, slag from the smelters, wooden blocks, concrete, asphalt, and even sawdust. Most of the streets weren't paved at all, unless it was with good intentions. They meandered uphill and down, plunging from hilltops to rocky gulches and back again.

Cabins and shacks lay scattered across the slope with no apparent plan, and buildings of brick stood proud above the wagon ruts. The city boasted electric and gas lights, telephones, and a water system, but a sewer service was yet to be.

Jack turned his team south on Arizona and

Utah Streets, drove across the Great Northern tracks, and rumbled over the Harrison Avenue Bridge. A few blocks later, Jack drew rein and pointed.

"You're lookin' at Butte City's new racetrack," he said. "As if a man can't lose *enough* money just playin' *faro*."

Ahead, across the flats below the city proper, stood a handsome grandstand alongside an oval racing strip. Stables, paddock, and tack rooms were scattered throughout the grounds. Grooms stood at stable doors, combing and currying the thoroughbreds. Out on the track, workout boys warmed up the horses.

"You sayin' you don't bet the ponies?" I asked.

"Oh, I bet on 'em," Jack said. "I just don't win. Those hot-bloods may be money makers for high rollers like Daly, but they are liabilities to me."

"Well, if they're costin' you money, why do you bet on them?"

Jack shrugged. "God help me," he said. "I love horses."

Reining the team about, Jack turned the carriage back toward the business district. "And it ain't just thoroughbreds, either," he said. "I love horses in general. Horses work hard their whole lives, but nobody gives *them* a testimonial or a raise in their pay."

I grinned. "Maybe they need a good union."

Jack ignored my remark. Holding the reins in

his left hand, he indicated the entire city with his right. "This city owes plenty to horses," he said. "From the camp's first days, horses helped sink the mines and haul the ore. Before the railroad came, horses brought everything and everyone to this place. Horses pulled the freight wagons, the stagecoaches, and the ore carts down in the mines. They graded and leveled the streets, and they hauled in the paving stones, bricks, and lumber that built the city.

"Today, horses pull delivery wagons for dozens of stores in this town. They pull the milk wagons, the ice wagons, the buggies, hacks, buckboards, spring wagons, and carts. High-steppin' Clydesdales pull the beer wagons. Horses pull the fire engine, the water wagon, the paddy wagon, the ambulance. And when a man finally breathes his last, horses in black harness and funeral regalia take him to the graveyard.

"Fifteen livery stables serve this camp. People rent horses for weddings, church picnics, political rallies, and miners' field days. Fancy women from the parlor houses rent saddle horses in their leisure time. And poor devils like me lose their hard-earned wages bettin' on the bangtails back there at the racetrack.

"The bald eagle is our national symbol and a handsome bird he is, but what did that high-flyin' fish eater ever do for this country? Nothing!

"America's symbol *should* be the critter that

51

built the nation, carried its armies, brought its settlers west, herded its cattle, and plowed its fields! America's symbol should be . . . *the horse!*"

I smiled. "Amen, brother," I said. "But you're preachin' to the choir."

A short drive later, Jack drew the team to a stop at the corner of Granite and Main and turned in his seat to face me. "You said a good hotel. The Centennial there, across the street, should meet your needs. Tell 'em I sent you."

"Now," he said, "about those questions you wanted to ask me. A deal's a deal."

"I'm lookin' for a man," I said. "I'm told he may be here to visit his brother. In a part of town called 'the Cabbage Patch.' "

Jack's eyebrows lifted slightly. "The Cabbage Patch is the city's shantytown," he said. "It began as a squatter settlement over on the east side, and it went downhill from there. There are some decent folks in the district, but most of the inmates are drunks, hopheads, burned-out whores, and other assorted low lifes."

He stroked his goatee and studied me thoughtfully for a moment. Then he said, "You say you're a lawman. Just what kind of rascal *is* this man you're lookin' for?"

"He's not wanted for any crime," I said. "I just want to ask him a few questions."

"And his name?"

"Digby O'Dhoul. I'm told his brother is a hard-rock miner called 'Scrapper' O'Dhoul."

For a long moment Fat Jack was silent. When he spoke again, his voice was somber. "I know Scrapper," he said, "but he doesn't live in the Cabbage Patch. He works at the Mountain Con mine and he lives nearby with his sister, Molly.

"And . . . I *met* his brother, Digby. You're a little late, Deputy. Night before last, Digby O'Dhoul *killed* himself."

Digby O'Dhoul, a *suicide!* I had trouble getting my mind around the news. I searched Jack's face, trying to convince myself his announcement was some kind of poor joke, but his expression was deadly serious.

"How . . . how did it happen?" I asked.

"Digby came to Butte a week ago. Moved in with Scrapper and Molly. He seemed nervous. He told wild stories about overhearin' a murder plot. Somethin' about a paid assassin comin' to kill Marcus Daly, of all people!

"Every week or so, I spend a few hours in a stud game with Scrapper down at the Copper Penny. Night before last, Scrapper brought his brother Digby to the game. A gloomy man, Digby was. Always lookin' over his shoulder, as if the devil was chasin' him.

"I don't like to speak ill of the dead, but I have to say I didn't like him much. He wasn't much

53

of a poker player, either—he kept talkin' all the time 'til a man couldn't concentrate on the game.

"That night Scrapper and me left early. We tried to get Digby to come with us, but he wouldn't. For all his bitchin' and moanin' he was ahead of the game. Said he didn't want to break his winnin' streak."

"Policeman found his body two hours later in an alley. There was a bullet hole in his right temple, and a revolver in his right hand. Digby O'Dhoul bought himself a one-way ticket to hell."

"You talked to the police?"

"Yesterday. They questioned everyone who took part in the game."

"What about Digby's poker winnings?"

"He lost it all after we left. Boys in the game said he was pretty drunk. Said he just staggered out the door and into the night."

Fat Jack frowned. "Scrapper and me should have made him come with us. We shouldn't have left him, in the mood he was in."

"You couldn't have known," I said. "Where is the body now?"

"Bowes's Mortuary. Mourners can pay their respects at Scrapper's house in the mornin'. Then it's off to the graveyard."

"No church funeral?"

Fat Jack shook his head. "The church has strong opinions about suicide."

I thought about Jack's report. With the death of
Digby O'Dhoul, my assignment was over. I
could go back to Ridgeway. I could tell him a sad
and troubled man was dead by his own hand. I
could dismiss Digby's wild tale as a product of
his fevered imagination. Yes, I could do that.
And yet . . .

What if the story *wasn't* a tall tale? What if
Digby *had* seen and heard everything just as he
said? Another thought came. What if his death
was *not* a suicide, but murder?

I made my decision. I didn't know enough to
stay, but I didn't know enough to leave, either.

I turned back to Jack. "You'll be at Scrapper's
house tomorrow?"

Jack nodded. "I will."

"I'll see you there," I said.

FOUR

A WAKE FOR DIGBY

The desk clerk at the hotel greeted me with a
practiced smile. "Yes, sir," he said. "Welcome to
the Centennial."

"I need a single room for a week," I said. "Fat
Jack said to tell you he sent me."

The clerk's smile widened. Clearly, he knew and
liked the hack driver. "That's all right, sir," he

said, chuckling. "We'll treat you right anyway."

"Single rate is two dollars a day," the clerk said. "What would you say to twelve dollars for the week?"

I smiled. "I guess I'd have to say you treated me right." I handed him a double eagle and signed the register. He gave me a five dollar note and three silver dollars in change, and handed me the room key. "Number fifteen, Mr. Fanshaw. Second floor, end of the hall. Enjoy your stay."

I climbed the stairs and let myself into my room. A porcelain basin was built into the wall, and I took the occasion to scrub the grime of travel from my face and hands. Making my way back downstairs, I stepped out into the smoky air. The day had been long, but I still had more to do.

I remembered I hadn't eaten since my early breakfast in Helena. Passing a Chinese restaurant on Granite Street, I turned in and treated myself to chow mein and all the trimmings. My hunger pacified, I paid my bill and made the waiter smile with a two-bit tip. Then I walked up to Park and Main and caught a trolley to City Hall. Minutes later, I passed through a wide oak door and found myself inside the city police station.

Butte's policemen were a natty bunch. When I walked into the station house that afternoon I saw two officers seated at desks, both clad in uniforms of stylish blue serge. Brass buttons marched down the fronts of their single-breasted frock coats, ending at a military-type belt buckle of the same metal. Five-pointed stars, the department's badge of office, were pinned to their coats, and stand-up shirt collars of white linen gave the boys a dapper appearance.

Behind a low wooden fence that set his work space apart from that of his men sat the police chief. He was a burly, red-faced man with graying hair and a walrus moustache, and his gimlet eyes seemed to follow my every move. Like his men, he wore a uniform of blue serge, but his coat was double-breasted and his badge was not a star, but a shield.

"I'm Chief McGinnis," he said. "What can I do for you, cowboy?"

I drew aside the lapel of my coat and showed him my deputy's badge. "Merlin Fanshaw, Chief. Deputy U.S. marshal out of Helena."

McGinnis nodded. "My mistake. What can I do for you, *Deputy?*"

"Marshal Ridgeway sent me here to question a man named Digby O'Dhoul. Turns out I'm a day late and a dollar short."

McGinnis nodded. "Sad but true," he said. "If dead men tell no tales, they also answer no questions. And what, if I may ask, is Chance Ridgeway's interest in the late Mr. O'Dhoul?"

"Digby O'Dhoul lives . . . *lived* . . . in Helena.

He came to the marshal's attention when he began talking about overhearing the hiring of a professional assassin."

McGinnis picked up a half-smoked cigar and put it in his mouth. "He told the same story here," he said. "Ten thousand dollars for the murder of Marcus Daly. Quite a fanciful tale."

The Chief struck a match on the sole of his brogan and lit his cigar stub. "The ancient Romans used to say *in vino veritas*, which means in wine there is truth. However, I've always found the opposite to be true. In wine and in overindulgence therein, there is *bullshit*."

At their desks, the other policemen laughed. I smiled politely. "Tell me, Chief," I said. "Did O'Dhoul ever show signs of suicidal behavior?"

Chief McGinnis exhaled a stream of cigar smoke. "Just once," he said. "Night before last, he shot himself in the head. I take that as a sign of suicidal behavior."

Again, the policemen laughed, louder this time. I bode my time, waiting until the laughter stopped. "Who found the body?" I asked.

One of the policemen, a red-haired youth with bad skin, leaned forward in his chair. "Me, Ned Kelly. I was makin' me rounds. Found O'Dhoul face down in an alley, a block from the Copper Penny."

"Bullet hole in the right side of his head? Gun in his right hand?"

"Yeah." Looking at the chief, he grinned. "More signs of suicidal behavior—right, chief?"

"What about the gun?" I asked.

The chief frowned. "Smith and Wesson pocket .32."

"Was it Digby's gun?"

"Must have been. Wherever it came from, it got the job done."

Chief McGinnis stood up. "Look here, Deputy. Scrapper O'Dhoul is a hell of a man, and one of our own, but his brother Digby was—well, he was a man of unsound mind. He had one too many drinks of the hard, and killed himself in an alley. Case closed."

Clearly, the chief and his officers were not pleased by my presence. I understood; local policemen tended to resent questions by visiting lawmen, especially federal lawmen. *A soft answer turneth away wrath* says the Good Book. I smiled, and asked a soft question.

"Thanks for your time, Chief. Mind if I have a look at the body?"

"Be my guest. He's on a slab, at John Bowes's Mortuary. Or you can see him laid out at his brother's house tomorrow. Pay your respects."

"I'll do that," I said, and turned away. At the doorway, I paused and looked back. "Oh, by the way," I said. "Did you boys know Digby O'Dhoul was *left-handed?*"

Then I walked out into the twilight.

• • •

Nightfall came late to Butte. High on a hillside, the city clung to the light long after darkness filled the valleys. Out on the Flats, smelter fires blazed red, belching fire and smoke into the sky. On the hilltops, gallows frames straddled mine shafts and sent the night shift down in cages. In the city, both gas and electric lights flickered on as dusk gave way to full dark. I moved through the crowds that filled the sidewalks in the business district, turned a corner, and walked down Main Street until I came to John Bowes's mortuary.

The sign above the door read J. M. BOWES FURNITURE EMPORIUM—UNDERTAKING AND EMBALMING A SPECIALTY. Gaslight glowed in the window. I stepped up to the front door and rang the bell. Moments later, I heard footsteps from inside. Then the door opened a crack, and a man who appeared to be in his early sixties looked out. "Yes?" he said.

I showed him my badge. "Merlin Fanshaw," I said. "U.S. deputy marshal. Are you John Bowes?"

"I am," said the man. He opened the door wider, inviting me inside. "What can I do for you, Deputy?"

"I'm investigating the death of Digby O'Dhoul," I said. "I understand you have his body here at your emporium."

"I do. I'll be taking it to his brother's home tomorrow morning."

"Yes," I said. "Well, I won't take up much of your time. I just have a few questions."

Bowes nodded. "Certainly," he said.

"I understand police found the body night before last in an alley off Galena Street."

"That's correct. Chief McGinnis called me. He asked me to pick up the body and bring it here."

"How long had O'Dhoul been dead at that point?"

"About two hours. Rigor was just beginning to appear. The face, neck, and shoulders were starting to show the effects."

"What was the position of the body when you found it?"

"The body was face down, in the alley. Cause of death was a gunshot to the right temple, apparently self-inflicted."

"Apparently? Is there some doubt?"

Smiling, Bowes shook his head. "No, no . . . not really. A .32 caliber revolver was in the man's hand. One cartridge had been fired."

"Did you find the bullet?"

"Yes, it was lodged inside the cranial cavity. The bullet was rather badly mushroomed, I'm afraid."

"Did you notice anything at the time that seemed unusual? Out of the ordinary?"

Bowes frowned. He looked past me, toward the street. For a moment, he was silent. Then he said, "I'm not sure. At one point, I had a feeling the body might have been . . . *moved*."

"Moved?"

"Yes. When the heart stops, the blood remaining in the body begins to respond to gravity and settle. This process is called 'lividity.' Because O'Dhoul was found face down, blood should have pooled in those parts of his body that rested on the ground."

"And it didn't?"

"That's just it—I'm not sure. There seemed to be signs of lividity on *both* sides, as if someone moved the body sometime after death. But I really can't say."

I smiled. "You've been very helpful, Mr. Bowes. I appreciate you sharin' your knowledge."

"Not at all. I've been an undertaker here in Butte for over twelve years now, and I'm always surprised by how little I've learned. Fact is I was Butte's first undertaker when I came here back in '76. Now there are several in town."

Bowes favored me with his friendly gaze. "Would you like to see the body?" he asked. "It's just downstairs."

"No thanks," I said. "I'll stop by his brother's house tomorrow and pay my respects."

"I understand. You'd prefer to think of him as you remember him."

Yes, I thought. *I'd prefer to think of him as still alive.*

Back in my room at the hotel, I lay on the bed and stared up into the darkness. I tried to tell myself I had no reason to think Digby O'Dhoul's death was anything but a suicide. Digby was a lonely, unhappy man, addicted to booze the way a horse gets addicted to loco weed. His life was shabby and drab. Like many a man before him, he simply chose to end it.

And yet . . . what if he really *did* overhear the hiring of an assassin? And what if that assassin was even now in Butte, preparing to take Marcus Daly's life? Or what if the man who *hired* the killer was here, too? Did Digby's wild tale, told too often and too free, cause someone to silence him for good?

I rolled over in the bed and tried to punch some comfort into the hotel's bed pillow. It occurred to me that the trouble with playing the "what if" game is that it tends to keep a man from getting his rest.

Morning came early, and found me still half asleep. Through the room's lone window, sunlight struggled to penetrate the haze of smelter and mill smoke. The hammering of the stamp mills echoed across the valley, and the rumble of ore dumped from skips into bins made a sound like distant thunder. I swung my legs over the side of the bed, and made ready to meet the day.

The Centennial Hotel provided hot water for its guests, and I took advantage of the offer to wash up and shave. Then I brushed my clothes and hat, and headed downstairs. The Centennial had a good restaurant just off the lobby, and I put away a breakfast of hotcakes, ham, eggs, and half a pot of coffee before venturing onto the street. Once outside, I squinted against the brightness.

"Top o' the mornin' to you, Deputy." The voice was familiar, cheerful. I shaded my eyes. There, at curbside, was Fat Jack's four-passenger rockaway, with Jack himself at the reins. Dressed entirely in white from his top hat to his gloves, he grinned around his inevitable cigar.

"I wear this outfit for funerals and weddings," he said. "And also for drivin' visitin' peace officers like yourself. Get aboard, if you're goin' to Scrapper's house. No charge, seein' as I'm goin' there anyway."

I stepped up and took a seat beside Jack. "I never turn down a free buggy ride," I said. "Besides, I was just wonderin' how I'd find the place."

"It's an Irish funeral," Jack said. "We'll just follow the sound of keenin' women and the smell of whiskey."

Jack turned the team uphill, toward the mines that overlooked the town. High on the ridge, the Mountain Con buildings and gallows frame stood stark and bold against the sky. Below, miners' homes huddled along the steep and rocky slope. I saw houses and cottages, cabins and shanties, some with fenced yards and some without. Barefoot children played on the hillside. Laundry flapped in the breeze on clotheslines, and smoke drifted from chimneys and stove-pipes.

Directly ahead, men and women trudged up a rutted pathway toward a small, whitewashed frame house. Other men stood in the yard, talking and drinking. Jack nudged me with his elbow and pointed. "Another way to find Scrapper's house," he said, "would be to look for John Bowes's hearse."

I looked where Jack was pointing. A matched team of black geldings in funeral regalia stood near the house, hitched to a polished hearse with plate glass windows. A gray-haired woman, passing the hearse, made the sign of the cross and looked quickly away. Jack reined his team to a stop, and we stepped down. As we approached the front door, men nodded at Jack and greeted him by name. Then they glanced at me, questions in their eyes.

Inside the front door, a stocky man with a fighter's face met us with a cool, unblinking gaze. "Jack," he said. "Good of yez to come."

"Not at all," Jack replied. "Sorry for your trouble, Scrapper."

Turning to me, Jack said, "This is Merlin Fanshaw, from Helena. Merlin, meet Scrapper O'Dhoul."

Scrapper's calloused hand grasped mine with an

honest grip. "Good to meet you," I said. "Sorry about your brother."

Scrapper looked me in the eye. "From Helena, are ye? How did ye know Digby?"

With this hard-eyed old fighter, I thought, nothing but total honesty will do. "I didn't really know him at all," I said. "I'm a deputy U.S. marshal, sent here to ask him some questions."

Scrapper's hard face softened. "Ye're a bit late for questions, Deputy. But it's kind ye are to pay your respects."

Behind us, other visitors approached. Jack and I doffed our hats and went into the parlor. Men and women sat in chairs and stood in small groups, their expressions somber and controlled. As they had outside, most of the men in the room seemed to know Fat Jack and they drew him aside to share a word or two. I looked around the parlor. The room was clean and tidy, its furniture modest but in good repair.

On the mantle above the fireplace, an antique clock stood silent, its spidery hands unmoving. Another clock, a railroad-style Regulator, hung on the opposite wall, and I noticed it too had been stopped. Years before, during my summer with the Starkweather gang, the outfit's cook, Shanty O'Kane, told me of Irish funeral customs. Among them, he said, were the stopping of all clocks and covering of all mirrors in the house to show respect for the deceased.

Across the parlor, through a wide doorway that led to the dining room, I could see the open casket that held Digby O'Dhoul's mortal remains. Banks of flowers filled the space on each end of the casket, their odor too heavy and sweet for the small space. The curtains in the room were drawn, and candles flickered in the gloom.

Seated nearby was a woman with a shawl about her shoulders, and I watched as a burly man bowed low to speak to her. After a moment, the man turned and knelt on a bench before the coffin, his head bowed and a rosary in his hands.

Fat Jack was still talking to a group of men in the parlor, towering over the tallest of them by a head. He caught my eye, nodded toward the dining room, and turned in that direction. I followed him, and we entered the room together.

The woman was pretty and clear-eyed. I judged her to be somewhere around thirty. Smiling at Jack, she looked past him at me. "Sorry for your trouble, Molly," Jack said. "God bless all here." He stepped aside and turned to me. "Molly is Scrapper's sister," he said, "and Digby's sister as well, of course. Molly is mistress of the house, and it's her place to receive visitors."

Turning back to the young woman, he said, "This gentleman is my friend, Merlin Fanshaw. He's come to pay his respects."

I nodded. "That's right, ma'am . . . I mean, Miss O'Dhoul. I sure am sorry about your brother."

Molly O'Dhoul looked up at me and smiled a sweet, crooked smile. Her eyes were large, and cornflower blue in color. Auburn curls cascaded below her slim shoulders. Scattered freckles danced across her nose and cheeks, and her lips framed even, white teeth. "Thank you for coming, Mister Fanshaw," she said. "'Tis a sad time, indeed. Like our blessed Lord, my brother Digby was a man of sorrows."

She looked out at the people gathered in the parlor. "He worked as sexton for a church over in Helena," she said, "but he wasn't a social man. Most of the visitors who came today didn't know him at all. People came because they're friends of my brother."

"I didn't know Digby either," I said. Then, remembering my talk with Bucktooth Betty, I told Molly what I hoped would be a comfort. "His friends in Helena were worried about him. One of them told me he might have come here for a visit. I'm a deputy U.S. marshal, and my boss sent me to find him."

Concern was plain on Molly's face. "He . . . wasn't in trouble with the law, was he?"

"No, not at all. He just seemed . . . a mite confused."

"Ah. You mean the story he told about hearin' a man hire a killer. Yes, he *did* seem a bit addled."

Fat Jack knelt before the open coffin. His prayer was brief. Quickly, he crossed himself and

68

unfolded his long legs as he stood up from the kneeling bench. There was no getting around it; it was my turn. I took my place on the bench.

John Bowes had done his work well. The late Digby O'Dhoul lay nestled in the satin lining of his coffin, gloved hands crossed upon his chest and eyes closed. His thinning hair was neatly combed, and his face was clean-shaven and composed. The mortician's art hid every trace of the bullet wound that ended his life. I looked at the body and felt like a hypocrite. What was *I* doing there? I was no mourner, no friend of the deceased or his family. I was a lawman, come to follow a lead.

My prayer was even shorter than Jack's. I got to my feet and went into the parlor. I did glance back at Molly as I left the room. I can't be certain, what with the candlelight and all, but I believe she smiled her sweet, crooked smile at me.

In the kitchen, Jack introduced me to several gents whose names I caught and then as quickly forgot. They were passing a jug around and trying to outdo each other with tales of how close they were to Scrapper O'Dhoul, and what a fine man he was.

One of the men, a heavyset pug with a scarred face and a fighter's nose, said he was Scrapper's closest friend, and he'd whip any man who said he wasn't.

Another was a paunchy man in his fifties who

spoke in grave, ponderous tones and who seemed to think his mission in life was to inform and correct everyone else. A priest—I think his name was Finley—was also in the group. He would, he said, conduct a brief service at graveside later that afternoon. Because Digby was a suicide, he would not be buried in consecrated ground. However, Butte City boasted several cemeteries. Father Finley said he was certain the Lord could find Scrapper's brother on Resurrection Day, wherever he might be buried. As for me, I had my doubts that Digby was a suicide, but I couldn't prove he wasn't.

The jug came around to Fat Jack. Getting into the spirit, he said, "To Scrapper O'Dhoul and his house. May God keep the soul of Digby, his brother." Jack took a hearty pull on the jug and passed it on to me. From somewhere, I recalled an Irish toast, and applied it to the dead man. I raised the jug, said, "May Digby be in heaven an hour before the devil knows he's dead," and drank.

There's a price to be paid for sociability. Whatever was in that jug blazed a fiery trail down my gullet, caused my eyes to water, and took my breath away completely. I thought for a moment I might be joining Digby on his trip to the graveyard.

The paunchy man took it on himself to scold me for the toast. "Now ye've went and done it," he said. "Ye've said out loud that Digby's dead! We can only hope the divvil wasn't listenin'!"

All of which may give you some idea of what passes for logic when the jug gets passed around. The boys raised a few more toasts, sang a song or two, and told some scandalous jokes designed to get Father Finley's goat. They praised Scrapper and his sister to the skies, and by the time the jug made a few more rounds they nearly conferred sainthood on Digby O'Dhoul. I decided they owed their high opinion of Digby, a man hardly anyone knew, to their admiration of his brother Scrapper, a man everyone seemed to know.

At last, Father Finley declared it was time to depart for the cemetery. Pallbearers loaded Digby's coffin into the waiting hearse. Other carriages arrived, also provided by the funeral parlor, and everyone going to the graveyard took their leave. Fat Jack was in favor of continuing the celebration at one of the local saloons, but I begged off, saying I had to write a report for my boss.

As Fat Jack and several other well-fortified celebrants set out in his rockaway, I turned to go back to my room at the hotel. And then, just as I began to walk down the hill, I noticed something strange. Behind me, walking stealthily away from the house, was the shifty-eyed cardsharp I saw earlier that week on the train from Great Falls!

FIVE

A HORSE AND A HANGOVER

Back at the hotel, I borrowed pen, ink, and paper from the desk clerk and wrote a report for Marshal Ridgeway. I offered no conclusions in my report because I had none. I simply wrote of Digby's death and said the Butte police had ruled it a suicide. I included no information as to when I'd be coming back to Helena, saying I still had some loose ends to tie up. Buying a stamp from the front desk, I committed the letter to the U.S. mail and climbed the stairs back up to my room.

Once there, I shucked my boots, stretched out on the bed, and thought about those loose ends. According to Fat Jack, five men were players in the poker game the night Digby died. They were: Fat Jack, Scrapper, Digby, and two others. Jack hadn't told me the names of the others, but whoever they were I wanted to talk to them.

Besides the two players, who else had been there? Did the game have a house dealer? Had a barkeep or barmaid served drinks? Scrapper and Fat Jack left the game early. Who had remained? How long after Digby left did the others leave?

And what about Digby's so-called suicide? He came from Helena to be with his brother and his sister. And yet he left no note, no explanation as to why he decided to take his own life. Digby was left-handed, yet he apparently shot himself with his *right* hand.

Then there was the story he told—a wild tale about overhearing a man hiring a killer—to murder Marcus Daly! A killer named Charon, Digby said. Unbelievable, people said. A made-up name to go with a made-up story. A fantastic story, told by a wet-brained drunk, meaningless words from a drinker's delirium.

Except . . . there was Ridgeway's telephone call to Abigail Bannister. The marshal passed along the name Digby said he heard. And Abby told Ridgeway there *is* a professional assassin who goes by that name—there *is* a contract killer who calls himself Charon!

Restless, I got up and began to pace the floor. I had too many questions without answers, too many pieces of a puzzle that didn't fit. My hotel room felt airless and stuffy, cramped as a prison cell. I felt the need to get out and walk it off, to corral my thoughts and see if I couldn't put them in some kind of order. Outside, I crossed the street and began walking south. I recalled passing a livery stable during my tour of the city. I wondered if I could find it again.

Ten blocks from the hotel, I came to the stable I was looking for. Located on lower Main Street, a two-story brick building boasted sixty feet of frontage and a sign that read FOGARTY'S

LIVERY—FRANCIS FOGARTY, OWNER. The big doors of the stable were open to the street, and the familiar odors of hay, leather and horse verified Fogarty's sign. I didn't need to see his sign; I'd have known I was near a livery stable even if I'd been blindfolded.

A wizened older man with flyaway white hair stepped out of the office and approached me. Behind gold-rimmed spectacles, his eyes were frank and friendly. A half-smile seemed to speak of a general good humor. Without seeming to, he looked me over carefully, appraising me like a jeweler studying a diamond. His eyes paused ever so briefly at the deputy's badge on my shirtfront, and then lifted to meet mine. Through it all, the half-smile never changed.

"Good day to you, sir," he said. "I'm Francis Fogarty, owner and general manager of this fine equine hotel. And what can I do for you today?"

I smiled. "I'm Merlin Fanshaw," I said. "A visitor to your beautiful city."

Fogarty laughed. "'Tis a wicked sense of humor you have, sir! This city is many things, but 'beautiful' is not among them."

"Maybe not," I said, "but I reckon beauty *is* in the eye of the beholder. I have an idea W. A. Clark and Marcus Daly think she's beautiful."

"Surely not," said Fogarty, "but they may well think there is a certain beauty in the ore that lies *beneath* the city."

"Men find beauty where they can, I guess. If beauty is only skin deep, as the sayin' goes, I reckon ugly is, too."

Fogarty's half-smile doubled. "You have the very soul of a philosopher, Mr. Fanshaw."

I got down to business. "Like I said, I'm new to Butte. Fat Jack Jones gave me a tour of the city my first day here, but I'd like to look things over by myself. Do you rent saddle horses?"

"I do indeed. I have horses that range all the way from *reluctant* and *recalcitrant* to *reliable* and *remarkable.*"

"That's quite a range of 'Rs'," I said. "And the price is . . ."

"Reasonable."

"Of course. And you . . ."

"Recommend them."

"All right," I said, laughing. "Trot 'em out. As long as they're not *rowdy* or *rank,* I expect I'll find somethin' that'll do."

Fogarty's string of saddle horses turned out to be pretty ordinary, but I figured most of his customers were people just looking for a gentle animal to help them get around. Out of the dozen or so hay burners the liveryman offered, only about three appeared to be good all-around mounts. I chose a six-year-old sorrel quarter horse with good legs and a nice way of carrying himself. I figured him to weigh about eleven hundred

75

pounds, and he seemed steady and sensible. When I told Fogarty my choice, he seemed to look at me with new respect.

"You know horses," he said. "That gelding is the best horse in my string."

"How much to rent him?" I asked.

Fogarty stroked his chin and frowned, as if no one had ever asked him that question. Then he smiled. "Sixty cents for a half day," he said. "All day for a dollar."

"Done," I said. "I'll have him back here before sundown."

I stroked the animal's neck. Even in the half light of the stable, the sorrel's hide shone like a new penny. "What's his name?" I asked.

"I don't know," Fogarty said. "He never told me."

I laughed. "All right. I'll call him *Centavo*, after the Spanish word for 'cent.'"

"Divvil I know if he speaks Spanish either," Fogarty said. "But call him what you wish. He's yours 'til sundown."

Fogarty's stableman saddled and bridled the horse, and led him outside to the street in front of the stable. Minutes later, sitting a rented saddle on a rented gelding, I rode out to see the city and get my thoughts in order. It was good to be horseback again.

I turned the sorrel south, toward the flats. On all sides, smoke and flame billowed up from the stacks of the smelters and thickened the afternoon air. Stamp mills thundered, pounding silver ore to powder before passing it on to the roasters and finally to the settling pans, furnaces, and coldwater pipes that bring the ore to a state of pure metal.

According to Fat Jack, there were some 340 stamps operating in Butte, treating 500 tons of ore every day. The clamor was tremendous; I thought the noise might spook my horse, but the gelding jogged along at a smooth foxtrot, head high and steady. I guess he had grown accustomed to the racket, but I hadn't. I couldn't imagine ever getting used to the din.

"It's a real pleasure makin' your acquaintance, Centavo," I said. "You're a good-lookin' animal, and you carry yourself with pride." The sorrel held to his smooth gait, but he cocked one ear back at the sound of my voice. "Fact is," I said, "you look like you belong in this minin' camp. Your hide shines just like burnished copper."

I slowed the gelding to a walk at a street called Clear Grit, and crossed the railroad tracks. High atop the hill, gallows frames loomed ghostly through the haze. Turning the gelding, I headed west.

Below the mine dumps, gray-green and yellow tailings crowded the miners' homes and sprawled in growing piles along the hillside. Ahead, a half-dozen children played king-of-the-hill on a steep mound, one husky, red-haired boy defending his turf against all comers. I thought of W. A. Clark and Marcus Daly, who played a grown-up version of the same game.

The youngsters stopped to watch as I rode past, studying me with sober, curious faces. I smiled and waved to them.

"Those kids think I'm talkin' to myself, Centavo," I said. "They don't know you and me are havin' a conversation."

Ahead, teamsters drove high-sided ore wagons downhill to the railroad, the heavy loads held back by big, blocky four-horse teams. I drew rein, watching the drivers ride the brakes as they guided the horses down the steep and rutted road.

I touched the sorrel with my heels and turned him uphill toward the heart of town. "All right," I mused. "If a paid assassin *is* gunning for Marcus Daly, the next question is *who* hired him, and *why?*"

The horse tossed his head from side to side, almost as if answering my question. I laughed. "Don't know, huh? Neither do I. But I have to wonder—who wants Daly's death enough to hire a professional killer?

Looking up toward the ridge, I saw a group of miners walking down the hill. As they drew near I reined Centavo off to the side and gave the men the right of way. "Afternoon," I said.

Some of the men replied, "Afternoon." Some

nodded, looking away as they passed. Others met my eyes, sizing me up. Most just seemed glad to be off-shift for the day, with maybe time for a beer or two, a hearty supper, and a good night's sleep. I was surprised to find I envied them.

The miners had their own concerns, and dangers to face deep below the surface of the earth. But they didn't have to worry about keeping a killer from taking the life of one of the camp's most important men. They had to mine copper ore and send it to the surface. *I* had to find a needle in a haystack.

Turning onto North Montana Street, I rode past the courthouse and looked out toward the mountains. A strong west wind swept across the valley and, for the moment at least, cleared the city of smoke.

Behind the courthouse, on Granite Street, gaslight shone in the lower windows of Marcus Daly's home. I wondered: Is Daly inside? Is he looking forward to supper with friends and family? Is he thinking about his holdings and considering how he might advance his empire?

I felt uneasy. Daly had no idea a killer was coming to take his life. Even if he heard Digby's wild story, it's not likely he believed it. I slowed the sorrel as I passed the house, my eyes still on the front door and the windows.

"Why *should* he believe it?" I asked aloud.

"There's no proof an assassin exists, and there's no motive for murder a man can point to. Daly has his rivals, no doubt. He has enemies, certainly. Men of his caliber play a high-stakes, no-holds-barred game of money and power. But they don't generally murder one another. I reckon that would spoil the fun."

Across the valley, a red sun burned low and dropped behind the mountains. Brick buildings glowed warm in the day's last light and then quickly faded to gray. Music halls and saloons made ready for the evening. Gas and electric light brightened windows and doors, projecting squares of yellow out onto the streets. Miners trooped along the sidewalks, their wages burning holes in their pockets. Through the open doors of dancehalls came the sound of female laughter, and hurdy-gurdy music jangled out into the evening.

I leaned forward in the stirrups and patted Centavo's neck. "Well," I said. "It's been nice talkin' to you, but I need to get you to the stables."

Gaslight flickered outside Fogarty's Livery when I rode Centavo across the cobblestones and stepped down before the open doors. Fogarty was waiting. "Ah! Good evenin', deputy," said he. "And how did you two get along?"

"We had us a fine ride and a long conversation," I said. "The sorrel is a good listener."

Fogarty's smile widened. "Sure and I hope you

didn't expect him to be much of a *talker.* He's an *introvert,* you know."

I laughed. "Yes, he is," I said. "Sorry I didn't bring him back sooner. Time got away from me."

"Tis the horse's fault. If he'd been more of a *talker,* he could have reminded you."

A stableman walked toward us and took the sorrel's reins. I watched as the man led the horse away, back toward the stalls. Turning to Fogarty, I handed him a silver dollar. "I want to pay you for the full day," I said. "I did have a fine ride."

Fogarty refused the money. "Not at all," he said. "It's a pleasure to do business with a man who appreciates a good horse."

"Besides," he said. "I have a feelin' you'll be takin' him out again while you're here."

I found sixty cents in change and paid him the half-day rate. "You're right," I said. "How about tomorrow mornin'?"

The liveryman took a small note pad from his pocket and pretended to study it. "You're in luck," he said. "*Señor* Centavo has no previous appointments. He'll be ready at seven a.m."

I was about to walk away when I turned back. "I do have a question, Francis."

Fogarty's eyebrows went up. He peered owlishly at me over the top of his spectacles. He said, "Here at Fogarty's horse hotel, we aim to please. Answers to all questions are free. Not necessarily *correct,* but *free.*"

"Do you know where Fat Jack Jones lives? I thought I might look him up tomorrow."

"Jack lives in a cabin on Basin Creek, two miles south of here. He has a carriage shed there, and a barn for his horses. That's where you'll find him, unless of course he's someplace else."

"Where else would he be?"

"Well, now. It's hard to say with Jack. Sometimes, when he's flush, he'll spend the night with one of those harlots over on Galena Street. Sometimes the police give him a ride in the hurry-up wagon and provide him with free lodgin' at the city jail. Back in eighty-two he left his team and carriage tied to a hitchin' post in front of the Arcade Saloon and hopped a stagecoach to the Coeur d'Alenes. Didn't come back for nearly a year."

Fogarty lowered his voice and assumed a confidential manner. "Jack's a terrible gambler, you know. Faro. Poker. Horse racin'. He never met a game of chance he didn't like. Sometimes he wins, but mostly he doesn't. Jack's a grand hack man, though, and a credit to his profession."

"Much obliged," I said. "I guess I'll find him at his cabin then. Unless I find him someplace else."

"See?" said Fogarty. "You're gettin' to know Jack already. Until tomorrow."

"Until tomorrow," I agreed, and we shook hands.

Turning north on Main, I walked up the street.

Thinking about seeing Jack the next morning, I took myself uptown, bought a few items, and went on to my hotel.

Morning dawned clear and bright. Sometime during the night, a steady rain had swept through the valley, and for the moment at least the city and its buildings appeared new-washed and sun-bright. Rainwater stood in puddles, reflecting the sky. A fresh breeze blew cool from the west. I stepped out of the hotel and took a deep breath. The air smelled faintly of earth and sagebrush. I turned south and walked down to the livery stable.

Fogarty was expecting me. His stableman brought the sorrel out again and saddled him. I led the horse up the street for several steps, untracking him out of habit. Then I swung up onto his back and took him away at a trot on the Basin Creek road.

Fat Jack's place turned out to be a sagging, sod-roofed cabin on the banks of Basin Creek. The logs that made up its walls were silver-gray with age, and there were gaps in the chinking that must have let in both critters and weather. Jack's four-passenger rockaway stood next to the cabin, the horses still in their traces. I frowned; since childhood I'd been taught that a man takes care of his horses first, before attending to his own needs.

Dismounting, I tied Centavo to a hitch rack in

front of the cabin, and knocked heavily on the door. "Jack!" I said. "Open up—it's me, Merlin Fanshaw!"

No answer. I knocked again, harder. "Come on, Jack!" I said, nearly shouting. "Let me in!"

Again, there was no answer, no sound inside the cabin. Worry troubled the edges of my mind. Had something happened to Jack? Was he sick—or worse? I tried the door, but found it locked from within. I took a step back. Just as I was about to break in with a well-aimed kick, I heard it. Something inside—a chair, maybe—fell heavily to the floor. I heard the shuffle of footsteps, and the scrape of the latch. Then the door opened, and Fat Jack stood in the sudden sunlight, blinking at the glare and showing his teeth in a grimace of agony. "Can't you let a man die in peace?" he whimpered. "There are *demons* inside my head— with *sledgehammers!*"

I grinned, relieved. "And you've got a breath on you like a hot fruit cake!" I said. "You had me scared for a minute there—I thought you were *dead!*"

Jack stumbled inside and slumped into a chair. "I *am,*" he muttered. "What brings you out here, anyway? You come to torment me?"

"I came by to ask how your evenin' went," I said, "but you've pretty well answered *that* question."

"Merlin," he groaned. "You . . . you wouldn't

have a wee dram of the creature on you? Just a touch—a drop or two—might save my life."

Living with my pa taught me well about the misery of a drinker's morning after. In those years, I learned to hide "a drop or two" to help relieve Pa's whips and jingles after a big night in town. Although I seldom drink whiskey myself, I do sometimes carry a pint for emergencies. Jack's condition seemed to fit the definition.

Taking the bottle from my coat pocket, I said, "As it happens, I did pick up a pint last night. A man never knows when he might need to save a life."

Jack took the whiskey with a trembling hand. "God *bless* you," he said. "May God and all his holy angels *bless* you, Merlin."

Tilting the bottle up, he took a long swig. Then he closed his eyes and took another. When he opened his eyes, Jack looked like a man just rescued from a cave-in. Droplets of whiskey, caught in his moustache and chin whiskers, sparkled in the sunlight. His eyes were red-rimmed and haunted.

"God, I was flamin' last night," he said. "Don't know how I even got home."

"Your horses brought you," I said, "and they haven't been fed or watered. They're still standin' out front in their harness."

"Ah, Jaysus. I clean forgot. My poor beauties."

I stood. "Get yourself together," I said. "I'll take care of the team."

Jack struggled to his feet. He still looked shaky, but he'd been moved to action. "Wait," he said. "I'm comin' with you."

Outside, we stripped the harness from the horses and Jack led them down to the creek for water. I found a barrel of oats in the barn and poured each horse a ration. While I forked hay into their mangers, Jack brushed and combed them until they shone.

Back at the cabin, I took the bucket outside, filled it at the pump, and treated myself to a dipperful of cold, fresh water. Jack watched me, his face haggard and pale. I could see by the careful way he held his head that he was hurting, and hurting bad. He shuffled over to the cabin's covered porch, closed his eyes, and sat down. After a moment, I took the water bucket and sat down beside him.

For a few minutes, we just sat there in the shade together, listening to the sound of the creek. Jack said nothing, suffering in silence like a wounded animal. In the end, I took pity on him. I slid the pint from my coat and offered him one more hair of the dog.

Jack grunted his gratitude and drank. Taking the bottle back, I corked what was left of the whiskey.

"That's enough," I declared. "Young Doctor Fanshaw says you should go to drinkin' water now. Plenty of water."

Jack opened one eye. *"Water?* For a hangover? What the hell happened to black coffee?"

"Coffee will just make you feel worse," I said. "Trust me."

For a time, neither of us spoke. Then Jack said, "All right. What brings you out here? Besides playin' doctor, that is."

"I need your advice. Not about drinkin.' I already know enough about that."

"What then?"

"I need to set up meetings with W. A. Clark and Marcus Daly. What's the best way to do that?"

Jack considered my question. "They both spend at least some of their time in Butte City," he said. "I'd say your federal badge makes a pretty fair letter of introduction."

Curiosity overcame Jack's misery. He frowned, studying me closely. Then he asked, "Does this have anythin' to do with what Digby was talkin' about? Some mystery man comin' to kill Marcus Daly?"

"I figure I have to look into it."

"You think Clark might know somethin'?"

"I don't know. If Digby was right, somebody is spending ten thousand dollars to hire a killer. Not many men have that kind of money to spend on a murder. From what I hear, Clark and Daly hate each other."

"You hear right," Jack said. "But I doubt Clark would go to the expense. He's a fussy little skinflint of a man, proud as a peacock and feisty as a banty rooster. He never spent a nickel unless he knew it would bring back a dime."

"Maybe he figures Daly's death is worth the cost. How much do they hate each other?"

Jack shrugged. "Pretty damn much, I'd say."

"How did they get that way?"

Jack assumed a pathetic look. "I could tell you that, and more besides," he said. "But my poor throat is terrible dry . . ."

His eyes were fixed on my coat pocket, where the pint bottle lay. I raised a forefinger and adopted a stern tone. "All right," I said. "One more drink. A small one."

I gave him the pint. His hands shook as he uncorked the whiskey and drank deeply. They still trembled when he handed the bottle back.

"W. A. Clark is a man with no vices, no humor, and a pinched little soul the size of a walnut," Jack said. "He came to the Territory during the gold strikes of sixty-three with nary a penny to his name. He bargained and borrowed, worked and schemed, and he prospected the miners who prospected for gold. He became a merchant and a money lender, and finally a partner in a Deer Lodge bank.

"He scrimped and scratched 'til he could buy his partner out, bought a silver mine here in Butte called 'the Original.' Then he acquired some other silver properties."

"An ambitious man," I said. "A captain of industry."

"Ambitious, and smart," Jack said. "Clark realized he needed to know more about how to manage his enterprises, so he took himself east and studied for a year at the Columbia School of Mines. When he came back, he acquired a silver stamp mill, another mine, and finally a smelter.

"He rode roughshod over his rivals, and built his profits up into the millions. Word has it he's now part owner of some forty-six silver or copper properties in the area. He also owns his own newspaper, the Butte *Miner*."

"Sounds like one of those Horatio Alger stories," I said, "where the hard-workin' lad with pluck and a pure heart goes from rags to riches."

"That ain't how it's worked for me," Jack said. "So far *I've* gone from rags to *rags*."

"I asked you how Clark and Daly came to be enemies," I said.

"Hell," Jack said. "How could it be otherwise? Two hard-drivin' high rollers, both hankerin' to be king of the mountain, and neither man willin' to take second place."

Fat Jack dropped his eyes to my coat pocket again. "My headache is still bad," he said. "You couldn't let a man have one more wee drop, could you?"

I shook my head. "I didn't help cure your

hangover just to start you on a new one," I said. "Tell me more about Daly."

Jack's shoulders slumped. He shrugged. "Daly came here in seventy-six to look at a mine his backers were interested in. The mine was called the Alice, and it was a silver mine up on the hill. On the strength of Daly's report, the brothers decided to buy the mine. Daly bought a one-third interest in it himself. That's when the trouble started."

Jack broke off his story then and searched his pockets until he came up with a half-smoked cigar. Looking as pleased as a prospector with a nugget, he clamped the stub between his teeth and struck a match on the sole of his boot. The stub was short, Jack's hand was shaky, and it was touch and go for a moment whether the match would ignite the stub or Jack's chin whiskers.

The stub won. Jack puffed away, producing clouds of white smoke. I waited.

"Where was I?" Jack asked.

" 'That's when the trouble started.' "

"Oh, yeah. Daly picked up an option from the seller on the Alice, and gave a draft on Clark's bank in Deer Lodge. Clark had plans of his own to acquire the Alice. He refused to honor Daly's draft. He said Daly had no authority. So Daly gave the seller an express order through Wells Fargo. Clark had no choice; he had to honor the order. Daly bought the mine, and the feud began."

"Later, Daly sold his interest in the Alice and bought a mine called the Anaconda. The Anaconda produced enough silver to pay Daly's backers a handsome profit and make him rich as well, but at the three-hundred-foot level, the silver ran out.

"That didn't bother Daly. He saw that the ore beyond was rich in copper. He quietly closed down the mine, and rumors spread that the Anaconda was worthless. Some of the boys laughed at him. Daly said nothing.

"Meanwhile, his agents quietly bought up most of the adjoining claims at very low prices. Then he reopened the hill, and brought in miners. He built a smelter to handle the ore, and a railroad to haul it from the hill.

"Clark pitched a fit. He called Daly uncouth and ignorant. He said Daly only stumbled onto the copper deposit by dumb luck. Well, it's not true, of course. Daly knows mining and mines better than most men, and he knows and loves his miners. Daly has the common touch. On any given day you can find him down in the mines with his men, or sittin' on a curb with one of his muckers, talking and sharing a chaw of tobacco.

"Some say Clark and Daly were friends in the early days of the camp, but it ain't likely. I think they hated each other at first sight. Daly is down to earth, full of Irish charm and wit. He is generous to a fault to the men who work for him, but he has a hot temper and he never forgets an insult. Clark has offered him several insults over the years."

Jack took a final drag on his cigar butt and ground it out in the dirt beneath his boot heel. "Anyway," he said. "That's how the feud began. The whole camp's waitin' to see what happens next."

Jack fell silent then, and so did I. Sunshine warmed the morning. A breeze sighed down the gulch, setting the leaves of the aspen trees to pattering. Basin Creek's icy waters chuckled over their rocky bed. Somewhere nearby, a bird warbled a bright song.

Jack said, "You remember I told you I play poker at the Copper Penny a couple of times a week?"

"I remember. You said you play with Scrapper O'Dhoul."

"That's right. Well, we're playin' again tonight. The same players as the night Digby was killed. Maybe you'd like to sit in on the game."

"I sure would," I said. "I want to meet the men who were there that night."

"Occurs to me *one* of those gents might be a real help to you. His name is Cecil Hardesty, and he's one of Clark's top lieutenants."

Jack stood up. "I'll come by for you," he said. "A quarter to eight at your hotel. Bring your money and your luck. There's a fifty dollar buy-in."

I untied Centavo and stepped up into the saddle. As I rode away, I looked back. Jack was on his feet, drinking water from the dipper.

SIX

FIVE CARD STUD

It was exactly 7:45 that evening when Fat Jack reined the bay team to a stop in front of the Centennial Hotel. I had just stepped outside and was looking at my watch. I didn't see him right away, but he saw me.

"Checkin' the time, are you?" Jack asked. "Save yourself the trouble, lad. It's a quarter to eight exactly. You can set your watch by Jack Jones every time."

Jack sat straight as a picket pin on the driver's seat of his rockaway. Dressed in top hat and double-breasted coat, he grinned around his cigar. He looked rested and well groomed. I found it hard to believe he was the same man I'd seen in the grip of a killer hangover that morning.

"Well, maybe not *every* time," I said. "You're lookin' good, Jack."

"Three hours in the Chinese baths," he said. "Sweated out most of the pizen."

Jack gave me his hand, and I climbed up beside him.

"So," he said. "Are you ready for a few hands of stud?"

"I hope so," I said, "but I'm just a poor country boy, new to city ways."

Jack gave me a sideways glance. "*Sure* you are," he said.

The Copper Penny turned out to be a tough saloon on the north side of Galena Street, a stone's throw from Butte's red-light district. As we drove up the street, it seemed to me that nearly every building we passed was some kind of saloon, dance hall, or gambling joint. "This part of town," Jack said proudly, "is wild and woolly indeed. Some say it's as wide open and tough as the Barbary Coast out in Frisco."

He drew rein and turned to me. "One thing," he said. "Strict rule. No weapons at the game. Are you packin', Merlin?"

I nodded. "I am. Goes with my job."

"Not if you're a player in the card room. You'll have to leave it here."

I thought about it. Banning weapons at the game made sense. I had a few misgivings, but I unbuckled my gun belt and handed it to Jack. He tucked it under the seat cushions of the rockaway and grinned. "It'll be right here after the game," he said. "In case you lose everything and feel a need to shoot yourself."

"Speaking of that," I said. "How did Digby get a gun inside the night he died?"

Jack shrugged. "Nobody knows. Maybe he picked it up after he left the game. Scrapper told me he never knew his brother to own or use a gun."

Stepping down, Jack tied the team to a hitching post on the street. "The game is in the back," he said. "Follow me."

Inside, drinkers stood elbow to elbow at the bar. The room smelled of whiskey, stale beer, and sweat. Cigar smoke eddied in layers beneath the tin ceiling. Hard-eyed men sat at oilcloth-covered tables, watching us as we passed. A few recognized Jack. They nodded and called him by name, and Jack returned their greetings.

Then, at the end of a short hallway, Jack opened a door and we stepped into the card room. Under a shaded electric bulb, a poker table was the single bright spot. A sallow-faced dealer in shirtsleeves and vest sat against the opposite wall, racks of blue, white, and red chips on the green felt before him. Two other men occupied chairs at the table, a tall man in a lounge suit and silk cravat, and Scrapper O'Dhoul.

Scrapper looked up as we came in. "Evenin', Jack," he said. "Have ye brought me money?"

Jack shrugged out of his coat and hung it on a peg. He grinned as he shook Scrapper's hand. "It ain't your money yet," he said. "You'll have t' win it."

Turning to me, Jack said. "I brought a friend, though—Merlin Fanshaw, from Helena. Maybe *he's* got your money."

Smiling, Scrapper gripped my hand. "Do ye, lad? Do ye have me money?"

I returned his smile. "Time will tell, Scrapper. Time will tell."

The tall man watched me intently, his expression serious. His eyes seemed to follow my every move. I was a stranger to him. He was just sizing me up, I figured.

Jack said, "And this well-dressed gent is Cecil Hardesty. Cecil, meet Merlin Fanshaw." We shook; Hardesty's eyes never left mine.

Jack pulled out a chair next to the dealer, and sat down. "And Ed Ferris here is dealin' for us tonight," he said.

We took our places at the table, Jack at the dealer's right, then Cecil, an empty chair, and me. The two places directly to my right were empty, too, and Scrapper took his seat on the dealer's left. Each of us bought in for fifty dollars, and the dealer gave us our chips. I looked around, wondering: where is the fifth man?

I tugged my hat down to shade my eyes from the electric light's glare. Beyond the table was only darkness. Then I heard the door behind me open and close. I heard footsteps approaching the table. The other players raised their eyes.

"About time you showed up," Jack said, and I knew the fifth man had arrived. I heard the scrape of wood on the card room floor as he drew out the second chair on my right. He came into the light and sat down. I *recognized* the man! Player number five was the cardsharp I'd seen on the train from Great Falls—the same man I saw walking away from Scrapper's house after Digby's wake!

The cardsharp's eyes widened. They were that peculiar green color I recalled. I knew he recognized me, too. I took the bull by the horns. "Howdy," I said. "I'm Merlin Fanshaw. I believe we rode the train down to Helena together last week."

The cardsharp made no reply. Maybe he was trying to think of one.

"I don't believe I caught your name," I said.

His eyes narrowed. "I don't believe I *threw* it," he said. "But it's Durand. Lucas Durand. And I don't recall seein' you on no train."

I hadn't pinned on my deputy's badge that evening, but I saw Durand glance at the place on my vest where I usually wore it, and I knew. Durand remembered me, all right.

I was not the best poker player in the world, but I was no fish either. Because five card stud is the only poker game where a player can see all but one of his opponent's cards, a man needs to watch the table like a hawk. No mistake is worse than staying in the game looking for a card that has already been played.

Besides keeping track of the cards, it's also important to watch the play carefully, not only to learn the other players' styles, but also to learn their "tells" and to become aware of your own. A "tell" is a habit—something a player says or does that tips off his hand to his opponent. One man may grow more talkative when he has a good hand. Another may play with his chips, or drum with his fingers on the table top. Or maybe he fidgets in his chair or grows quiet when he's running a bluff. Knowing a man's "tell" gives you an edge.

Most players stay in a hand too long. Learning when to fold and when to stay takes a lifetime, I suppose, but knowing how to calculate the odds can at least keep you from getting skinned. As a general rule, I fold if I don't have a pair or better in the first three cards, and I don't even start a hand unless my hole card is higher than any up card at the table. Also, I never play for straights or flushes. Well, almost never.

My cards were run-of-the-mill for the first hour or so, and I took the time to study the other players. Fat Jack appeared to love the game for its own sake, and he played with a reckless abandon that had little to do with the quality of his cards. The stacks of chips before him declined with each hand dealt, and finally disappeared altogether. Jack laughed off his losses, bought in for a second fifty dollars, and continued to play fast and loose. He would not, I decided, be among the winners that evening.

Ed Ferris, the dealer, was good at his trade. He shuffled and dealt, called the cards as they fell, and made sure the pot was right at all times. He didn't play himself, but took a fifty-cent rake for the house from each hand played, and kept the cards moving. Five card stud is a fast game; as many as sixty hands can be dealt every hour. At four bits a hand, the Copper Penny stood to earn thirty dollars every hour we played.

Cecil Hardesty was cautious. He seldom spoke, folded often, and kept his bets and calls low. In his stylish suit and silk cravat, Hardesty seemed out of place in the back room of the Copper Penny. From time to time I caught him watching me out of the corner of his eye in a way that made me feel uneasy. There was something in his stare that felt a little like suspicion—or fear. I decided it was because he knew I was a U.S. deputy marshal, and the knowledge made him nervous. Not that it meant anything—even the most innocent folks sometimes act edgy around a lawman.

Scrapper O'Dhoul played no-nonsense heads-up poker, calm and unruffled against even the toughest competition. I figured Scrapper's experience as a fighter no doubt stood him in good stead. He was pleasant and smiled often. I rarely saw him run a bluff, but he had no trouble calling those who tried to bluff him.

Lucas Durand was a professional gambler, and cold as a glacier. For the most part, he played his cards by the book, calling and folding according to the odds and the strength of the other hands. Durand was something of a mystery to me. I recalled watching him play Solitaire on the train from Great Falls, and remembered how he'd cheated at the game. He'd left the train at Helena, as I had. My guess was that he tried and failed to find a game in that city that interested him, and so caught the train to Butte a few days later.

Apparently, he'd found a place in the game at the Copper Penny with Fat Jack and Scrapper. With Hardesty, he'd played on the night Digby O'Dhoul met his death. Now, I watched as he played, and wondered. Was he only another drifting gambler and nothing more? Or was he a possible suspect in Digby's murder? All I knew then was that he played his cards close to his vest, and that I seemed to make him nervous.

There were no big hands during the first few hours, but by nine-thirty I found myself nearly two hundred dollars ahead of the game. Fat Jack was down nearly a hundred, and Hardesty had lost maybe forty or forty-five. He bought in for two hundred more and began to push his cards, betting, raising, and re-raising in an effort to keep as many other players out as possible. I stayed with him when I believed I had the cards, and folded when I didn't. Then, at about ten-thirty, I spotted his "tell."

Hardesty and Fat Jack were the only players left

in the hand. By the third face-up card, neither hand showed a pair. Jack's door card was a ten, and from the way he played his hand I figured him for pocket tens. Then, on the final round, Hardesty caught a queen. He glanced at his hole card and bet fifty dollars. Already down for the night by nearly a hundred, Jack folded. Showing off, Hardesty turned up his hole card. His winning hand was not a pair of queens, as he wanted Jack to believe, but only a queen high, no pair. He'd taken the hand on a bluff.

"Deal me out," Jack said. "I'm busted."

Hardesty allowed himself a smug grin, making a show of raking in the pot. But his grandstanding would cost him. Several times that night I'd noticed that just before betting he toyed with the flashy diamond ring he wore on his right hand. He had done so again when he bluffed Jack out. I knew his tell, and he was mine!

Fat Jack consoled himself with whiskey and watched the game for a while. I hoped he would be around to see me take Hardesty down, but it was not to be. We heard a general commotion from the bar next door—excited voices, a chair or table falling, men shouting—and then the bartender threw open the door to the card room and fixed his eyes on Jack. "Tony Sanchez and Big Joe Campbell just had a helluva fight," he said. "Tony pulled a knife and cut Big Joe quick, deep, and frequent!"

He caught his breath, and continued. "Big Joe's bleedin' like a stuck pig, and we got to get him to a croaker! Is your hack outside, Jack?"

Jack stood up. "It is," he said, striding toward the bar. "I'll bring it to the front door."

"What about Tony?" Scrapper asked.

"He's out cold. Big Joe hit him a lick that could have dropped a bull. I sent my swamper up to get the coppers."

Fat Jack was gone, the back door closed behind him.

"Anything we can do?" asked Scrapper.

"No," said the barkeep. "Go back to your game, boys." And then he, too, was gone.

We heard Jack's hack clatter off up the street on its errand of mercy. Minutes later, the paddy wagon arrived and patrolmen loaded the unconscious Tony Sanchez inside. The boys in the bar picked up the furniture and swept up the broken glass. The drinkers returned to their drinking, and we went back to our game.

I looked at Hardesty. "Jack tells me you're one of W. A. Clark's top lieutenants," I said. "Is that true?"

Hardesty's eyes narrowed. "I'm not here to socialize," he said. "Let's play cards."

"Fine by me," I said. "Any objection to raising the ante?"

Scrapper shrugged. Durand lit a cigar, and didn't bother to reply. "Make it easy on yourself," Hardesty said.

"Let's make it ten."

"Done," said Hardesty.

We took our places. Ed Ferris broke out a new deck, broke the seal, and shuffled. Cards snapped across the green felt, and we resumed our game.

For the next two hours the play see-sawed back and forth, with nobody holding an advantage. Scrapper was ahead for a while, and then he lost a big hand to Durand and went back to slow play. I lost a few small hands to Hardesty, deliberately playing poorly when the pots were small. I even let Hardesty bluff me out of a pot I knew I could win. Hardesty played with his ring, and tossed in a fifty-dollar bet. I folded my hand, running like a scared rabbit.

"He who fights and runs away," I said, "lives to fight another day."

Hardesty sneered and stacked his chips. "Let me know when you're ready," he said. "I can beat you *any* time."

The hand I was waiting for came at about one-thirty in the morning. Hardesty's door card was the ace of diamonds. Mine was the jack of spades. Durand showed the eight of clubs, and Scrapper caught a low card, the four of diamonds. I checked my hole card—it was the jack of hearts! I had pocket jacks, back to back.

Hardesty bet twenty dollars, an amount that told

me he either had aces back to back or he was betting on the come.

I called, and raised twenty dollars. Durand called. Scrapper folded. Hardesty re-raised another twenty. I called, as did Durand.

On the third round, Hardesty caught a three. No apparent help. I picked up a seven. Durand paired his eight. He bet ten dollars. Hardesty raised another twenty, and I called the raise. So did Durand.

Fourth round brought Hardesty a second three—two treys and an ace showing. I picked up the jack of diamonds, giving me two jacks showing and one in the hole.

Durand showed a pair of eights and a ten. I bet twenty dollars. Durand called, and raised thirty dollars, which I took to mean he held two pair or three eights. Either way, my jacks had him beat. Hardesty called. I saw Durand's thirty and raised him thirty.

Durand called. Hardesty saw my thirty and raised twenty more. I called the raise, and so did Durand.

Then came the fifth and final round, and the game suddenly got interesting. Hardesty caught the ace of spades, giving him two pair—aces and treys—showing. I caught another seven, giving me two jacks and two sevens showing. With my jack in the hole, I had a full house!

Durand caught the queen of clubs, which meant

the best hand he could have would be three eights. Hardesty's aces and threes gave him the bet, and he shoved out a stack of ten five-dollar chips. "Fifty to the losers," he said.

Durand called, and I knew he had three eights. He was reading Hardesty's hand as two pair. Hardesty's face was a mask, showing nothing. He looked at the pot, the biggest of the night. He looked at his hole card. Again, he toyed with his ring. *Hardesty was bluffing!*

"Call," I said, "and raise you two hundred." Durand read my hole card as clearly as if he could see it. He was a professional, and he trusted his instincts. He turned his cards over and tossed them to the center of the table. "Fold," he said.

Hardesty looked at my hand. My full house was coming down on him like an avalanche, but he didn't know it. He had believed he could buy the hand. All his chips were in the pot. He reached for his wallet, but found only a hundred dollars there. Hardesty frowned. "I'm short a hundred," he said, "but I'm good for it."

Ed Ferris, the dealer, spoke up. "Table stakes, Hardesty," he said. "You play what you have."

"Damn it, Ed," Hardesty said. He turned to me, almost pleading. "I *am* good for it—Jack told you right, I *do* work for Clark."

"Tell you what," I said. "Put up that fancy ring you're wearin' and I'll call it good."

Anger blazed in Hardesty's eyes. He worked at

the ring, twisting until it came free of his finger. His voice was tight as he pushed the ring into the pile of chips at the table's center. "There, damn you," he said. "I call!"

I turned up my hole card. "Full boat," I said. "Jacks over sevens."

Hardesty froze. I waited. Ferris reached over and turned up Hardesty's hole card. The cards told their story. "Aces and treys," Ferris said. "Two pair."

Hardesty trembled like an aspen tree in a breeze. I trembled some myself, raking the chips toward me. There was well over a thousand dollars in that pot.

Hardesty's eyes blazed. *"Dumb luck,"* he muttered.

I thought of all the nights I'd spent with "Bones" Belcourt back in Dry Creek, learning how to play the big hands and learning when to fold. "Bones" was a good teacher, but he never put much store in luck.

"There's all kinds of luck," I replied. "There's dumb luck, beginner's luck, luck of the Irish, and better luck next time. Whatever kind I had tonight, I'm grateful."

Scrapper grinned. "Hell of a hand, boy-o," he said. "Glad I got out when I did."

Durand pushed his remaining chips over to Ferris. "That's all for me," he said. "Cash me in, Ed."

Hardesty stared as I picked up his ring. I could see he was replaying the last hand in his mind, wondering what had gone wrong. He frowned, concentrating. And then, suddenly, awareness flared in his eyes. Hardesty *recognized* his own *tell!*

"I'll keep this ring 'til you redeem it," I told him. "I can see it's important to the way you play the game."

"Damn you," Hardesty said.

I just smiled. I could afford to.

SEVEN

FOOTPADS AND FRIENDS

Without another word, Cecil Hardesty marched stiffly out the back door of the card room and into the bar. Lucas Durand smiled a wry smile and followed him. Scrapper took his coat from a wall peg and put it on. At the table, Ed Ferris counted my chips and cashed me in. "Eleven hundred and thirty-two dollars," he announced.

Scrapper whistled. "Nice piece o' work, that last hand," he said. "Winnin' at poker sure beats muckin' ore in a copper mine."

Carefully, I put the money in my pocket. "I guess it would," I said, "if a man could do it every time. But at least for me, winnin' at poker is a sometime thing."

Scrapper opened the door that led to the bar. He nodded. "For me, as well. I think I'll have another whiskey and then take meself home."

He paused in the doorway. "Will ye join me, Merlin?"

"Another time," I said. "I won't rest easy until I get this money locked away in the safe at the Centennial."

"Can ye find yer way? There's no tellin' when—or if—Fat Jack will come back."

"I just walk west on Galena 'til I hit Main Street, and then go north to my hotel. Is that right?"

"That's right. Watch yerself, lad. Some o' them streets out there are terrible dark."

Turning, Scrapper entered into the barroom. I followed, walking past the Copper Penny's few remaining customers, and went outside.

At two in the morning, many of the saloons and gambling halls on Galena were still open. Away from the lighted windows and doorways, the street was dark as a mineshaft. Music drifted out of the dancehalls and died in the gloom.

Directly in front of me, a heavy-set drunk stumbled through saloon doors and into my path. He nearly fell, but he caught himself and stood swaying on his feet. He stared at me, his bleary eyes trying to focus. "Steady, pardner," I said. "Steady as she goes." He made no answer, but mumbled a half-hearted challenge as I passed.

Darkness deepened. Sulfur and arsenic fumes

from the smelters joined the smoke of burning ore dumps to cast a foul fog over the city. Light from the beer joints and saloons faded into the distance behind me, and the street seemed darker than before. Passing an alley, I heard the clatter of a trash can and the high-pitched yowl of a cat. I took its cue and walked cat-eyed in the middle of the sidewalk and away from the blackness of alleys and doorways. The sound of my own boot heels echoed on the planks of the sidewalk. Twice, thinking I heard someone following me, I glanced back over my shoulder, but saw nothing.

I missed the familiar weight of my .44, and remembered the gun was still in Jack's hack. The pocket that held my winnings seemed to glow in the dark. I imagined thieves jumping me, taking my money. At a darkened building, I sat down on its steps and pulled my boots off. Dividing the bank notes into two roughly even stacks, I placed a stack inside each boot and pulled them on again. I thought: *These are the most expensive boots I ever wore.*

By the time I turned onto Main Street I'd begun to chide myself. *You're spookin' at shadows,* I told myself, *like a green-broke horse in bear country.*

I had almost shamed myself out of my dread when I looked ahead and saw a narrow alley coming up on my right. I slowed, listening. I heard movement, a scuffling sound. And then, suddenly, a big man and two smaller men stepped out of the shadows and blocked my path!

"Where you *goin'*, cowboy?" asked the big man. His voice was sly, mocking.

I stopped, held my breath. The pounding of my heart was loud in my ears.

The man's voice took on an angry tone. "You damn cowboys can't walk here for *free,* you know. You got to pay a *toll.*"

I glanced to my left, at the silent buildings across the street. There was still time to make a break for it.

The big man stood facing me on the boardwalk. Beside him, one of the other two stepped into the street to block my escape. The third man sidled toward me, his back against the building. *Can't let him get behind me,* I thought.

Somehow, I tamed my voice. "I didn't know," I said. "How much is the toll?"

"All you got!" exclaimed the big man, and all three came at me!

Suddenly, I wasn't afraid any more. Three men were about to beat hell out of me and take my money. There wasn't much I could do about that, but I wasn't going to make it easy for them.

The big man came in fast, too fast for his own good. He drew back a fist that looked as big as a ham, but I didn't back away. Instead, I stepped inside his swing and hit him on the nose with everything I had. My blow didn't stop him, but it caused him to break his stride. I turned away, letting the man's momentum carry him past me, and ducked in time to avoid a roundhouse swing by the second man. I aimed a sidewise kick that caught him full in the belly and slowed him down some.

I didn't even see the third man, but I felt his fist slam hard against my jaw. Bright light exploded inside my brain, and my knees buckled. Blows fell like hail as the other men recovered and joined the fray. They were on me then, slugging and striking. I covered my face, keeping my chin down and taking their punches on my arms and shoulders. The big man was prone to telegraph his punches, and I managed to block most of the blows he aimed at my face, once by taking the full force of his right fist on the top of my head. Sure, it hurt— the shock stunned me and scrambled my vision— but striking my skull with his fist hurt the big man more than he hurt me.

I fought to stay on my feet. The men grabbed at me, tried to pry my arms away so they could do some real damage, but I turned turtle and stayed inside my shell. In the end, I knew I couldn't defend myself against six fists with only two of my own. My arms were getting numb. I was gasping and wheezing, fighting for breath. More of the men's blows were getting through. I took a hard one to the face. I felt my nose break, felt the hot rush of blood, and I knew the game was ending.

One of the men caught my legs and jerked me off my feet. Falling, I curled up in a ball, waiting for the stomping and kicks I knew would come. They came, all right, hard kicks that robbed me of breath and shook my body. I took one to the back of my head, another to the ribs, and several to the deep muscles of my butt, legs, and arms.

Gasping for air, I felt the shock of the kicks and blows, but surprisingly little pain. The real hurt, I knew, would come later. I began to fade in and out of consciousness, my eyesight growing dim. I knew I couldn't hold on much longer.

And then I heard a startled cry, and the hammering and stomping stopped. All at once, my attackers left me! I stared in the direction they'd gone, my vision filled with strange and shifting forms. Wiping my eyes with my shirtsleeve, I stared.

Scrapper! The Irishman held the biggest of the three thugs by the collar and dragged him out into the street. The other two men stepped away from me, their eyes on the struggle.

"Three ag'in one, is it?" Scrapper said. "Give *me* a go, ye yellow bastards!"

Scrapper released his hold on the big man and stepped back. Rising quickly, the man made what turned out to be a serious mistake—he swung on Scrapper O'Dhoul. Calm as a monk at his prayers,

Scrapper ducked the man's big fist. Setting his feet, the Irishman struck him hard with three rapid left jabs to the face. The right cross that followed seemed to come out of nowhere. It connected solidly against the man's jaw and dropped him like a felled tree.

The other two would-be thieves had been moving in on Scrapper. Seeing their companion sprawled in the street made them hesitate, but for one of the men hesitation came too late. He was already in range of Scrapper's deadly right hand when he stopped and tried to back-pedal away from danger. Scrapper stung him with a left jab and then stepped in and delivered a hard right that knocked the man off his feet and sent him reeling.

Scrapper's feet were spread wide in a fighter's stance, his fists cocked and ready. The last man lost his nerve. Jittering backward in panic, he turned and dashed away down the street.

"Run, ye gobshite!" Scrapper said. "Go get ten more o' yer kind and come back for an even fight!"

I tried to get up. I *wanted* to get to my feet, but my legs had other ideas. Now that the fight was over, the pain was setting in with a vengeance. I wasn't about to let my body quit on me, so I pushed it and ignored the hurt. Like a tired mule, my body had the last word. Just as I managed to get up on my hands and knees, all my strength left me. I felt I was spinning into the eddy of a cold, dark river, and I passed out.

I came awake slowly, coming up from darkness into light like a man rising from the bottom of a pool. I was still on the street where I'd fallen. Scrapper bent over me, worry plain on his honest face. "Merlin," he said. "Are ye all right, lad?"

The eddy was pulling me down again. "Don't . . . know," I said. "Do . . . I still . . . have my boots on?"

"Aye, lad. A fine high-heeled pair they are, too."

I closed my eyes. "Then . . . everything's all right," I said.

I lay on my back in a place of darkness and peace, but my pain would not leave me alone. It tormented me like a terrier worries a rat, prodding me to wakefulness. My face felt like it was on fire, and my head throbbed with every breath I took. I opened my eyes a crack and light stabbed in and punished me. Remembrance came, and with it the hurt of the beating. My breathing quickened. I moved, trying to escape the remembered blows and kicks. I cried out, and sat up.

Gentle hands pushed me back down. "Easy, Mister Fanshaw," a soft voice said. "'Tis only me, Molly O'Dhoul. You've been through a bit of a storm, but you're in safe harbor now."

I opened my eyes. Scrapper's sister Molly smiled as she stood looking down at me. Through the narrow window behind her, sunlight turned her auburn hair to flame. I glanced about, trying to get my bearings. I lay, covered by a patchwork quilt atop a painted iron bed. The room was small, and sparsely furnished. I tried again to sit up, but grew lightheaded and lay back again. When I spoke, my voice was hoarse. "Where . . . ?"

"You're in our house, and welcome," Molly said. "My brother brought you here in the wee hours of this mornin'."

My broken nose was tender to the touch, and the skin around my eyes felt puffy. "Scrapper straightened your nose, and put a bit o' plaster to hold it," Molly said. "He says 'twill be good as new."

"I sure am grateful," I said. "If your brother hadn't come along when he did . . ."

It hurt me, but I smiled anyway. "I had a few more playmates than I could handle," I said. "I think they were after my *lunch* money."

Molly's laughter bubbled up like water from a spring. "So I understand," she said. "But be of good cheer. Scrapper found your 'lunch money' in your boots. 'Tis safe, and there seems to be enough to buy you many a lunch, and of the finest kind."

"Some of my playmates were unlucky at poker."

"Including my brother?"

"He lost a few dollars."

Molly sighed. "Yes, he usually does. And yet he

115

loves the game so. Why is it we love the things that treat us badly?"

"Beats me, Miss. Maybe we're just born contrary."

I turned, resting on my elbow. "Where is Scrapper?" I asked. "I'd like to thank him for savin' my bacon."

"He works the day shift at the Mountain Con. He'll be back this evenin'."

I didn't really feel like it, but I made another try at sitting up. When I did, my body protested. A stabbing pain shot through my head, and I felt like I'd been run over by a beer wagon. Through clenched teeth, I heard myself say, "I should be gettin' back to my hotel. I don't want to put you folks out."

"Don't be daft," Molly said. "Lie back and rest. You'll only be puttin' us out if you don't do as I say."

I closed my eyes. "Well," I said, "All right. Maybe I will rest a little while."

When next I awoke, it was evening.

"Evenin,' boy-o," said Scrapper O'Dhoul. I opened my eyes to find the miner standing beside my bed, a lighted kerosene lamp in his hand. "Are ye after sleepin' your life away, or would ye join Molly an' me for a bit o' supper?"

I smiled. Fresh from his bath, Scrapper's hair was neatly parted and lay plastered against his skull. He smelled of lye soap and hair oil, and his skin was pink as a baby's. "Evenin', Scrapper," I said. "Fact is I *could* eat a bite. I have decided to put off dyin' until a later time."

In the lamplight, Scrapper's craggy face was a riot of wrinkles. He set the lamp down atop the bureau and glanced back toward the kitchen. "It's glad I am ye've chosen to live," he said. From behind his back, he produced a small pottery jug and pulled its cork. "To celebrate your momentous decision, may I offer ye a sip of *poteen*?"

I took a sniff of the jug. I'd never heard of poteen, but I knew homemade whiskey when I smelled it. I raised the jug, braced myself, and drank.

I was surprised. The whiskey went down smooth as silk, and warmed me from the inside outward. "That's good moon," I said.

" 'Tis *Irish* moon," Scrapper said. "We use it in the old country to revive corpses."

I sat up. "Speakin' of corpses," I said, "thanks for what you did to keep me from becomin' one."

Scrapper seemed embarrassed. "Not at all," he said. "I'm just glad I could give ye a hand. There's many a bold thug prowlin' the streets of this camp, just waitin' to waylay the unwary."

"Or even the *wary*," I said. "What made you follow me?"

"I suppose it was the thought of ye walkin' the dark streets with all that money from the game."

He grinned. "Or maybe I was aimin' to rob you meself. Eleven hundred dollars is a terrible temptation."

"Eleven hundred and thirty-two," I said, correcting him.

"Sure and I'm not greedy," he said, laughing. "I'd ha' let ye *keep* the thirty-two."

I had no idea how bad I looked until I washed up for supper. In the beveled mirror above the wash stand, my battered face stared back like an accusing ghost. Both my eyes were puffy and swollen, and a purple bruise marked my cheek. Beneath the plaster strip, my nose was red, and tender to the touch. I had a cut lip, loose teeth, and a knot on the top of my head. Scrapper was sympathetic, but matter-of-fact.

"I spent half me life lookin' the way ye do," he said, "and the other half healin' up again. I took up boxin' when I was but a lad, and found I had a talent for it. I was quick on me feet, bulldog stubborn, and I loved to fight."

Scrapper paused, remembering. Then he said, "Digby and me went to work in the mines near Allihies in West Cork as soon as we could hold a shovel. The work was hard, and the pay small, but the miners were fond of sport. When they saw me fight, they took to settin' up matches between me and the other lads. Mostly, I won, and our fortunes improved.

"I worked double shifts at the mines, and I boxed whenever we could promote a match. Before long, I was earnin' more money with me fists than with me muck stick. A good thing, too, because Digby came down with pneumonia and was no longer able to work.

"He got better, but he was still sickly, poor lad. He worked as a clerk, a dustman, a gardener— anything he could find. Then the metals market went belly up, and most of the mines closed. Like many another mucker, I lost me job. Like Digby, I worked at whatever I could find. I still fought sometimes, but with the miners gone there were fewer and fewer bouts.

"Me sister Molly was cleanin' houses in Allihies and takin' in washin', but when the bosses and their families moved on she was out of a job herself. Then we heard about the great copper discoveries in far-off Butte City, and of the need for hard-rock men. We booked passage for America."

Scrapper grinned. "At any rate," he said, "it took years of fightin' to give me this face. Keep walkin' the streets alone at night and one day ye'll be as handsome as *me*."

I gave his grin back. "I wouldn't mind the *result,* but I don't think I could handle the *process.* I think I'll just stay homely, the way I am."

When Scrapper led me into his kitchen, I went along more from politeness than hunger. But as I

119

sat down at the table, the smells of rich stew, soda bread, and black beer persuaded me I was hungry, and hungry indeed. At Molly's urging, I filled my plate not once but twice, and went back for yet a third helping. I praised her cooking until she blushed, and Scrapper laughed aloud, enjoying his sister's happiness.

"Ah, go on with you now," she said. "It's a wicked man you are, Merlin Fanshaw, filled with flattery and honeyed words!"

"Not at all," I said, imitating her brogue. "I'm filled with your savory stew, and bewitched by your soda bread!"

Obviously trying hard not to smile, Molly appealed to her brother. "The man is mad as a hatter," she said. "Sure and that beatin' he took has robbed him of his senses entirely!"

Scrapper assumed a serious expression. "Aye," he said. "Too many beatin's are what did it to *me*."

Sitting there at the O'Dhoul's table was mighty pleasant. The soft glow of lamplight, the simple but tasty supper, and the warmth of our conversation made the evening special. For a few hours, I nearly forgot my lingering aches and pains and my need to thwart an assassin.

But all good things have to end. As the hour grew late, I thanked my hosts again, and told them I needed to go back to my hotel. They urged me to stay, but I knew morning would bring Scrapper another hard day's work at the Mountain Con. He would need his rest. In the end I prevailed, but even then they insisted on walking with me.

We said good-bye at the hotel's front door. "Good night, Merlin," said Molly. "Don't be a stranger."

"Aye, lad," said Scrapper. "Tap 'er light."

I picked up my room key at the front desk and asked the clerk to lock my poker winnings in the hotel safe. He did so, and I asked him if I had any messages.

"No sir," he said, "but Fat Jack Jones left this for you this morning." Gingerly, like a man handling a snake, he took my belted revolver from beneath the counter and passed it over to me.

"Much obliged," I said. "If I'd had this the other night I might not look the way I do today."

The clerk stared at my battered face, and I knew what he saw. I had cuts and bruises from forehead to chin, a red nose, and two black and swollen eyes. I answered the question he was too discreet to ask.

"I cut myself shaving," I said, and walked away toward the staircase.

EIGHT

A DIAMOND RING AND
A COPPER MINE

Until 1888, W. A. Clark made his home in Deer Lodge, a pleasant, tree-lined community some forty-odd miles from Butte. For years, he had managed his enterprises from his bank in that town, but now he was spending nearly all his time at his branch bank in Butte. His holdings in and around the hill had grown, and it only made sense for him to make his headquarters where most of his investments were. Two days after my run-in with the would-be robbers, I walked down to his bank and asked to see him.

The branch manager was a pleasant man with careful eyes. He smiled politely as he looked me over, from my battered face to the .44 on my hip. His eyes paused briefly as they took in the badge on my vest, and then rose to meet mine.

"May I tell Mr. Clark the nature of your business?" he asked.

"Official business," I said. "U.S. marshal's office. I'm conducting an investigation."

The manager looked me over again, in case he missed something the first time. Then he said, "Wait here" and walked toward the offices at the far end of the building. Taking a stand near the front windows, I did as directed, and waited.

Clark's bank was fairly typical of the time and place. The sign out front read: W. A. CLARK & BROTHER, BANKERS. Stone columns framed the double doors that led inside to the spacious lobby. Topped by ornate grillwork, a raised counter of polished wood set the tellers and clerks apart from the bank's depositors. Potted palms, oaken desks and chairs stood like islands on the lobby floor, providing meeting spaces for loan officers and borrowers. Ceiling fans stirred the air, turning lazily under a tin ceiling.

The branch manager returned. "Please," he said, "come with me."

He led me to an office at the rear of the bank and opened the door. "Five minutes," he said. "Mr. Clark is a very busy man."

I nodded, and walked inside.

Three men were seated at a conference table. Papers and charts were spread out before them. W. A. Clark sat at the table's head; I recognized him from photographs, and from Fat Jack's description. A small man, he was dressed in the latest style, from his dark business suit to the pearl stickpin in his silk cravat. He sported a bristling moustache and chin whiskers, and his pale eyes glittered like ice.

I glanced at the other men, and saw that I knew one of them. Cecil Hardesty stared intently at me, his mouth a bitter line. I smiled. Cecil hadn't forgotten our poker game, or the way his "tell" had cost him its final pot.

"Yes?" Clark said. "You wish to see me?"

I turned my attention back to Clark. "Yes, sir," I said. "I'm Merlin Fanshaw, U.S. deputy marshal out of Helena. I'd like to ask you a few questions, if I may."

"Yes, yes," Clark said. "Get on with it, man."

"All right. Last week, a visitor to Butte named Digby O'Dhoul was found dead in an uptown alley. Before he took the big jump, he told everyone who'd listen that he overheard a conversation in which a man hired an assassin to kill Marcus Daly."

Clark's eyes flashed. "Yes," he snapped. "I heard that story. What's your question, Deputy? Did *I* hire an assassin? The answer is no. Do I think killing that bog Irish bastard is a good idea? The answer is yes. Now, is there anything else?"

The third man at the table leaned back in his chair and smiled. He was a young man, well groomed and handsome. I figured him for another of Clark's lieutenants. Behind him, leaning against the wall, was a huge man with a fighter's face and arms nearly the size of my legs. His eyes hadn't left me since I entered the room.

Bodyguard, I thought.

Cecil was staring at me, too. He seemed nervous, uncertain. Little beads of sweat appeared on his upper lip. He lowered his eyes.

"Howdy, Cecil," I said. "Good to see you again. You still interested in buying your ring back?"

"This is neither the time nor the place," he muttered. "I'll talk to you later."

"You're right," I said. "I apologize."

I turned back to Clark. "No, sir. There's nothing else, not at this time. Thank you for seein' me."

Cecil got to his feet. "I'll show the deputy out, Mr. Clark."

"Be sure to show him all the *way* out," Clark said, and turned his attention back to his charts and papers.

Cecil walked me through the lobby and opened the door leading to the street. I passed through and stepped outside. To my surprise, Cecil followed me. He stood for a moment, his head bowed and his eyes closed. Then he raised his head and looked at me. "Seems we've got off on the wrong foot," he said. "I'm sorry, Fanshaw."

"Don't mention it," I said. "Tempers can run high at a poker table. I get carried away sometimes."

Cecil smiled. He drew out a leather wallet from the breast pocket of his jacket. He said "If you have my ring with you . . ."

"Sure," I said. Reaching into my pocket, I brought out the ring. The diamond sparkled in the sunlight.

"How much?" Cecil asked.

"You were a hundred light," I said.

He took a hundred dollar bill from his wallet and

handed it to me. I gave him the ring and pocketed the bill.

Cecil slipped the ring on his finger. "I appreciate your letting me redeem this," he said. "Sentimental value, you know."

I grinned. "You bet. *I'm* sentimental about money, too."

He laughed, and the tension between us eased. "I'm sure I have other tells," he said, "but I don't think I'll be wearing this ring on poker night anymore."

"Good idea. No hard feelings?"

"None," he said. He held out his hand. "Shake?"

I gave him my hand and we shook. His grip was firm and his smile was friendly.

I couldn't help wishing his *eyes* were friendly, too.

Back at my hotel room, I shucked my boots and stretched out atop the bed. My meeting with W. A. Clark had been brief. His comments had been curt and to the point. Yes, he despised Marcus Daly, but he did *not* pay an assassin to kill him. End of story, Deputy Fanshaw. I'm a busy man, so if there's nothing else . . .

Before I met Clark, I considered him the most likely suspect. He and Daly were business rivals and personal enemies; neither would grieve the sudden death of the other. Clark certainly had ample finances to pay ten thousand dollars for the job. And yet his manner had been cool and matter-of-fact. He freely admitted he detested Daly but denied plotting his death.

I was inclined to believe him. Maybe, I thought, there *was* no hired assassin. Maybe the entire incident was only a hallucination on the part of Digby O'Dhoul, a delusion brought on by booze and his own imagination.

And yet . . . what about Ridgeway's telephone call? According to Abby, at the Pinkerton Agency, there really *was* a contract killer named Charon. How could Digby's imagination have come up with *that* detail? Now Digby was dead, a supposed suicide. But he was a man who never owned or used a firearm, a left-handed man who allegedly shot himself in the temple with his *right* hand.

Had Digby been murdered? Had powerful men killed him because of the story he told? And if his story *was* merely fantasy, who would have cared?

I sat up. My thoughts only dug the mystery deeper. Like a dog chasing its tail, I was chasing answers and not catching them. I needed to clear my mind. I needed to get away from town for an hour or two, maybe take a ride up into the mountains.

I heard someone knocking. Walking quickly to the door, I opened it to find Scrapper O'Dhoul standing in the hallway.

"Scrapper!" I said. "Come in! What brings you out this way?"

"I've got a day off from me shift," he said. "But I was wonderin'—would ye like to see the workin's of a copper mine?"

"I would," I said. "When?"

"Right now, if ye've a mind to. Big Jim Brennan, the shift boss, says I can give ye the grand tour."

"All right," I said. "What do I need to do?"

Scrapper held up a metal lunch pail. "Molly made ye a lunch," he said. "Just put the bucket under your arm, and follow me."

The lunch pail had a handle. I picked it up by its handle and donned my old hat.

"Nivver carry your lunch pail by the handle," Scrapper said. "The boys will take ye for a greenhorn. A miner tucks his lunch bucket under his arm like a football."

"The boys will take me for a greenhorn no matter what I do," I said. "I *am* one. I've never been down in a mine in my life."

"Just watch what I do, and do what I tell ye," Scrapper said. "When the day ends ye'll still not be a minin' man, but ye'll look the part."

The gallows frame and buildings of the Mountain Con stood stark against the sky on a low hill above town. Scrapper and me rode a street car to the end of Main Street, and trudged up the hill to the mine yard.

The office stood just inside the gate. Scrapper

128

opened the door and spoke to a sandy-haired man at the desk. "I'm takin' a guest down today, Murph. Big Jim says it's all right."

"Yeah," said the man. "Jim said you'd be comin' through."

Outside in the yard again, I watched the cable from the shaft house roll through the flanges of the gallows frame wheel, lowering cages inside the mine shaft.

"The engineers run the skip cages from the shaft house there," Scrapper said. "They have marked the cable with paint for each level the hoist reaches."

A line of miners stood waiting to board the cages. Scrapper led the way to a weathered supply building. Shelves along the wall held shoes, hats, jumpers and such. "Ye'll be needin' miners' boots," he said. "Let's find ye a pair."

I pulled off my riding boots and tried on miners' boots from the shelf until I found a pair that fit. They were well worn, with a hard toe cap and hobnail soles for traction. I had worn riding boots since I was a kid, and at first the flat-heeled miners' boots made me feel like I was falling over backward.

Scrapper handed me a jumper from the pile, and I put it on. Then he handed me an odd-looking lamp. "They'll be lightin' all the mines with electric lights soon," he said, "but some of us old-timers still carry our candlesticks and candles.

Today ye can carry this safety lamp. 'Twill give ye light without riskin' a blow-up."

The steam whistle shrieked, announcing the noon hour. The long line of miners began to move, entering the cages. Scrapper and me took our places at the line's end. At the edge of the shaft, a husky worker was loading men into the cages. He packed in nine men to a cage, then closed an iron gate and secured it from outside. He gave a tug to a signal rope, the cage went down ten feet or so, and the loader packed the next cage as he had the first. There were three cages, stacked one on top of the other like floors in a building.

Scrapper and me got on the last cage of the third tier, jammed in with other miners like steers in a cattle car. The station tender said, "Tap 'er light, boys" and the cages dropped down the shaft like a rock. I leaned back, looking up into the darkness, and prayed the cable would hold. Down we went, fast as an express train, the cages rumbling and shaking.

Lights flashed as we dropped. Jammed close beside me by the bodies of the other men, Scrapper spoke into my ear. "Them lights ye see come from the main tunnels, every hundred feet. We're goin' down to twenty hundred."

"Twenty hundred . . . *two thousand feet?*" I said. "Lordamighty!"

The cage slowed, then stopped with a jerk and sprung up and down in the shaft. A big, redheaded worker opened the cage door, and Scrapper took hold of my arm. "Step lively, lad," he said. "Here's where we get off."

We were in a big, well-lit room Scrapper said was the station. Maybe two dozen miners were there, moving out into the tunnels that opened off the room. Everybody seemed to know Scrapper; from the easy way they spoke to him I could tell they liked and respected him.

A bandy-legged man with a big belly spotted Scrapper and greeted him with a grin. "Scrapper!" he said. "I thought you weren't workin' today."

"I'm not," Scrapper said. "I'm takin' a visitor through. But I could use a good Number Eight shovel, if ye have one. It don't feel right, bein' down in a mine without a muck stick in me hand."

"This is me friend, Merlin Fanshaw," he said. "Merlin, meet Bill Mulcahy. He's nipper here at the Mountain Con."

"Howdy, Bill," I said. "What's a nipper?"

Scrapper answered my question. "A nipper is a fat man in charge of the tools down here," he said. "He stashes 'em where no man can find 'em and saves the good ones for his friends."

Mulcahy laughed, and his belly shook. "Keep it up," he said, "and I'll be givin' you a broke-handled canal wrench with loose rivets." But he handed Scrapper a new shovel from a stack beside the entrance to the tunnel, and Scrapper nodded his thanks.

131

Scrapper filled a water bag and slung it over his shoulder. He lit a candle, helped me light my safety lamp, and led the way off into the darkness. I followed him close, like a calf following its mother; I wasn't about to get lost in some durned copper mine if I could help it.

We walked a piece; I don't know how far. We didn't talk much, but when we did our voices had a hollow sound, the way they sometimes do in a big cave. The air smelled musty and stale, like it does in a root cellar, and the farther we walked the hotter it got.

Scrapper said the tunnel was called a drift, and that a drift ran parallel to, or inside, a body of ore. Rails ran down the center of the drift, and I learned they were tracks for the ore cars that were hauled to the station by horses and mules.

A short time later, we saw a string of six fully loaded cars coming our way. The ore train was pulled by a single mule and driven by a dirty-faced kid who looked to be no more than twelve years old. The young skinner grinned as he met and passed us, his teeth and eyes shining in the light of my safety lamp. The mule must have been strong as an ox, I thought, to pull those heavy cars. Scrapper said the animals spent five or six years working underground, and then the company took them up and put them out to pasture.

"Sure and wouldn't it be grand," he said, "if they'd do the same for us miners?"

I heard dripping and splashing in the darkness. Lifting my lamp, I saw where water had mixed with copper ore to form rock icicles of amber, green, and red. Copper water stood in pools along the sides of the drift, and I walked wide of it. Scrapper said the water was a deadly poison, and that if it even dripped on your skin it would give you sores.

We walked on for maybe another ten minutes and then climbed a ladder up into another kind of hollowed out space, this one composed of solid rock overhead and a long slope of dirt, boulders, and broken timbers. It was a scary-looking place, and it appeared the whole shebang, rock ceiling and all, could come crashing down any minute. Scrapper explained this was a "rill stope" and said we were going to see miners "bar down a rill." I nodded my head, as I did when I was a kid and Pa was trying to teach me something, but at that point I had no idea what a "rill stope" was.

It turns out a rill stope is an excavation, sort of like an upside-down pyramid, where miners stand on ore they blasted loose the day before and send it tumbling down to a chute mouth. I watched as two miners went to work with long iron bars, poking and prying down big sections of loose rock and dirt. They kept at it until they were satisfied the whole place was barred down and free of loose rock that could fall and kill a man. Scrapper said the company liked rill stope mining because it didn't require much timbering. I took his word on that, but kept an eye on the tons of rock and dirt above my head. All things being equal, I said, I'd just as soon not have half a mountain to fall on me.

We took time to eat our lunches, and I found that Molly had sent us both out with the meat pies the Cousin Jacks, or Cornishmen, called "letters from home." Pasties were a full meal in themselves—beef, potatoes, and onions all diced up and baked in a pie dough crust. From what Scrapper told me, Cousin Jacks and Irishmen didn't get along all that well, but I guess Cornish and Irish women did. Enough to trade recipes, anyway.

The pasties had been hot when Molly put them in our lunch pails, but they'd long since gone cold. That didn't bother me; I wolfed mine down and cleaned up every crumb. It was different with Scrapper.

"I like me lunch *hot*," he said. Placing the pasty on the blade of his shovel, he held his lighted miner's candle beneath it until he judged the meal warm enough. Then, taking his time, he ate his pasty, saving the last corner of its crust to crumble and scatter in the drift. "An offerin' for the mine spirits," he explained.

When we'd finished our lunches, Scrapper lit his pipe and puffed away for a while. He told me stories of his days as a miner, both in Ireland and there at Butte Hill, and he spoke of the changes he'd seen.

"Back in the mines of West Cork," he said, "we used hand drills and black powder, and a divvil of a time that was! It took a two-man team ten hours just to drill a four-foot hole. And then, when a man went to charge the holes and tamp in the fuses he nivver knew whether the damn powder would go off in his face!

"Now we've got the new one-man 'buzzy' drill. The 'buzzy' runs on compressed air and is faster by far than hand-drillin' but terrible dusty. Some of the boys call the 'buzzy' the 'widow maker' because of the rock dust that gets in a man's lungs.

"And we don't use black powder any more. Now it's dynamite in the holes, but a powder man still has to take care. He needs to 'tap 'er light' when he tamps in the charge, and count the blasts before goin' back to the rock. Many a powder man has met his maker when a slow-burnin' fuse joined forces with a poor count of charges blown."

Scrapper took a swig of water from the bag and passed it over to me. Getting to his feet, he picked up his shovel and said, "We'd best be goin' on. I've got more to show ye."

We turned up a drift and found a man shoveling loose rock into an ore car. "That's Ole Svenson," Scrapper said. "One of the best muckers on the hill. I'll give him a hand."

The man looked up as we drew near. He had a

round face and quick blue eyes. Seeing Scrapper, he stopped shoveling and grinned. "What the hell you doin' down here on your day off?" he asked. "I t'ink you *miss* me, by golly."

Scrapper grinned. "Meet me friend, Merlin Fanshaw," he said. "Merlin, this is Ole Svenson, dumbest Swede in Silver Bow County. I taught him everything I know and he *still* don't know nothin'."

Ole shook my hand with a grip that could have crushed granite. "What he yust said maybe gives you some idea how little this ugly Mick *knows*," he said.

Scrapper's grin widened. "Pay him no mind, Merlin. Dumb Swede's just jealous because he ain't Irish."

"My people were *Vikings*," Ole said. "They sailed over to Ireland and made babies with the Irish ladies, by golly. Where you t'ink all them blue-eyed, redheaded Irishers *came* from, anyway?"

Scrapper spat into his palm and rubbed his hands together. Taking a firm grip on his shovel, he said, "Stand back, lad. I have to show this greenhorn how to load an ore car."

Ole took a grip on his own shovel and bent his knees. For a moment the two men paused, their eyes locked. Then, at the same time, they started shoveling rock into the car. For the next five minutes they made the ore fly, loading one cart and then another. Then they stopped, as if someone called time, and stood grinning at each other with sweat streaming down their faces.

"You're slowin' up, Ole," Scrapper said. "But you're still faster than me."

"No, by golly," Ole said. "You beat me by two shovels."

Scrapper pulled a bandanna from his jumper and mopped his brow. "So long," he said. "See you tomorrow. We'll muck out that new drift together."

"You betcha," said Ole. "See you tomorrow, Scrapper."

Scrapper continued his tour for another hour, guiding me through a day's work at the Mountain Con. Then, at quitting time, we made our way back to the station and joined the men going off shift. Once again, we found ourselves packed into the cages. The station tender rang the bell, the engineer set the hoist in motion, and we shot up two thousand feet, rattling and banging back to sunlight and cold mountain air.

We parted with a handshake outside the mine yard. Scrapper was my friend, and he'd shared his world with me. I thanked him and told him good night, and he said, "Not at all" and "Tap 'er light."

I took a deep breath, felt the sunlight warm upon my face, and walked away down the hill to the streets of Butte City.

NINE

A PICNIC LUNCH AND A NEW HAT

Early the following week, I lay atop the bed in my hotel room and thought about the goodness of Scrapper O'Dhoul and his sister Molly. They were the kind of folks I savvied, folks who think of strangers as merely friends they haven't met yet.

When the street toughs jumped me the night of the poker game Scrapper had come to my aid without hesitation in a fight that was not his own. Ignoring the risk, he laid into the would-be thieves and drove them away. He brought me into his home. There, he and Molly fed me, nursed my wounds, and treated me as an honored guest. Now Scrapper had taken me two thousand feet below ground into a copper mine to show me something of the dangerous work he and the other miners shared.

I was impressed by what I saw. The miners reminded me of cowpunchers I knew, men who were proud of their skills, loyal to their companions and the outfit they worked for.

Scrapper and Molly said little about their grief at the loss of their brother, but I knew their hurt ran deep. As a lawman, I saw Digby's death as something I needed to investigate and resolve. To

Scrapper and Molly, Digby's death was personal, and a loss to be mourned.

I lay back on my bed and gave some thought to what I could do for my new friends. Then I sat up, pulled my boots on, and took a walk down to Fogarty's Livery.

When I drove up to the O'Dhoul house in a rented buggy, Molly was hanging out her washing on the backyard clothesline. The day was hot, and a sullen wind drifted smoke and ash from the smelters over the homes and commercial buildings of the town. There was little left of the forenoon, but I paid tribute to it anyway. I tipped my hat and smiled. "Top of the mornin', Molly," I said.

Molly smiled in recognition, but a slight frown furrowed her brow as she finished pinning a bed sheet to the line. "And the rest of the day to yourself," she said.

Bending, Molly picked up her empty laundry basket. "I think the wind knows when it's wash day," she said, "and sifts the black smoke over our house just for spite."

"I don't mean to complain," she said. "The mines give Scrapper a decent wage and we have a good life here, but sometimes I can't help wishin' for the fair skies and green hills of Ireland."

"Especially on wash day," I said.

She laughed. "Yes," she said. "Especially then."

139

"Well, I can't give you Ireland, but I can take you out of the smoke for an hour or two. Will you come away with me for a picnic, Molly O'Dhoul?"

"A picnic?"

I turned, and showed her the hamper behind the buggy seat. "You bet. Fried chicken, green beans, biscuits, lemonade, and apple pie. I had the hotel put a basket together."

Molly smiled her crooked smile, and her frown disappeared. She said, "Back in Allihies, an old priest told me Sunday is 'one day in seven to save us from our selfish selves.' Two hours in twenty-four away from this dreary camp just might save *me* from goin' *loopers*."

For a moment, she hesitated. "I will need to be at home when Scrapper comes off shift at five," she said. "Do you suppose . . ."

"You'll be back with time to spare," I told her.

Molly turned to enter the house. "I'll just fetch my shawl and my bonnet—and a bit of jam for those biscuits," she said. Pausing at the doorway, she looked back. "Thank you for the askin'," she said. "You've a sweet spirit, Merlin Fanshaw."

Minutes later, with Molly beside me, I turned the carriage horse away from the city and drove north to a broad meadow known as Elk Park. The noise and smoke of the camp fell away behind us, giving way to green grass and wildflowers under clear blue skies. The area had been heavily logged, but islands of ponderosa and lodgepole pine stood tall at the edges of the meadow, and a mountain stream danced in the sunlight.

Molly seemed to drink in the sights and smells of the countryside, finding joy at each bend of the road. It was she who chose our picnic place; a grassy slope above the creek, at the foot of an aspen grove. I stopped the buggy and helped her down.

"Oh, my," she said. "How grand it all is! I nearly forgot there could be such loveliness in the world!"

I had borrowed a blanket from the hotel, and with Molly's help I spread it on the grass beneath the aspens. Then I placed the basket on the blanket, and Molly busied herself in laying out our lunch. We filled our plates, and I poured us each a glass of lemonade.

"You must think I'm bold as brass," she said, "comin' out buggy-ridin' with a well-favored man like yourself on barely a moment's notice. Sure and my neighbors will think I'm a shameless hussy!"

"No one would ever think that of you, Molly," I said.

Seated on the blanket, Molly leaned back on her hands and looked out across the meadow at the mountains. Her face was relaxed, her expression one of simple wonder. "Ah, they could and they would," she said, "but just bein' here on such a day is more than worth the risk."

I raised my glass in a toast to the day. "Here's how," I said.

"*Sláinte,*" said Molly.

We drank together, and Molly met my eyes. " 'Twas kind of you to think of me," she said. "I'm grateful, Merlin."

I looked away. Molly's gratitude made me uneasy. Asking her to come away from the city for an hour or two was my way of returning her kindness. It was a small thing. I was being a friend, and nothing more.

"I'm obliged to you and Scrapper," I said. "Kindness begets kindness, I reckon. But don't make it sound like charity. I asked you out because I wanted to be with you."

Molly's laughter was like music. "And why wouldn't you?" she asked. "I'm an elegant spinster lady and a fine washerwoman. Also, I eat chicken with my fingers and drink lemonade in the great out-of-doors."

Talk came easy that afternoon. I told Molly about my growing up back in Dry Creek, and of my mother's passing when I wasn't but ten. I spoke of running mustangs with my pa, and of our gentling those wild ponies for sale to the cow outfits along the Little Porcupine.

I also told Molly about the summer Pa died in

142

his horse wreck at the home place, and how I went on to become first an outlaw and then a deputy marshal under Chance Ridgeway. I even told her about my longtime sweetheart, Pandora Pretty Hawk, and how she had fell in love with Johnny Peters and married him. I never meant to run on so, but for some reason I was a regular chatterbox that day.

Through it all, Molly just sat there with her blue eyes big and friendly, and listened. When I finally ran down some, she smiled and said, "Ah, Merlin. 'Tis a true *Irish* story you've told me, full of love and sadness."

She spoke of her own life then, covering some of the same ground Scrapper had the night he told me about working the mines back in west Cork. Molly's voice was steady and matter-of-fact when she talked of taking in washing and cleaning the houses of the mine owners. She told of Scrapper's hard work in the mines, and his determination to make a new life with his brother and sister in America.

"We were happy as larks to be comin' here," Molly said, "but there was sadness, as well. We were leavin' Ireland and the only life we knew for the hope of a better life in America. And Scrapper was leavin' part of his heart behind, as well."

Molly paused. She seemed to be gathering her thoughts, looking back to another time and another world.

Then she said, "Scrapper has a sweetheart, you see, a lovely girl from our village named Eileen O'Grady. Scrapper wanted to marry Eileen and bring her with him to America, but the poor lad had scarcely two pence to rub together, and Digby and me to care for besides. So Scrapper and Eileen parted, but he vowed he'd send for her when he'd made his stake.

"We came to Butte, and Scrapper worked hard and saved his money. I have done, as well. Digby found work at St. Elmo's in Helena, but he still had trouble makin' ends meet. Scrapper and I helped him out from time to time."

With the mention of her other brother, Molly's eyes grew misty.

"Poor Digby," she said. "He had such a wretched life. First he drank from the bottle, and then the bottle drank from *him*. When he came to visit this spring, I thought we'd have a week or two as family once again, but Digby was troubled in his mind, and haunted by phantoms."

The frown on Molly's brow was back again. Her eyes met mine and held them. "Tell me," she said. "Do you believe Digby really overheard a plot to kill Mr. Daly? Or was it only a mad delusion?"

"I don't know," I said. "But you didn't ask what I *know,* you asked what I *believe.* Yes, I believe your brother really *did* hear what he said he heard."

Like storm clouds overshadow a sunny day,

Molly's next question stole the joy from the afternoon. She turned her head away, but not before I saw the tears brimming in her eyes.

"And his death?" she asked. "Did he take his own life, or was he murdered?"

"Again, Molly, I don't know. But I promise you I won't rest until I do."

Our conversation turned to other things. We continued to act as if our outing was as light-hearted as before, but we both knew it wasn't. After a time, we packed up our dishes and silverware and shook out and folded the blanket. Molly stood, her shawl about her shoulders, gazing out at the green meadows and forested hills of Elk Park. I helped her into the buggy, climbed up beside her, and swung the rig around for the trip back to Butte City.

I was as good as my word. Just as we pulled up at Molly and Scrapper's house, I heard the steam whistle at the Mountain Con announce the end of the day shift. Soon, miners would ride their crowded cages up to the surface and step out into sunlight again. I gave Molly a hand down. "Just in time," I said. "I expect Scrapper will be home directly."

Molly raised an eyebrow. "He will, if he doesn't stop for a beer with the lads first. But it's seldom these days that he does that without lettin' me know."

She looked up into my eyes. "Thank you again for our picnic," she said. "'Twas a lovely time."

"For me, as well," I said. "Tell Scrapper I said hello."

"That I will," Molly said. Turning to enter her yard, she stopped and looked back at me. Her face was flushed from the sun, and once again, her blue eyes found mine. "Merlin," she said. "If you don't get a better offer, why don't you come over for Sunday dinner? Scrapper would like that."

Then she smiled. "And so would I."

"That makes three of us," I said. "I'll be here, with bells on."

She had nearly reached her front door when I called her name. "And Molly," I said. "There couldn't *be* a better offer."

I spent the next few days catching up on my housekeeping and getting better acquainted with the town. Seeing Molly hang out her washing the day of our picnic reminded me that my own dirty clothes needed attention, so early Saturday morning I bundled them up and took them to a Chinese laundry on East Galena.

The shirt I wore the night of my run-in with the street toughs was too badly torn for mending, so I decided I'd buy myself another. On East Park Street, a fair piece from Chinatown, and beyond the cribs and parlor houses of the Red Light District, stood the retail emporiums and clothing stores of the camp's Jewish merchants. It was to that quarter I made my way.

Storekeepers were cranking open their awnings and sweeping the sidewalks when I walked up that morning. Their doors were open to the street, and clerks were busy stocking the long benches in front of the store windows with merchandise of every kind. I saw shoes for women and men, stacks of caps and hats, piles of underwear and socks, lunch buckets, shirts, pants, overalls, slickers, and rubber boots. There weren't many shoppers out at that hour of the morning, so I took time to look the offerings over. That's when I met Solomon Shapiro.

"Good morning, Mister Cowboy," he said. "Welcome to Shapiro's. If you ain't finding what you want out here, it's because I got it inside. Best prices in Butte, everything a bargain."

He leaned against the door jamb, watching me over the tops of his spectacles. He was a tall man and gaunt, with a long face and quick, clever eyes. He wore a skull cap, a dark woolen vest over a collarless cotton shirt, and he sported a short, neatly trimmed beard.

"Mornin'," I said. "I'm lookin' for a shirt. You got one that'll fit me?"

Shapiro studied me for a moment, measuring me with his eyes. "You need a work shirt, best quality and price. Sixteen and a half neck, thirty-four sleeve, but never mind the sleeve length. Longer sleeves I'll sell you. You wash the shirt, the sleeves shrink to fit.

"Also you need a dress shirt, fancy with a pleated front. Dress shirts I got, too. Finest in Montana. You came to the right place, Mister Cowboy."

I grinned. "I just came in for the one shirt. I don't need . . ."

The storekeeper took me by the arm and led me inside. "Worry you shouldn't," he said. "Two shirts you need, two shirts I'll sell. But at such a price you couldn't buy even one cheap shirt someplace else."

Now I'm not saying I'm perfect. I have been fleeced a time or two, and I've been skinned more than once. But I didn't just fall off the pumpkin wagon. I've dealt with a wide variety of horse traders, peddlers, and flim-flam artists in my time. I know how to turn down a sales pitch. And so the only way I can explain how I came to buy two shirts, three pair of socks, a suit of underwear, and a new pair of California pants is that I must have *wanted* to. Shapiro was a likeable cuss, and I admired his style.

He wrapped my new duds in paper from a roll and tied the bundle with string. Then, as he was adding up my bill, he stopped short.

"Say, Mister Cowboy," he said. "Some of my business it ain't, but I got to be honest. Forgive me for saying it, but that *hat* you're wearing makes you look like a *schlemiel*."

148

"A what?"

Shapiro stepped back. "I ain't saying you are! I'm just saying how it looks. A *schlemiel* is a person who ain't so smart. A *chump*."

I took my hat off and looked it over. It was sweat-stained and dirty, from trail dust, smoke, axle grease, and other things I didn't even want to think about. Horses had stepped on it. Too many snows and too much rain had altered its shape. The hat had taken on a form John B. Stetson never intended. I had to admit the old conk cover had seen better days. "I've wore this Stetson for years," I said. "It's like an old friend."

Shapiro looked at it, too. "Such a *friend*," he said. "Your *friend* is making you *look* bad. A handsome cowboy like yourself should wear a fine-looking hat."

"I suppose you just happen to *know* of such a hat," I said.

Shapiro shrugged. "For you, the *perfect* hat. But I understand. A slave to fashion you ain't. You are loyal to your old hat. You don't care what people think. You don't care *how* bad you look. A new hat you wouldn't want."

"Now hold on . . . I never said that. I suppose a man could own *two* hats . . ."

Shapiro disappeared into the back room and came back seconds later carrying a dusty hatbox. "Here," he said. "It couldn't hurt you to look, could it? I ain't saying you should buy, but you can look, can't you?"

The storekeeper blew dust off the box and removed the lid. Like a bishop at a coronation, he carefully lifted out the hat inside and held it up for me to see. I saw it was a genuine "Boss of the Plains" Stetson, silver belly in color, with a four-inch brim and crown. I have to say it was a fine-looking hat.

"To tell the truth, I mostly stock hats for miners. This is the only cowboy hat I have," Shapiro said. "Size seven and a quarter, red silk lining, leather band, finest nutria fur. It has your name on it."

I was beginning to get my feet under me. I knew what a good Stetson was worth, and I was set to haggle. "I don't know," I said. "I don't really need another hat. How much are you askin'?"

"I'm losing money, but what can I do? Gentleman cowboys don't come along every day. Twelve dollars and I'm giving it away."

"*Eight* dollars and you're giving it away."

"Mister Cowboy! *Eleven,* and you're robbing me!"

I started for the door. "Well, like I said, I don't really need another hat."

"*Ten!* Ten dollars and my kids will starve for a week or two."

Shapiro looked at me, his eyes big behind the lenses of his spectacles. He smiled, waiting for my reply.

"Sold," I said. "You drive a hard bargain, Mister Shapiro."

"You don't know the heff of it, Mr. Cowboy. My kids ain't starved yet."

I shaped my new Stetson in the steam from Shapiro's teakettle, and set the hat squarely atop my head. Looking at myself in the mirror, I thought: *This surely is a handsome sombrero. Makes me look like I am somebody.*

As a man might pick up a dead skunk from the roadway, Shapiro gingerly picked up my old hat and placed it inside the hatbox. I paid my bill, gathered up my purchases, and sauntered out into the morning. As I walked away from his shop, I figured Shapiro was already in the back somewhere, scrubbing the dirt of my old hat from his hands.

With my arms loaded with packages, I caught the streetcar across town to Main and hiked the two steep blocks up to my hotel. As I neared the hotel's front door, I saw Fat Jack Jones out in front, his four-passenger rockaway parked at the curb. A well-dressed gent I figured was Jack's passenger stood on the hotel's gallery, his luggage on the pavement beside him. The gent paid his fare and turned to enter the hotel as a bellhop scurried out and picked up his bags.

Jack saw me and grinned. "Well, if it ain't the

same old Merlin Fanshaw, in a brand new hat," he said. "Are all them packages for me?"

I smiled. "It's not Christmas time yet," I said, "but if you'll wait 'til I take this plunder up to my room I'll buy you a beer at the blind pig of your choice."

"I never turn down a free beer," Jack said. "It's a matter of principle."

The Blue Frog Saloon was neither the best nor the worst drinking place in Butte City, but it had the advantage of being the closest. Jack and me stepped inside its front door, out of the sun's glare, and made our way to the bar more by feel than by sight. I gave my eyes time to adjust to the gloom, and sized the place up with my nose. The familiar smells of stale beer, sawdust, and tobacco smoke brought back memories of my pa. I guess they always will.

The saloonist wiped the hardwood before us with a bar rag, and asked our order.

"Two beers," I said.

"I haven't seen you since your big win at the Copper Penny," Jack said. "I heard you got jumped by thieves."

"Yeah," I said. "It was touch and go for a while, until Scrapper showed up. Whoever named him 'Scrapper' sure knew what they were talkin' about."

The barkeep drew two scoops and set them

before us. I raised my stein to Jack and said, "How."

"How," said Jack, and we drank.

Jack frowned, his eyes on his stein. "Damn street toughs are gettin' worse all the time. I should have been there to drive you back to the hotel."

I shook my head. "No way you could have known," I said. "Besides, you were gone by then, takin' Joe Campbell to the doctor."

"Yeah. Joe's comin' along. He was tender for a while where the doc sewed him up, but he's doin' all right now."

"I sure could have used my .44 that night," I said, "but it was still in your hack. Thanks for bringin' it back to the hotel."

"Lockin' the barn door after the horse is gone. Never occurred to me you'd need a gun that night."

"A man never needs a gun until he *needs* one. Trouble is he never knows when that time will come."

Jack took a sip of his beer. "Makin' any progress on your investigation?"

"Not much. I did talk to W. A. Clark, at his bank. He denied hirin' an assassin, but he did say he thought killin' Marcus Daly was a good idea."

"No love lost between those two. I hear Clark's runnin' for territorial representative to Congress this year. No politics for Mr. Daly, though. He'd rather *buy* a bureaucrat than be one."

Jack finished his beer and ordered another round. His elbows on the bar, he turned and fixed me with a quizzical stare. "Have you heard about Cecil Hardesty?"

"I saw him at Clark's bank last week. He redeemed the ring he lost to me. What about him?"

"W. A. Clark fired him. Cecil Hardesty has joined the ranks of the unemployed."

I was surprised, and I guess it showed. "I hadn't heard," I said. "What happened?"

Jack shrugged. "Beats me. I ran into Cecil at the Four Jacks Club. He said Clark sacked him and showed him the door. Didn't say why."

"He'll likely hire on with some other mining mogul. Clark and Daly aren't the only high rollers in town."

"No," said Jack, "but they roll a hell of a lot *higher* than the others."

"I still need to meet Marcus Daly," I said. "Any idea how best to do that?"

"Mr. Daly ain't hard to meet," Jack said. "He's got an office over on Mountain Street, a mile east of the post office. He lives in that West Granite Street mansion I showed when you first hit town. He spends some of his time overseein' his interests at Anaconda. And he'll be runnin' his thoroughbreds down at the racetrack when the season opens.

"Right now I hear he's in New York, hob-nobbin' with the other high rollers. But I expect he'll be back any day now. Butte Hill is where the goose that laid the copper egg lives, and Mr. Daly likes to keep an eye on the goose.

"Like I said, Mr. Daly ain't hard to meet. You just have to catch him standin' still for a minute."

I have to confess I was on my guard with Jack that morning. Knowing his liking for strong drink, I was fully prepared for our few beers to become more than a few *whiskeys*. I was relieved when that didn't happen. Jack fished a pocket watch from his vest and snapped open the case.

"No rest for the workin' class," he said. "The noon train is due in ten minutes, and I need to be down at the depot with my hack."

"See you," I said. "Tap 'er light."

Jack grinned. "You're pickin' up the lingo," he said. "Know where that expression comes from?"

"No," I said. "I had supper last week at Scrapper's house. That's what he said as I left."

"Down in the mines, powder men drill holes in the rock and tamp dynamite in the holes before they touch off a charge. They tamp the dynamite sticks into place, but they tap 'em *light,* if they're interested in stayin' alive. 'Tap 'er light' is how a miner says 'take it easy,' or 'be careful.'"

"Good advice," I said. "So long, Jack."

"Tap 'er light, Merlin," Jack said.

TEN

THE NAKED TRUTH

The weather was hot and sultry that Saturday, and I spent most of the afternoon in my room at the Centennial. I pulled down the window shades and laid back on the bed, trying to recall the cold weather I complained about last February. It didn't help much. Sweat rolled off me like rain off a roof, and I came to believe I had the town's Finlanders beat—I didn't even need to build a fire to have my own sauna.

I cracked open a window, thinking I might pick up a cooling breeze, but all that came in was smoke from the smelters. Figuring I'd rather broil than suffocate, I closed the window again and tried to think about polar bears.

One good thing about mountain country is that it tends to cool off when the sun goes down. By eight that evening the temperature outside had dropped to the sixties, while my room still resembled a pressure cooker. Worst of all, I caught a whiff of myself, and I sure didn't smell like a spring bouquet. I think I druther have smelled the fumes from the smelters, sulfur, arsenic, and all.

I was looking forward to Sunday dinner with Scrapper and Molly, but I figured it wouldn't be right to inflict myself upon them in my present condition. At around eight-thirty, I gathered up my clean clothes, put on my new hat, and headed out to find an all-night bath house.

Turning east on Galena, I left the darkness and silence behind. Dance halls and hurdy houses were open and going strong, with electric light and jag-time music pouring out onto the street. Passing a brightly lit saloon, the murmur of men at their drinking nearly drowned out the sound of a tinny piano. Somewhere inside, a woman laughed, her voice too shrill and too loud.

I recalled seeing a barbershop and bath house somewhere along that street the night of my poker game, but as I passed the Copper Penny and a gambling hall I began to doubt my memory. Then, at the end of the block, I saw it—a barber pole out front and a sign reading: NAPOLI BARBERSHOP & PUBLIC BATH. GIUSEPPE MORELLI, PROP.

As I approached the barbershop, a ragged scarecrow of a man stepped out of the shadows and shuffled toward me. His dirty overcoat had long since lost its buttons and his left hand clutched its collar in an effort to keep it closed. The man's eyes were red-rimmed and haunted, and his right hand reached out palm up. When he spoke, his lips pulled back to reveal yellowing, rotting teeth. "Spare a dime, mister?" he asked. "I'm down on my luck . . . ain't et in a while."

I gave the man a dollar and turned away. Neither

of us said anything, but he gripped the coin tightly and thanked me with his eyes.

When I reached the barbershop door, I stopped and looked inside. A single barber chair stood in the center of the room, directly beneath a green-shaded electric light bulb. A brass cash register crowded a mirrored counter of hair tonic and bay rum bottles, and ranks of shaving mugs filled a special case on the wall.

A small man I took to be the barber was sweeping up hair from the linoleum floor. In a mistletoe moustache and with his hair pomaded and slicked back, he was a walking advertisement for his shop. Seeing me standing in his doorway, he looked up and smiled.

"Come in, come in," he said. "You need a haircut; you come to the right place." His eyes dropped to the bundle of new clothes I carried, and he offered me a seat in his chair with a wave of his hand.

"Maybe you need a shave, and a *bagno*, maybe—a bath, no? I'm a take care of you, whatever you need."

The sign on the wall listed his services: HAIRCUT 35 CENTS, SHAVE 25 CENTS, BATH 50 CENTS.

I laid my bundle on a bench inside the open door and hung my new hat on a hook above it. Then I sat down in the barber chair. "You sold me, pardner," I said. "I'll take the works."

A tin sign above a doorway at the rear of the room read: BATH. Giuseppe opened the door and looked back at me. "I'm a just go build a fire in the stove," he said. "Heat up some water. Make a you very nice *bagno*, OK?"

I closed my eyes, waiting for Giuseppe to return. I could still hear the music from the dance halls up the street. A cool breeze swept in through the open door. I opened my eyes and looked outside. The panhandler I gave the dollar to stood near the barber pole, staring. I thought about telling him to take the money and go get himself some food, but I thought better of it. He might be a drunk or a hophead, I thought. Food may be the last thing he wants, or needs.

Just then Giuseppe came back into the shop and saw the man loitering outside. *"Andare!"* he said. *"Go!* You want me to call the coppers? *¡Lárgate! Go away!"*

The beggar slunk away into the darkness like a whipped dog. I was sorry for the poor devil, but I felt smug as well. After all, I had set him up with the price of a meal, hadn't I?

Giuseppe cut my hair and gave me a close shave. When he handed me the hand mirror so I could see the back of my head I figured I looked about as good as ever I could. He brushed the loose hair off my shoulders and snapped the cloth away with a flourish, like one of them Mexican bullfighters. Not only was Giuseppe a good barber, he had a sense of style besides.

I paid him for the shave, haircut, and bath, and walked into the back room. Inside, I hung my new clothes and hat on a peg near the alley door and stripped buck naked while Giuseppe filled the tub with water from the stove. I laid my belted six-gun on a low bench next to the tub and slipped into the hot, steaming water. Giuseppe laid out a couple of big Turkish towels and tossed me a new cake of lye soap.

"Enjoy your bath," the barber said, "but be careful. Watch your *vestiario*—your clothing, and your *capella*—your hat. Sometimes a thief, he's a maybe break in and steal."

Already steam was filling the room. The bathwater felt mighty good; if it had been one degree hotter I couldn't have stood it. I reached over to the low bench and patted my .44. "Thanks for the warnin'," I said, "but I've got it covered."

Then I laid back in the water until just my nose and mouth cleared and closed my eyes again. I heard the door to the barbershop close as Giuseppe left the room. Then I just wallowed in the good all-over feeling and sort of dozed off.

It was the water that woke me. I must have slid deeper into the tub as I slept, but anyway I woke up sputtering with a snoot full. For a moment I had no idea where I was. The bath water had cooled some, but the copper boiler atop the stove was steaming like a locomotive and the room was filled with vapor.

I glanced at the bench beside the tub. My .44 rested there in its leather, just as I'd left it. Looking across the room at the pegs where I'd hung my clothes and hat, I squinted as I tried to see through the steam. Then the fog lifted and I was struck speechless. The bum I gave the dollar to stood inside the bath's alley door, wearing my new hat! His ragged clothes lay in a pile on the floor before him, and he was dressing himself in my new clothes!

I stood up, and water splashed from the tub. *"Hey!"* I shouted. "What do you think you're doin'?"

Startled, the man turned and bounded through the door into the alley. I pulled my pistol from the leather and started after him, slipping and nearly falling on the wet floor. *"Stop, thief!"* I yelled. Thinking about it later, I decided I'd never said more foolish words in my life. The beggar had hit the jackpot when he found my clothes and hat; he was not about to stop. And as for my calling him a thief, I don't reckon that was news to him either. All he knew was he'd been caught in the act and that he was being chased by a bare-assed man with a gun.

I stepped out into the alley just as the thief dashed across the street, running away from the barbershop. I was about to call out again, maybe fire a shot into the air, when I saw gunfire flash from the side of a building directly in front of the man. The roar of the shot was loud, and the muzzle blast lit up the darkness like a lightning flash. *Shotgun,* I thought, just as the buckshot struck. I saw the thief blasted off his feet, saw my hat fly free.

Then I was in the street, racing toward the source of the shot. From the corner of my eye I saw the thief crumpled on the cobblestones. Ahead, the figure of a man stepped out of the shadows and turned toward me. The shotgun in his hands glinted in the half-light, coming up. I snapped off a shot on the run, felt the .44 buck in my hand, and saw my bullet strike the building wall.

The shotgun belched fire again; buckshot lashed the pavement beside me like sleet. Gripping my pistol in both hands, I centered on the shooter and fired. He staggered, dropped the scattergun, and toppled backward into the darkness.

A moment later, and I was inside the alley and standing over him. The man lay on his back, shoulders against the wall. He was alive, but hard hit. I saw him struggle to sit up, one hand reaching inside his coat.

"Don't try it!" I said. "Show me your hands!"

The man raised his free hand. The hand inside his coat came out slowly, some kind of hideaway gun slipping from his fingers and falling away. I pointed my .44 at him, leaning closer. I stared hard at his face, but I couldn't make out his features in the gloom. "Who *are* you?" I asked.

The man grunted, coughed. "Easy, mister," he said. "I'm bad hit. Don't shoot me again."

My eyes were adjusting to the dim light. The man's face turned away from the shadows, looking up at me. There was something familiar about him. He was someone I'd seen before, someone I *knew* . . .

And then I recognized him—the green-eyed gambler from the train, and from the poker game at the Copper Penny! *Lucas Durand!*

I guess *he* was adjusting to the light, too. His eyes widened, staring. "Gawdamighty," he said. "You're naked as a jaybird!"

Up the street, people were coming out of the saloons and dance halls. From somewhere in the distance, the jangling bell of the hurry-up wagon told me the police were on their way. It occurred to me I had enough to explain without adding indecent exposure to the mix.

Giuseppe the barber had come out of his shop and was staring wide-eyed at the bloodied body of the beggar. He looked like he was about to be sick. In the alley, I picked up Lucas Durand's hideout gun. I had my .44 in my right hand and Durand's derringer in my left, with neither belt nor pocket to put it in.

"Giuseppe!" I called out. "I'm a peace officer and this man is my prisoner. I can't leave him, but I'm sort of on display out here. My old clothes are next to the bath tub. I sure would appreciate it if you'd fetch 'em for me."

The barber seemed to notice my nudity for the first time. He clapped a hand to his forehead and his eyes got big. *"¡Mama Mia!"* he said. *"¡Si, si!* Wait there, mister!" and he dashed back to his shop as if his shirttail was on fire.

He was back in seconds, and I was able to get into my shirt and pants just as the first gawkers showed up. Bare of head and foot, I knelt by Durand's side and examined his wound. My bullet had struck him high in the chest, a few inches below the collar bone, and had passed through to the other side. The gambler was bleeding heavily, and I used one of Giuseppe's towels to stanch the flow.

I don't know if clothes make the man like people say, but putting on a shirt and a pair of pants seemed to help Durand recognize me. Then, too, my shirt had my badge pinned to it, and I'm sure *that* helped.

"Fanshaw!" he said. His eyes darted to the shattered body sprawled on the cobblestones. "But . . . who . . . I thought *he* was *you!* You went in . . . to the barber . . . that hat . . ."

"If I was you, I'd save my talkin' for later," I told him. "Lie still."

164

By that time, maybe two dozen people had gathered in the street, and more were coming. I retrieved Durand's shotgun, and then walked over and picked up my hat. "Move back now," I told the crowd. "Break it up, folks. There's nothing for you to see here."

Bell clanging and the hooves of the horses clattering on the paving stones, the paddy wagon rumbled up the street and stopped. Two uniformed city policemen stepped down and pushed their way through the onlookers. One of them was the red-headed kid with the bad skin I met my first day in town. *"You,"* he said. "What's goin' on here, Deputy?"

"It's a short, sad story," I said. "The dead feller yonder stole my clothes while I was yonder at the Napoli, takin' a bath."

Turning to where Durand lay in the alley, I said, "And *that* man cut him down with a scattergun. When I came out, he turned the gun on me. I fired back, and put him down."

The kid frowned. "You got any witnesses can back that up?"

"I'm a lawman, like you. Do I *need* witnesses?"

"So you *don't* have any." Turning to his companion, he said, "Take his gun and put the irons on him, Pat. We'll sort all this out back at the station."

I nodded at Durand. "That man is my prisoner," I said. "He needs a doctor."

The redheaded kid pulled his truncheon and tapped it against the palm of his hand. "*You'll* need a doctor if you don't shut up," he said. "Get in the damned wagon."

"Take it easy, kid," I said. "You won't be near as snotty once your face clears up."

The kid's face didn't exactly clear up right then, but it did turn beet red. Teeth bared, he jerked his club up to hit me, but the cop called Pat grabbed his arm. "Jaysus, Ned," Pat said. "The man's a federal deputy!"

Ned was so mad he couldn't speak, but there was doubt behind his bluster. I gave him my best smile, and stepped up into the paddy wagon.

Chief McGinnis was waiting at the station when we arrived. He listened to Ned's and Pat's accounts of what they found at the crime scene and had them take Durand to the hospital. Then he took my irons off, allowed me to finish getting dressed, and poured me a cup of coffee. "Now let's hear *your* version," he said.

Clearly and simply, I described the night's events pretty much as they occurred. I didn't exactly dwell on my nakedness during the shootout, but I could tell by the way McGinnis tried to keep from smiling that he got the picture anyway.

"You seem to be having more than your share of trouble lately," he said. "I heard about your big win at the poker table and your run-in with that street gang a while back."

"Yeah. I don't think that has any connection with what happened tonight, but I can't say for sure. What I do know is Durand killed that panhandler with a shotgun, apparently because he believed the man was *me*. What I *don't* know is why he would want me dead. Durand is my prisoner, Chief. I need to question him as soon as I can."

"I want to be there when you do," McGinnis said. "All right, let's go. I have a horse and buggy around back."

Chief McGinnis led me to the rear of the station and out the door. In the alley, a handsome black gelding stood hitched to a light buggy. McGinnis stepped up and took the reins as I took a seat beside him. Turning the rig about, the chief started the gelding away up the street with a crack of his whip. "This town has two hospitals," McGinnis said, "the St. James Home and Doc Whitford's private hospital. The lads took your man to Doc's place."

Minutes later, the Chief reined the gelding to a stop in front of a two-story log building with a white-painted fence. The building's pitched roof displayed brick chimneys at each end, and Old Glory flew briskly from a staff in the middle. Parked just ahead of us at the curb was the hurry-up wagon from the station. McGinnis set out the weighted tether to secure the horse and rig and rang the door bell. He paused, and then rang it again.

A stout woman in a starched apron and cap unlocked the door. "Good evening, Captain McGinnis," she said. "Your men are inside, on the second floor. Doctor Whitford is with the patient."

"Thank you, Maggie," the chief said.

McGinnis led the way across a polished wood floor to a staircase at the end of the building. The smell of disinfectant was strong in the air. Stairs creaked as we climbed to the second floor.

The redheaded cop called Ned was seated in a chair outside the door of a private room at the end of the building, but he jumped to his feet when he saw Chief McGinnis.

"The prisoner's inside, Chief," he said. "Doc Whitford and a nurse are workin' on him. Pat's in there, too, keepin' watch."

McGinnis nodded, and opened the door.

Lucas Durand lay propped up on the pillows of a hospital bed, his face gray as ashes and his green eyes open and wary. Beside him, a nurse with salt-and-pepper hair gathered up blood-stained bandages and cloths and dropped them in a hamper. Picking up the hamper, she carried it past us and out of the room.

The policeman called Pat had been sitting in a chair beside the bed. As the red-haired cop had done, Pat quickly got to his feet when he saw

Chief McGinnis. To the right, near the room's single window, a man I took to be Doc Whitford scrubbed his hands in a basin. He wore a white doctor's coat over a dark business suit and a stand-up collar of white linen. His hair was curly and unkempt, and a heavy moustache and beard hid most of his necktie.

"Your malefactor is going to live," he said. "Officer Pat tells me the man killed a panhandler with a shotgun."

"Case of mistaken identity," McGinnis said, "or so it appears." The chief turned to me. "This is Merlin Fanshaw, U.S. deputy marshal out of Helena. Merlin, meet Doc Whitford. Doc is the proprietor of this hospital. He was *mayor* of Butte City a few years back."

The doctor shook my hand. "Good to meet you, Deputy. So you're the man who put a bullet through my patient."

"I am. All right if I ask him a few questions?"

"I'd say that is your right. You bagged him."

I walked over to the bed. Durand's eyes followed my every move. "First question," I said. "Why did you kill that man back at the barbershop?"

"Never meant to," Durand said. "He was wearin' your clothes and your hat. I thought he was you."

"Second question. Why were you gunnin' for me?"

Durand closed his eyes. For a long moment, he said nothing. Then he spoke, his voice tense with pain.

"I believed . . . you were fixin' to arrest me. I kept runnin' into you. On the train. At O'Dhoul's wake. At the stud game. I didn't want to go back to that damn prison at Deer Lodge."

"So . . . *you're* the assassin hired to kill Marcus Daly. You gunned down Digby O'Dhoul because you thought he could identify you."

"*What?* Hell, no! I don't know nothin' about all that! I figured you were doggin' me for that shootin' back in Benton."

"Fort Benton? Remind me . . . what shooting was that?"

"*You* know. I killed a man over a card game in Benton a while back. Turned out I had a gun and he didn't. I lit a shuck for Great Falls and caught the train to Helena. That's when I saw *you.* Saw your damn *badge. You* know."

I shook my head. "I *didn't* know, but I do now. I guess we *all* know now—me, Chief McGinnis, Officer Pat, and Doc Whitford.

"Doc says you're goin' to live, and I'm glad about that. But you're lookin' at a trial for a killin' in Fort Benton and another for a murder in Butte City. If you know a good lawyer, you might want to get in touch with him."

ELEVEN

SHARING AND CARING

When I first met Chief McGinnis I have to confess I didn't like him much. But as we talked together back at the station house, I was learning he was a tough cop with a wry sense of humor. After returning from the hospital, he poured me another cup of coffee and pondered the fate of Lucas Durand.

"If you'd been a better shot," he said, "we could just bury Durand, and get on with our other duties."

McGinnis sighed. "But you only wounded him. Now we have to wait 'til he heals up so we can try him for murder and *hang* him."

I grinned. "Maybe if you slip Doc Whitford a double sawbuck he'll smother him in his sleep."

"No chance. Doc's got ethics. Hippocratic Oath, and all that. Besides, the county is payin' Doc for his care."

"Well, maybe Choteau County will extradite Durand for that killing in Fort Benton."

"Why would they? He only killed another gambler. It's not like he gunned down a taxpayer, or a decent woman."

There was a part of me that *needed* the banter with Chief McGinnis. Like miners laughing away the pressure after a hard shift, the chief and me were laughing away the tension of the shootout. But as I thought about all I'd been through during the past few hours, I suddenly felt jittery, and tense as stretched wire.

"I can see the situation calls for desperate measures," I said. "If you'd break him out of the hospital, maybe I could take another shot at him."

McGinnis chuckled. "Might be worth a try. Chances are you shoot *better* with your *clothes* on."

I looked down. The hand that held my coffee cup trembled slightly. All at once, the cup seemed to weigh twenty pounds. I felt bone weary and sad.

The chief took my belted revolver from a desk drawer and slid it across to me. "You're free to go, Deputy," he said. "If I need you, I know where to find you." I stood up. Out of nowhere, sharp and clear in my mind's eye, I recalled the face of the bum who died in my place. As in life, I saw his red-rimmed eyes, his rotting teeth, the way he almost seemed to apologize just for being alive. Well, I thought, he doesn't have to apologize for *that* any more.

"What about the vagrant?" I asked. "Do you know anything about him?"

McGinnis shrugged. "Local character. Beggar and small-time thief. Lived in a tumbledown shack over in the Cabbage Patch. Claimed he was a soldier in the 'War Between the States,' so he was probably a Reb. If he'd been a Yank he'd have said 'Civil War' or 'War of the Rebellion.' "

"In a way, I almost feel like *I* killed him. Poor devil died because Durand thought he was me."

McGinnis frowned. "You take a lot on yourself," he said. "The man died because he stole your clothes, that's all."

I nodded. "I know that," I said. "I just don't *feel* it, somehow."

"Coroner says he was probably dead before he hit the ground. That first charge of buckshot hit him like a wall. Think of it this way, Deputy—he's better off."

"Yes," I said. "We could put that on his tombstone, if he could *afford* a tombstone. 'Here lies good old Nobody. Died 1888. He's better off.' "

I made the first telephone call of my life that night, to my boss, U.S. Marshal Chance Ridgeway. I held the receiver up to my ear and spoke into the mouthpiece, only I had to speak a little louder than usual. Our voices faded in and out some, but I was able to give a clear report of the shooting. Ridgeway's voice sounded concerned.

"You all right, Son?"

"Yes, sir. Just a little tired."

"Do you figure this Durand feller had anything to do with O'Dhoul's death?"

"He says no, and I believe him. I asked the Butte City police to look through their old wanted circulars. Sure enough, there is a poster out of Fort Benton on Durand. He shot a man in a poker game and headed out for the tall and uncut."

"Why do you suppose he came after you?"

"Seein' me made him nervous. He thought I was fixin' to arrest him for murder."

Ridgeway's voice turned soft. Either that or the telephone line faded again. "Like the Good Book says, 'The wicked flee when no man pursueth.' "

"Yes, sir. I'll send you a full report by telegraph tomorrow."

"I appreciate that. Take care, Son. Get some sleep."

In my room at the hotel, my body and my brain had an argument. More than food, water, or strong drink, my body wanted sleep. On the other hand, my brain wanted nothing more than to stay awake and rehash the evening's events. To that end, it tormented me with guilt pangs, thoughts of my own mortality, and complaints to the Almighty. The argument was a good one. It went on like a bare knuckle prize fight for nearly two hours, but finally my body won. At about 2:30 in the morning, I fell asleep at last.

Sunday dawned clear, and much too early. Born of the dawn, a strong west wind swept over the camp, and—for the moment, at least—blew away the sulfurous smoke that was such a permanent part of life on Butte Hill. I sat up on the edge of my bed, thinking about the shooting and its aftermath until I forced my thoughts onto a different track.

I remembered with some surprise that I had accepted Molly O'Dhoul's invitation to Sunday dinner that day. My surprise was not because I remembered the invite but because I nearly forgot it. I had looked forward to dinner with Molly and Scrapper since she and I had our picnic at Elk Park. The gun battle on Galena Street drove every other thought from my mind. I washed up at the basin in my room and dressed in a pair of clean California pants and my one remaining new shirt from Shapiro's. Out on the street, I treated myself to a steak-and-eggs breakfast and enough strong coffee to wash away most of my cobwebs. I bought daffodils for Molly at a greenhouse on Madison, and some of Scrapper's favorite pipe tobacco at a cigar store a block away. Then I went back to the hotel, where I wrote a full report on the drifter's death and the shooting of Lucas Durand.

I sent my report off to Ridgeway by telegraph and rented a horse and carriage at Fogarty's. Then I turned the rig up toward the gallows frame of the Mountain Con Mine, and the home of my friends which lay in its shadow.

• • •

Scrapper was waiting on the porch when I pulled up. He stood, an easy grin on his weathered face as he squinted against the sun. "Is that you, lad? *Fáilte*, Merlin . . . welcome!"

I stepped down and tied the buggy horse to the gatepost. Carrying Molly's flowers and Scrapper's tobacco, I walked toward the porch.

I smiled. "It's me, all right," I said. "I come bearin' gifts . . . and the appetite of a wolf!"

Scrapper chuckled. "Sure and ye've come to the right place then," he said. "Molly's cooked enough food for an army . . . or one hungry young deputy marshal."

As I walked toward him, I noticed that while Scrapper seemed to be looking my way, he wasn't looking at me directly. Instead, he tilted his head as if relying more on his hearing than his vision.

"How are you, Scrapper?" I asked.

"Well enough, lad," he said. "A little trouble with me eyes, but well enough."

The screen door opened and Molly stepped out. She smiled in greeting, but she seemed somehow distracted, and tense. "More than a *little* trouble, I fear," she said, "but welcome . . . come in."

She brightened when I handed her the flowers. "Why, thank you, Merlin," she said. "What lovely daffodils!" Then she turned to put them in water. I watched her walk away, and breathed in the good smells that came from her kitchen.

I looked at Scrapper, thinking he might say more about his eye trouble, but he did not. Handing him the pipe tobacco, I watched as he took it in his big hands. He lifted the package to his nose and sniffed it. "Ah," he said. "The good Erlichs! How did ye know it was me favorite brand?"

"I can't take the credit," I said. "They told me, down at the cigar store."

Scrapper produced the poteen jug I recalled from our last meeting, and two glasses. "Pour your own," he said, "and one for me as well. We'll drink a toast to friendship."

We had our drink—all right, we had *two*—and then Molly called us to the table. I was so busy looking at the great platter of ham, the serving bowl of sweet potatoes, the turnip greens, and the basket of cornbread that I nearly forgot my manners. Luckily, I saw Molly bow her head, and did the same. She quietly offered a table grace, and we all said "Amen" together.

The dinner was perfect. Molly had prepared a fine meal, and I savored every bite. When a man eats out at chop houses and noodle parlors every day, he comes to appreciate home cooking.

I wasn't slow to express my appreciation, either, and my words seemed to have at least two positive results. First, the more I complimented Molly, the more she encouraged me to go back for another helping. And second, my praise caused her to blush and smile like a schoolgirl. Molly O'Dhoul looked downright fetching with the high color in her cheeks and her eyes a-shining.

"Aw, go along with you now," she'd say, and then "Would you be after havin' another piece of cornbread, Merlin?"

Finally, when even I could eat no more, we moved to the parlor for coffee and conversation. Scrapper sat across from me, a work-hardened hand on each knee, and looked at me through narrowed eyelids. "Well, how's it goin', lad?" he asked. "What's the news?"

I paused. Then, choosing my words carefully, I said, "Sometimes a peace officer's life is slow and tedious. Nothing much seems to happen for days. And then, all of a sudden . . ."

Keeping the story as matter-of-fact as I knew how, I related the events of the previous night. I told them about my bath, and about the vagrant who stole my clothes. I spoke of his murder at the hands of Lucas Durand. And I told of my shooting Durand after he fired at me.

I described my arrest and transport to the City Jail and told of my meeting with Chief McGinnis. And finally, I recounted my questioning of Durand at the hospital.

"Doc Whitford says Durand will recover," I said, "but he'll stand trial for murder, either here in Butte City for killin' that poor drifter or for another man he killed up at Fort Benton."

The silence in the parlor was nearly total. I heard the ticking of the mantel clock. The distant hammering of the stamp mills out on the flats came faintly to our ears. Molly sat on the divan, her eyes wide and her coffee untouched. Scrapper sat across from me in a parlor chair, still and unmoving.

He had been holding his breath. Now he let it go in a long sigh and shook his head. "Faith," he said. "Lucas Durand, and him a murderer. And weren't we playin' poker with the blaggard just a few weeks ago!"

Scrapper leaned forward. "He was in the game the night Digby was killed, too. Ye don't suppose . . ."

"I asked him directly about Digby. He says he knows nothing about your brother's death. I tend to believe him."

Scrapper slumped back in his chair. "Poor Digby," he said. "God knows I'm not a superstitious man, but sometimes I can feel me brother's soul wanderin' lost and lonesome in the dark. I'm thinkin' his ghost won't rest until his killer is brought to justice."

"For what it's worth," I said, "neither will I."

I sipped my coffee and found it cold. As if sensing the problem, Molly brought the pot in from the kitchen and added fresh coffee to each cup. I thanked her, and turned my attention back to Scrapper.

"Now what's this about 'a little trouble' with your eyes?" I asked.

" 'Tis nothin'," Scrapper said. "It's only that I'm not seein' as well as once I did."

Molly frowned. " 'Tis a bit more than that," she said. Turning to me, she added, "Scrapper's been laid off at the Mountain Con because of a serious problem with his eyes. Jim O'Grady, the shift boss, gave him the pink slip."

I turned back to Scrapper. "Have you seen a doctor?"

"Aye," he said. "He said me vision is goin', but divvil if he knows why. Too many bare-knuckle fights, maybe.

"Jim Brennan said to me, 'You're the best mucker on the hill, Scrapper, but I can't let you go down in the mines no more, not until your eyes get better. You'll get hurt, or you'll hurt one of the other boys. I've got to lay you off for your own sake.' "

Molly broke in. "And then last Friday who should show up here at the house but Marcus Daly himself! He told Scrapper to rest easy, that he'll continue to receive his full wages. He also said he's expectin' visitors soon from back east, and that one of his guests is a famous New York eye doctor! Mr. Daly said when his doctor friend gets here he'll ask him to examine Scrapper, and he'll see that Scrapper gets everything he needs."

Molly seemed to choke up then. On the verge of

tears, her eyes shone in the late light. "Marcus Daly is a saint," she said.

"He is that," Scrapper said. "And a great man entirely."

Scrapper pushed his chair back and stood up from the table. "I hope ye'll excuse me, lad," he said, "I'm fair knackered. I need a bit of a lie-down."

"But stay," he said. "Keep Molly company. And don't be a stranger. Ye're always welcome in this house."

"Thanks," I said. "I'll give Molly a hand with the cleanup."

Molly was indignant. "You will *not!* You're our *guest!*"

I stood and began to clear the table. "Yes, I am," I said, "and you're too good a hostess to *argue* with me."

Molly continued to protest, but I knew she was only going through the motions. Her eyes shone, and her crooked smile told me this was an argument she wanted to lose. Standing together at the kitchen sink, I washed the dishes while Molly dried and put them away. We stood close beside each other, laughing and teasing. And when at last I went to take my leave, Molly stood on tiptoe to kiss my cheek.

As I turned my rented buggy down toward Fogarty's, my belly was full, my heart was light, and my fingernails had seldom been so clean.

• • •

Early the following week, a coroner's jury was convened at the courthouse to look into the cause of death of the unfortunate vagrant. Chief McGinnis and his officers were called to testify, and so, of course, was I.

Giuseppe Morelli, the barber, told of seeing the beggar often on the street near his shop. He told investigators he knew him to be a nuisance and a small-time thief, and that he'd warned me about the man the night of the shooting.

I told my story again, and gave the jury a copy of my report to Marshal Ridgeway. As the only witness to the actual shooting, I told of seeing the man steal my clothes and run out of the bathhouse into the night. I pursued him, I said. I did *not* say I was stark naked at the time. When I looked across at Giuseppe and saw his knowing smirk, I favored him with my scariest glare and he sobered up fast.

I told of seeing the muzzle flash and hearing the shot from the alley across the street. I said I saw the buckshot strike the thief. I said I fired at the man in the alley and missed him with my first shot, whereupon he turned his shotgun on me and fired the other barrel.

My second shot put him down, I said, and I took him into custody. The man with the shotgun was a wanted killer, I explained, and he feared I was coming to arrest him. He fired at the thief who wore my clothes, believing he was shooting at me. The vagabond thief, I said, was a victim of mistaken identity.

The coroner said he examined the body. He said he observed that the thief was riddled with double-ought buckshot and apparently died almost instantly.

In the end, the inquest officially ruled that the vagabond sure was dead all right, and that nobody much cared. His corpse was taken away and buried in Potter's Field at county expense.

I wondered about the dead man. Who had he been in better days? Surely he'd *known* better days. He'd been some mother's baby once, somebody's boy.

Had he ever had a wife? Children of his own? Had he been a hero in the war, or a coward and deserter? And what had brought him to panhandling and petty larceny on the fringes of life, and sudden death by misadventure on the streets of Butte City?

I couldn't help wishing I knew more about him. It should *matter* to someone when a man dies.

TWELVE

LOOKING FOR ANSWERS

The headline ran bold and black on the front page of Monday's Butte *Miner*:

U.S. DEPUTY MARSHAL
APPREHENDS MURDER SUSPECT
GUN BATTLE CLAIMS LIFE OF
INNOCENT BYSTANDER.

Well, I thought, I don't know how *innocent* he was, but he sure was a *bystander*. The story went on to get my name wrong, as well as some of the facts.

"On Saturday night, U.S. Deputy Marshal Melvin Farnshaw arrested suspected murderer Lucas Durand after a brief gun battle on Galena Street. According to Police Chief John McGinnis, Durand is wanted for questioning in Fort Benton in regard to the unlawful death of a Choteau County citizen.

"Also according to Chief McGinnis, a local transient was slain in the shooting affray when he was caught in the crossfire between Deputy Farnshaw and the suspect. A coroner's inquest has ruled the cause of death to be accidental, by misadventure."

To tell the truth, I was not all that offended by the newspaper's write up. At first, I was annoyed because the reporters messed up my name and left out some of the incident's more pertinent details.

A few years earlier, Clifford Bidwell, editor of the Medicine Lodge *Star*, told me the practice of journalism wasn't all that difficult. "All you have to do is report the facts and spell the names right," he said.

The Butte *Miner* had missed the mark on both counts, but when I thought about how the story would have read if the writers *had* reported all the facts and spelled my name right, I pulled in my horns and thanked my lucky stars.

Later that day, I was reminded of the difference between what a newspaper prints and what the man on the street thinks. The afternoon was hot, and I turned in at the Blue Frog in search of a cold beer and some quiet time. I got neither. The barkeep was out of ice, and the beer was lukewarm. And as for quiet time, the first person I ran into was Cecil Hardesty, my opponent from the big poker game and a man with a natural gift for rubbing me the wrong way.

As usual, Cecil was dressed like a dandy in top hat, frock coat, and fancy vest, which made him stand out from the Blue Frog's regular customers like a peacock in a chicken house. He was reading the *Miner* at a table near the front door, and he recognized me the minute I walked in.

"Well, if it isn't Melvin Farnshaw, shootist extraordinaire!" he said. "I hear you were in your birthday suit when you shot Durand."

"I like to keep the blood off my clothes," I said. "How are you, Cecil? I heard W. A. Clark tied a can to your tail."

Anger flashed across Cecil's face. "Clark's loss is Jim Murray's gain. I'm working for Murray now. Better job. Better pay."

"I knew you'd land on your feet," I said. "There's always a demand for flunkies."

I smiled when I said it. Cecil laughed as if he took my remark as a joke, but anger smoldered behind his eyes.

"I was surprised to learn that Durand is wanted for murder up in Fort Benton," he said. "We've been in several poker games together. I thought he was just another tinhorn gambler."

"Life is full of surprises," I said.

Hardesty's stein was nearly empty. I was feeling guilty about my "flunkies" remark.

I smiled. "Can I buy you a beer, Cecil?"

The anger faded from his face. "If you'll have one with me. Sit down."

I caught the barkeep's eye and held up two fingers. He nodded, drew two beers, and brought them over to the table. I raised my stein, and took a sip. That's when I found out the beer was warm.

I looked up to find Cecil watching me. "Barkeep

says he ran out of ice," he said. "Another of those surprises life is full of."

Cecil stared into his stein, like a fortune teller reading tea leaves. When he spoke again, he asked the same question Scrapper asked.

"Do you think Durand killed Digby O'Dhoul? He was in the game the night Digby died."

I shrugged. "So were you," I said. "You, and Fat Jack, and Scrapper. When I questioned Durand at the hospital, I asked him that directly. He said no."

"Well," said Cecil, "he *would* say that, wouldn't he?"

I was growing tired of the conversation. "Yes, he would," I said. "He'd deny it if he *was* involved, and he'd deny it if he *wasn't*. I think he wasn't."

"I mean no offense, Fanshaw. I'm curious, that's all."

"Find something else to be curious about."

"Sure. No offense."

Cecil smiled his practiced smile, but once again, I saw the anger behind his eyes. Since the night of the stud game when I read his "tell" and took him down, I'd felt his dislike for me. I was annoyed with myself for letting him get to me. I hated the smug way he smiled when I insulted him. Why did he hide his feelings behind that phony smile instead of calling me out like a man?

I finished my beer and set the stein down on the

table. Taking my watch from my vest pocket, I snapped open the case. "Well, look at the time," I said. "I had no idea it was so late."

"It isn't late," Cecil said. "What's your hurry?"

I stood up. "Maybe it's just me," I said, "but it seems to get late *early* when I'm around you."

Out on the street, I thought again of Digby O'Dhoul. I had not gone to the cemetery when he was buried but I knew its location from Molly's description. For maybe the hundredth time, I wished I could talk with the man.

After my pa was killed back in Dry Creek, I used to go out sometimes and visit his grave. At such times I'd hunker down and talk to him like he was still alive, but mostly I'd just think about him and sort of listen with my heart.

At such times I'd often recall something Pa said, or maybe I'd remember how he did certain things. And sometimes a thought would come that was almost like Pa talking to me.

Now I never held much with spiritualists and such who claim they can talk with the dead. From all I can make out, we can talk to them all right, but the conversation is likely to be pretty much one-sided. When a feller is gone, I figure he's gone for good. All his notions and memories are buried with him and that's the end of things, at least until Judgment Day.

On the other hand, I had no leads at the moment.

Having a chat with Digby could do no harm. I caught a streetcar and headed out to the bone orchard.

The last resting place of Digby O'Dhoul was lonesome and bleak by any standard. The smoke-poisoned grass of the graveyard was stunted and sparse, and even the weeds struggled to survive in the rocky soil.

Half a hundred graves lay scattered across the flat. Sunken earth and weathered markers of wood and stone revealed the sites of older burials, but the soil atop Digby's grave was still mounded and fresh. A simple stone of white marble stood at the head of the grave, and wilted flowers in a fruit jar gave evidence of a sister's devotion.

I read the stone's inscription:

DIGBY DANIEL
O'DHOUL
Beloved Brother
1853–1888
A Man of Sorrows

A man of sorrows indeed, I thought. Haunted by sinister words he overheard in a silent church. Frightened by those words and yet driven to tell others. And now dead by his own hand, or murdered to protect a conspiracy.

He wasn't that old, I thought. *Only thirty-five.*

I took the photograph from my vest pocket and looked at it again. Digby's troubled eyes stared back from the image, seeming to plead for help and understanding. Tight-lipped and tense in the photograph, his mouth formed a bitter line.

I wish I had known you, I thought. *I wish I knew what you knew.*

I must have spoken aloud, because a soft voice from behind me replied, "I wish you could have known him, too."

Startled, I turned. Molly O'Dhoul stood an arm's length away, fresh flowers in her hands.

"I'm sorry if I surprised you, Merlin," she said. "Sure and you were that deep in thought."

Molly was dressed in a pale green walking suit with a bustle and she wore her black woolen shawl draped over her shoulders as a wrapper. A matching green hat, decorated with ribbons and lace, perched atop her auburn hair. She smiled, touching my arm. "I bring Digby fresh flowers from time to time," she said. "Why are *you* here, Merlin?"

I felt foolish, and a little off balance. "Still looking for answers," I said, "even in the graveyard."

Molly nodded. "Aye. I come because he was my brother," she said, "and because I loved him."

She knelt beside the headstone and replaced the wilted flowers in the fruit jar with the fresh ones.

Then she stood, and for a time neither of us spoke.

"Molly," I said at last, "Is there anything Digby told you about that night at the church—anything you haven't told me?"

She frowned. "I can't think of anything," she said. "Digby was so frightened. I'm not sure he remembered every detail himself."

"No," I said. "I don't expect he did."

Molly looked down at her brother's grave. For a moment, she was silent. Then she raised her head and her blue eyes looked into mine.

"There is one thing," Molly said. "I'd almost forgotten. Digby said he saw the man who came to the church, but he never saw the *other* fella—you know, the assassin.

"But he heard his voice, and he heard it clearly. The killer had a cruel, mocking voice, he said, but there was somethin' else. Digby said the killer spoke with a lisp!"

"With a lisp?"

"Aye! Just a soft lisp when he made an *s* sound, Digby said."

Molly looked into my face, her expression earnest. "Do you think that's something that might help you, Merlin? Could it be important?"

I smiled. "Could be, Molly," I said. "It's more than I knew before."

We stood together in the pale sunlight, each of us warmed by the presence of the other. Molly spoke of Scrapper's failing eyesight, and of her hope that Marcus Daly's doctor friend could help him. She spoke of Digby, and of the memories she held of him from childhood.

Kneeling, she cleared the dead grass and weeds away from his headstone and bowed her head in prayer. I didn't kneel with her, but I took off my hat and offered up a prayer of my own. *Whatever she wants, Lord. I want that, too.*

Afterward, I walked Molly back to the trolley stop and we rode uptown together. I bade her good-bye at the corner of Granite and Main, and was crossing the street to enter my hotel when I heard someone call my name.

"Merlin! Wait up!"

I turned to see Fat Jack Jones rein his four-passenger rockaway to a stop in front of the hotel. He was wearing his buffalo coat and his top hat, and the color of his nose told me he was at least two sheets to the wind.

I walked over to the curb. Jack swayed in the driver's seat, his eyes trying hard to focus.

"Howdy, Jack," I said. "One thing's sure. That rig you're drivin' is *not* the water wagon."

Jack gave me a boozy grin. "Course not," he said. "I got news!"

The smell of Jack's breath hit me like a fist. It even cut through the stench of the smelter smoke.

"All right," I said. "What is it?"

Jack swayed again on the carriage's seat. "Wha's *what?*"

"What's your news? You said you have *news.*"

He frowned, considering the question. "Oh," he said. "Oh, yeah! Mr. Daly . . . he's back from New York! He brought some people with him. I just took 'em up to his house."

"People, huh? What kind of people?"

"Oh . . . you know. High rollers. Rich people. One fancy-dressed gent. Bald as a cue ball. An' another stuffed shirt . . . a banker, maybe. An' a real . . . purty . . . lady! Mr. Daly paid me fifty dollars! He said, 'Keep the change, Jack. Buy yourself a drink.' "

"I see you followed his advice."

"I had . . . one or two," Jack admitted. "But I wanted . . . let you know. Mr. Daly will be down at the racetrack tomorrow. Be a good time for you to meet him."

"Thanks," I said. "I'll be there."

"Tha's good. I wanted . . . to let you know. Goin' home now. It's quittin' time."

"Can you make it all right, Jack?"

"Course I can! Horses . . . know the way. I'll . . . pick you up in the mornin'. Ten o'clock sharp."

"All right, Jack. I'll see you then. Tap 'er light."

Jack slackened the reins and the bay team— Jack's "beauties"—moved out. As I watched the rockaway ramble down the street, it occurred to

193

me that another good thing about horses is that when they have to they can take their driver home.

Jack was as good as his word. When I walked out of my hotel the next morning, his team and carriage were parked at curbside and Jack was in the driver's seat. He greeted me with a broad grin. It was exactly ten o'clock.

"I really didn't think you'd make it," I said. "What's your secret?"

"Hair of the dog and the Chinese baths," Jack said. "That, and clean livin'."

I swung up onto the seat beside Jack. He shook the reins, and the team moved out. We were off, as the saying goes, to the races.

As we made our way to the racetrack and grounds, it seemed nearly everyone in Butte City was doing the same. Streetcars of the Butte City Railway Company, packed with passengers, sparked their way along the tracks. I saw people in buggies and hacks, riders on horseback, men and women walking, children running, and even one sport astride a high-wheel bicycle, the first one I ever saw.

Outside the main entrance gate, the form men and tipsters were selling their tips and selection sheets to anyone who'd buy. A big feller in a checkered vest and derby hat made a strong move toward us, but changed his mind when Jack drew back his buggy whip.

"The grounds are owned by the West Side Racing Association," Jack said. "The association runs mostly harness races now, but runnin' races are comin'. Mr. Daly has a pacer in the races, a mare called Yolo Maid."

Jack drove slowly through the crowd, which moved around behind the grandstand to the stables, paddock, tack rooms, and other buildings on the grounds. I saw drivers in their silks walking and running, working to harden their leg muscles. Others were squeezing hand grips and exercising with dumbbells to strengthen their arms.

I watched as the workout boys warmed up the horses, getting them ready for the upcoming races. Drivers polished their harnesses and carefully examined their sulkies. At the stables, grooms washed, curried, and brushed the horses until they gleamed like polished silk.

Outside one stable, grooms held a handsome chestnut filly by its halter. A short, stocky man seemed to be pointing out the animal's finer points to a well-dressed group of men and women. The man appeared to be somewhere in his mid-forties. His hair and moustache were silver-white, but his face was unlined and ruddy. I'd have to say he was a good looking man.

"Now's your chance," said Jack. "Come on over and meet Marcus Daly."

THIRTEEN

A DAY AT THE RACES

Fat Jack stepped down from the carriage and led the way toward Daly and his party at a brisk walk. Seeing Jack shambling toward him, Daly raised his head and smiled. The men and women in his group turned, their eyes widening as they saw Jack. Behind Daly, a mountain of a man with close-cropped red hair moved quickly to his side. Tense and alert at our approach, he appeared to recognize Jack. The man relaxed, but his eyes never left us.

I don't know what the other people with Daly thought, but seeing a cadaverous character in a top hat and buffalo coat ambling their way with a buggy whip in his hand may have caused them some alarm. Lanky and lean, with his bushy goatee and weather-beaten face, Jack was what some folks called "picturesque," which in Jack's case I think meant "scary."

Daly stepped forward to meet us. "Good morning, Jack," he said. "Here for the races, are you?"

"That I am," said Jack. "Racin' is better for losin' money than Faro. I lose either way, but racin' is quicker. I don't have the terrible suspense of thinkin' I might win."

Daly's laugh was hearty and honest. "You're a true original, Jack," he said. "If you think *racing* is a quick way to lose money you should give the stock market a try."

He turned to his companions. "No need for fear, my friends," he said. "You remember Jack Jones. He's quite the celebrity. Jack has driven all the important people who've come to Butte City, including you folks. He drove the four-passenger rockaway that brought you to my home last night."

Daly's guests seemed reassured. Two of the men fit Jack's description. One was a portly gent who sure did look like a banker; the other removed his silk hat and mopped his hairless head with a handkerchief. *Bald as a cue ball indeed,* I thought.

Marcus Daly was speaking to his guests, but he was watching me. He looked me over carefully, his eyes pausing briefly at the badge on my vest before moving on.

Jack turned to me. "This here's a friend of mine, Mark," he said. "Merlin Fanshaw, U.S. deputy marshal."

Recognition dawned in Daly's eyes. "You've been in the newspapers of late," he said. "That business with the man from Choteau County."

He offered his hand, and I took it. Marcus Daly's grip was as hearty as his laugh.

I smiled. "A peace officer's life is mostly long periods of dull routine," I said, "but it's those sudden moments of sheer terror that make it all worthwhile. I'm pleased to meet you, Mr. Daly."

"None of that now," he said. "Call me Mark. Tell me. Do you feel the same about racing as Jack does?"

"No, sir. I take no pleasure in losing money. But I agree with the old saw, 'There's something about the outside of a horse that's good for the inside of a man.' "

"Well said." Daly turned to the chestnut filly. "What do you think of my Yolo Maid?"

"She's a real beauty. Strong of leg, and well muscled in the forelegs and stifles. She has the long top line of a true standardbred."

Daly looked at me with what I took to be new interest. "You do have an eye for horses," he said. "Have you worked with blooded stock?"

I smiled. "I owned a thoroughbred stud once, a long time ago. Mostly, I've worked with mustangs and cow ponies."

"It's grand to meet a man who appreciates fine horseflesh." Daly beamed at the filly. "Yolo Maid isn't running today, but she will, and soon."

He turned to the portly gent. "This is Otto Van Dorn, with J. P. Morgan's bank in New York. Otto, meet U.S. Deputy Marshal Merlin Fanshaw."

Van Dorn's handshake was just a touch of the fingers. I fought the urge to count my own fingers to see if I'd lost a few.

The bald man wore a top hat and those pince-nez eyeglasses that clip to the nose by a spring. Daly turned to him. "And this is my friend, Dr. Charles Lambert. Charlie, meet Deputy Fanshaw."

"A pleasure," the doctor said.

Fat Jack stood apart from the group, talking with the huge man who apparently worked for Daly. Jack seemed to be telling a joke; the man bent his head toward Jack, grinning. He may have been listening, but his eyes were alert and watchful.

Daly was talking to one of the women. I gave him—and her—my attention.

"Miss Killgallen," Daly said. "May I present Deputy U.S. Marshal Merlin Fanshaw? Merlin, Miss Karen Killgallen."

She was a woman of average height, maybe five feet four or five, with small feet and a narrow waist. She wore a tailored suit of emerald green and carried a matching parasol. Beneath a hat that also matched her suit, her jet black hair was pulled back at the sides and worn in an upswept style. She smiled, and held out her hand.

I haven't been around all that many high-class ladies. I never know what to do when a lady holds out her hand, palm down. I've watched gents take a lady's hand and bend over and kiss it, and I've seen some who just bend over and *almost* kiss it, but I'm hanged if I know which is right.

Miss Killgallen wore snow-white gloves that day, so I decided on the *almost* option. I was taking no chance of leaving a smudge of leftover ketchup or mustard from my breakfast on that spotless glove.

"Miss Killgallen is a celebrated actress from the New York stage," the banker said. "She just completed a long run as Ophelia in Shakespeare's *Hamlet.*"

She did appear to be in good shape. I figured it must be on account of all that running.

"I sure am pleased to make your acquaintance, Miss," I said. "Is this your first time in the west?"

Her cool blue eyes appraised me. Her smile widened. I don't believe I ever saw teeth so white. "No," she said. "I've performed in plays throughout the west. My first time in Butte City, though."

Close up, I looked at her face and caught my breath. Now I don't claim to be much of a hand at judging a lady's fine points, but I thought Karen Killgallen was just about the most beautiful woman I'd ever seen. Her oval face featured a smallish nose and chin, set off by high cheekbones and forehead. Full lips framed her perfect teeth, and her skin seemed to glow in the late morning light.

But it was her eyes that caught my attention. I said they were a cool blue, but as I looked closer they seemed to change color, fading to a sort of smoky purple. And then I noticed a strange thing. Karen Killgallen's eyes appeared to be *older* than the rest of her, as if a young woman had somehow been given the eyes of a wise female elder.

Under the strength of her gaze I commenced to feel nervous and off balance. My ears felt warm, and I knew I was blushing. I tried to turn away but could not. Looking at her cool, beautiful face was like looking at the moon, and I was moonstruck.

Marcus Daly was speaking to me, his voice sounding faint and far away. I turned my attention to his words and broke the spell.

"Jack tells me you're a friend of Scrapper O'Dhoul's," he said. "Scrapper is a good man."

"Yes, sir. He sure is."

"I don't know if he told you, but he's been having a bit of trouble with his eyes. I said my friend Dr. Lambert was coming soon, and would have a look at him."

"He told me," I said. "Scrapper does miss working at the Mountain Con."

Daly nodded. "He's a grand old Scrapper. I'll do what I can for him."

"I know you will," I said, and in that moment I did know it. I decided I liked Marcus Daly.

I cleared my throat. "Mr. Daly," I began.

"None of that, I said. Call me Mark."

"All right . . . *Mark*. I'm conducting an investigation on a legal matter. Not now, not today, but when you have the time I'd like to talk with you."

Daly drew a small appointment book from a vest pocket and consulted it. "I'm taking my guests on a mine tour tomorrow," he said. "Later, I'll be at my office on Mountain Street. Why don't you meet me there at, say, one-thirty?"

"I'll be there, Mr. . . . *Mark*. Thank you, sir."

"Not at all. Good to meet you, Merlin. Enjoy the races."

I remembered my manners. Turning to Daly's guests, I told each of them I was glad to meet them. It was true in the case of Dr. Lambert, it was not so true in the case of the New York banker, but it was definitely true in the case of Miss Killgallen. As I walked away toward the grandstand I could swear I was blushing again.

From our seats in the stands, I had a good view of the track. A one-mile oval, the racing strip circled the infield and was used for both harness racing and thoroughbred flat racing. Runners and bookies from the betting circle gathered along the rail at trackside and made their way into the grandstand taking bets from the players, and Jack kept them busy.

Seated in the light two-wheel carts called sulkies, drivers lined up their horses behind a tape to begin each race. With a pistol shot, the horses exploded out onto the track, dashing away in a pacer's smooth gait. Watching the drivers urge their horses to their fastest speed as they neared the finish was enough to make a man's heart pound even if he had no bet on the outcome, and all the more if he did.

Fat Jack enjoyed the day. Between betting every race and taking frequent belts from a whiskey flask, Jack threw himself into the afternoon. He bet on every race, he cheered for his favorites, and he cursed when they lost. He even *won* a bet or two. In any case, Jack was so caught up in the excitement I think he forgot I was with him. And that, I thought, was just as well.

I was caught up in excitement of my own, but it had nothing to do with fast horses on a racetrack. The memory of meeting Karen Killgallen stirred my senses like a drug, and I could scarcely think of anything but her.

Instead of being moved by the sight of sunlight shining on horsehide, I recalled the way Karen's skin seemed to glow with a light of its own. As others thrilled to the pennants that fluttered above the grandstand and the colorful silks worn by the drivers, I thought of Karen's tight-fitting green suit. And when the crowd roared as a driver brought his horse and sulky across the finish line, I remembered a smile that lifted my heart and made my throat grow tight.

After the races, I helped guide Jack through the crowd and back to his team and carriage. His money was gone, and so was his whiskey. He drove me back to my hotel, complaining all the way. He cursed his bad luck and his lack of self control. He ranted about the folly of betting on horses: *Horses are smarter than we are; you never hear of a horse betting on a man, do you?*

When I arrived at Marcus Daly's office the following afternoon, I found him seated behind a massive oak desk, talking to his aides. The red-haired giant who'd been with him at the track met me just outside the office door.

"Good day to ya, Deputy," he said. "I'm Oodles O'Brian, and I watch out for Mr. Daly. I need to frisk ya a bit before ya go in."

I was carrying my .44 in an open holster. I held my arms out from my body and smiled. "I'm only packin' my belt gun," I said.

Oodles' pat-down was quick, and smoothly done. "Ya'll have ta leave it with me, sir," he said. "No weapons allowed in the office."

I understood the precaution. I even approved of it. But I was just a bit rankled by the implied mistrust. I remembered the times I'd let myself be separated from my revolver only to find I needed it, and fast.

"The gun goes with the badge," I said.

"Maybe so, sir," said Oodles, "but it don't go in the office."

I felt my temper rising. "My purpose is the same

as yours," I said slowly, "protecting Mr. Daly."

Oodles blocked my way, a huge, living door. "I am glad to hear it, sir."

I decided to try reason. "What if Ed McGinnis, the chief of police, came to see Mr. Daly? Would you ask *him* to surrender his gun?"

"That I would, sir. If Pope Leo himself came to call sure and he'd have to leave his guns at the door."

I laughed. The image of the Pope of Rome, bristling with weapons and being turned away from Daly's door, was so preposterous I could do nothing else. "You win," I said, and unbuckled my gun belt.

Daly was waiting for me. He dismissed his aides and stood as they left the room. Then he looked up and welcomed me. "Merlin!" he said. "Come in, lad—pull up a chair."

We shook hands and I sat down across from him. "Thank you for seein' me," I said. "I know you're a busy man."

"You said you were conducting an investigation," Daly said.

"Yes, sir. The U.S. marshal's office has reason to believe your life may be at risk."

Daly rested his elbows on the desk top and steepled his fingers.

"I'm listening," he said.

Over the next several minutes, I related the entire story as I knew it—the story Digby

O'Dhoul told of the late night meeting in St. Elmo's Church, the conversation he overheard, Marshal Ridgeway's telephone call to the Pinks in Chicago, and the report that an assassin called "Charon" did indeed exist.

I spoke of Digby's death, and said I believed he'd been murdered. "Digby told his brother, Scrapper, the story, and he told his sister, Molly. He told a good many people. I believe someone killed Digby to shut him up. I also believe you are in mortal danger, and I believe the assassin may already be here in Butte City."

Daly sat calmly at his desk, apparently unruffled by all I'd told him. I paused briefly, and then continued. "My question, sir, is do you know any reason someone would want to take your life?"

"Well," he said, "as to that. I have my enemies, as any man does. I believe there may be some who might like to see me dead. But I know of no one who'd take steps to *cause* my death."

"Yes, sir," I said. "The trouble is, not knowing of such an assassin doesn't mean there *isn't* one. I urge you to take every precaution."

Daly smiled. "My good wife, Margaret, seems to believe I lack culture," he said. "Lately, she's taken to instructing me in the writings of William Shakespeare. To please her, I've even committed a few passages to memory.

"For example, there's this from *Julius Caesar*:

206

*Cowards die many times before their
deaths;
The valiant never taste of death but
once.
Of all the wonders I yet have heard,
It seems to me most strange that men
should fear;
Seeing that death, a necessary end,
Will come when it will come.*

"I'll take precautions as you suggest, but I don't plan to lose any sleep over the matter. Oodles O'Brian is a good man and loyal as a hound. Keepin' the bold and rowdy at bay is what I pay him for. Now you tell me it's one of the things they pay *you* for."

"That's right," I said.

"So with a childlike faith I entrust my protection to Oodles O'Brian, the U.S. marshal's office, and the Almighty—though not necessarily in that order."

Daly leaned back in his swivel chair and gazed at the mountains beyond his office window. When he spoke again, it was as if he was seeing all the way back to his beginnings in Ireland.

"I've had a fine run of luck so far," he said, "but it hasn't been *all* luck, as some would have it. I was only fifteen when I left County Cavan, and all I had were the clothes on my back. I had no money, no education, and no skills at all.

"America gave me my chance, and I took it. I worked as a stable hand and messenger, saved my money, and booked passage to California. There, I worked at whatever job I could find—ranch hand, logger, section hand, common laborer. I didn't go to diggin' for gold right away, but earned a stake by diggin' *potatoes* near San Francisco!"

Daly chuckled, remembering. "The gold rush was over by then, but I teamed up with another lad from Ireland and gave mining a try. That's when I found my vocation.

"I seemed to have a gift for findin' the ore— somehow I could almost *sense* the way the metal lay in its veins beneath the earth! I studied the mines, and they gave up their secrets. For a time I worked as an ordinary digger, and then I became a mine foreman and began to attract the notice of the owners. I went to work for Walker Brothers, a mining syndicate in Salt Lake City. I married Margaret, and became a citizen.

"In 1876 the Walkers sent me here to Butte City to look into a silver mine called the Alice. I did so, and gave them a good report. I bought the mine for the company and kept a one-third interest for myself. I moved my family here, and we settled in."

"I know what happened next," I said. "You bought a silver mine called the Anaconda, and everything changed."

Daly nodded. "Indeed it did. When we reached

the mine's three-hundred-foot level the silver played out, but I found veins of copper so rich I thought the hill must be solid copper! I bought up most of the ground around the Anaconda and we went to work."

"The mountain surrendered her wealth," Daly mused. "I built my smelter and I built Anaconda, the town I named for the mine. Built a railroad to transport the ore. I prospered beyond my dreams."

"And now?" I asked.

Daly's eyes brightened. "And now I'm building a stock farm up in the Bitterroot Valley," he said. "I'm going to raise and train thoroughbreds, and standardbreds like Yolo Maid, the filly you saw yesterday."

He smiled. "I love and admire horses," he said.

"It shows," I told him.

I pushed back my chair and stood up. "I've taken up more of your time than I meant to," I said. "Thanks for answering my questions."

"Not at all," Daly said. "We'll have to talk more about thoroughbreds and racing sometime. Horse racing really is 'the sport of kings,' you know."

"Sure seems to be the sport of one particular *copper* king," I said. "I've always wondered. Why is racing called the sport of kings?"

Daly's laugh was a hearty guffaw. "Because only kings can afford it, I suppose!"

He stood and came around his desk to see me

out. Beyond the office door, Oodles O'Brian waited, my belted six-gun in his hand.

Daly's hand gripped my shoulder. "Wait a minute, lad," he said. "Do you have any plans for Friday evening?"

"Why, no, sir," I said. "I haven't."

"We're havin' a few friends over to the house for supper. Margaret calls it dinner, but it's still supper to me. The young actress you met at the track, Karen Killgallen, has promised to give us some readings from Shakespeare. I'd be pleased if you could come."

"I'd like that," I said. "I'll be there."

An invitation to Marcus Daly's home! I was surprised to be asked, because I sure wasn't in the man's social circle. When I began my interview with him, I thought Daly would consider me an annoyance, but instead we had hit it off like friends.

Maybe, I thought, it's just the power of men who share a love for horses. In any case, I would attend. I could hardly turn down such a gracious invitation.

You don't fool me, said a small voice in my mind. *Daly had you when he mentioned Karen Killgallen.*

FOURTEEN

DINNER AT DALY'S

After breakfast the next morning I was sitting in the hotel lobby reading the Anaconda *Standard* when a boy walked in and approached the front desk. Like many another youngster on the streets of Butte City, the boy wore knickers and a cloth cap, and might have been a newsboy except that he carried no papers.

I watched as he spoke earnestly to the desk clerk and I was about to go back to my reading when I saw the clerk point across the lobby at me. I stood up as the boy walked toward me, and I saw that he held a small white envelope in his hand.

"Mr. Fanshaw?" the boy said.

"You bet," I replied.

"Man said to give this to you personal," he said. "Must be important. He gave me four bits."

I took the envelope and dug in my pocket. "In that case," I said, "I'd better match it."

The boy's eyes widened as I gave him the half dollar. "Thanks, mister!" he said, and hurried away, back out onto the street.

Opening the envelope, I drew out a handwritten card that read:

Mr. and Mrs. Marcus Daly
request the pleasure of your company at
a dinner honoring the celebrated actress
Karen Killgallen
on Friday evening at seven o'clock
Black tie R.S.V.P.

I took another look at the envelope to make sure it had my name on it, and sure enough it had. *Merlin Fanshaw* was written there in flowing black script.

My hand shook and my mouth went dry. My ears felt hot. I had a nervous feeling in my belly as if I'd just bet the limit in a high-stakes poker game.

I don't know why I was so stirred up; Marcus Daly had already asked me to come to his house for supper Friday night. The formal invitation just confirmed it.

The desk clerk's name was Clyde Bellingham. I sauntered casual-like over to the desk and showed him the card.

"Say, Clyde," I said. "What does this part mean—where it says 'black tie' and 'RSVP'?"

Clyde's eyebrows went up like window shades. "Marcus Daly!" he said. "My goodness!"

He got hold of himself and looked again at the invitation. " 'Black tie' means you're expected to wear formal clothing. 'RSVP' means you should let them know if you're coming."

"Shoot," I said. "Why wouldn't I come? I already told Mark I'd be there."

"*Mark?*" Clarence said. "You call Mr. Daly '*Mark*'?"

"Sure," I said. "We're old friends, Mark and me." Now I was telling whoppers to impress desk clerks. I began to worry about myself. "Well," I said, "we're good enough friends that he invited me to his house, anyway."

My first concern was how I was going to get myself decked out in formal clothes. Never mind that I'd never *worn* a full dress suit, I didn't even know where to *look* for one. Butte City was full of places where a man could buy overalls, work shirts, and such, but it was a mite short of stores that catered to nabobs and tycoons.

Luckily, before I could work myself into a lather I came up with an idea. I would go back to Shapiro's, the place where I bought my new hat. If Solomon Shapiro couldn't help me I figured nobody could. With my dinner invitation in my pocket, I lit out for East Park Street.

Shapiro's hadn't changed much since my last visit. The doors stood open to the street as before. Under the striped awning, the benches out front were piled high with merchandise of every kind. Inside, clothing for men, women, and children filled the shelves and hung from the ceiling.

Solomon Shapiro himself stood behind the counter, drinking hot tea from a glass. He peered over the tops of his spectacles and smiled.

"Mister Cowboy!" he said. "So why ain't I seen you lately? So many clothes you've got you couldn't use some more?"

"That's why I'm here, Sol," I said. "I need a dress suit for a formal dinner . . . at Marcus Daly's house!"

"*Mazel tov!*" said the storekeeper. "Dress suits I got, the finest. Not *shmatta*, but quality goods, sewed by a tailor."

I showed him the invitation. "I'll need the works," I said, "whatever a man wears to a shindig like this."

Shapiro stepped out from behind counter. He began making notes with a pencil and pad. "So!" he said. "You'll need pants, a coat, a vest, dress shirt, and a necktie. Also a top hat, suspenders, and patent leather shoes. As the old saying goes, *Klader machem dem mentshem* . . . clothes make the man."

"Whoa, pardner!" I said. "There's another old sayin' I just made up—high-priced clothes make the man *broke.* How much is all this goin' to cost me?"

"So cheap you couldn't believe it. The whole *shmeer*, only fifty dollars."

"Fifty dollars! That's pretty steep for an outfit I only figure to wear once. How about thirty?"

"For thirty, I couldn't include the pants."

"Then I guess I wouldn't need the *suspenders.* Work with me here, Sol—make me a price."

"Forty-two fifty and I'm giving it away."

"Not to me you're not." I walked to the door and looked out. Next to Shapiro's was another clothing store. The sign out in front read: SQUARE DEAL DRY GOODS AND GENTLEMEN'S FURNISHINGS. BENJAMIN GOLDSTEIN, PROPRIETOR.

I turned back to Shapiro. "I see your neighbor, Benjamin Goldstein, is still open. Maybe he can help me."

"*Goldstein!* That *macher* should have a bigger store, and whatever people ask for he shouldn't have, and what he does have people shouldn't ask for!"

"Yeah," I said, stepping out through the doorway. "Well, thanks anyway."

Shapiro shambled after me. "*Wait,* Mister Cowboy! So maybe I got an idea. In my back room I got *such* a suit! Finest broadcloth, satin lining! Only worn once! I could *rent* it to you cheap!"

"*Rent* it to me? *How* cheap?"

Shapiro shrugged. "Fifteen . . . twelve . . . all right, *ten!* Ten dollars, alterations free! A stitch here, a tuck there, take it in a little at the waist . . ."

"Well," I said. "Maybe I *could* come up with *ten* dollars. Worn only once, you say?"

"Worn once by a rich man for a special occasion."

"Uh-huh. What was the occasion?"

"I'll tell you the truth, Mr. Cowboy. It was his funeral."

"His *funeral?* You mean the suit was worn by a *dead* man?"

Shapiro nodded. "A practical woman his widow was. After the funeral she had the undertaker take the suit off from her husband, may the poor *shlemiel* rest in peace, and she sold it to me. As the saying goes: *Fyn a kargn gvir in fet bok genist men ersht nukhn toyt!* 'A rich miser and a fat goat are of no use until they are dead.'"

"Yeah," I said. "And 'waste not, want not.' All right, Sol—show me the suit."

Shapiro was as good as his word. He took me back to his work room and had me try the suit on. After a few alterations, it fit me like it was tailor made. I drew the line at wearing a top hat and patent leather shoes. Instead, I donned my "Boss of the Plains" hat and paid a boy at the hotel to put a mirror shine on my boots.

At any rate, that's how I came to be standing outside Marcus Daly's front door on a soft Friday night, wearing a dead man's suit and clutching a formal invitation. I took a deep breath, rang the bell, and waited.

Seconds later, the door opened and I found

myself face to face with a tall, gray-haired gent I took to be Daly's butler. The man wore white gloves, a dark broadcloth suit, and a striped vest. He sized me up with a glance, and I gave him my name to go with his appraisal. "Merlin Fanshaw," I said. "Here at Mr. Daly's invitation."

The butler—if butler he was—had done his homework. "Yes, indeed, Deputy," he said. "Mr. Daly is expecting you."

I stepped inside and the butler closed the door behind me. "Mr. Daly and his guests are in the drawing room, sir," he said. "May I take your hat?"

"If you promise to give it back, pardner," I said. The butler almost smiled, but not quite.

Marcus Daly's drawing room turned out to be what most people call a parlor, but it was the most elegant parlor I ever saw. Roomy and spacious, with a white-painted fireplace and high ceiling, the room held enough furniture, carpets, drapery, and knick-knacks to outfit a small museum.

Daly and the New York banker stood near the fireplace, deep in conversation. Two older ladies, wearing gowns of purple and black, sat talking together on a large upholstered sofa. Other gents and ladies sipped champagne and wine from stemmed glasses and chatted all friendly-like and social, but it was Karen Killgallen who caught my eye.

Seated in a wing chair beneath a crystal chandelier, the actress wore a stylish dress of lime green with emerald accents. Her hands and arms were covered from fingertips to above the elbows by long white gloves, and her sleek black hair gleamed like obsidian in the chandelier's light. Diamonds glittered at her throat, wrist, and earlobes. Men in claw-hammer suits and cutaways stood nearby and sat at her left and right hand, seeming to hang on her every word. Somehow, the picture they made put me in mind of a huddle of penguins surrounding a bird of paradise.

Karen looked up and smiled as I entered the room, and it was clear she recognized me. I returned her smile, stricken by wonder. How anyone could recognize me in my rented suit was a mystery to me. I felt like a kid wearing his grandpa's Sunday-go-to-meeting clothes. It was all I could do to recognize myself.

The men attending Karen turned, to see who she was smiling at, I guess. Seeing me, one gent looked puzzled, as if he couldn't understand Karen's apparent delight. Another scowled, his face hard as flint. I didn't know either man, and from the looks they gave me I decided I had no wish to. The third man turned out to be Doc Lambert, the eye specialist I'd met at the track. The doc smiled, too, but his smile didn't light up the room the way Karen's did.

I made my way through the crowd toward her,

hoping I'd think of something to say by the time I reached her, but the closer I got the more tongue-tied I became. My throat felt dry. I felt a blush climbing up my neck. I hadn't stuttered in years, but I feared I was about to take it up again.

"Deputy Fanshaw," Karen said. "How nice to see you! I hoped you'd be here."

She held out her hand in that palm down manner high-class ladies seemed to favor. Once again, I took the 'almost' approach, bowing over her gloved hand like I was fixing to kiss it but not quite doing so.

"M-Miss Killgallen," I said. "I walked in here feelin' like a fish out of water, but that smile of yours sure makes me glad I came. I wouldn't want to be any place but here in its light."

I hardly knew what I was saying, but in case it was something wrong I apologized in advance. "I-I hope I'm n-not bein' too forward."

Karen looked into my eyes. She smiled, and her smile was even brighter than before. I wouldn't have thought that was possible.

"On the contrary," she said. "Thank you for a lovely compliment."

Marcus Daly was at my side. "Merlin!" he said. "Glad you could come, lad. You look almost as uncomfortable in that monkey suit as I am in mine."

The spell broke. I turned away from Karen's eyes and smiled at my host. "I didn't know it showed," I said, "but you're right—I feel like a broomtail scrub at the Kentucky Derby. I am glad to be here, though. Thanks again for invitin' me."

Daly turned to Karen. "Mind if I borrow Deputy Fanshaw for a minute, Miss Killgallen? I'd like to introduce him to my wife, and to the other guests."

"If you must, Mark," Karen said. "It shall be my sacrifice."

Daly took my arm and led me to the ladies seated on the sofa. "Margaret," he said, "this is Merlin Fanshaw, the young man I told you about. Merlin has an eye for good horseflesh. Merlin, my wife, Margaret."

Margaret Daly was a handsome woman with intelligent eyes. She smiled, and held out her hand. "Welcome to our home, Mr. Fanshaw," she said. "Mark has told me of your interest in thoroughbreds."

I gave Mrs. Daly my compliments, bowing over her hand and giving it the "almost" kiss I'd learned. The other lady on the sofa turned out to be Doc Lambert's wife, and I passed a few pleasantries with her as well. I have to say I found talking to those ladies easier than talking to Karen Killgallen. With the other ladies I was hardly flustered at all.

By that time there were a dozen or so people in the drawing room and Marcus Daly took me around, introducing me. I remembered my manners, making small talk and expressing interest in each person, but I have to confess my mind was not fully present in the meetings. Instead, my thoughts—and my eyes—kept drifting back to the lady in green who sat beneath the crystal chandelier.

I was putting on the dog and living high. I was in a situation and with people I wasn't easy with, but I believe I'd have clumb the social ladder to its top rung and done a dry dive into an ore dump just to be in the same room as Karen Killgallen.

Daly led me to a dapper little man who seemed as comfortable in his formal clothes as I was not. "This is my friend John Maguire," Daly said. "John is Butte City's showman. He came here in 1875, a year before I did. John has brought many a top entertainer to the camp."

"That I have," Maguire said, "including the celebrated actress who seems to have so thoroughly captured *your* interest."

He smiled. "I mean no offense," he said. "We're all captivated by Miss Killgallen. And I dare say there's many a man in this room who envies the smiles she has for you."

"John is manager of the Grand Opera House here," Daly said. "Unfortunately, the Grand burned down recently, but it's already being rebuilt. Meanwhile, John has opened a playhouse called the Lyceum at the corner of Granite and Alaska."

"That's right," Maguire said. "I've booked Miss Killgallen for a two-week engagement beginning tomorrow night. She'll be doing selections from the Bard."

"The Bard?"

"The Bard of Avon, another name for the immortal William Shakespeare. Miss Killgallen has an extraordinary vocal range—she'll perform parts written for both men and women, in voices ranging from a bass to a lilting soprano. Really quite remarkable."

Daly smiled. "Miss Killgallen has agreed to give us a sampling of her talents after dinner," he said. "I'm looking forward to her performance."

The gray-haired butler I'd met at the door walked into the drawing room just as the mantel clock chimed eight. Bowing slightly to the Dalys, he said, "Ladies and gentlemen, dinner is served."

The guests finished their drinks and stood with their eyes on Marcus and Mrs. Daly. Then everybody began to form up two by two, as if it was raining and Noah had just called "All Aboard." I learned later that the host at such dinners enters the dining room first with the female guest of honor on his right arm, and that's how it was at the Daly's. Karen took Marcus Daly's arm and they led the procession into the dining room.

The other guests followed as couples, a man and a woman, but more men had been invited than women and I wound up walking with John Maguire. Bringing up the rear was Mrs. Daly, on the arm of Otto Van Dorn, the banker.

We entered the dining room to find the table prepared and set. Candles lit the table itself, while gaslight guttered in the chandelier above. Hand-lettered cards marked the places, and china, silverware, and crystal reflected the light. Servers in white gloves and livery flanked the mirrored sideboard where tureens and platters of food stood waiting. We found our places, the gents seating the ladies, and Marcus Daly took his place at the table's head, seating Karen on his right. Mrs. Daly took her place at the table's foot, with Van Dorn on her right.

I looked at the dishes in front of me and like to froze with bafflement and the fear of making some god-awful mistake. There was a folded white napkin on the plate that was cleaner than anything I ever owned. Three silver forks were lined up on the left, and I had no idea what they were all for. For no particular reason, I thought of the three forks that made up the Missouri River—the Gallatin, the Madison, and Jefferson. They had nothing to do with the confusion I felt, but I took comfort in the thought that most people at that table likely couldn't name *those* forks.

To the right of my plate were a couple of knives, a spoon, and a little do-funny of a tool I learned later was an oyster fork. Four glasses occupied the space above the plate on my right. Add a butter knife on a bread plate on the left, and I was well-nigh paralyzed by confusion.

"I perceive you are something of a stranger to formal dining," McGuire said. "Don't be alarmed. Food and drink will be served and the ceremonies will be observed. Growing up in County Cork, we had scant use for such folderol. We simply ate what little we had, usually with our hands.

"But I've now become accustomed to the rituals of the Golden Age. Just watch me and do as I do. I shall guide you through the mannered maze."

I found I'd been holding my breath. I let it go, and went back to normal breathing. "Much obliged," I said. "I was commencing to feel nervous as a bronc in a round corral, but I'll be all right now."

I was, too. The servers brought the wine and the food course by course, and I tackled everything as it came. I may not have been an experienced diner, but I had always been a champion eater.

Following McGuire's lead, I made my way through the raw oysters, clam chowder, pickles, radishes, cucumbers, and pickled herring, then took on some croquettes, sweetbreads, and such, and moved on to the prime rib, venison, and ham. I put away some Roman punch and a glass or two of wine, and finished off with plum pudding and fruit.

Every now and then I'd dabble my fingers

dainty-like in the finger bowl and wipe them dry with my napkin. Once, I dropped my fork on the floor, and before I saw McGuire shake his head I bent down to pick it up. Before I knew what was happening, one of the servers snatched it away and handed me a clean one. It sure was one highfalutin' feast, I can tell you.

Some of the meals I had as a cowpuncher came to mind—sitting hunkered in the sagebrush on a windy day, the beans sprinkled with sand while I tried to shoo the blowflies away, and all the while eating beef so tough you couldn't get a fork in the gravy. I remembered my tour of the mine with Scrapper O'Dhoul and watching him heat his pasty on the blade of his shovel. At one point, I looked at Marcus Daly in his place at the head of the table, only to see him shake his head and make a face, as if he remembered such times, too.

Of course, I spent much of the meal watching Karen. She was so graceful and elegant in everything she did that I felt like some kind of gorilla from the jungle by comparison. From time to time our eyes met across the distance, and even though we could not speak to each other our eyes did the talking for us. When she looked at me and smiled, I felt lightheaded just knowing her smile was all for me at that moment.

Finally, as we sat finishing the last of our pudding and sipping our coffee, I saw Karen rise from her place and leave the table. At first I thought she might not be feeling well, but she smiled and spoke to Marcus Daly as she rose, and then left the room.

I pushed my chair back; I was fixing to go after her and find out what the trouble was, but McGuire touched my arm and shook his head.

"She's going to prepare for her performance," he said. "In a few minutes we'll all go into the drawing room and take our places. Be patient."

I sat back down, looking at her empty chair and missing her. Even in the light of the candles and chandelier, the room seemed darker with her gone.

FIFTEEN

ALL THE WORLD'S A STAGE

For a time we remained at the table while folks finished their pudding and their fruit. Coffee was served, and I found out what the fourth glass was for when a waiter came by and poured sherry into it. I had drunk water from the first glass, champagne from the second, red wine from the third, and finally sherry from the last. I had et my way through the courses like an old-time Roman, and I was full as a tick and pleased with myself. Thanks to McGuire's example, I'd made no major social blunder during the dinner, leastways nothing bad enough to get me cast out from polite society or tarred and feathered.

Not that I was home free at that point. I seriously considered letting out my belt a notch or two to ease my paunch. Then I remembered I wasn't *wearing* a belt. So I just sat up straight as a ground squirrel on a cow chip, stifled a belch, and tried to look stylish.

Up at the head of the table, Marcus Daly caught McGuire's eye and nodded. The showman stood up, and the diners fell silent.

"Dear friends," he began, "Mr. and Mrs. Daly have asked me to announce the *pièce de résistance* of the evening. We shall now retire to the drawing room for a special preview of Miss Killgallen's upcoming engagement at my theater, the Lyceum.

"Miss Killgallen will enact scenes from several of Shakespeare's plays, displaying her remarkable vocal range by performing both male and female roles. You're in for a rare treat, and we all owe the Dalys a debt of thanks."

The guests applauded politely. Because most of us wore gloves, the applause was kind of muffled but that made it all the more polite, I guess.

Entering the drawing room, we found the lights had been dimmed and the chairs arranged in a semicircle. An upholstered chair stood alone in a circle of light. We took our seats, and waited.

"Ladies and gentlemen," McGuire said. "Please welcome Miss Karen Killgallen!"

Again, enthusiastic but muffled applause.

And then a sort of collective gasp went up from the watchers as Karen stepped into the light. Gone was her lime green gown; gone the diamonds. Dressed in black tights and a white shirtwaist, she stood in the light and waited until the room was completely silent. Then she sat, half reclining in the chair, and in the voice of a young man began:

> *To be, or not to be: that is the question:*
> *Whether 'tis nobler in the mind to*
> *suffer*
> *The slings and arrows of outrageous*
> *fortune,*
> *Or to take arms against a sea of*
> *troubles,*
> *And by opposing end them?*

She went on that way for a while, appearing to be deep in thought as if she was all alone and fretting about something. Turned out she was portraying an old-time prince name of Hamlet who was thinking about doing himself in. I can't say I understood all the words, but I found I was so caught up in the prince's problems I nearly forgot it was playacting.

Next, Karen did a part from *Romeo and Juliet*, or rather *two* parts, for she played a scene where the two young lovers are talking to each other, first, in Romeo's voice:

Lady, by yonder blessed moon I swear
That tips with silver all these fruit-tree
tops—

And then, in Juliet's voice:

O! swear not by the moon, the inconstant
moon,
That monthly changes in her circled orb,
Lest that thy love prove likewise variable.

Karen took on a speech from *Julius Caesar*, speaking as Mark Antony in a bold man's voice:

Friends, Romans, countrymen, lend me
your ears;
I come to bury Caesar, not to praise him.
The evil that men do lives after them,
The good is oft interred with their bones.

And a scene where old King Lear goes plumb loco when his daughter dies:

And my poor fool is hang'd! No, no, no
life!
Why should a dog, a horse, a rat, have
life,
And thou no breath at all? Thou'lt come
no more,
Never, never, never, never, never!

Well, I tell you the way Karen wept and carried on, fussing and grieving and such, nearly broke my heart. She went on to do other Shakespeare characters, including Lady Macbeth (*Out, damned spot! Out I say!*), Othello (*Ah balmy breath, that dost almost persuade*), and Richard III (*A horse! A horse! My kingdom for a horse!*).

I never knew much about Shakespeare's writings before that evening, but it seemed to me a lot of his characters are nutty as a squirrel's pantry. I suppose that's one of the things that makes them interesting.

As the evening ended, I thanked Marcus and Mrs. Daly, and fell in line with the other guests as we filed past Karen to tell her how much we enjoyed her performance. When it came my turn, I sort of stammered a little and said I thought she was wonderful. She smiled her radiant smile and took my hand in hers. "Thank you, Merlin," she said.

Out on the street, the stars overhead shone bright as cold fire and seemed close enough to touch. I don't recall how I got back to my hotel, but I believe I may have flown.

I attended Karen's show at the Lyceum the following night, and marveled at her skills. She performed many of the same passages from Shakespeare as she did at the Daly's, but she included longer works as well. A string quartet backed her up with some high-class music, and colored lighting added to the show.

She appeared in costume, a different one for each character, and she changed outfits as quick as she changed voices. She'd act out a passage, say while wearing Juliet's gown, and then the lights would go dark for what seemed only a moment. When they came on again, there she'd be, wearing armor or the royal robes of a queen. Folks in the audience clapped like crazy and hollered with delight. Many, like myself, maybe didn't savvy all that much Shakespeare, but we liked what Karen did and the way she did it.

I have to admit I pretty much liked the way Karen did everything. I didn't really know her, of course, but I sure liked what little I did know. Twice more that week, I attended her performance, and I never tired of watching her use her voice and her body to make the works come alive.

The third night, as I came out of the Lyceum with the rest of the crowd, I found Fat Jack parked out front in his rockaway, and of course he had to comment on my frequent theater going.

"Hark!" he bellered. "Is that a Fanshaw I see before me? Merlin, Merlin, wherefore the hell art thou, Merlin?" Then he grinned, and added, "I swear, I never seen *anybody* as crazy about Shakespeare as *you* are."

"I just may have to shoot me a skinny hack

driver," I grumped, "soon as the *season* opens." Of course, that only pleased him all the more, knowing he'd got to me.

Also that week, I paid a visit to Chief McGinnis at the police station to find out how Lucas Durand was making out.

"A Choteau County deputy came by and collected him," McGinnis said. "He's healin' up nicely from that .44 slug you put in him. He's almost healthy enough to hang."

"Doc Whitford does good work," I said, "but I don't think he'd better plan on a testimonial from Durand."

"Durand wouldn't give him one anyway. The man has no gratitude. He didn't thank you for puttin' that bullet in him, and he didn't thank Doc for takin' it out."

I assumed a disappointed look. "I'm afraid you're right," I said. "I'll bet he won't thank the Choteau County judge, jury, and hangman either."

The chief was quiet for a moment. Then he said, "Do you recall that Smith and Wesson .32 we found with Digby O'Dhoul's body?

"Yes," I said. "Your man Kelly found it in Digby's right hand, you said. What about it?"

McGinnis frowned. "When you asked me that day if it was Digby's gun I said, 'it must have been.' I gave you that answer because I *assumed* the gun was Digby's, not because I had any evidence. That was poor police work, and I apologize.

"This week I sent Kelly out to check the hock shops and secondhand stores, to see if somebody might recognize the weapon."

"And?"

"And . . . somebody did. Charley Potts, proprietor of Cheap Charley's Pawn Shop, in Walkerville. Got time for a buggy ride, Deputy?"

"You bet," I said.

A short drive north of Butte City brought us to the independent town of Walkerville, and to a ramshackle building marked by peeling paint and barred windows. Above the front door, the traditional three gold balls announced the nature of the business inside, and a painted sign reading CHEAP CHARLEY'S PAWN SHOP repeated the message.

Chief McGinnis brought the buggy to a stop, and we stepped out onto the boardwalk in front of the building. Behind the window's dirty pane, a display of musical instruments reflected sunlight. Pawn shops always give me a sad feeling. The trumpet, trombone, and tuba in the window made me think of abandoned pets waiting for their owners' return.

Inside, merchandise of nearly every kind hung from pegs and filled display cases. Dolls and dishes, guns and watches, jewelry and clothing filled every nook and cranny of the shop. Behind a high counter, a balding man with a two-day growth of beard studied a ring through a jeweler's loupe. He placed the ring back in its box as we approached.

He nodded at McGinnis. "Chief," he said.

McGinnis returned the nod. "Hello, Charley. How you keepin'?"

"Not bad," the man said. He looked at me, questions in his eyes.

"This is Merlin Fanshaw, Charley—deputy U.S. marshal out of Helena. Merlin, meet Charlie Potts."

"Deputy," said Charley.

McGinnis drew the revolver from his coat pocket and laid it on the counter. "Remember this gun?" he asked.

The pawnbroker glanced down. "Thirty-two caliber Smith & Wesson," he said. "You showed it to me that other time. I told you. I sold it to a feller a month ago."

"Tell me again," McGinnis said. "What did the man look like?"

"Fancy dressed dude. Sandy hair, clean-shaven. Maybe thirty or thirty-five years old. He wore a frock coat and a showy embroidered vest. Black silk necktie. Top hat. He wore kid gloves and carried a walkin' stick."

"Anything else?" McGinnis asked.

"Yeah. He took his gloves off to look at the gun.

That's when I saw he was wearin' a big diamond ring on his right hand. Kept fiddlin' with it while we talked price."

The chief turned to me. "Sound like anyone you know?" he asked.

I caught my breath. "Cecil Hardesty," I said.

Back in Butte City we found Cecil nursing a hangover at a table in the Four Jacks Mess Club. The club was supposed to be for high-class gentlemen only, but they let Chief McGinnis and me in anyway.

Cecil's eyes were red and haunted. He sat slumped in his chair, with his elbows on the table and his head tilted to one side. From the face he made when we approached his table Cecil must have had the granddaddy of all headaches. When he raised his hands to massage his temples the ring reflected sunlight.

McGinnis was short on sympathy. He leaned over and slammed the revolver down between Cecil's elbows. "Ever see this gun before, Hardesty?" he asked.

Cecil stared, but he said nothing.

"That's the pocket .32 officer Kelly found in Digby O'Dhoul's hand the night he died. Charley Potts, over at Walkerville, says he sold the gun to you."

Cecil continued to stare at the weapon. At last he nodded. "Yes," he said. "I bought the gun from

Charley. Digby was obsessed with the idea someone was out to kill him. He was driving us all crazy. I thought maybe if I got him a gun, he'd feel safer. It never occurred to me he'd use it on himself."

"Why didn't you come forward at the time of his death?" McGinnis asked.

Cecil lowered his eyes. "I felt bad, Chief. To tell the truth, I thought I might be blamed for his death. I was working for W. A. Clark then—I felt if word got out I'd given Digby the weapon I'd lose my job."

I said, "As it turned out, Clark fired you anyway."

Cecil bared his teeth in a bitter grimace, and lowered his eyes. "Yeah," he said. "Ain't life a bitch?"

Nervously, Cecil toyed with the ring on his right hand. Then he raised his eyes and looked at McGinnis. "I just felt *sorry* for the poor bastard, Chief . . . all I did was lend him a weapon to give him a little confidence . . . I *swear!*"

"How do we know you didn't kill him and plant the gun on him afterward?" McGinnis asked.

Cecil shrugged. "I guess you don't. But why *would* I? O'Dhoul was just a troubled soul with a worried mind. I had no reason to wish him harm."

"Still," McGinnis said. "You can't prove you didn't kill him."

Some of Cecil's old arrogance returned. "No, I can't," he said, "but then I don't *have* to. Under our system of justice, I don't have to prove I'm innocent; the law has to prove I'm guilty."

"Now," he said, "Unless there's something else, I'd appreciate it if you'd go away and let me suffer in peace. And take that damned gun with you—if this hangover doesn't let up soon I just may follow Digby's example."

Out on the street, I climbed up on the buggy seat beside McGinnis. "Well," he said. "What do you think?"

"Another piece of the puzzle has come to light," I said. "But we're no closer to solvin' it than before."

McGinnis clucked to the buggy horse and we moved out up the street. "Another day in the good old law and order business," he said. "As Cecil said, 'Ain't life a bitch?' "

Late Friday morning, I picked up my shirts from the laundry and was on my way back to my hotel when I nearly collided with Molly O'Dhoul. Molly was just coming out of O'Malley's Grocery with a full shopping bag, and the sun was in her eyes.

"Merlin!" she said. "I'm sorry—sure and I'm daydreamin' instead of watchin' where I'm goin'!"

I smiled and tipped my hat. "My fault, Molly," I said. "I didn't expect a pretty girl to cross my path today."

"Go on with you now," she said. "I'm thinkin' pretty girls must cross your path on a regular basis."

Molly looked into my eyes. "I've not seen you since that day at the cemetery," she said. "How are you?"

"I'm well," I said, "but it has been too long. Have you had your lunch today?"

"Not yet. I just now finished me my shoppin' and I'm on my way home."

"Tell you what," I said. "Lee Sun's noodle parlor is in the next block. I'll buy you lunch and we'll catch up on all the news."

Molly smiled her crooked smile. "Well," she said. "I am hungry—and my feet could use a bit of a rest."

I took her shopping bag from her. "Then come with me, Molly O'Dhoul," I said, "and together we'll sample the delights of the Orient."

Molly giggled. "Aw, go on with you now," she said.

Like many of Butte City's restaurants, Lee Sun's Noodle Parlor was open twenty-four hours a day. Long and narrow, the interior consisted of a hallway lined with individual booths, each containing a table and four chairs. A muslin curtain on a wire closed off the entrance to each booth, affording privacy for the customer and access by the waiter. A busy kitchen occupied one end of the restaurant, where Lee Sun ruled over his staff of cooks and waiters in a bedlam of fire, smoke, and steam. Molly and me walked in off the street and were met by Lee Sun's daughter, Susie.

Susie showed us to a booth and offered us each a bill of fare written in English. I looked at Molly. "I already know what I'm havin'," I said. "Lee Sun's chow mein is the best in town."

Molly studied the list. "I'll have the wonton soup," she said, "and a nice cup of tea."

I turned to Susie. "Wonton soup for the lady," I said, "and a pot of tea. I'll have your chow mien and a double order of egg rolls."

Susie nodded and turned away toward the kitchen. I looked at Molly and smiled. "Well," I said, "How are you, Molly? How is Scrapper?"

Molly's blue eyes were troubled. "I'm well enough," she said, "but Scrapper . . ."

The curtain parted. Susie set a hot teapot and two cups before us and left. I filled Molly's cup, and then my own.

"It's been hard for Scrapper," Molly said. "His eyes are no better, and he misses his job at the Mountain Con. Some days he walks up to the mine yard and talks to his friend Murph at the office, or whoever will give him the time o' day. Some days he just follows me about the house, drivin' me *loopers*."

Molly sipped her tea and placed the cup back in her saucer. "Oh, he's doin' his best to keep his hopes up, but it's hard for a man when he can't work. A man's work is who he is."

I tried to lighten the mood. "That's true," I said. "I know *I* get restless when a week goes by and I haven't gunned down an outlaw or two."

Molly's merriment was my reward. "God love you, Merlin," she said. "You do know how to make a girl laugh."

Susie brought our orders and placed them before us. Molly bowed her head and said a silent table grace, after which she raised her head and thanked me, too. Then we took up our eating tools and set to with a will.

"There is good news," Molly said. "Doctor Lambert, Mr. Daly's friend, came to the house last week. He spent nearly an hour examining Scrapper, and he'll be comin' back again this week."

"I met the doctor," I said. "I think he's a fine man."

"Scrapper likes him. He seems confident the doctor can restore his sight—maybe *too* confident. It's almost as if he wants to be healed so much that somehow it *must* happen."

"I've always believed confidence in a person's doctor is a good thing, Molly."

She raised her head and smiled. "I believe that, too," she said. "It's just that Scrapper's my brother and I worry. It's an old habit."

Molly raised her teacup to her lips. "Maybe it's the fighter in him," she said, "but he is determined to manage his life and shape his future. He wants his eyesight restored, his job at the mine back, and he wants to marry Eileen O'Grady, the girl he left behind in Ireland.

"Scrapper wrote her this week. He sent her money for the passage and asked her to come to Butte City and marry him. He told her he's having 'a bit of trouble' with his eyes but said he was sure they'd be fine by the time she gets here.

"I'm fond of Eileen, Merlin. She's beautiful both inside and out, and she has the face of an angel. She and Scrapper have waited so long for each other, and they deserve their happiness. But there is a wee, small part of me that asks 'What if his eyesight is *not* better?' What if he loses his vision entirely? How then could he support a wife?"

"Scrapper is a strong man, and I have no doubt he can rise above many a woe and misfortune," she said. "But not, I think, with a broken heart."

"Somebody reminded me once that today is the tomorrow we worried about yesterday," I said. "Most of the things folks worry about never happen."

I reached across the table and took her hand. "Believe me, Molly," I said. "Everything is going to be all right."

Molly nodded, and hope shone brighter in her eyes. For the moment at least, my words seemed to calm and convince her.

Now if only I could convince *myself,* I thought.

SIXTEEN

MUCH ADO ABOUT HORSES

The horses broke from the starting line like buckshot from a gun, exploding out and away in a riot of color and motion. The people in the grandstand and along the rail whooped their approval, cheering their favorites and rising to their feet. Sunlight on horseflesh and the silks of the jockeys dazzled the eye, and the thunder of galloping hooves caused the hearts of the spectators to beat faster.

As they passed the grandstand the first time, the seven thoroughbreds thundered down the track, matching stride for stride. The favorite in the race, a chestnut named Diamond Jim, pulled ahead as the horses swept into the first turn, and by the quarter led the field by a length and a half. At the half, Diamond Jim continued to hold his lead, with his jockey moving him to the inside rail and pushing the animal to still greater effort.

Then, at the three-quarter mark, Marcus Daly's horse, a handsome bay named Warlock, began to close the gap. He gained a half length on the leader, then a full length, and by the mile marker Warlock and Diamond Jim were neck and neck. Diamond Jim's jockey went to the bat, but Danny O'Dea, Warlock's rider, urged the bay to his best speed, gave him a crack or two with the bat, and he swept past the leader to win by two lengths.

The crowd was on its feet and so was I. Warlock had won at the fast speed of 2.07 for the mile and a quarter. At odds of two to one, I had bet twenty dollars from my poker winnings. I was richer by forty dollars.

Fat Jack stood beside me down at the rail. Disgusted, he tore up his ticket and scattered the pieces. "Lucky!" he snorted. "I've bet every race today and I've *lost* 'em all. You've bet only *one* and you're *up* by forty bucks!"

"And that's not the half of it, Jack," I said. "I'm not bettin' again, so I'm walkin' *away* with my forty bucks."

"You're disgustin,' Fanshaw! What kind of sport are you, man?"

"No kind," I said. "If by 'sport' you mean somebody who bets every race and loses all his hard-earned wages."

"You don't understand! The whole *point* of gamblin' is to lose, and to keep losin' until some day you win, and win big!"

"Now that doesn't make any sense at all," I said. "Anyway, my weakness is women, not race horses."

Jack grinned. "Mine, too!" he said. "Who says we're only allowed one weakness?"

Across the way, Marcus Daly waited for O'Dea to bring Warlock into the winner's circle. Daly stood, his hat in his hand, smiling broadly. Doc Lambert was beside him, as were Van Dorn the banker and Oodles O'Brian. Other men gathered to congratulate Daly and shake his hand. I scanned the crowd, but to my disappointment saw no trace of Karen Killgallen. Making my way to where Daly stood, I offered my own congratulations.

"A race to remember," I said. "Your Bitter Root Stock Farm is a winner, if Warlock is an example."

"Good of you to say so," Daly said. "I'm glad you were here to see him run."

I showed him my ticket. "Me, too. I profited by the experience."

Daly laughed. "Good for you! Wait here a minute—I'll be right back."

O'Dea rode Warlock into the winner's circle. Breathing heavily and sweated from the race, the bay's sleek hide shone in the afternoon light. Daly reached up and shook the jockey's hand, and then he stood at the horse's head while a photographer captured the moment on film.

Daly's face was flushed when he returned, and his eyes twinkled with pleasure. The man loved his thoroughbreds, and on that day, in that race, one of his own had loved him back. Taking me by the arm, he led me away from the others.

"I've a favor to ask," he said. "Some of my guests have expressed interest in going for an extended horseback ride tomorrow. Charlie

Lambert, his wife Gwendolyn, and Karen Killgallen tell me they'd like to explore some of the local trails.

"I'm tied up all day tomorrow in business meetings, so I can't go. Would you consider taking them out?"

I didn't hesitate. "Sure, Mark," I said. "Truth is I was thinkin' about goin' out myself tomorrow anyway. What kind of ride are they lookin' for?"

"Charlie and Gwen do a bit of riding back east, bridle trails mostly. They tell me they'd like to make a day of it."

"What about Miss Killgallen . . . Karen?" I asked. For a mercy my voice held steady when I spoke her name.

"She feels as the Lamberts do. The theater is dark tomorrow night, so Karen will not be performing. She tells me she's an experienced horsewoman. In light of her many other accomplishments I'd be surprised if she weren't."

Daly paused. Thoroughbreds and their jockeys were forming up for the final race of the day, and the excitement distracted him for a moment. He turned back to me.

"Tell Francis at Fogarty's Livery I want good horses and tack for my guests. Pick the animals out yourself—not too spirited, but no crow bait or plugs, either."

"I'll take care of it," I said. "Any suggestions as to where we should ride?"

Daly considered my question. Then he asked, "Have you been to Highland City?"

"Can't say as I have," I said.

"It's an old gold camp, about fifteen miles from here. Between sixty-five and seventy-five it was something of a boomtown. A few people still live there, but the town is mostly a ghost now. Abandoned cabins, a cemetery—it sits right at the top of the Continental Divide.

"I'll send a man ahead of you with food and drink. When you arrive, you'll find a hot meal waiting."

"Sounds good," I said. "Ask Miss Killgallen and the Lamberts to be at Fogarty's by seven-thirty. If we can get started before eight we should make Highland City around noon, depending on the trail and how many stops we make."

Daly shook my hand, as if he'd just finalized a business deal. "I'm obliged to you, Merlin. Here's to a pleasant outing for all concerned."

It will be for me, I thought. *If Karen is there.*

Francis Fogarty sat in a chair outside the open doors of his stable when I stopped by that afternoon. He smiled as I approached, and peered at me over the tops of his spectacles.

"Welcome back, Deputy," he said. "Sure and I thought you'd given up horses entirely, it's been that long since you were here."

"I've been usin' public transportation," I said.

"With a streetcar, there's neither hay to pitch nor poop to scoop. And yet somehow *ridin'* on tracks just ain't the same as *makin'* tracks."

"Not even close," the liveryman agreed. "Once a horse man, always a horse man."

"You bet. Which brings me to the reason for my visit. I'll be needin' Centavo tomorrow, and three more of your best horses. For Marcus Daly."

Fogarty's eyebrows went up. "Well, well!" he said. "Marcus *Daly,* is it? Is the great man riding himself?"

"Nope. Mr. Daly has asked me to take his guests out for a day-long excursion. I'm thinkin' Highland City."

"The very place," Fogarty said, getting to his feet. "Come, let us visit the corral."

A dozen horses milled in the thick dust of Fogarty's corral as he walked slowly among them. I stood outside, my arms resting on the top rail, and listened to the animals with my eyes.

Horses don't talk, as far as I know, but that doesn't mean they can't let a person know how they feel. The way a horse holds his head and neck, the way he uses his ears, and the way he moves his legs and tail can tell you volumes about what's on his mind and how he's likely to behave.

A friendly horse will face you, ears forward and his muscles loose and easy. His eyes will show interest, and he may stretch his neck out toward you and give you a friendly sniff. A horse that's not friendly can run the gamut from cranky and out of sorts to waspish and downright ornery. At such a time he may show you his teeth, and it won't be because he's smiling. His eye will be cold as a hangman's heart, and he might even have a hind leg loaded and cocked.

If he holds his head high and tosses it in a restless kind of way, your equine barometer is telling you to batten down the hatches; a storm's a-coming.

Want to know what a horse is thinking? Watch his ears. If one or both are loose and floppy, a horse is easy in his mind and plumb peaceful. If his ears are up and pointed straight ahead, he's giving something or someone his full attention. And if his ears are laid flat back, the message is clear—your horse is saying "leave me alone" or "beware."

Like people, horses show their feelings mostly through their eyes. When all is right with his world, a horse's eye has a sort of soft and dreamy look. When he's in a hostile mood, those warm and gentle eyes turn hard as flint. They hold a warning and a threat, and you have to either let him have his way or be prepared to call his bluff.

Add to all this the thousand other ways a horse tips his hand—the way he stands and moves, the way he switches and wrings his tail, and even the noises he makes—and you can see there's not much your horse isn't telling you.

All these signs and more are things I looked for in choosing mounts for Doc and Mrs. Lambert and for Karen Killgallen. I chose a long-legged Morgan gelding for the doctor, and a sensible gray mare for his wife.

A high-headed black filly with a silken mane and tail caught my eye. The quick, dancing way she moved put me in mind of Karen herself. For a moment I nearly chose her for Karen's mount, but there was a nervous, edgy quality about the animal that troubled me. In the end I passed her by and chose a steady bay mare instead.

"We'll need two good ladies' sidesaddles," I told Fogarty, "one for the gray and one for the bay. Put an English saddle on the Morgan, and the rig I use on Centavo. Have the horses saddled and ready by seven-thirty; I want to be on the road by eight."

"I suppose you want me to promise good weather, too," said Fogarty. "I can, but it will cost you extra."

I laughed. "Never mind, Francis," I said. "We'll take what we get."

Daybreak came soft the next day. Beyond the sawtooth edge of the eastern mountains, darkness faded from the sky until at last sunlight topped the ridge and put a run on the stars.

In my room at the hotel I shrugged into my

brush jacket, picked up my saddlebags, and walked out into the new day. Above the flat, smoke from the smelters stained the morning, and the hammering of the stamp mills broke the stillness. I caught a quick breakfast of ham and eggs at a Greek café on Main Street and walked down to Fogarty's.

The liveryman and his hostler were waiting when I got there. The horses I'd chosen were saddled and loose-tied at the hitch rack out front, and Fogarty was in a good mood. He smiled a sly smile as he saw me walking toward him, and directed his comments to his hired man.

"Never mind calling out that search party, Bob," he said. "Deputy Fanshaw is here at last! Sure and wouldn't it be grand to be a federal marshal and sleep late every morning?"

"We live in a wonderful country," I said. "I used to work in a livery barn myself, but I aspired to better things. Through pluck and industry I rose above the peon class."

I walked over to the horses. The Morgan I picked for Doc Lambert wore an eastern-style bridle and an English saddle. Both the gray mare and the bay sported three horn ladies' sidesaddles, built on Somerset trees. I have to admit I didn't know much about sidesaddles, although I did clean and restore a couple when I worked at Walt's Livery in Dry Creek.

In those days no self-respecting lady would ride

any way but aside, and only Indian maidens and some ranch women rode astride. Wasn't considered decent; I don't know why.

I guess side saddles of one kind or other have been around about as long as ladies have rode horses, but they improved some in the 1880s. A balance strap was added to help keep the back of the saddle from shifting and causing a sore-backed horse. The cutback head was invented, which allowed the saddle to set lower on the horse and thus gave the rider a more level seat. The lower pommel—called the "leaping head"—was added to give ladies' limbs a better grip. And various so-called safety stirrups and safety bars—designed to release the stirrup leather in case of an emergency—were added. Some worked. Some worked sometimes. And some didn't work at all.

I looked the saddles over and checked their girths and their fit to the horses' backs. Marcus Daly had given me the responsibility of guiding his guests on their outing, and I meant to make sure they enjoyed their ride and came back safe.

When I finished my inspection and was satisfied with the horses and their rigs, I eased up some. Fogarty poured me a cup of coffee, and I stood there in the cool of the morning and passed the time of day with him and Bob, his stable hand.

At exactly 7:30, Fat Jack pulled up in his rockaway with Daly's guests. Doc Lambert stepped out first and greeted me with a smile.

"Good morning, Deputy," he said. "Good of you to serve as our guide."

"Mornin', Doctor," I said. "I'm lookin' forward to it."

Doc Lambert was dressed in what the gentry considered informal clothes in those days. He wore a short-tailed wool jacket of dark wool, and trousers of the same material. He wore English riding boots, and a patterned vest over a shirt with a stand-up collar and cravat. Tight-fitting leather gloves and a top hat completed his outfit. I was beginning to think a gentleman of that day pretty much dressed up all the time, whether his outfit was practical or not. I can't say whether those high-class dudes wore a boiled shirt and necktie to bed, but it wouldn't surprise me none if they did.

I noticed the doctor also carried his medical bag. I nodded toward the bag and grinned. "I hope you didn't bring that bag because you're worried about my ability as your guide," I said.

Doc Lambert laughed. "Not at all, Deputy. It's just that I don't feel dressed without it."

The doc offered his hand to the ladies, helping them down from Jack's carriage. First, he assisted his wife, Gwendolyn ("Please," she said to me later, "you simply must call me 'Gwenny'!" I didn't, of course. Mostly, I called her Mrs. Lambert).

Then Doc assisted Karen from the rockaway, and I caught my breath. The actress wore a powder blue riding habit that fit her like a second skin. A high collar graced the bodice of her dress, and a score of tiny buttons marched down its front to end in a cutaway flare, like a man's vest. Brown leather gloves, soft as butter, protected her hands, and a silk top hat with a veil sat squarely above her eyes. She met my gaze with her bright smile, and I felt my heart leap like a deer clearing a four-wire fence.

"Good morning, Merlin," she said. "What a lovely day for a ride!"

I wanted to say yes it sure is, but I didn't trust my voice right then. I'd spent years getting rid of a stutter that used to come on me whenever I got nervous. Until Karen showed up I thought I was cured.

I led the Lamberts and Karen over to the tethered horses and took care of the introductions. "This big feller is yours," I told the doctor. "He's of the Morgan persuasion, and he's strong and steady. I think you'll like him."

Doc seemed pleased with my choice. He stroked the animal's neck, getting acquainted.

"And this gray mare is a real lady," I told Mrs. Lambert. "She's modest but reliable, and she has excellent manners."

"I like her," Gwendolyn said. "I'm sure we shall get along famously."

I turned to Karen. She stood beside the bay mare, but there was disappointment in her eyes.

"The bay seems to be a reliable animal," she said, "but I must confess I had something a bit different in mind. Mr. Daly was kind enough to take me on a tour of the city this week, and we stopped briefly here at Fogarty's."

Karen turned to the stable's owner. "Mr. Fogarty," she said. "I have to confess that I rather fell in love with that black filly you have in your string. Is she available by any chance?"

Fogarty looked as fuddled as most men did in Karen's presence. He glanced at me as if he expected me to throw him a lifeline. "Why, yes," he said, "but she is . . . that is, Deputy Fanshaw chose . . . but yes, to answer you directly, she *is* available."

Karen beamed. "That's wonderful!" she said. "Merlin . . . can we make the change? I'd be *ever* so grateful!"

I was outmatched, and I knew it. Karen smiled the hopeful smile of a schoolgirl making a small and reasonable request. I stood in the light of that smile and tried to stand firm on my original decision. There was still something about the black filly I didn't quite trust. I meant to stick to my guns. I meant to turn Karen down, I really did.

And then I opened my mouth and words I had not intended came out. "W-Why, sure, K-Karen," I said. "I d-don't see why not."

It was not the first mistake I ever made.

Fogarty sent his hired man to the corral to bring the black filly out and stripped the bridle and sidesaddle from the bay. With the good manners of the gentry, the Lamberts waited patiently at the hitch rack, talking quietly to each other.

Karen paced to and fro in front of the livery stable, impatient to set out on our trip. She was full of questions about Highland City and its history—was it a true ghost town? Did people still live there? What was the surrounding countryside like? At what altitude did the town lie?

I did my best to answer her questions, but I had to admit I hadn't seen the former gold camp myself. All I could do was repeat what Marcus Daly told me and what I'd heard from others. I had no firsthand knowledge of the region, and that left me feeling off balance and edgy.

As we waited for Karen's mount, I found myself growing impatient. Pa's old silver watch read 7:50, then 8:00, and then 8:15. *We need to get going!*

Highland City was supposed to be only fifteen miles from Butte City but mountain miles, I knew, are longer than prairie miles. I knew nothing about the condition of the trail that led there, or if trying to reach the town and come back the same day was practical or not. I took to pacing up and down myself.

I ran over my check list in my head—I had

sandwiches and first aid supplies in my saddle bags. A full canteen of water hung from the forks of my saddle. I had matches in my pocket. *Come on, Fogarty—we're burning daylight!*

I heard the rumble of hooves on the barn's plank floor. Fogarty jogged outside, leading the saddled filly. He was disheveled and his expression was grim.

"About time, Francis," I said. "What kept you?"

"Some horses catch easy and some do not," he said. "This filly does not."

Karen was all smiles. "Oh, she is beautiful," she said. "Please—may I mount her now?"

I caught the animal's bridle. "Let her settle down a minute," I said. "Just talk to her easy 'til she calms a bit."

Standing at the animal's side, Karen stroked its sleek neck, speaking quietly. "Perhaps if I recite a sonnet for her," she said, smiling. "Shall I compare thee to a summer's day . . ."

A few minutes later, the filly was more peaceable and so was I. "All right," I said. "Take the reins. I'll give you a hand up."

My hands at her waist, I helped Karen into the saddle. Her smile was warm, but there was mischief in it. "Your stuttering is much better," she said.

The remembered touch of her body and the fragrance of her perfume lingered. I turned away to mount my own horse. "N-no, it's *n-not,*" I said.

256

SEVENTEEN

AN OUTING INTERRUPTED

We struck out on the Basin Creek road, riding south toward Highland City and Red Mountain, which lay just beyond. According to the rules of etiquette, a man accompanying a woman is supposed to ride on her right hand side, and Doc Lambert took that position beside his wife either by instinct or because he knew the rule.

Normally I would have taken the lead, but I held Centavo back for the first few miles so I could see how the horses and riders got along. Doc Lambert rode in the English manner, with a great deal of bobbing up and down; *posting,* I believe, is what he called it. Gwendolyn, his wife, was less active, riding aside without fuss or concern. Gwendolyn smiled a good deal, a toothy smile of pleasure at the sight of songbirds and scenery. Leaving the smelter smoke and the din of the stamp mills behind was enough to make anyone smile.

I held Centavo back so I could keep an eye on the black filly—yes, all right, and on Karen, too. Erect in the saddle, her shoulders back, and moving with the filly as if the two were one, Karen seemed a kind of joyful spirit. The sleek hide of the animal shone in the sunlight, its mane and tail flowing like silken banners in the breeze.

Watching Karen's confident way with the filly, I felt my concern fade. Yes, the filly still tended to be something of a shadow jumper, and yes, it used twice the nervous energy to travel the road it needed to, but Karen seemed to have the animal in hand. I stopped worrying, sat back, and admired the view.

Perhaps because she is a trained actress, I thought, Karen seems fully in control of her body, commanding it as she does the filly, with poise and an easy grace. I touched Centavo with my spurs, and rode up alongside her.

"We'll stop up ahead and let the horses drink," I said. "Then we'll push on to Highland City."

Karen slowed the filly to a walk. She leaned forward and stroked its neck. "Thank you for allowing me to ride her," she said. "She is a lovely and spirited animal."

"I thought at first she might be *too* spirited," I said. "I didn't know you rode so well."

I turned Centavo off the road and down to the fast-flowing waters of Basin Creek. Close beside me, Karen followed.

"I didn't mean to tease you about your stuttering this morning," she said. "I meant to compliment you on how well you control it."

I gave her a rueful grin. "Used to be a lot worse," I said. "It still comes on me from time to time."

Behind us, Doc and Mrs. Lambert followed us

down to the water. Karen said, "You'd be surprised how many people in history have suffered from speech impediments. The Bible tells us Moses had a speech problem."

"Yes, and Thomas Jefferson and John Adams, I hear. I don't know whether they stuttered or lisped, but apparently they learned to control the problem, whatever it was. Gave me hope that I could, too."

Basin Creek ran fast and clear over its gravel bed. Centavo stretched his neck out above the water, sniffed it, and lowered his head to drink. Karen's filly followed his lead.

"When I was a child, I had a lisp," Karen said. "My teacher told me about Demosthenes, the ancient Greek orator. Seems he had a serious speech problem—people laughed when he stammered at his first assembly.

"Demosthenes worked hard to change things, speaking with pebbles in his mouth and reciting verses while running uphill. He strengthened his voice further by speaking at the seashore over the sound of the waves. And he went on, the story goes, to become one of the greatest orators of ancient Greece."

Karen smiled. "I decided if Demosthenes could do it, I could too. I spent hours each day working to overcome my lisp. It still returns from time to time, but never when I'm on stage."

"It's hard to believe you *ever* had a speakin'

problem," I said. "You're able to hold a whole theater full of people spellbound by the way you speak English. What's more, you do it in a whole range of voices."

Karen lowered her eyes. "I very much wanted to be an actress. It's amazing what determination can do."

The Lamberts reined up beside us and allowed their horses to drink. Doc Lambert shaded his eyes, looking away toward the mountains. "This is remarkable country," he said. "Wild and open, solid and unchanging. Makes a man feel free. Makes him feel younger, somehow."

I turned to the Morgan and the bay the Lamberts rode, drawing the saddle girths taut. "Sometimes it takes a visitor to help us natives see with fresh eyes," I said. "We tend to take all this for granted."

Dismounted, Karen and Gwendolyn stood talking together near the creek. Like Demosthenes, I raised my voice to overcome the sound of the water. "We'll take a short break here," I said. "It'll give us a chance to stretch our legs—excuse me, ladies, *limbs*—before we go on."

I filled my canteen and looped its strap over the forks of my saddle. Doc Lambert watched as I tightened Centavo's cinch. "That's a good looking animal," he said. "Strong, stout, and well muscled. Would you say he's a typical western cow pony?"

I nodded. "He's a quarter horse," I said. "I rent him from Fogarty whenever I need a saddle horse around Butte City. And yes, quarter horses make good cow ponies."

"What exactly *is* a quarter horse?"

"A quarter horse is a horse that can run a quarter-mile faster than any other breed. Quarter horses are quick off the line, and faster than thoroughbreds for the first quarter to a half mile."

"My word! Faster than Daly's racehorses?"

"For the first quarter to a half mile. Thoroughbreds start slower, but they can maintain a fast speed for a longer period of time."

Doc Lambert noticed the catch-rope strapped to the forks of my saddle. "Do you always carry a lasso?" he asked.

"Not when I'm just ridin' around Butte City," I said, "but we're headin' up into the mountains for the day. I'm workin' on the 'have and need' principle."

"Have and need?"

"That's right. As a kid, my pa taught me it was better to *have* a thing and not *need* it than to *need* a thing and not *have* it. He was talkin' about packin' a gun, but the principle applies to other things, as well."

Doc Lambert laughed. "Being prepared," he said. "I understand. Wise man, your father."

I smiled, remembering. "Sometimes. Like the rest of us, Pa was a blend of wisdom and folly. He mostly learned things the hard way, and he was always his own worst enemy. But he did leave me the 'have and need' principle."

Karen and Gwendolyn came walking toward us from a nearby patch of willows. Gwendolyn carried a small bouquet of wildflowers.

"All right, ladies," I said. "Shall we resume our journey?"

The road ahead grew dim and grass grown, winding steadily upward into the Highlands. Scattered pines grew on the hillsides, and sagebrush-studded meadows sloped down to the creek. We rode in silence now, each alone with our thoughts, as the sun climbed higher and warmed the morning.

As before, Karen led our small procession, riding maybe forty yards ahead of me, following the road across a side hill. Doc Lambert and Gwendolyn were perhaps twenty yards behind me. I watched as Karen turned the filly down onto the meadow to take advantage of easier travel. The sun was warm. We relaxed in the languor of the morning. Even the horses seemed half asleep, plodding along with their ears flopping off to the side.

To say that trouble comes when we least expect it is at best a half-truth. Expected or not, trouble comes when it will, but it is true that it often surprises us. That morning it did so again.

I saw the filly, black hide shining in the light. I watched its nervous feet dance through the grass. Then I saw the mounded dirt of a badger hole at the filly's feet, its opening a dark wound in the meadow. There, in the grass—movement! Something was coming toward Karen and the filly! It broke out into sunlight—a badger, hurrying toward its burrow!

Fast it came, its open mouth pink in the sunlight, its teeth flashing! I smelled the badger's musky stink, heard its angry squeal. The filly stared, startled. Karen braced herself, her foot thrust hard into the iron stirrup of her sidesaddle, her eyes wide with surprise.

The filly lurched sharply, a startled leap uphill, away from the badger. Karen fought to stay in the saddle but was shaken free. For a moment she seemed to hang in mid-air. The badger scurried into its burrow, and Karen fell heavily to the ground!

The bridle reins burned through Karen's fingers. *Her foot was caught in the stirrup!* Panic exploded in the filly's brain; the animal bolted and raced away toward a grove of aspens at the end of the meadow.

I was late, but catching up fast—my spurs drove Centavo into a high lope. I slipped the strap that held my coiled lariat and built a loop as we tore a hole in the wind. Ahead, Karen was dragging head down through the sagebrush and bunch grass, her face inches from the filly's hooves. She threw her arms up to protect her face, and in that split-second I saw her clearly. Her eyes were wide and staring, and her mouth was a thin, tight line.

Centavo's muscles rippled and bunched beneath me; he was giving me everything he had. I bent low over his neck, swinging the loop above my head. The wind of our passage buffeted me; I felt it push against my rope arm.

The filly dashed pell-mell toward the tree line, its fright made even greater by the strangeness of Karen's dragging, bouncing body. Centavo's burst of speed closed the gap. I threw the lariat hard and watched the noose settle about the black's neck.

Quickly, I took my wraps, dallying the home end of the rope around the saddle horn. Centavo remembered his training; already the sorrel was bracing for the catch. The noose tightened, closed about the filly's neck. The black reared, front legs pawing at the air. Fighting the rope, the filly twisted, tossed its head, and stopped. Moving toward the animal, I gained enough slack to throw a half-hitch atop my dallies and step down. I was at Karen's side in an instant; my hands trembled as I opened my jackknife. The sidesaddle's stirrup leather was stretched taut by Karen's weight against it. I slashed the strap and she was free.

I held my breath. Karen lay perfectly still, her left foot still caught in the stirrup. Her riding habit was torn and streaked with dirt, and her glossy black hair had come loose from its pins and lay tangled and lank about her shoulders.

Kneeling, I cradled her head against my chest. Bright blood flowed freely from a cut above her temple, and I took the bandana from my neck and used it to stanch the flow.

Nothing bleeds like a scalp wound, I thought. Pale as a morning moon, Karen's perfect face held no expression at all.

"Karen," I said. "It's me, Merlin. It's all right now. You're safe, Karen."

She gave no sign she heard me. With her eyes closed and her lips slightly parted, she seemed deep in a peaceful sleep.

Behind me, I heard the clatter of horses' hooves on the rocky ground. Turning, I saw the Lamberts draw rein at the top of the rise. Doc Lambert dismounted quickly and loosed the strings that bound his doctor's bag to the saddle. A moment later and he was kneeling beside me. Gently, the doctor held his fingers to the pulse at Karen's throat. "Faint, but steady," he said. "She's unconscious, and no wonder."

He turned his face to me. "Extraordinary, the way you caught Karen's horse and stopped the runaway," he said. "You saved her life."

"I got lucky," I said. "Sometimes a man can even do the impossible if he has to."

Doc Lambert smiled. "A principle well known to doctors," he said.

His fingers probed Karen's scalp wound. "Her head probably struck a rock," he said. "Effusive bleeding, but there's no apparent fracture. Concussion, however, is another matter."

Holding my bloody bandana firmly in place, the doctor asked, "Do you have clean water in your canteen?"

I told him yes, I did. "It's on my saddle," I said. "I'll fetch it."

When I returned with the canteen, Gwendolyn knelt beside her husband. She reached out to smooth Karen's hair. "Poor dear," she said. "Poor darling."

Doc Lambert poured water on a cloth and wiped away the blood and dirt from Karen's face. He cleaned her scalp wound, and covered it with clean compresses and a bandage. Through it all, Karen neither moved nor spoke. I was worried.

"You mentioned a concussion," I said. "That can be pretty serious, can't it?"

The doctor dried his hands and closed his bag. "It can be," he said. "There are two types of concussion, simple and complex. In a simple concussion, the patient is disoriented and may experience dizziness, headache, and nausea. Those symptoms generally go away in a week or ten days and the patient returns to normal function.

"In a complex concussion, the symptoms may continue for weeks, even months, and the patient's thought processes are affected, sometimes permanently."

Doc Lambert gave me a long, searching look. "You've had a brain concussion yourself, haven't you, Deputy?"

I nodded. "More than one. Since I pinned on this badge I've been kicked, clobbered, and cold cocked by all manner of good horses and bad men. I have yet to find a way to enjoy it."

"I recommend you avoid it in the future," the doctor said. "In my opinion, you're a prime candidate for a complex concussion."

"I'll try, Doc. But askin' a lawman to avoid gettin' his bell rung is like askin' a copper miner to avoid consumption. In neither case do we seek the experience, but it does seem to come with the job."

At that moment Karen moaned and tried to raise her head. Her eyelids fluttered and she opened her eyes. She seemed confused, unaware of her surroundings. When she spoke her voice was hesitant, uncertain. "Where," she said. "What . . . ?"

"It's all right, dear," Gwendolyn said. "We're here, Karen."

"We need to get her back to Butte City," Doc Lambert said, "and to a hospital."

"That won't be easy. I could ride her filly and put her on my sorrel, but I'm not sure she's ready to get on *any* horse just yet."

Karen lay back in the grass, her eyes tightly closed and her teeth bared in a grimace of pain. Her hands were clenched and she trembled, but she didn't moan again or cry out. *Tough lady,* I thought. *She's no crybaby.*

I looked beyond the sagebrush flat to the aspen grove. *We might be able to make a travois for her,* I thought. *We don't have a saw or an axe, but maybe I can rig something.*

And then, like the answer to a prayer, I heard the wagon. It came rattling up the road toward us, drawn by a team of bay horses and driven by a man in a derby hat. I walked out to meet him.

"Merlin Fanshaw, U.S. deputy marshal," I said. "I sure am glad to see you, pardner."

The driver craned his neck, looking past me at the Lamberts and Karen. He nodded toward the back of the wagon. "Barney Hobbs," he said. "I'm takin' food and wine up to Highland City for y'all. Mr. Daly's orders."

"Change of plans," I said. "We have a lady over yonder who's hurt bad. We need to get her to a hospital."

Barney frowned. This new information seemed to confuse him. "You ain't goin' to Highland City?"

"No. Back to Butte."

Barney fingered his beard stubble. "I don't know. Mr. Daly said . . ."

I turned so as to let the sun reflect off my badge,

and rested my hand on the butt of my holstered .44. Looking Barney in the eye, I said, "The lady is a very important guest of Mr. Daly's. I know he'll appreciate you helpin' her."

"Oh," Barney said. "Sure, Deputy . . . whatever you say."

Minutes later, lying in the back of the wagon, Karen Killgallen began her trip back to Butte City. Gwendolyn knelt at her side, and Doc and me served as outriders, leading the filly and Gwendolyn's gray.

I used myself hard concerning Karen's injury. As we traveled, I thought about all the things I might have done to prevent her horse wreck, but after a mile or so I commenced to feel I was wallowing in guilt to an unreasonable degree. That's when my *other* side came to my defense.

I'm getting a little tired of this beat-up-on-yourself business, it said. What happened back there was an accident, nothing more. You shouldn't blame yourself.

Then who *should* I blame, I replied, the durned *badger?*

Arriving back in Butte City, Barney Hobbs and the Lamberts took Karen directly to St. James Hospital where the doctor arranged to have her admitted. Meanwhile, I returned the horses to Fogarty's and caught a streetcar back to the hospital. Once there, I took the stairs two at a time up to the second floor and found Gwendolyn waiting outside Karen's room.

I was restless, pacing the floor like a first-time father expecting triplets. I was dusty from the trail, still wearing my leggings and spurs, and the front of my brush jacket was crusted with Karen's blood. I felt as out of place as a hog in church in that spotless hallway, and the nurses and orderlies all gave me a wide berth.

Gwendolyn sat primly on a padded bench against the wall and gave me one of her toothy smiles. "This hospital is an excellent facility, and my husband is a skilled physician," she said. "Karen will be fine."

I stopped my pacing for a moment. "Yes'm," I said. "I just feel like I shouldn't have let her get hurt in the first place."

"Pish tosh!" Gwendolyn said. "You couldn't possibly know a badger would startle her horse! Your quick action almost certainly saved her life!"

Two nuns—Sisters of Charity, the order that ran the hospital—came toward us down the hallway. One looked to be little more than a girl, and the other maybe ten years her senior. The younger nun smiled, while the older one tried not to. I doffed my hat and stepped aside. The sisters swept past me and glided on down the corridor as if they were on wheels.

"Well," I said. "At least they didn't fumigate me or ask me to leave."

Gwendolyn gave me a knowing glance. "It just dawned on me why you're so fidgety," she said. "You have, shall we say, certain *feelings* for Karen."

"What?" I asked, though I'd heard her perfectly well. "Why . . . no such a *thing,* missus! I just feel sorry for the poor thing—pretty lady like her gettin' hurt and all . . ."

Gwendolyn gave me one of those I-know-what-I-know looks. She smiled without showing her teeth. My ears felt hot and I knew I was blushing. I have no idea how our conversation would have gone from that point because right then the door opened and Doc Lambert came out.

"Karen is sleeping soundly," he said. "Her head injury is severe, but there's no evidence of a skull fracture. Her vital signs are good. I've prescribed tincture of aconite, one drop each hour, and all the bed rest and quiet she can endure."

He turned to me. "I expect a full and speedy recovery, Merlin. Thanks, in no small part, to you."

I didn't trust my voice so I just nodded. After a moment I said, "When do you suppose she can have visitors?"

"Give her a day or two. If I know the Dalys, they'll take Karen back to their house as soon as she can be moved, and care for her there."

"Yes," I said, "I expect they will."

I walked over to the window. Down the hill,

beyond the buildings of the town, the valley sloped away toward the distant mountains. Before we set out on our excursion Marcus Daly told me he'd be in business meetings most of the day. I turned back to Doc Lambert and Gwendolyn.

"Well," I said. "I'd rather take a beatin', but I'm off to find Mark Daly and admit my shortcomin's."

"There's no need," Doc Lambert said. "I telephoned Mark when we arrived at the hospital. Gave him a full report. He asked me to tell you he finds your prompt action in stopping Karen's runaway to be commendable—*highly* commendable. He gave me the definite impression he is not interested in any sort of confession or apology on your part."

I was relieved, of course, but disappointed somehow. There I was, all nerved up to confess my poor judgment, and now Doc was saying I didn't need to.

I felt like a man with a wagon full of horse manure and no place to dump it.

EIGHTEEN

SCRAPPER DECIDES

Back at the hotel, I spent the next few days catching up on my paperwork and sending an expense report to Ridgeway. I tried to reach the marshal by telephone at his office in Helena, but the deputy on duty said he was out of town. The marshal was working on a case, he said, and wouldn't be back until the following week.

Karen was much on my mind. Sharp and clear in every detail, I recalled the black filly's panic, jumping out from under Karen at sight of the badger. I saw again in memory her fall, her foot caught in the stirrup, spooking the filly even more. Then the race for the aspens, Karen dragging through the rocks and sagebrush and her head mere inches from the filly's pounding hooves.

Riding hard until I was close enough to rope the filly, I'd made my cast. My hoolihan throw was more luck than skill, but it stopped the runaway and gave me the time I needed to cut Karen free. There in the short grass, holding her close to me, her beautiful face seemed peaceful, even serene. Her body was warm in my arms, and the blood from her injured head soaked my jacket and my shirt.

Like a sudden storm on a sunny day our carefree outing had changed, bringing danger and the threat of death. Trouble ofttimes comes that way, I thought, so sudden it takes a man's breath away.

As Doc Lambert predicted, Marcus and Margaret Daly took Karen into their home, providing round-the-clock nursing care in a pleasant room at the rear of the house. When I asked the doctor again when I might visit her, he said soon, in another day or so. She was healing nicely, he said. She would recover completely, he said. I was not to worry, he said.

Two out of three is pretty good. Karen was healing, she would recover, but I would still worry. I reckon a person can't have everything.

I caught up on the local news by reading both the Butte *Miner* and the Anaconda *Standard*. If you're wondering why I read two different newspapers reporting pretty much the same news it's because the *Miner* was owned by W. A. Clark and the *Standard* by his rival, Marcus Daly. The news was pretty much colored by the special interests of each tycoon, and the only way for a person to come anywhere near the truth was to read both papers. Reading the news that way was more like watching a bare-knuckle prizefight than simply becoming well informed.

Anyway, I was reading the *Standard* on the Saturday after Karen's horse wreck when I heard a knocking at my door. "Who's there?" I asked.

"It's me, Mr. Fanshaw—Clyde Bellingham, the desk clerk. You have a telephone call downstairs."

I opened the door. "Who's calling?" I asked, as if I had telephone calls every day.

"A young Irish lady, from the sound of her," said Clyde. "I think she said her name is Molly O'Dhoul."

"I'll be right down," I said.

The hotel boasted one public telephone for the

convenience of its guests, and it was located on a wall in the lobby near the front desk. I pulled my boots on and followed Clyde down the stairs.

The receiver rested atop the oak box that housed the telephone's workings. I put it to my ear and spoke into the mouthpiece. "Hello, Molly?" I asked. "How are you?"

Molly's voice sounded a bit strained, but she seemed pleased to hear from me. "I'm grand, Merlin," she said. "What about yourself?"

"Fine, Molly, just fine."

"Merlin," she said, "Scrapper and I were wonderin' if you can come over for dinner tomorrow. We'll eat about noon. It will be lovely if you can join us."

"Thanks, Molly. I'd like nothin' better. I'll come on one condition."

"And what is that?"

"That you let me bring a nice ham. I know you already have your dinner planned, but I'd like to contribute somethin' to your pantry."

"Tis thoughtful you are," Molly said, "but there's no need. Just bring yourself."

"I'll be there," I said. "I'll be the hungry lookin' cowboy with a ham under his arm."

"What am I goin' to do about you?" she said. "Good-bye, Merlin."

"Good-bye, Molly."

I hung up the receiver and then lifted it again. The city directory showed a listing for the Palace

Meat Market on Park, and I waited for the operator.

"Number plee-iz," she said, in a kind of singsong voice.

"Number seventy-five, ma'am," I said. "I'm callin' the butcher."

"One moment, plee-iz," said the operator, and I heard the phone ring once, twice, a third time.

Through the receiver I heard a click and then a deep voice. "Hello," the voice said. "Palace Meat Market. What can I do for you?"

"This is Merlin Fanshaw, up at the Centennial. Have you some good hams for sale?"

"We sure do. How big a ham you lookin' for, sir?"

"Big enough for a Sunday dinner. Maybe twelve pounds."

"We can sure handle that, Mr. Fanshaw. Would you like the ham delivered?"

"No thanks. I'll pick it up later today. I'll see you directly." Then I hung up the receiver, and marveled. Here I'd spoke to Molly somewhere across town and called a feller at a meat market clear over on West Park Street, and it was just like they were there in the hotel lobby with me. It was not like those were my first telephone calls but I couldn't help thinking: *What will they think of next?*

As familiar to me now as the way to my hotel, the dirt road that led to Scrapper and Molly's house unfolded before me. Schoolboys played shinny along the road, free at last after a long Sunday morning with their parents at Mass. The boys paused in their play to let me pass, and returned to their game. The savory smells of home cooking wafted through the open windows of the miners' homes and reminded me of Molly's skills in the kitchen.

I carried a twelve-pound ham in the crook of my arm. I had to smile; hard-rock men on their way to the mines carried their work clothes in a bundle they called their "turkey." I was carrying the ham in the same way, but it struck me funny to think of a "turkey" made of pork.

Scrapper was waiting for me as I neared his house. He stood perfectly still outside on the porch, listening.

"Hello the house," I said. "God bless all here."

Scrapper broke into a smile that took years off his weathered face. "Merlin!" he said. "Welcome, lad! Ye come too seldom, and ye leave too soon."

I opened the gate and stepped inside. Scrapper took a careful step away from the porch and stuck out his hand. I grasped it and marveled at his strength.

"Man, the grip on you," I said. "All those years with the muck stick have given you a mitt that could crush rock!"

"Ah," he said. " 'Tis but the strength of me welcome. Is that ham I smell?"

"It is. I told Molly I might bring a friend."

His chuckle was quick, but it broke off too soon. His expression grim, Scrapper turned back toward the house. I helped guide him toward the doorstep. His vision was worse than before; it seemed he had become almost completely blind.

Molly met us at the door. Beneath her apron she wore the green-checked dress I liked, and her face was flushed from the kitchen's heat. Her eyes were red, too, from crying, I thought.

She smiled her crooked smile, but like Scrapper's chuckle, it ended too soon. Molly reached for Scrapper's arm to help him inside, but he jerked it away. "Let a man be, can't you?" he muttered.

I gave Molly the ham and kissed her cheek. I had a lump in my throat the size of a hen's egg, but I had to ask the question.

"So, Scrapper," I said. "How is it with your eyes?"

Feeling his way into the parlor, he found a chair and sat down. "Well," he said, "Let me put it this way. It's a good thing I've seen as much as I have in me life, for now I'll be seein' no more."

Inside the kitchen, at the pantry door, I saw Molly's back stiffen. She put the ham on a shelf inside the pantry and buried her face in her hands. She was weeping, I knew, but she didn't make a sound.

"Molly," Scrapper said. "Would ye bring the

poteen, darlin'? Pour us a wee drink, won't ye?" His voice was gentle, as if he was sorry about his brusque words at the door.

"I met Doctor Lambert," Scrapper said. "He's a good man, and he seems to know a great deal about diseases of the eye. He took me over to Doc Whitford's hospital. 'Twas there he examined me and asked about me vision.

"I answered him as best I could. Sure and he seemed as troubled as if he had the condition himself. He gave it to me straight. 'Ye have detached retinas,' says he, 'and your condition is too far advanced for any medical solution I know of.'"

"He said he was sorry, and I believe him. I could hear the sorrow and the anger in his voice. 'Someday,' says he, 'surgery may restore vision in cases like yours. But that time is not yet.'"

Molly filled two small glasses from Scrapper's poteen jug and placed her brother's glass in his hand. "To friendship," said Scrapper. "Friendship," I said, and we drank.

"Now," Molly said. "Would you two great lummoxes wash your hands and come to the table? I've made chicken and dumplings and I'll not see my dinner grow cold."

Scrapper grinned. "Sure and I have no need ever to marry," he said. "I already have me *sister* to nag me."

I don't claim any special knowledge as to how

to keep the peace with womenfolk, but the fire in Molly's eyes told me I'd better put on my poker face and keep my mouth shut. Meek as a lamb, I hung my hat on a peg and washed up at the basin in the kitchen. Scrapper scowled, and followed suit.

As we took our places at the dining room table I was careful to mind my manners. I drew out Molly's chair and seated her, and then sat down myself. Scrapper found his chair by feel and joined the circle. I was just reaching for a biscuit when a glance from Molly stopped me cold. She bowed her head, offered a silent table grace, and crossed herself. Then, with a toss of her auburn curls, Molly smiled brightly and said, "Eat hearty, gentlemen."

She didn't have to tell me twice. I fell to eating with my usual enthusiasm, hampered only by my resolve to be mannerly. Molly's dumplings were light and fluffy, the gravy was larrupin', and the chicken tender and moist. Except for such comments as "pass the biscuits, please" and "this sure is a fine meal" nobody talked much during dinner.

I thought about the feast I'd took part in at Marcus Daly's house—the highfalutin' grub, the fancy wines and appetizers, the white gloves and finger bowls, and all the while trying to figure out which fork to use—and I found I enjoyed Molly's dinner more. Molly and Scrapper were solid folk and the salt of the earth. They were my kind of high society.

I couldn't help thinking it was because of men like Scrapper that Marcus Daly and W. A. Clark could live as high on the hog as they did. Every day, more than four thousand miners went down into the mines of Butte to bring out the ore. They risked their lives for wages and they were killed in rock falls, explosions, and fires. Somewhere on Butte Hill a miner died each and every day, and the men who didn't go sudden and hard perished slow from the rock dust they inhaled.

I'm not saying Daly, Clark, and the other mine owners neglected or mistreated their workers; they didn't. Daly provided his miners with jobs, top wages, and the best working conditions he could manage. He even encouraged their membership in the Butte Miners Union.

Now one of his men—Scrapper O'Dhoul— faced blindness and the end of the work he'd followed all his life. Daly sent his friend, eye specialist Charles Lambert, to examine Scrapper. The verdict was bleak. Scrapper's world was going dark. Nothing could be done.

What caused the problem? Was it something in the work itself? Was it a blow to the head? Was it all those years of bare-knuckle fights in mining camps from Ireland to Montana? Nobody knew. No one could say.

I felt sorry for my friend, but I couldn't show it. Scrapper wanted my friendship, not my pity. He was proud, and he was tough. Scrapper was a survivor. He was a man.

Just when I thought I couldn't eat another bite, Molly changed my mind. She brought in a hot apple pie, fresh from the oven, and cut us each a generous slice.

When I was a kid I used to wonder about the story of Adam and Eve and how they got kicked out of the Garden of Eden just for snitching an apple. I mean that seemed like pretty harsh punishment even if the Almighty did put up a no trespassing sign on that particular tree.

According to the Good Book, Adam and Eve behaved pretty well right up until the serpent gave them that big sales talk. It just didn't make sense to me that they'd risk losing the farm over such a small thing. I don't care how good a salesman that snake was, I wouldn't have been tempted by a durned apple.

But if Old Scratch had come at me with a fresh-baked apple pie, hot from the oven and smelling of sugar and cinnamon and all, well I'm not so sure.

I looked at that wedge Molly set before me and I protested. I said I was too stuffed to eat another bite. And yet somehow I managed to put away that entire slab of pie, right down to the last crumb on the plate and a couple of strays I found on the tablecloth.

Another thing I've learned about females is that when you offer to help them clear the table and they protest, they don't really mean it.

"Not at all," Molly said. "You men take your coffee into the parlor and leave the clearin' to me. I'll join you directly."

I made no reply, but stacked the crockery and silverware and carried them over to the sink and scraped them. As I may have indicated previously, I didn't have to scrape my plate very much.

Molly scolded me for my action, but her protest was lame. Her cornflower blue eyes sparkled, and she looked at me as if I'd hung the moon. It was like when a dog barks at you as if he was fixing to eat you alive, but his tail is wagging like sixty all the while.

Molly and me took our coffee into the parlor and sat together on the settee. Scrapper eased himself into a well-worn wing chair facing us. Filling his pipe, he struck a match and lit the briar, puffing patiently until it was going well. Blue smoke drifted in eddies above his head. Scrapper closed his eyes and seemed to marshal his thoughts. Then he cleared his throat and spoke in a firm, clear voice.

"I've a thing or two to tell ye both. I need ye to hear me well, for I'll only be sayin' it this once."

"First, the good news," he said. "Marcus Daly,

may all the saints and holy angels preserve him, has offered me a new job. I'd be workin' with his racehorses as a groom at his Riverside Stock Farm, I'll be makin' the same wage I made as mucker in the Mountain Con."

He paused. " 'Tis a job I can do," he said, "and I've told the great man I will."

Scrapper turned his head toward me. "Molly says she's told ye about Eileen O'Grady and me. She told ye, no doubt, of Eileen's faithful heart and her great beauty."

"Molly tells me she's beautiful both inside and out," I said.

Scrapper smiled, and the hard lines of his face seemed to soften in the lamplight. "Sure and didn't she tell ye the gospel truth entirely. I've loved Eileen and her only since I was a young mucker in the mines of West Cork.

" 'Twas ever our dream to be married, and yet when Molly and Digby and me left Ireland we were poor as dirt. I couldn't bring Eileen with me. So I vowed that when I made me stake I'd send for her."

Scrapper puffed on his pipe, but it had gone out. Gently, he laid the briar on the table beside him. "When we came here it seemed like one thing led to another," he continued. "I did well in the mines and Molly worked besides, but then Digby needed our help and somehow it seemed I nivver had the money I needed to send for Eileen.

"This year, at last, I had me stake. I sent the money and asked Eileen to come to me as soon as she could book passage. I was a happy man."

Scrapper sighed, and the hard lines of his face returned. "But now I've learned I'm losin' me sight and nothin' can be done about it. I'll nivver see a robin or a sunset or Eileen's beautiful face again. 'Tis the greatest sadness of me life, but even that I could live with.

"What I can't and *won't* live with is bein' less than a whole man! Eileen would say me blindness doesn't matter to her—she would marry me anyway. She'd spend her life takin' care of me, cuttin' up me food, leadin' me by the hand so I wouldn't fall in a ditch . . . she'd do all that and nivver complain . . . but I won't *allow* it!

"If Eileen comes here, I'll not marry her. If she asks for me, I'll not meet with her. And if she finds me somehow, I'll send her away. That's me decision, and I'll brook no argument."

Turning toward Molly, Scrapper asked, "Do ye *hear* me, sister?"

Molly's eyes shone in the light of the lamp. She set her jaw, trembling. And in the end she nodded. "Damn you for a proud, cruel man, Scrapper," she said. "Yes. I hear you."

Scrapper shifted in his chair. "And ye, Merlin. I think of ye as me friend. Do *ye* hear me?"

"I hear you," I said.

Scrapper sagged. All at once he seemed older

than his years, and weary. When he spoke again, his voice was faint and filled with pain. "For that, much thanks," he said. A man must do what he believes is right, unless it be against the laws of God and nature. This decision is against neither."

"Perhaps not," Molly said. "But it *should* be."

NINETEEN

THE LANGUAGE OF FLOWERS

Monday morning dawned gray and overcast, and it wasn't just smoke from the smelters either. Looking out the open window of my room at the Centennial I watched the clouds build above the camp and smelled the coming rain. Fog drifted and eddied, erasing the looming gallows frames and the upper floors of buildings. Even the clamor of the stamp mills seemed far away and muffled, like a covered cough.

I thought again of Karen. When last I spoke to Doc Lambert he said I might visit her at Daly's in a day or two. By my count "a day or two" had come and gone. Clean shaven and dressed in my best, I made my way downstairs and out onto the street. I was eager to see Karen again.

By the time I reached the florist's shop on Madison, a light rain was falling. I stepped off the trolley and ran the fifty yards or so to the shop's front door. Inside, I shook the water off my hat and stepped up to the counter. A pink-cheeked older lady smiled in greeting.

"Good morning," she said. "I see the rain has begun."

"Yes, ma'am," I said. "I never know whether to run or walk when it's raining. If I run I get where I'm goin' sooner, which means I really should stay drier. But it also means I'm runnin' *into* raindrops I might miss if I was walkin'. It's quite a dilemma."

The lady laughed. "Indeed," she said. "Of course, you could just stay inside until the rain stops, but then you wouldn't be coming to my shop. What can I do for you, young man?"

I looked around. Banks of flowers stood in displays throughout the shop. They were of many kinds and colors, and their scent in that closed space was more like the music of an orchestra than of a single melody.

"I'd like to buy some flowers for a lady," I said. "She had a bad horse wreck last week. I figured some posies might help cheer her some."

"I see," the lady said. "Did you know that flowers have meanings? For example, Balm of Gilead means 'healing'—or 'I am cured.' And the Sweet Pea means 'Good-bye, Blissful Pleasure' or 'Thank you for a lovely time.' "

"That's mighty interestin', ma'am," I said, "but I just want somethin' to brighten up a sick room."

A display of yellow and orange flowers caught my eye. "Somethin' like these, maybe," I said.

"Oh my, no," the lady said. "Those are marigolds. They mean 'Cruelty, Grief, and Jealousy.'"

"I sure don't want to send *that* message. Well, how about those yellow tulips?"

The lady smiled. "Certainly," she said. "Those come from our hothouse. Yes, they might be just the thing."

I bought twelve yellow tulips and watched as the lady wrapped them in paper. "Thank you, young man. I hope your friend has a speedy recovery."

"Yes'm. It may be rainin' outside, but I figure these flowers will bring a little sunshine to her room. Much obliged, ma'am."

Outside, the rain fell steadily. I took refuge under an awning on Madison until I heard the streetcar coming, and then swung aboard and rode all the way up to the courthouse on Granite. Minutes later I bounded up the front steps of the Dalys' house and rang the bell. I pulled my head down inside my coat as I waited, listening to the patter of rain on my hat. It seemed longer, but it could only have been half a minute or less before the door opened and the butler stood looking at me.

"Howdy," I said. "It's me, Merlin Fanshaw. I'm here to see Miss Killgallen."

The butler smiled. "Yes, sir. We met the evening

of the Dalys' dinner party. I asked if I might take your hat, and you said I might if I promised to give it back. Please—let me have your wet things. I promise to return them, and in a somewhat *drier* condition."

I gave him my hat and coat, watching as he hung them on a coat tree in the hall. "Thanks, pardner," I said. "I'm sorry, but I don't recall your name."

"Perfectly understandable, sir. I don't believe I gave it to you. My name is Malachi. Malachi O'Keefe."

He turned, leading the way to a wide staircase. "Doctor Lambert said you might be calling," Malachi said. "I'll show you to Miss Killgallen's room."

My wet boots squishing with each step, I followed Malachi up the stairs and down a broad hallway. Stopping at a paneled door near the end of the hall, the butler knocked softly.

"Miss Killgallen," he said. "It's Malachi, Miss. You have a visitor—Deputy Fanshaw. May we come in?"

The reply came quickly. "Certainly," Karen said. "Please do."

Malachi opened the door and indicated that I should enter. I walked in and looked around. The room was spacious and comfortable, and furnished with a canopied bed, wardrobe, washstand, and vanity, all of a dark wood I took to be mahogany. Patterned rugs in shades of red, green, and gold gave color to the floor, and matched the drapery, canopy, and wallpaper.

Dressed in a high-collared gown and a robe of green silk, Karen lay beneath the coverlet, propped up against oversized pillows in the huge four-poster bed. An upholstered wing chair stood nearby. Smiling, Karen held out her hand, beckoning me to come closer.

"Merlin," she said. "I'm so glad you're here— please, sit beside me."

My throat tightened. I was having trouble swallowing. Except for the bandage at her temple Karen seemed even more beautiful than I remembered. Her hair lay loose against the pillows, and her cool blue eyes seemed to shine in the lamplight. I felt awkward and shy as a school boy. It was all I could do just to meet her gaze.

My hand trembled as I handed her the flowers. "These are for you," I said. "I figured they might brighten your room some."

"Yellow tulips," Karen said. "Thank you, Merlin . . . they're lovely!"

Malachi was at my side. Speaking to Karen, he said, "With your permission, Miss, I'll put those in water for you."

"Yes, please, Malachi. And then . . ."

"And then," the butler said, "unless you need something else, I'll simply disappear and leave you two alone."

Karen laughed. "You are the perfect butler, Malachi."

I thought so, too.

I looked into Karen's eyes. I said, "I've wanted to come and see you ever since the accident, but Doc Lambert asked me to wait a day or two. How are you, Karen?"

"Good as new, actually. Charlie—Doctor Lambert—is a sweet man, but he is a *terrible* tyrant. He tells me I must continue to rest in bed and remain quiet for a few more days."

Karen took hold of my sleeve and drew me closer. She smiled a sly smile, and put a forefinger to her lips as though she was letting me in on some sort of conspiracy. "But just between us," she whispered, "I think I may make a break for it *tomorrow*."

I tried to put on a stern face, but all I could think of was how Karen's fingers felt on my arm and how close my face was to hers. I closed my eyes and breathed in the scent of her perfume. I knew that women use perfume to arouse a man's interest and gain his attention. Well, Karen already had my attention. Mainly, what her scent did for me was make me *nervous*.

Just then Malachi came back into the room carrying the tulips in a blue vase. He placed the vase on Karen's side table and quickly left the room. Karen looked at the flowers and then at me. There was mischief in her eyes as she said, "You brought me *yellow* tulips."

"Uh . . . yes, I sure did."

"Did you know that each flower has its own special meaning?"

"That's what the lady at the flower shop said, but she didn't tell me what yellow tulips mean."

Karen's smile widened. "Would you like to know?"

"Sure . . . I reckon . . ."

"Yellow tulips say, 'There's sunshine in your smile. Are you my love?'"

"They do? I-I didn't realize . . . that is, I just thought they were sort o' cheerful, and . . ."

Karen's laughter was like music. "I'm only teasing," she said. "The flowers are beautiful. It was sweet of you to bring them."

"I surely didn't intend to be forward, Karen. I never meant . . ."

The fingers of her right hand caressed my face and rested on the back of my neck. "I know that," she said. "I don't believe you *could* ever be forward."

Karen leaned toward me, her lips parted and her eyes half-closed. "But," she said, "I'm a brazen New York actress, and I *can* . . ."

And she drew my head down to hers and gave me a long, lingering kiss!

When Karen finally let me up for air I didn't know whether rain was wet or if snow was hot or cold. To tell the truth, I was stirred up considerable and more than a little confused.

"Lordy," I said.

Looking deep into her eyes again, I had that same strange feeling I had the day I met her. Karen's eyes seemed mysterious and somehow *older* than the rest of her. Again, her fingers brushed my face. "Doctor Lambert and Gwen told me how you rescued me that day," she said. Then her expression changed. The teasing mood turned serious.

"I owe you a life," Karen said.

It was my turn to try to keep things light. "Now don't be *too* grateful," I said. "First thing you know I'll be comin' on bold and cheeky, and forward as all get-out."

Slowly, Karen's expression changed. Her smile returned, and the peculiar depth faded from her eyes. And then her light, teasing manner came back as well. "Thank you for the rescue, kind sir," she said.

Karen looked at the tulips on the table beside her bed. "Back to floriography, the language of flowers," she said. "As Otto Van Dorn told you the day we met, I recently finished a rather long run on the New York stage as Ophelia in Shakespeare's *Hamlet*. In that role I delivered Ophelia's flower speech every evening, and I'm afraid it's embedded in my memory:

> *There's rosemary, that's for remembrance;*
> *pray, love, remember: and there is pansies,*

that's for thoughts. There's fennel for you,
and columbines; there's rue for you; and
here's some for me; may we call it herb of
grace o' Sundays. O! You must wear your
rue with a difference. There's a daisy; I
would give you some violets, but they
withered when my father died . . .

"To tell the truth," I said, "I don't understand much of Shakespeare's writing. But it sure sounds fine when you say it."

"He often wrote of flowers in his poetry and plays," Karen said. "In his time, audiences understood his references because they, too, knew the meanings of flowers."

We went on to speak of our horseback outing and of Karen's accident. I played down my part in her rescue, but accepted her praise and her gratitude. I remembered all too well the part luck played in roping the black filly, and I shuddered inside at the knowledge of how near to death she came.

Karen spoke of her plans to continue her performances at the Lyceum when she was fully recovered. When I asked how long she expected to remain in Butte City she gave no definite reply, but indicated it would very likely be only a matter of weeks. I was sorry I asked.

I told her something about my background. I spoke of growing up with my dad at Dry Creek and my later years with the marshals' service. Karen seemed interested, asking questions, but as I now recall she said almost nothing about her own family and her life before the theater.

We talked of horses, of the weather, of books we'd read. As thunder rolled outside and raindrops rattled on the window pane, we talked as people do when they're getting to know each other. We spoke lightly, of everyday things. *As if we'd never kissed.*

There is this about that. Karen's kiss was strong in my memory. I was surprised at how much it moved me. All through that morning I recalled the moment and the feelings that came with it. And yet neither of us spoke of it or gave any outward sign the kiss had occurred. I wondered: Did the kiss mean nothing to Karen? Had it been only a meaningless gesture? I'd heard that people in the show business sometimes used intimate terms and caresses in a casual manner. Had that been the case with Karen?

Maybe so, I thought, *but that was not a casual kiss.*

A short time later I heard the sound of footsteps in the hall. I looked up to see Malachi framed in the doorway, a covered tray in his hands. "I beg your pardon," he said. "I've brought Miss Karen's lunch. Will you be staying too, Deputy?"

I got to my feet. "No," I said. "I have to be

goin'. I wouldn't want to overstay my welcome."

Turning back to Karen, I said, "I'm glad you're doin' well, Karen. I hope you'll think twice about breakin' out before the doctor says you can."

Mischief was in her laughter. "These days I think of nothing else," she said.

Back in my room at the hotel I stretched out atop my bed and tried to make sense of my scattered thoughts. I came to Butte City to follow up on a lead that was scarcely more than a rumor. Digby O'Dhoul, sexton at a Helena church, claimed to have overheard the hiring of an assassin to murder Marcus Daly. My assignment was to locate the man, question him, and determine whether there was anything to his story. It all sounded pretty simple at the time.

Almost the first thing I learned when I hit town was that Digby O'Dhoul was dead. A suicide, some said. Murdered, others believed. I talked to the city police and the coroner. I went to the man's funeral. I met his brother and sister, thinking they might provide me with answers, but they only left me with more questions.

Then I took their questions and my own to the people who knew Digby—to the men who played poker and drank with him, to copper king W. A. Clark, to Marcus Daly himself—and now I felt I was no closer to the truth than when I first came to the city.

My accomplishments were few. I'd won a pile of money in a poker game. I'd been set upon by robbers and lived to tell the tale. I'd shot it out with a gambler and killer while wearing nothing but a scared expression. I'd courted Digby's sister—sort of—and I'd toured a copper mine with his brother.

I had worn a rented monkey suit to a mogul's dinner party, and I'd gone silly as a schoolboy over a New York actress. Now, she was on my mind more than my work. I was losing my edge, drifting. The trail had gone cold, and I didn't know what to do next.

Maybe, I thought, it's time to throw in my cards and quit the game. Digby's death has been ruled a suicide and there's nothing to say it wasn't. There has been no attempt on Marcus Daly's life and I had no real reason to think there would be. Daly has his own security, I thought. He doesn't seem to be worried. Why should *I* be?

I answered my own question. Because my gut *tells* me I should be, that's why. Yes, Digby's tale is fantastic, I thought. It's overblown and unbelievable and highly unlikely, but all that doesn't mean it couldn't be true.

The summer before my pa died I was hunting alone in the Brimstone Mountains, just north of the home place. I had tied my saddle horse in an aspen grove and gone off to scout the country.

297

Thirty minutes later a heavy fog rolled in. Almost before I knew it I could hardly see my hand before my face.

Well, at first I just kept a-walking. I thought the fog would lift any minute, but it didn't. Finally I turned around, figuring I'd go back to my horse and let the animal take me home. An hour passed, then two, and I still hadn't found my horse or the aspen grove either. I began to have doubts. Had I got myself turned around somehow? Was I lost?

I tried to walk a straight line, but I commenced to believe I was walking in circles. I was confused and growing tired. I told myself I'd just go another twenty minutes and see if I couldn't find my way.

And then the strangest thing happened. I had a powerful feeling I should stop walking that very *minute.* My gut told me I should sit down and wait until I could see where I was. I didn't really understand it, but the feeling was so strong I had no choice but to obey. A big old pine tree took shape out of the gloom. I crawled beneath its spreading boughs, curled up, and fell asleep.

It was sunlight that woke me. I blinked my eyes and crept out from under the tree. The fog had lifted and the sky was crystal clear. I shaded my eyes and tried to get my bearings. And then I froze! The tree I'd chosen as my resting place clung to the rocky ground at the edge of a cliff maybe three hundred feet above the valley below. If I'd gone past it I'd have walked right off the edge!

My heart beat like a trip hammer as I backed away from the precipice. I found the aspen grove, and my horse, maybe ten minutes later. But the lesson wasn't lost on me—paying attention to my gut had saved my life. Now my gut was telling me to wait, and wait I would.

I sat up in my bed and took hold of the floor with my feet. I thought, *Come morning I'll rent Centavo from Fogarty's and ride him out into the country. I'll take some bottles and cans along and do a little pistol practice. And I'll look for a quiet place in my mind where I can wait for the fog to lift. When it does, I'll know what I need to do. I'll be confused no more.*

At least, that's what I thought at the time.

TWENTY

CATCH ME IF YOU CAN

Early the next morning I picked up Centavo from Fogarty's and struck out on the Basin Creek road. Tied behind my saddle was a sack of empty airtights and bottles I'd scavenged from the trash bin behind the hotel. They rattled and clattered like a tinker's wagon, which irritated the sorrel some. He neither shied nor spooked, but rolled his eyes and blew his nose as if to say he'd heard better music.

Yesterday's fog had burned away with the

morning sun, and the fog in my mind was clearing as well. It felt good to be going back to simple, familiar things—riding out into new country on a good horse, scouting out a place for some long-neglected pistol practice—and I was looking forward to spending some time alone. The road was still muddy after the rains of the day before, and raindrops clung to the grass like diamonds in the sunlight.

A mile or two beyond Fat Jack's place, I came to a clearing that seemed the perfect place. Backed by a raised cut bank, a grassy meadow slept in the sunlight just off the road. Trees bordered the open space, and a big fallen pine lay along the meadow's far side, bleached white by the sun and rotting into the dirt. Short stubs jutted out from the trunk where branches once were, and pine cones and bark littered the ground.

I dismounted near the tree and loosened the saddle strings that held my targets. Unbuckling the saddlebags, I took out two boxes of .44 cartridges and filled the pockets of my brush jacket. Then I led Centavo back across the meadow and hobbled him. As I walked back to the fallen tree I took note of the cut bank beyond. It would make a perfect backstop for my shots.

Placing the cans and bottles about three feet apart along the log, I paced off thirty yards. Then I turned, drawing and firing my revolver in a single smooth motion. I was rusty from lack of practice. At first my bullets missed as often as they struck their targets, blasting chunks of the toppled tree out into the sunlight and throwing up dirt clods at the cut bank beyond. Then, as I set my mind to the task, my shots began to strike home. I practiced both aimed fire and point and shoot, and within the first half hour saw my shooting begin to return to my old standard.

Gunsmoke drifted above the meadow. Time and again I emptied my gun and reloaded. I went through my first box of cartridges. I began to work on my speed, getting the weapon into action fast and from different positions. My shots rang out across the meadow and shattered the stillness.

I was resetting the targets along the log when I heard the sound of a horse coming fast up the road. Grazing in his hobbles, Centavo jerked his head up at the sound and stared through the trees in the direction we'd come. I holstered my revolver and followed the sorrel's gaze. The hoof beats grew louder.

Then, across the meadow, a horse and rider galloped into view. *Karen!* The actress was dressed for freedom, not for style, and she reined her mount to a stop and rode onto the meadow toward me. She was not wearing the powder blue riding habit she wore the day of our outing, of course; it had been torn and bloodied by her accident and had no doubt been thrown away at the hospital.

She wore a white shirtwaist with full sleeves beneath a velvet jacket and the short dress and Turkish style trousers some ladies called "bloomers." Most shocking of all for that day, she rode *astride* like a man!

Karen smiled as she came toward me across the meadow, and I saw she was mounted once again on the black filly from Fogarty's. I caught my breath at her daring. Riding any horse so soon after her accident struck me as reckless. I still believed the black filly to be more snorty than reliable, and an accident waiting to happen. The animal had spooked during our ride to Highland City. It had jumped out from under Karen and had nearly dragged her to death. But as I watched Karen ride the black toward me with confidence and flair, I have to admit I felt a grudging admiration. Karen and the filly were well matched. Both were beautiful and high-spirited, and both were wild cards.

Karen drew rein and swung down from the saddle with a bound. Strands of her long black hair had pulled free of their pins and lay unrestrained across her face. She smiled again, mischief in her eyes. The filly was lathered and breathing hard. I caught the reins and looked at Karen. "Aren't you pushin' your luck just a little?" I asked.

Karen took out her remaining pins and let her hair fall free about her shoulders. She shook her head. "Just following the old horseman's rule," she said. "If you're thrown, get back on again right away."

Her eyes dropped to the holstered .44 at my waist. "I heard shooting," she said. "Was that you?"

I nodded. "Figured I could use the practice. It's not good for a peace officer to lose his edge."

"I don't know much about guns," Karen said. "Shakespeare's plays have more to do with swords and daggers. Could I . . . could I see it?"

I had emptied the revolver at the targets and had not yet reloaded. "Sure," I said, and drew the weapon from its holster. I showed it to Karen.

"This is a Colt's Peacemaker, .44 caliber," I said. "It belonged to a friend of mine until he drew it too slow one day."

Karen frowned. "Guns are ugly," she said. "They frighten me."

"A gun is a tool," I told her. "I grew up knowin' a gun can save a man's life on the range. A hungry man can use it to shoot a rabbit. He can stop a runaway horse, if he needs to, in a situation like you were in the other day."

"All guns seem evil to me. Like deadly snakes."

"A gun is neutral, as good or bad as the hand that holds it." I held the revolver out toward Karen. "Go ahead," I said. "Take it."

Gingerly, she picked up the .44 with her left hand, wrapping her fingers around its ivory grips.

Her thumb found the hammer and drew it back to half cock. Her hand trembled as she opened the loading gate and turned the cylinder. Karen had always seemed so confident, so bold. Seeing her fearful and uncertain was new to me.

"It's not loaded," I said. "Would you like to fire it?"

"No," she said, thrusting the weapon back into my hands. "Put it away. Please."

I reloaded the revolver and slid it back into the leather. "All right," I said. "What brings you out this way—were you lookin' for me?"

Her eyes were frank. "I woke up this morning and I thought of you. You, at my bedside. You, bringing me yellow tulips. You, kissing me."

Karen paused. Somehow, she had moved closer to me. I felt crowded, off balance.

She closed her eyes, and then opened them wide and looked into mine. Her voice was soft when she spoke. *"Remember?"*

I felt the heat of her body, smelled her perfume. Oh, I remembered, all right.

I did my best to keep things light. "So you woke up in your big bed at Daly's and decided you'd go for a horseback ride, did you?"

Karen smiled. "Yes," she said. "Malachi tried to stop me. He said the doctor insisted I remain in bed another day or two. I'm afraid I bullied the poor man terribly. In the end, he wound up helping me make my getaway."

"You must have bullied Fogarty, too," I said. "How did you persuade him to let you take the black filly out again?"

She laughed. "I *charmed* Fogarty. Told him I forgave the filly and wanted to let her know we were still friends."

"And when you told him you wanted to ride astride rather than sidesaddle?"

"He took it well. He even told me you'd been in earlier. He said you'd taken Centavo out on the Basin Creek Road."

"So you rode out to see me."

She nodded. "When you visited me at Daly's I felt thomething happen inside me," she said. "Thomething I can't explain. I wanted to thee if it would happen again."

I smiled. For just a moment the daring, free-spirited actress seemed to disappear, leaving only the little girl she must once have been. "Your lisp is back," I said.

"Yeth. *Yes.* And that thing I felt is happening again." Karen took my hand and pressed it to her bosom. "Feel my heart beating?" she asked.

I felt more than that. My own heart was racing. A ripple of heat turned over in my belly. I drew my hand back.

And then Karen's arms were around my neck and her body was hard against me. Her lips found mine and drank me like wine. Hot and fierce, she kissed me as if she was laying a claim to me somehow, and I began to pull away. But in that moment her lips softened, and her kiss turned tender, deeper. She was giving then, not taking, and all at once I burst into flame like a crown fire in a forest.

Karen struggled, and pushed back out of my arms. Dancing away, she picked up the filly's reins and swung into the saddle. Her devil-may-care look was back as she turned the horse away. "Catch me if you can," she said.

The filly broke away like a racehorse leaving the starting line. Karen bent low over the filly's neck, her smile taunting me. She didn't turn back to the road, but rode into the woods beyond the meadow. I was already moving toward Centavo.

My hands fumbled with the sorrel's hobbles, but he soon was free and I was mounting on the run and hot on Karen's heels. Ahead, the filly zigzagged through the trees, its black rump gleaming in the sunlight. Branches slashed at my arms and shoulders as I crouched low over Centavo's neck. Then we were out of the woods and racing across another meadow, with Karen clinging to the galloping black.

The meadow swelled and became a knoll, and then a hill. Ahead, Karen's hair trailed behind her like a flag as she gave the filly its head. Up they went, over the hill top, the black's hooves gouging up clods of mud as it dashed away. Seconds later, Centavo topped the hill as well, and we sailed up and over with Karen and the filly just feet away. I caught a glimpse of log buildings at the bottom of the hill, a cabin fallen in on itself and a weathered barn in a weed-grown lot. I thought: *abandoned homestead.*

Centavo was closing the gap. His quarter horse bloodline kicked in, and the little sorrel turned on a burst of speed that put him right on the filly's heels. I saw Karen glance over her shoulder at me, then pull hard on the reins and turn the black away. I tried to rein the sorrel around as well, but the rain-slick earth made for poor footing. Centavo slid past Karen and the filly, checking and fighting to keep his balance. By the time I slowed him and turned to follow Karen again, the filly was slipping, too. Karen left the saddle in a bound and raced downhill toward the old homestead.

I jerked the sorrel's head up to keep him from falling and stepped down onto the hillside. Below, at the foot of the hill, Karen ran into the barn. Slipping and sliding in my boots, I made it down to level ground and ran after her.

When I entered the barn I stopped to get my bearings. It was dark inside, and after coming in out of the sunlight it took a moment or two for my eyes to adjust. I stood still and listened. I heard the beating of my heart and the heavy sound of my breathing; all else was silence.

Gradually, details formed. The square-hewn

logs of the barn had lost most of their chinking, and sunlight slanted through in bright stripes. Overhead, pigeons rustled and fussed in the rafters, cooing softly. Below, two stalls occupied the front part of the barn. A homemade milking stool lay amid the dust and litter on the hard packed floor. On the wall, rusty horseshoes, strung on a wire, hung above a broken pitchfork.

In the back, gloom shrouded my view. The loft had long since collapsed, spilling loose hay into the barn's lower level. I narrowed my eyes, looking for Karen. Holding my breath, I strained to listen.

Where was she?

Then I heard a rustling sound from the back, and Karen moved into the light. She stood at the edge of the fallen hay, her eyes locked on mine. I stepped forward, but just as we stood face to face I stopped.

Karen's fingers trembled as they touched my face. She came into my arms and kissed me with a passion that took my breath away. If her kiss back at the meadow had seemed to stake her claim on me, this time it spoke of surrender and submission.

My lust was strong; I wrapped my arms around her waist and pulled her to me. We kissed again, deeper and more ardently than before, and I felt the rapid beating of her heart keeping time with my own. With a soft moan, she let herself fall backward into the loose hay and pulled me down with her.

And then there was neither barn nor meadow nor woodland. There was only Karen and me, and the singing in the blood, and a growing dance of passion as old as time itself.

The world came back slowly, moving from the faint and shadowy into the solid and real. Sunlight slanted in through the spaces in the logs as before. A hole in the barn roof revealed a patch of sapphire sky. In the rafters, pigeons scuffled and talked about what they'd seen. I caught the scents of weathered wood, musty hay, and the bouquet of Karen's perfume.

She lay close beside me in our dusty bower, and I raised myself on an elbow and looked at her. Smiling, I picked hay stems from her raven hair. She closed her eyes and nestled closer.

"A question," I said.

She opened her eyes. "Yes?"

"Why me? I'm a two-dollar-a-day peace officer from a hick town in Montana Territory, and you're Karen Killgallen, celebrated actress and the toast of New York. You must have dukes and earls standin' in line to give you diamonds and pearls. I expect you could have most any man you wanted, and yet you chose me. I guess what I'm askin' is how come?"

Karen rolled away and sat up. "Don't sell

yourself short," she said. "You have some very endearing qualities, and they're rarer than you might think."

"Such as?"

"You're generous and strong, and you care about people. You don't seek power over others or personal fame. You're a man of character, a man of your word. Those are rare qualities indeed."

She smiled. "Besides, you're really very nice to look at."

"Even in my rented monkey suit?"

Karen laughed. "All right," she said. "You're nice to look at *most* of the time."

She got to her feet, brushing hay from her jacket and trousers. "Perhaps," she said, "we should find our horses now, if they haven't gone back to town on their own."

I wanted to ask her to stay, to linger in the barn that had become our trysting place. I wanted her to spend the day in my arms and watch the sun set and the stars come out. But she had made her decision, and I knew our day was ending.

I stood up. "All right," I said. "Let's go round up those ponies."

The horses hadn't gone far. They grazed in the high grass at the foot of the hill, glad for the change from their livery stable diet. I caught Centavo easy enough, but when we went to catch

Karen's horse it was a different matter. When the black filly saw us coming she laid back her ears and threw up her tail as if to echo Karen's earlier challenge: *Catch me if you can.*

"She's playing hard to get," Karen observed.

I took my rope down and built a loop. "Wait here," I said. "I'll see if I can't overcome her maidenly modesty."

"I'm sure you can," Karen said. "You overcame mine."

The filly made it clear she did not intend to be caught, but I touched Centavo with my spurs and dabbed a loop on her just as she started up the hill. There was nothing wrong with her memory. When the loop settled about her proud neck she stood stock still and didn't budge until I picked up her reins and led her back to Karen. I figured the filly recalled how the rope had choked her down that day on the trail to Highland City and she wanted no more of that.

Karen had pinned up her hair again while I was catching the black. She looked much as she had that morning when she rode onto the meadow. She took the reins from me and stepped up into the saddle. "It might be best if we don't ride back to Fogarty's together," she said. "A lady's reputation is a fragile thing."

I nodded. "All right. I'll pick up my targets back at the meadow and ride in later. Can I take you to supper this evenin'?"

"I can't this evening, darling. I'm dining with the Lamberts," she said. "Charlie will be furious that I disobeyed his medical advice. I need to smooth his ruffled feathers."

I was disappointed, but Karen had smiled and called me "darling." *My* ruffled feathers were easily smoothed. "Tomorrow night then. I'll pick you up at Daly's at seven."

"I'm so sorry, Merlin, I can't. Mr. Daly has invited me to accompany the family on a visit to his stock farm at Riverside. We're taking the train tomorrow morning."

"Oh. Well . . . how long will you be gone? I want to be with you."

"As I do with you. I'll telephone you the instant I return."

Karen turned the filly toward the road and smiled at me over her shoulder. "Catch me if you can," she said, and rode away at an easy lope.

TWENTY-ONE

A BREAK IN THE CASE

Back in Butte City, I treated myself to supper at a noodle parlor in Chinatown and a bath at the Yellow Dragon bath house. Fat Jack Jones, my hack driving friend, swore by the Chinese baths. Jack said, "Merlin, if you ain't had a Chinese bath, you just ain't had a bath."

Well, I knew Jack was prone to exaggeration at times, but I'd seen him go from hung over and sick to pink-cheeked and perky with one visit to the Yellow Dragon, and I figured he might be on to something.

The Chinese say "you put water in your skin in the morning and you put your skin in water in the evening." Near as I can figure, that translates—sort of—to "you should drink a cup of hot tea in the morning and take a hot bath in the evening." Anyway, Chinese folk are big believers in the pleasures of the bathhouse and I decided to give it a try.

The Yellow Dragon was located in the basement of a building in the Chinese quarter. I found my way there by going down a narrow stairway and passing through a corridor to its entrance. An old Chinese gent met me at the door and showed me by signs that I was to take off my boots and put on a pair of sandals. I also gave him four bits and told him Fat Jack had sent me. Hearing Jack's name really set the old gent off. He grinned from ear to ear and kept nodding and saying, "Ah, yes! Fat Jack very good customer! Fine fellow, Fat Jack!"

He gave me a key with a number on it and sent me on to a locker room. Once there, I stripped down to my birthday suit and put my clothes and hat in the locker that matched my key. A boy I figured was some kind of attendant double-locked the locker and sent me on to the bath room.

The room was filled with steam when I walked in. A couple of Chinese men were standing in hot pools, taking showers under spouts shaped like dragon mouths. Elsewhere in the room, men soaked in big wooden tubs and others just sat on benches in the steam. I broke out into a full sweat just from the heat of the room, and I went over and stood under a water spout for the relief of it.

I guess I was sort of a novelty to the rest of the bathers as I was the only feller in there who wasn't Chinese. A big man with a build like a wrestler offered to give me a "first class, A-number one" rubdown. He said, "You friend Fat Jack *always* get rubdown." I figured if it was good enough for Jack it was good enough for me. I told him to do his worst, and he did.

For the next forty-five minutes I was scraped, rubbed, pounded and polished, and when the big feller finally turned me loose I felt like I no longer had any bones. I took another shower and settled back in a tub of hot water like a chicken in a stewpot. I inhaled the steam, closed my eyes, and remembered Karen Killgallen.

I thought: *What is it about Karen that makes me forget everything else when she's near?*

The answer came quickly. *She's beautiful, wild, and female—and she's different than any woman I ever knew.*

Ever since I was a kid I've felt there are two people living inside my skin. There's Merlin the

Dreamer, who figures if a bird can step off a limb and fly, so can he. And there's Merlin the Realist, who shakes his head and points out the rocky ground beneath the limb.

I can fly if a bird can, says Dreamer.

You'll break your fool neck, says Realist.

I closed my eyes. Dreamer was up to his old tricks, building castles in the air for Karen and me to dwell in. I heard Realist say: *You don't really know her.*

I know her well enough, Dreamer shot back. *I know her pretty durned well.*

There's more to know, Realist replied. *Look behind her mask.*

I sat straight up in my tub. Water sloshed over the side. "What the hell does *that* mean?" I asked aloud.

Other bathers stared at me. Some smiled. An elderly man made a face, and shrugged.

You're an investigator, Realist said. *Investigate.*

I tried to go back to my reverie, but the spell was broken. I stepped out of the tub and wrapped myself in a towel.

Investigate?

I don't always like what Realist says, but I have to admit he tends to be right most of the time. Castles in the air have poor foundations.

Next morning, I picked up the hotel telephone. I was still pretty much a greenhorn when it came to using that instrument, but the operator was helpful.

"Number plee-iz," she said.

"I don't know the number, ma'am," I said, "but I'd like to call the Pinkerton Detective Agency in Chicago, Illinois."

"One moment plee-iz," the operator replied.

Through the receiver I heard clicks and pops and a kind of high-pitched whine like a prairie wind blowing through a barbwire fence. I waited, listening. Then I heard another click and a faint voice said, "Pinkerton Agency. This is Agent Blair."

"Hello!" I hollered. "This is Merlin Fanshaw, U.S. deputy marshal. I'm callin' you on the telephone from Butte City, Montana. Is Abigail Bannister there?"

There was a long pause. I couldn't tell whether or not anybody was still on the line. Then I heard Agent Blair's voice again. "Agent Bannister will be back in the office at two o'clock. What's your name again?"

"Fanshaw. *Merlin* Fanshaw. I worked with Abby Bannister in Wyoming a few years back. She'll remember me. I'm at the Centennial Hotel in Butte City, phone number seventy-nine."

"I'll ask her to call you."

"Much obliged, pardner. Tap 'er light."

"Tap 'er *what?*" he asked, but I was already hanging up the receiver.

• • •

I was reading an old copy of *Harper's* in the hotel lobby when the telephone rang. I glanced up at the clock above the registration desk and saw it was only a few minutes past one, so I went back to my reading. Clyde Bellingham, the desk clerk, walked over to the telephone and picked it up. Putting the receiver to his ear, he listened for a moment. Then he turned to me and said, "It's for you, Deputy."

I took the receiver from Clyde's hand and spoke into the mouthpiece. "Howdy. Who's this?"

"Merlin?" said a sweet voice. "This is Abby Bannister. You called me?"

It was a good connection, clear as a bell. "Abby!" I said. "I sure did, but I didn't expect you to call me back until two! It's only one o'clock."

"It's *two* o'clock in Chicago. We have time zones now, remember? The railroads put them in back in eighty-three. You're an hour earlier there than we are here."

"Oh," I said. "Yeah, I knew that." (I *hadn't* known it, but I saw no need to advertise my ignorance.)

"I need a favor, Abby," I said. "I'm workin' a case here in Montana, and I need a background check. On an actress from New York—Karen Killgallen."

"What are you looking for exactly?"

"Whatever you've got. Personal history, trouble with the law. Anything."

The telephone went silent. I could almost *hear* Abby thinking.

"I had a call from Chance Ridgeway earlier this year," she said. "Questions about a professional assassin called Charon. Are you working on that case?"

"I can't talk about it just now," I said.

Again the telephone went silent for a moment or two. Then Abby said, "I'll see what I can find. It may take a day or two. Call you back at this number?"

"Anytime. I'm obliged to you, Abby."

"You *bet* you are. Be talking to you. Good-bye, Merlin."

The sun didn't come up the next morning; or if it did nobody saw it. During the night, storm clouds drifted in over the mountains, and by sunup rain was falling again on both the good and bad alike. I took breakfast in the hotel dining room and settled myself at a table in the lobby with coffee and a newspaper. I had no need to venture out into that downpour, nor any wish to do so.

Reading a newspaper is like eating at a café, I thought. You start by looking at the bill of fare— the headlines—and go on to sample an item that sounds good. If it turns out to be to your liking you might take in the entire story. If it doesn't— say, if the article is like Brussels sprouts or cumquats—you may taste only a line or two, or maybe not read the story at all. And if you're really starved you might consume the newspaper's entire contents, including advertisements for snake oil and cures for female complaints.

I guess I was hungry for news that morning. As I sat in a corner of the Centennial's lobby I was pretty much oblivious to everything but my reading. Clyde Bellingham passed through, turning on both gas and electric lights to counteract the gloom. From time to time a guest of the hotel would walk past, dressed for the weather, and go out onto the rain-wet street.

I took in the events of the day. Back east, the great John L. Sullivan had fought Charlie Mitchell to a draw in a thirty-round heavyweight boxing match. George Eastman was granted a patent for a new Kodak box camera. The state of California got its first seismograph, an instrument for measuring earthquakes. Two hundred and fifty people were killed by hail in the Moradabad District of New Delhi, India.

My coffee was cold. I had taken in all the news I cared to. I stretched, yawning. I thought I might go up to my room and take a short nap. And then, the door that led to the street swung open and everything changed.

Out of the rain and into the lobby came Cecil Hardesty, my old poker opponent. In spite of the umbrella he carried Cecil was wet and rumpled from the rain. He stamped water off his feet, furled his umbrella, and looked around. Usually dapper, Cecil seemed edgy and a bit run down. Stains marred his usually immaculate suit. He wore a two days' growth of beard, and his hair was long and unkempt. His eyes were red, and the cuffs of his shirt were frayed. Most telling of all was the absence of his showy diamond ring. Cecil Hardesty looked to me like a man on a downhill slide.

"Hello, Cecil," I said.

Cecil's eyes darted to me. "Fanshaw," he said. "I'm here to see you."

"I'm here to be seen," I said. "Sit down."

Drawing out a chair opposite mine, Cecil eased himself into it. "That's a damned cold rain," he said.

"I'll buy you a cup of coffee," I said. "That should help take the chill off."

Rainwater was running off Cecil and onto the hotel's Turkish carpet. His expression was grim. "If it's all the same to you, I'd rather have a brandy."

I caught Clyde Bellingham's eye and beckoned him over. He stepped out from behind the registration desk and walked toward us.

"Would you ask the bell captain to bring us a bottle of brandy and a couple of glasses?" I asked. "Tell him it's for snake bite. Ask him to fetch a snake, too, if he can find one."

Clyde was in no mood for humor. Clearly annoyed by the wet carpet beneath Cecil's chair, he scowled but said nothing.

Moments later, the bell captain came out of the dining room carrying a bottle and brandy snifters on a tray. Approaching our table, he poured two fingers of brandy into each glass and re-corked the bottle.

"Thanks, pardner," I said. "Tell Clyde to put it on my bill."

As the bell captain walked away I turned my attention back to Cecil. "What can I do for you?" I asked.

Cecil couldn't decide whether to look at me or the brandy. His hand trembled as he raised his glass, sniffed its contents, and took a careful sip. "I've got some news," he said, "about Digby O'Dhoul's death."

Suddenly, Cecil had my full attention. "I'm all ears," I said.

"I guess you know I'm working for James A. Murray now," Cecil said, "as supervisor at his Alice May mine. The Alice May was a good producer, but the ore played out and Murray is shutting down the operation.

"One of the miners came to me this week and hinted he knew something about O'Dhoul's death. He was nervous as a cat, looking back over his shoulder as if the devil himself was after him. I bought the man a drink—actually, I bought him a bottle—and he told me the rest. To make a long story short, he said he knew O'Dhoul was murdered. When I asked him how he came by that knowledge he said he knew it because he was there when it happened!"

I felt a chill run up my spine. Carefully, I set my glass back on the table and concentrated on keeping my voice steady. "I see," I said. "What did you say?"

"What do you *think* I said? I told him he should take his story to the police—I said if he saw a murder take place it was his duty to report it."

Cecil tossed back the brandy in his glass and reached for the bottle. "He said he didn't know if telling the police was a good idea. Said he'd had a run-in with Chief McGinnis, and he'd be damned if he'd tell him anything."

"When I said he'd be damned if he *didn't* tell what he knew he got that devil-over-his-shoulder look again. He said all right then, he would tell somebody—but not McGinnis."

I raised an eyebrow. "And you thought of me?"

"Yeah. Cut me some slack here, Fanshaw. I know we're not exactly friends, but I also know withholding evidence of a felony is a serious crime."

"All right," I said. "When do I get to talk to your witness?"

Cecil frowned. "There is a slight problem with that. The man is a walking case of nerves, afraid of everything and everybody. He says he'll only meet with you on *his* terms. I'm to take you to him, but *he'll* choose the time and place of the meeting. He'll talk to you and *only* you."

My heartbeat went from a walk to a gallop. Sitting across the table from Cecil Hardesty, I recalled our game at the Copper Penny and put on my poker face. "I guess I could meet him," I said. "Tell him I said yes."

Cecil nodded. Raising his glass, he downed the brandy in a single gulp. I didn't join him. I didn't need the stimulation.

Back in my hotel room, I listened to the rain rattle against the window pane and paced the floor like a cougar in a cage. After weeks of following every lead and rumor regarding the death of Digby O'Dhoul I had nearly given up. Now, suddenly, a closed case was open again. A man had come forward to say O'Dhoul had *not* died by his own hand but was the victim of a murder! Further, the man claimed to be an eyewitness to the killing and was willing to talk about what he'd seen!

True, Cecil Hardesty, a man I neither liked nor trusted, had brought me the news. His story might be less than reliable or an outright falsehood. But I had waited too long for a lead and I was in no mood to quibble with even a possible break in the case.

I cleaned and oiled my revolver and checked its

loads. I looked at the over and under derringer I carried as a backup weapon and returned it to its place in my boot. Ridgeway, my boss, had taught me well. A peace officer can't be too careful, especially when going forth to meet a stranger.

Making my way downstairs, I told Clyde at the desk that I was expecting Cecil Hardesty, the man I'd shared a brandy with earlier. I said I'd be in the dining room if he came back, adding that I'd appreciate it if he'd let me know when he came in. Clyde said he would, but he hoped my *friend* wouldn't drip water all over his carpet again. I said I hoped so too, but as long as the rain kept up we really couldn't be sure, now could we?

Seating myself in the dining room, I ordered a light lunch but found myself unable to eat it. I kept looking at my watch and waiting for Cecil to return. Finally, I pushed my plate aside and went back into the lobby. I took the seat I'd occupied earlier and vowed I wouldn't keep checking my watch every two minutes.

And from that moment on I didn't. Instead, I found myself glancing up at the big clock above the registration desk.

The time was nearly two o'clock in the afternoon when Cecil returned. He saw me and came directly over to where I sat. "He's agreed to meet you today," Cecil said, "but you'll never guess where."

"I'm not big on guessin' games," I said. "Where?"

"At the bottom of a mine shaft, deep in the Alice May."

Outside, a sway-backed horse waited at curbside, hitched to a buggy. Rain fell in sheets, lashing the cobblestones and spattering against the buggy's top. Hardesty climbed inside and picked up the reins. I took the seat beside him.

Lightning flashed overhead, and thunder rolled with a sound like gravel falling on a drumhead. Hardesty shook the reins and the trembling horse stepped reluctantly into the storm. We headed west to the edge of the camp, picking up a winding road that led to the buildings and gallows frame that marked the Alice May itself. As we passed through the gate, lightning flashed again and I saw the cable running over the big gallows frame wheel, bringing the cages up from the shaft.

"I see the lift is still running," I said. "I thought you said the Alice May was shut down."

Raising his voice in order to be heard above the storm, Hardesty said, "It is. There's just a small crew working cleanup."

Hardesty parked the buggy on the lee side of a shack near the mine shaft, and we stepped down and went inside. Fumbling in the darkness, he found an oil lantern. A match flared, revealing the room's contents. Tools stood against the walls. Shelves held candles and miners' lamps. Miners' boots lay jumbled in piles. Jackets and jumpers hung on nails along the walls.

I remembered my visit to the Mountain Con with Scrapper. I said, "No miners' work shoes for me. I'm used to my old riders' boots."

"Suit yourself," Hardesty said.

Seated on a bench, he pulled on a pair of miners' hard-toe boots. "Bring the lantern," he said. "I'll tell the engineer we're going down."

Minutes later, we stepped into one of the cages. Hardesty blew out the lantern, saying we'd light it again when we got off. The station tender closed the big steel door and dropped the iron bar. He rang the buzzer thirteen times, and I knew we were headed down to the thirteen hundred foot level. I took a deep breath.

The cage went down like a dropped boulder, lights flashing as we passed each hundred-foot level. My belly seemed to rise into my throat and I found myself holding my breath as we fell.

Then the cage slowed and bounced to a stop, and another station tender opened the cage and let us out. I saw only a few hard rock men. They glanced at us curiously, as if wondering what a couple of non-miners were doing down in the Alice May. The men's faces were sharp-edged in the lantern light, their eyes shining like polished stone.

One thousand three hundred feet down, I thought. *Long way from sunlight and rain. Long way from everything.*

Rails for the ore carts led off into the darkness of the main tunnel. Hardesty relit the lantern. "Follow me," he said.

"Seems to me your witness chose a mighty strange place for a meeting," I observed.

Hardesty shrugged. "I guess he wanted it to be on ground of his choosing."

"All right. Where to now?"

Hardesty took the lantern and turned away. "This way."

We walked for what seemed a long time. The air turned stale and thick. Walking behind Hardesty, I began to sweat. The tunnel was dark, and hot as a dragon's breath. I remember Scrapper telling me the deeper you went in a mine the hotter it got, and we were down thirteen hundred feet. I tried for a joke to lighten the mood.

"We must be gettin' close to hell," I said. "Feels like Lucifer has lit his boilers."

Hardesty made no reply. He walked along the tracks, the lantern held high. Inky shadows swelled and danced on the tunnel's sides, then were swallowed up in blackness. All was silence. Only the scuffle of our feet broke the stillness. The beating of my heart was loud in my ears.

We stopped. From some place ahead and above us came a grinding, groaning sound, as if the mountain itself was shifting. We stopped, listening. I heard water dripping. Pools of copper

327

water at the sides of the tunnel caught lantern light. The groaning sound ended, and silence came back to the Alice May.

I stood there, listening. Now I have to tell you I heard nothing and saw nothing that gave any hint of trouble ahead. But I've come to believe there is something that's built into all us humans—a wee, small voice, if you like—that warns us when danger is near. Call it instinct, a sixth sense, or a gut feeling. There in that silent drift, thirteen hundred feet below the surface of Butte Hill, I heard that voice inside my head. It was growing louder all the time.

Hardesty looked at me, then turned and walked away again. I took a deep breath and followed him. Twenty minutes later we came to a ladder that led up into a tumbledown cavern of rock, dirt, and debris. When Hardesty spoke it was in a whisper.

"At the top of that ladder is a rill stope. Do you know what a rill stope is?"

"Yeah," I whispered. "Scrapper showed me one at the Mountain Con. It's a big room full of ore that's been blasted out by powder men. Rill stopes slant downhill so miners can bar down loose rock and ore into a chute mouth."

Hardesty nodded. "That's right," he said. "Your witness is waiting for us just inside. We'll climb that ladder, and I'll let him know we're here."

Moments later Hardesty was at the top of the

ladder and inside the stope. I gripped a rung and began my own climb. Above us, the lantern cast an orange glow on boulders and rubble. Then I was at the top and facing Hardesty. Handing me the lantern, he said, "Here. Hold this a minute."

I reached out and took the lantern. The alarm bells inside my head were screaming. In the dim and smoky light Hardesty smiled a hard smile. Then I saw the revolver in his hand. It was pointed directly at my belly.

"I have a confession to make," Hardesty said. "*I'm* the witness."

TWENTY-TWO

A LITTLE MISUNDERSTANDING

"Unbuckle your gun belt," Hardesty said. "With your left hand and let it fall."

Taken by surprise in spite of myself, I faced Hardesty in the rill stope, still holding the smoky lantern in my right hand. The dim light picked up the glint of the gun in Hardesty's hand. I considered the odds. Hardesty was no *pistolero*; I could pull against his drawn gun and maybe take him down. Other men had done as much.

"What if I don't?" I asked. "Are you goin' to shoot me, Cecil?"

"Dead as yesterday's hash," he said. "Never bet the farm against a pat hand."

I eased my grip on the lantern's bail. I thought: *If I drop the lantern and dodge to one side . . .*

"I called your bluff once before," I said. "Besides, it's not that easy to kill a man."

Hardesty's face twisted. "It gets easier after the *first* time," he said. *"Shuck that belt!"*

I was surprised by how calm I felt. Hardesty was growing agitated, on the edge of losing control. I loosed the buckle on my gun belt and let it fall.

Hardesty leaned down and picked up my pistol and belt, keeping his gun pointed at me all the while. "Now put the lantern down," he said. "Do it easy!"

I bent my knees and set the lantern down in the dirt of the stope. "Sure thing, Cecil," I said. "Now do you want to tell me what this is all about?"

"You know damn well what it's about! You're planning to arrest me for O'Dhoul's murder!"

"Am I? Why would I do that?"

"Don't play dumb with me, you son of a bitch! You think I did it!"

"I think you *could* have, but I don't have enough evidence to arrest you."

Hardesty pointed to a boulder, surrounded by dirt and debris. "Sit!" he ordered. "Put your hands behind your head and your ass on that rock!"

I did as ordered. "You've gone to quite a bit of trouble to set his up," I said. "Want to tell me why?"

"Maybe I just brought you here to kill you," Hardesty said. "You ever think of that?"

330

"Sure," I said. "I thought of that. But if killin'
me was your only reason you'd have done it by
now. I think you brought me here to *talk*."

Hardesty scowled. His eyes burned. The gun in
his hand was a heavy Colt's Dragoon revolver.
Carefully, he shifted it to his left hand. He wiped
his right hand on his pants leg. Groping behind
him, he found another boulder and eased himself
down on it.

"What makes you think I want to talk to you?"
he asked.

"It's plain you want to talk to *somebody*," I said.
"My guess is you're a man who's carryin' a heavy
burden. I'd say you could use some help unloadin'
it."

Hardesty moved the pistol back to his right
hand. He looked from me to the darkness beyond
and back again. For several seconds he said
nothing. Then, as if he was talking to himself, he
said, "It all started with the old man, W. A. Clark.
When I worked for him it seemed he was mad as
hell most of the time."

"At you?" I asked.

Hardesty's eyes blazed. "No, damn it! Not at
me—at Marcus Daly! Clark was *obsessed* with
the man! Not that he didn't have his reasons. W.
A. Clark and Marcus Daly were rivals who
became enemies, and enemies who did everything
they could think of to harm each other.

"Daly would have his eye on a piece of

331

property; Clark would buy it out from under him. Clark would bring a case to court, only to learn Daly had bought the judge. The feud grew worse by the day.

"Then one morning we were in a meeting at Clark's office—lawyers, engineers, accountants, and the like—and Clark stormed in like a madman! He threw a temper tantrum for the record books. Kicked over chairs, cursed Daly, screamed like a little girl! You'd have thought Marcus Daly was the Antichrist!

"'How *long?*' Clark shouted. 'Will *nobody* rid me of that bog Irish bastard?' The old man was wound up like an eight-day clock.

"There was nothing for us to do but lay low and wait for the storm to blow over, which it did a few minutes later. Clark straightened his tie, combed his hair, and took hold of himself. He acted as if nothing had happened, and we got on with our work and forgot the incident."

Hardesty paused. He toyed absentmindedly with the revolver. Then he continued. "Except I *didn't* forget it. I began to think about ways someone *might* get rid of Daly. I thought if I could actually make it happen the old man would be so grateful he'd reward me with money, promotion, and honor."

From somewhere in the bowels of the mountain the deep groan of shifting rock came again. Loose dirt and gravel fell from overhead to the floor of the stope. Hardesty seemed lost in thought. Then he began to speak again.

"A drinking companion of mine had once worked for a private detective back east. He told me about an assassin he'd heard of who was supposed to be the best money could buy. My friend said this man killer could be reached by telegram at a New York City hotel, and that he called himself 'Charon.'"

At my feet, the lantern flame guttered and nearly died. Flickering, it caught and burned brightly again. Testing Hardesty, I moved my hands from behind my head to my lap. He didn't seem to notice. After a moment, he continued.

"I was a little drunk. On a lark, I sent a telegram to the hotel, addressed simply 'Charon.' I said something about needing his services and I asked about his fee. Then I pretty much forgot the whole thing."

"A week later, 'Charon' called me on the telephone. He asked the name of what he called 'the subject,' and confirmed the price. His instructions were specific. I was to meet him at ten p.m. the following Sunday at St. Elmo's Church in Helena. I was to bring five thousand dollars in bank notes. The church would be deserted at that hour. I was to go into the sanctuary and enter the confessional. 'Charon' would be waiting."

"Where did you get the five thousand?"

"From Clark. I took it out of his safe at the bank.

It was only right, seeing as he was the one who wanted to get rid of Daly."

"So you stole the money from your boss and went to Helena. Was 'Charon' waiting?"

"He was. I had a few drinks at a saloon and caught a streetcar that took me to within a block of the church. When I went inside it was pretty dark; only the sanctuary lamp and a few candles were burning. I made my way to the confessional and knelt inside. I saw movement beyond the grill that separates the priest from the confessor. I asked, 'Charon?' and a voice answered, 'Yes.'"

"I've got to hand it to you, Cecil," I said. "It took guts to meet a hired killer like that."

"Damn right," Hardesty said. "Son of a bitch was scary."

"What did he look like?" I asked. "Was he what you expected?"

"I couldn't see him. Too dark. I gave him the five thousand. He said it would cost another five when the job was done."

"Must have felt strange, hirin' a killer in a church. Are you Catholic yourself, Cecil?"

There was a pause. "Used to be," he said. "Parochial school."

"Look here," I said. "You don't need that gun. Why don't you put it up so we can talk a little friendlier?"

Hardesty leapt to his feet, cocking the big revolver and centering its muzzle on me. *"Shut up!* " he said. "Are you going to let me tell this or not?"

"I'm all ears," I said. "Take your time."

"I came back here to Butte City and waited. And then one day Digby O'Dhoul hit town. He started telling everybody about hearing a man hire a killer in a Helena church. I ask you, Fanshaw—what are the odds? The sexton of St. Elmo's just happens to be napping in a pew on the night I come in to hire an assassin! Mousey little drunk remembered every word! He could hardly remember his own name, but he recalled everything *we* said as if it was etched in stone!

"The more he talked the more I worried he might suddenly remember it was me he saw that night. Scrapper brought him to the poker game at the Copper Penny and the little bastard spent all night staring at me like he was trying to remember where he'd seen me!

Hardesty fell silent. Then he spoke again, and his voice sounded bitter and lost. "You can see why I had to kill him, can't you?"

I made no reply. Hardesty had only confirmed what I already believed. He resumed his seat on the rock. He said, "Then I heard from 'Charon' again. He called me on the telephone, saying he was in town and that he had the 'subject'— Daly—under observation. He said he'd 'fulfill the contract' at a time of his own choosing, and that he would expect the second five thousand then.

He also said there could be no change of mind, no 'cancellation of the contract.'

"Funny thing. When he told me I *couldn't* cancel the 'contract' that's when I suddenly *wanted* to. I guess remorse set in."

"Yeah," I said. "Parochial school. 'Thou shalt not kill' and all that. So then what happened?"

I hoped to keep Cecil talking. He seemed troubled by what he'd done. I figured talking to me would ease his mind some, and maybe buy me some time. I waited, careful not to make any sudden moves. He laid the revolver in his lap, but his finger was on the trigger and his thumb on the hammer. I waited.

"You're right, you know," Hardesty said. "It *is* hard to kill a man. Digby was a weak, frightened nobody, helpless as a lamb, and *still* it was hard to take his life."

Hardesty's glance was cold. He raised the Dragoon and drew the hammer back to full cock. "Like I said, killing is hard the first time. I think it'll be easier with you."

"Two questions first, Cecil," I said. "I don't want to make the big jump without knowin' a few answers. First, why did Clark fire you?"

"After I killed O'Dhoul I went to him. I told him I'd hired 'Charon' to get rid of Marcus Daly. I don't know—I guess I thought he'd be pleased. But he wasn't."

"Imagine that. Meanin' no offense, Cecil, but I

fear the jelly has slid off your cracker. I hereby place you under arrest for murder and conspiracy to commit murder. I believe it will be best all around if you hand over that horse pistol and come quietly."

Hardesty's eyes widened. His face twitched, and he swung the pistol up to take my life. Still seated on the boulder, I slipped my right hand into my boot top and found the grips of the derringer.

The Remington over-and-under derringer is small but mighty. Loaded with two .41 caliber soft-nose bullets, its range is just about the diameter of a poker table and maybe a foot or two more. Anything farther than that and you might as well be throwing rocks. But for the shorter distance, the gambler's favorite is a serious weapon. I slid off the boulder and triggered both barrels just as fast as I could.

Hardesty was quicker than me for the first shot, and if I hadn't ducked to the side that big pistol would have bored a hole in me big enough to plant the schoolhouse flag. Fire and smoke belched from the muzzle of his gun and the blast echoed off the rocks overhead. I threw myself away from the boulder, seeing Hardesty's eyes as my bullets slammed him back toward the chute that yawned at the foot of the incline.

I heard that groaning, grating sound above me again, this time louder and more ominous than before, and I scrambled back toward the ladder that led out of the stope. I swung out and into the drift beyond just as the entire mountain seemed to collapse in one mighty crash. Rocks smashed against each other, tumbling down in a choking cloud of dust and grit. It all happened so fast there wasn't even time to pray, so I stretched out on my belly in the drift beyond the stope, covered my head, and hoped for the best.

Rocks continued to fall. Lying there in the darkness, I listened to the rumble and thud of the rill stope's collapse, feeling the ground shake beneath me with the impact. Then, at last, all was quiet. I reached out in the total blackness and touched the wall of the drift. Getting to my feet, I took a quick inventory and decided I was unhurt and intact.

Not so Cecil Hardesty, I thought. Both my bullets had found their mark. In the moment of the overhead's collapse they had thrust him toward the chute of the rill stope. Tons of rock and dirt had fallen in that chamber; Hardesty would now lie dead beneath them, to be seen no more until judgment day.

Silence was complete again in the Alice May. I began a slow and careful walk along the drift, my goal the main tunnel and eventually the lift station. There would be light there, if nowhere else. Electric lights made visible the stations, at least. All I had to do was find my way there in the dark.

I continued my inventory. I had saved my life, but I had lost a few things. My .44 Colt revolver and its belt and holster; my .41 rimfire derringer, dropped during my headlong retreat; the smoky lantern that provided the little light we had; and last but not least the murderer of Digby O'Dhoul and the man who hired the mysterious "Charon," the late Cecil Hardesty himself.

Hardesty's rambling confession had brought some answers, but his death was not an end to the danger. Somewhere out there, a hired killer followed his own hard rule. There would be no "cancellation of the contract" for any reason. Marcus Daly walked each day in deadly peril, and would as long as "Charon" remained at large.

I moved carefully along the drift, my hand on the wall. I tried to recall how far we'd walked from the main tunnel but couldn't. I began counting my steps one by one until I reached fifty, then started over and counted to fifty again. The silence was total.

I have never been a smoker, but I've carried matches all my life. I searched my pockets and found a dozen or so phosphorous matches, and I decided I'd use them to find my way. From time to time I'd strike one and use it to light my path for as long as it lasted. But the life span of a burning match is short indeed, and I found the darkness all the deeper when the flame went out. I decided to save my dwindling match supply until I really needed a light.

I heard something up ahead—dripping water, faint in the distance. The sound grew louder as I walked. Dripping water for sure, splashing down from the ceiling. Then I could feel it—moisture in the air. I moved away from the wall, to the middle of the drift. Copper water was acid, Scrapper said. It could burn a man's flesh.

My mind began to play tricks on me. Had I really come this way before? Maybe I'd taken a wrong turn when I left the rill stope. Maybe I should . . .

Don't doubt, I told myself. *If you lose your way down here you could be lost forever.*

The air seemed to change, become cooler. The drift had grown wider! I moved further from the wall, tripped, and fell headlong. I lit one of my few remaining matches, saw it flare into flame. Before my eyes grew accustomed to the brightness, I reached out and touched something smooth along the floor of the passageway—rails! Tracks for the ore trains! I had reached the main tunnel—the lift station would be just ahead!

Now I walked faster, staring into the blackness, looking for a glimmer of light that would mean miners, a station tender anyway.

And then I saw it! Far down the tunnel—light! I saw men in the distance, heard their talking. Covered with rock dust and dirt from head to toe,

I stumbled into the lift station. The station tender's eyes went wide.

"What the hell happened to *you?*" he asked.

"Rill stope caved in," I said. "The feller I was with went down the chute."

"Jaysus, Mary, and Joseph!" the tender said. "You ain't likely to see *him* again!"

"Somehow," I said, "I don't really *expect* to."

At the police station, I sat across from Chief McGinnis at his desk and told him about my showdown with the late Cecil Hardesty. McGinnis tried hard to maintain his "I've seen everything and nothing surprises me" attitude, but my story of Hardesty's unsuccessful attempt on my life was a little too much even for him. What I said about the events in the Alice May was true as far as it went, but I have to admit I didn't tell the chief everything.

"Now let me get this straight," McGinnis said. "Cecil Hardesty told you a witness to Digby O'Dhoul's death had come forward. According to Hardesty, this phantom witness wanted to speak to you and *only* you."

"That's what Hardesty said. He took me out to the Alice May in a rented buggy, and we rode the lift down to the thirteen-hundred-foot level. Then Hardesty led me to a rill stope where the 'witness' was supposed to be waiting."

"Except there *was* no witness."

"Only Hardesty, and a big Colt's Dragoon pistol. Hardesty pointed the gun at my belly and confessed that *he'd* killed O'Dhoul."

McGinnis frowned. "He didn't happen to say why, did he?"

"I gather Hardesty thought O'Dhoul *had* something on him. Blackmail, maybe?"

"Could be, I suppose. Hardesty was no choir boy. But what did he have against you?"

I put on my poker face. "Beats me. Maybe he figured I had something on him, too."

The chief rubbed his jaw and fixed his gimlet eyes on me. "And *did* you?"

"Not until he told me about killin' O'Dhoul."

"So Hardesty takes your gun and cartridge belt and throws down on you with a cap and ball pistol. Then what?"

"He fires and misses. I pull my hideout gun from my boot and shoot him twice. Self defense, Chief."

McGinnis picked the coffee pot off the office stove and poured us both a cup. Setting my cup before me, he said, "Guess we'll have to take your word for that, won't we? Instead of having a witness to the shooting, we've got the testimony of the man who *did* the shooting. I know any number of hungry lawyers who'd love to get a crack at you."

I took a sip from my cup. "Good coffee," I said.

McGinnis leaned back in his chair. He drummed his fingers on the desk top. "What about the physical evidence? Hardesty's body. Hardesty's gun. *Your* gun."

"Well," I said. "There is a small problem about that. The rill stope hadn't been barred down. The whole place was full of loose rock—on the sides, overhead. It was a disaster waitin' to happen.

"When the shootout started the whole mountain seemed to fall in on itself. Hardesty and the guns are in there somewhere, but it may take some doin' to find 'em."

The chief sighed. "We have to try. I'll talk to Jim Murray and see if he can get his miners to do some prospecting for evidence."

"And in the meantime?"

"You know the drill. Don't leave town."

TWENTY-THREE

FACTS, RUMORS, AND WHISKEY

My telegram to Ridgeway was short and to the point: *Cecil Hardesty confessed murder of Digby O'Dhoul. Resisted arrest. Died.* The telegraph operator was impressed. "You're a man of few words, Deputy—exactly *ten* by my count."

"I like words," I said, "but I try not to use more of 'em than I need to. Send that to Chance

Ridgeway, U.S. marshal's office in Helena. Sign it 'M. Fanshaw, Deputy.'"

"I'll send it now," said the operator. "You want to wait for a reply?"

"No," I said. "Ridgeway knows where to find me."

Outside the telegraph office, I took a deep breath and savored it. After the rain, Butte City stood new-washed and golden in the late afternoon light. Painted clouds drifted over the mountains, clinging to their color against the coming darkness. I felt both guilty and glad to be alive. Cecil Hardesty would breathe no more mountain air and watch no more sunsets forever.

Facing me in the rill stope that day, Hardesty said killing gets easier after the first time. Well, maybe so. But living with the feelings that follow a killing gets harder, not easier. Now another man was dead because of me. Another face would haunt my dreams.

What a pity, said a mocking voice inside my mind. *Poor you.*

Covered by tons of rock and rubble, Hardesty's corpse lay somewhere in the thirteen-hundred-foot level of the Alice May. With it were my revolver, my gun belt, and the Remington derringer I'd used to take his life. Practicing my trade, I'd left its tools at my work place. Careless of me. Very unprofessional.

Be of good cheer, said the voice. *You have a spare revolver and more cartridges in your hotel room—enough to take at least another score of lives.*

I was passing a beanery a block from my hotel when the smell of beef stew drifted out through the open door and drew me inside. I'd had nothing to eat since breakfast, and my belly wasted no time in reminding me of the fact. *Play your head games all you like,* it seemed to say, *but attend to the basic needs.*

The place was nearly empty. I found myself a quiet table in the back and ordered a bowl of stew and a pint of ale. Then I turned my mind away from the troubling events of the day, and thought once more of Karen.

I recalled our meeting back at the meadow and the kisses that fanned our passion into a fire storm. I remembered Karen's words, both invitation and challenge: *Catch me if you can.* She had embraced me boldly but her fingers had trembled as they touched my face. And when at last we came together in the abandoned barn the hunger of our bodies swept away caution, and reason, and everything else.

Where was she now? Was she still with the Dalys at Riverside? Or was she back in Butte City? *I'll telephone you the instant I return,* she'd said. All I knew was that I wanted to be with her again and that I needed her like a drowning man needs dry. I was inclined to heed the advice of my belly: *Play your head games all you like, but attend to the basic needs.*

I was waiting on the porch of Scrapper and Molly O'Dhoul's house that evening when they returned from mass. Dressed in their Sunday best, they came walking up the steep roadway, and Molly's face brightened when she saw me.

"Merlin!" she exclaimed. Taking her brother's arm, she said, "It's Merlin, Scrapper—he's come to call."

I stepped down from the porch to greet them. "I have news," I said. "I wanted you to hear it from me before the rumors began to fly."

Molly's eyes searched my face. Her smile faded, but the warmth remained in her eyes. "Come inside," she said. "I'll make us a pot of tea."

Seated at their dining room table, I told Scrapper and Molly of the events at the Alice May. I told them how Cecil Hardesty lured me into the mine with his story of a mysterious witness to Digby's death. His story turned out to be true, I said, except that the "witness" was Cecil himself. Holding me at gunpoint, he had confessed to Digby's murder.

I told them their brother had died the victim of a coward, fearful his secret plot would be revealed. I said Cecil planned to kill me for the same reason, but a hidden gun and the collapse of a rill stope had ended his life instead.

When I had told it all, I raised my head and looked into their eyes. Molly was weeping softly into her handkerchief, and Scrapper's sightless eyes were wet as well. Scrapper breathed a long sigh, and I could hear the pain in it. His work-hardened hand grasped my shoulder with a grip of steel. " 'Tis grateful I am," he said. "Digby's death was an open wound that now may heal. And thanks to you, the gobshite who killed him is roastin' in hell."

I squeezed Molly's hand. "I'll be glad to write up a sworn statement you can take to the priest," I said. "It will show your brother was not a suicide. Maybe the church will allow him to be buried in hallowed ground."

Molly blew her nose and looked at me through tear-filled eyes. "That part doesn't matter so much," she said. "Just knowin' the truth is enough for now, and knowin' Digby's soul can rest at last."

Clyde Bellingham was not on duty when I walked into the hotel that night, but Bud Hollis, his young assistant, was. Bud was an affable youth, with the eager-to-please manner of a spaniel pup. When Bud saw me enter the lobby he scurried out from behind the desk with a big smile and a piece of paper.

"Good evenin', Deputy," he said. "How are you doin' this fine evenin'?"

"I've been better," I said. "How are you, Bud?"

"Finer than frog hair, Deputy, finer than frog hair! You had a telephone call while you were out this afternoon—a lady!"

Karen? I wondered.

Bud handed me the paper. "Lady from Chicago! Chicago, *Illinois!* Lady said telephone her at that number in the mornin'."

I smiled. "The only Chicago I *know* of is in Illinois. But much obliged, Bud. I'll return the lady's call first thing tomorrow."

Alone in my room, I sat on the bed and felt the tension drain from me like sand through an hourglass. My eyes seemed to have a will of their own to close, and I longed for sleep and forgetfulness. A nameless dread nibbled at the edges of my mind, warning me . . . of what? I had no enemies I knew of. The men who feared me because of my badge were gone, and gone for good.

I crossed the room and locked the door securely. Shuffling back to my bed, I pulled off my boots and stretched out full-length atop the coverlet. More than anything I wanted an easy mind and rest, but I didn't really believe they would or could be mine.

I prepared for a restless night. I waited in the

darkness for ghosts and guilt and the anger of God to trouble my thoughts. But instead came a gentle miracle. Against all odds, I drifted off into a deep and peaceful sleep.

I awoke early the next morning. After a quick breakfast in the hotel dining room I brought a cup of coffee with me back to the lobby and took my place at a table near the telephone. Equipped with several sheets of stationery and a pencil for note taking, I placed my call to the Pinkerton Agency in Chicago.

Through the receiver came the hiss and crackle of static as the call meandered east, and then I heard the brisk burr of a distant ringing. I looked at the lobby clock. Eight a.m. Nine o'clock Chicago time. *Ring-ring,* went the telephone. *Ring-ring.*

Then I heard a click, and a familiar voice. "Pinkerton Detective Agency," said the voice. Agent Bannister speaking."

"Good mornin', Abby. It's Merlin. What do you have for me?"

"Facts and rumors," said Abby. "Are you ready?"

"I'm all ears."

"I remember that about you," Abby said, "but even so you're not a bad-looking man."

"I didn't telephone you to be made sport of," I said. "Tell me about Karen Killgallen."

"All right," Abby said. "Here's what I found: Karen Killgallen, born Karen Roth in 1858 to Erebus and Clementine Roth at Brooklyn, New York. Her parents were vaudeville and circus performers, her mother a dancer and her father an exhibition marksman.

"At age five Karen joined the act, holding targets for her papa. By age six she was a crack shot herself."

"Hold it, Abby. Karen was a sharpshooter? Are you sure?"

"Regular Annie Oakley. Pistols, rifles, shotguns, you name it. That fact gets interesting later."

"All right. Go ahead."

"Parents separate when Karen is twelve. Allegations by Clementine of spousal and child abuse by her husband, Erebus. Clementine becomes an opium addict and prostitute, dies after a beating by person or persons unknown. Found in an alley a short distance from her rooming house. Erebus retains custody of Karen.

"When Karen is fourteen Erebus is murdered, shot once between the eyes. Karen tells police she found him dead when she returned home from school. Police theorize Erebus surprised burglars in the apartment he shared with his daughter and was killed by them. No arrests.

"That same year Karen becomes a ward of Charles Beldon Killgallen, Manhattan stockbroker and patron of the arts. She adopts his last name. Karen is educated in private schools, including a year in Switzerland. She studies theater in London, and is regarded as an accomplished actress, particularly in Shakespearean productions. She has a remarkable vocal range, and as a result is able to assume roles usually performed by men. In addition to English, Karen is fluent in French, Spanish, and Italian.

"Charles Killgallen dies of a stroke two days before Karen's nineteenth birthday. She is his sole heir. She maintains a brownstone in New York City and a second home in Denver. Critics consider her an accomplished if erratic classical actress, given to sudden and unexplained absences.

"She has never married; at least there is no record of a marriage under either her given or adopted name. She will be thirty years old in November."

"That's quite a report."

There was a pause on the line. I thought for a moment I'd lost the connection. "Abby?" I said. "Are you still there?"

"Merlin," Abby said, her voice serious now. "There's one thing more. I talked to an old leatherhead, a retired harness bull from the New York Police Department. He investigated the death of Karen's father, and he has his own opinions about the case. His exact words to me were 'Justice got done, and that's a fact. The little girl done him in. The nonce bastard had it comin'.'"

"No evidence, nothing that would hold up in court, but he believes Karen *killed* her *father!*"

Our telephone call had ended. If Abby was curious about my questions, and I believe she was, she was professional enough not to ask me about them. Somehow I found the words to thank her and hung up the receiver.

The hotel lobby seemed even more silent than it had before. The ticking of the clock above the registration desk was loud in the stillness. I heard hoof beats outside on the cobblestone street. And I heard the echo of Abby's words inside my head: *Regular Annie Oakley. Child abuse. Vocal range. Karen killed her father.*

Karen had lied to me about her familiarity with weapons. "I don't know much about guns," she'd said. "All guns seem evil to me." According to Abby, Karen was not only *familiar* with firearms; she was an *expert* in their use!

Other recollections came quickly. Karen had a broad vocal range. She could impersonate a boy's voice, a man's voice. With her acting skills, she could imitate my voice, your voice, *anyone's* voice.

Digby had described the voice he heard in that Helena church. The voice spoke with a lisp, he said. "Just a soft lisp when he made an *s* sound." Sometimes Karen spoke with such a lisp!

My train of thought was high balling down the

track. Hardesty had first contacted Charon, the assassin, at a New York City hotel. Karen, the actress, had a home in New York City.

Hardesty had contracted to have Marcus Daly killed. Karen had become part of the Dalys' inner circle, and their house guest!

Was it possible? Could "Charon" be—a *woman?* Was Cecil Hardesty's paid assassin Karen Killgallen? It was a hard thought to get my mind around—such a thing just couldn't be! And yet . . .

I took the stairs up to my room two at a time. Inside, I checked the loads in my spare revolver and picked up my handcuffs. Then I dashed downstairs again and out onto the street. Minutes later I climbed the steps of Marcus Daly's house on West Granite Street and rang the bell.

I waited. *Come on, come on,* I thought. *Answer the door, somebody.*

I rang the bell again. Listening for some sound of movement, I heard nothing. I was about to turn away when I heard footsteps inside the house. I heard the rattle and slide of the latch, and then the door swung slowly open. Daly's butler, Malachi, stood in the doorway with a bottle of whiskey in his free hand.

I looked at the whiskey and smiled. "For me?" I said. "You shouldn't have."

Malachi glanced down at the bottle in his hand

and then looked at me again. "Oh, my," he said. "I'm sorry, Deputy—I was about to prepare a hot whiskey for Mr. Daly."

"Mr. Daly is at home then," I said. "I understand he's been out of town this week."

"Yes, sir. At his stock farm in the Bitterroot valley, with Mrs. Daly and Miss Karen. They returned night before last.

"I'm afraid Mr. Daly is not presently receiving visitors. He has come down with a rather bad cold and has taken to his bed. Miss Karen brought him this special bottle as a gift, and she made him promise to drink a hot whiskey as a treatment and a preventative."

Beware of Greeks bearing gifts, the saying goes. Karen Killgallen wasn't Greek as far as I knew, but the principle still applied.

I pointed at the bottle. "You say that bottle is a gift from Karen?"

"Indeed it is," Malachi said. "A rare bottle of Hargrove's Irish Whiskey, a special blend and more than twelve years old. I was about to open it when you rang the bell. Miss Karen certainly is a thoughtful young lady."

"Yes," I said. "*Thoughtful.* Is she at home?"

"No, sir. Miss Karen has taken a suite at the Dorchester Hotel, on Park. She told Mr. and Mrs. Daly she has imposed on their hospitality long enough. The Dalys tried to dissuade her, but Miss Karen is very strong-minded, you know."

I sure do, I thought. *"I'll telephone you the instant we return,"* Karen said. I would almost believe she forgot to call me if I didn't know how *thoughtful* she is. Yes, and strong-minded.

"Look here, pardner," I said. "I'm going to ask you to do something you won't understand and something I can't explain. But take my word; it's for a very important cause. I want you to lend me that bottle for an hour or so and say nothing to Mr. Daly, Miss Karen, or anyone else until I return."

Malachi looked uncertain. *"Lend* you this bottle? I can't *do* that, Deputy—That is, I'd need to have a very good *reason . . ."*

I held out my hand. "Let me put it this way," I said. "It's for an investigation that affects the vital interests of your boss, Marcus Daly. As I see it you have two choices. You can lend me the bottle or I can *confiscate* it. And if you force me to do that you might well be liable to a charge of obstruction of justice. What do you say?"

Reluctantly, Malachi gave me the bottle. "Very well," he said. "I only hope granting your request doesn't lead to the termination of my employment."

"Don't worry," I said. "Termination is the very thing I hope to prevent."

TWENTY-FOUR

TO SERVE AND PROTECT

Stepping off the streetcar in front of Doc Whitford's hospital, I made my way toward the building's front door. As luck would have it, the doctor was talking with his head nurse Maggie at the front desk when I walked in, and he looked up and greeted me.

"Deputy Fanshaw!" he exclaimed. "Don't tell me you've shot someone else!"

"No one who's going to need *your* services," I said. "I tend to shoot straighter these days."

I cradled the bottle from Daly's in the crook of my arm. Curiosity was plain on Doc Whitford's face. "Then what can I do for you? Is that whiskey you're carrying?"

"I sort of hoped you could tell *me* that," I said. "I have an idea it's *mostly* whiskey . . . and maybe a bit of somethin' *else*."

Doc Whitford looked at me with sudden interest. "You suspect . . . *poison?*"

"You tell me, Doc."

"All right. Bring your whiskey and come with me. My laboratory is a bit primitive, but it should be sufficient."

I followed Doc Whitford to a small room on the first floor that seemed to be crowded with test tubes, beakers, and flasks of all sizes and shapes. A sturdy work table held a Bunsen burner, a mortar and pestle, and a microscope. Above the table, shelves displayed a variety of chemicals in bottles and jars. Doc turned on the light and examined the sealed whiskey bottle with a magnifying glass.

"Interesting," he said. "This bottle has been opened and carefully resealed. You'd never know it, though. Someone went to a lot of trouble to make it look safe and secure."

Doc uncorked the bottle and sniffed its contents. "Irish whiskey, all right," he said. "The good stuff."

Pouring a generous slug in a beaker, Doc lit the Bunsen burner and put on his lab goggles. "First, I'll do a test for metallic poisons—arsenic, antimony, and mercury, among others. Have a chair, Deputy—this may take a little time."

"I'm in no hurry," I said.

Over the next two hours I watched as Doc Whitford conducted his tests. From time to time, Maggie appeared at the laboratory door to ask him a question or call him away to attend to a patient, but each time the doc returned and continued his work. When the tests for metallic poisons came up negative he began a search for the volatile poisons, distilling the whiskey and condensing the vapors before analyzing them further.

I sat in my chair and watched him, not knowing what I was seeing but not wanting to break in on his work with questions, either. Doc Whitford was caught up in the search like a bloodhound tracking a jailbird, and he scarcely seemed to know I was in the room.

Finally, he stepped back from the table and took off his goggles. "I have the answer," he said. "The whiskey does contain poison, enough to kill a dozen men. It's an alkaloid with an interesting history—*Aconite*."

Doc took a heavy book down from a shelf and thumbed through its pages until he found what he was looking for. "Yes," he said. "Here it is.

"Aconite comes from a flowering plant called 'monkshood' or 'friar's cap' and it's one of the strongest poisons we know about. Also called 'wolfsbane' because folks back in the Middle Ages used it to poison wolves. Plant has blossoms shaped like a monk's hood, dark blue or purple mostly, but some varieties are yellow, pink, and white. Looks a little like a delphinium at first glance.

"Anyway, all parts of the plant contain a deadly poison. There are no known antidotes, and its victims usually die in agony in about an hour. And you don't even have to take it internally—just handling the plant can kill you!"

"Oh," Doc said. "And one thing more—the poison can't be detected in the bloodstream. A victim of aconite poisoning appears to have died of asphyxia. For these reasons, monkshood has been called the assassin's plant of choice."

Doc Whitford put the cork back in the bottle. "I can say *one* thing about your whiskey," he said. "Whoever takes a swig of *this* stuff will quit drinking within the hour—*forever.*"

By the time I got back to the Dalys' house night was falling fast. Darkness filled the hollows and chased sunlight to the ridges that topped Butte Hill. Overhead, color bled from the clouds and left them ghostly and gray. I stepped off the streetcar and raced up the stairs to the Dalys' front door.

Malachi must have seen me coming; he opened the door before I could ring the bell. Worry made his face a tense mask, and his eyes searched for mine and fixed on them.

"Two things," I said. "There's been an attempt on Mr. Daly's life, and the assassin is still at large. If Mr. Daly's bodyguard isn't here, send for him.

"Allow no one into the house except family, and don't give Mr. Daly anything to eat or drink you haven't personally inspected. I should be back here in a few hours, but if I'm not send for Chief McGinnis and tell him what I said. Have you got all that?"

Malachi nodded stiffly, his eyes wide. I gave him a smile I hoped would assure him, and bounded down the stairs and across Granite Street.

The Dorchester was the city's newest hotel, and in the opinion of its owners at least, its finest. Built of brick and boasting four floors above its spacious lobby, it stood tall on Park Street and offered a grand view of the valley. According to Malachi, Karen had moved out of the Dalys' house and had taken a suite at the Dorchester. I figured she'd done so at least in part to distance herself from the planned site of Marcus Daly's death.

I walked in through the side entrance and crossed the lobby to the registration desk. A door to one side bore a sign that read MANAGER and I stopped there and knocked. The door opened and a pigeon-chested gent with bushy eyebrows looked me over. His once over didn't miss much; I saw his eyes drop to the holstered revolver on my hip, then raise to take in the badge on my chest.

"Yes? How can I help you, officer?"

The man's voice was high, thin, and pompous. I kept mine genial and friendly. "I need to speak to one of your guests," I said. "Can you tell me how to find Miss Killgallen's suite?"

"Certainly not, unless you have a warrant. Miss Killgallen is a guest of the Dorchester, and we do not allow unauthorized visitors to intrude upon our guests' privacy."

What I really wanted to do right then was pull

out his bushy eyebrows and put a foot on his pigeon chest, but of course I did neither. Instead, I smiled, thanked him for his time, and walked away. The man had told me what I needed to know. Karen was a guest at the hotel, as Malachi said.

Across the lobby, a freckle-faced kid in a bellhop suit stood inside the open door of an elevator. I had not had occasion to ride in an elevator before, but I was about to do so. I stepped inside, and the kid closed the door. "What floor, sir?" he asked.

I folded a ten-dollar bank note lengthwise and held it before Freckles's eyes. "Whatever floor and suite number Karen Killgallen calls home," I said.

Maybe the Dorchester's manager didn't allow riffraff to pester its guests, but the elevator operator had no such compunctions. He took the ten-spot from my fingers with an appreciation bordering on reverence and put it in his pocket. "Fourth floor, Suite 4-B," he said. "Going up."

The elevator stopped at the fourth floor and I stepped out. Turning back to Freckles, I said, "You never saw me, pardner."

The kid stared past me, his eyes focused on nothing. "Never saw *who?*" he asked.

I waited until the elevator's doors closed and watched the pointer on the wall begin its countdown. Then I checked the loads in my revolver, took a deep breath, and cat-footed down the hall.

The door to Suite 4-B looked like every other door in the corridor, but I knew it was different, and far from ordinary. Beyond that door were Karen, her shadow self "Charon," and the end of a long trail. Memories of the meadow and of our afternoon together came back to sap my will, but I made my face like flint and hardened my heart.

The palms of my hands were wet, and I dried them on my thighs. The thudding of my heart was loud in my ears. I took another deep breath and knocked urgently. I waited, my six-gun in my hand. Seconds passed. Then I heard movement, and Karen said, "Yes? Who is it?"

Imitating the hotel manager's high, thin voice, I said, "Management, Miss Killgallen. I'm afraid there's been an emergency."

No answer.

My boot heel struck the door just above its brass knob and smashed it open. Karen stood less than eight feet away, her eyes wide. Her hand held a pocket-size revolver. I pointed my Colt at her head. "Drop it!" I said. "Don't make me kill you!"

Alarm left her face. She smiled, and let the pistol fall to the floor. "You certainly know how to make an entrance," she said. "I'm sorry about the pistol, but a girl can't be too careful."

I picked up her gun and stuck it in my waistband. "It's no good, Karen," I said. "I know who you are."

She wore a kimono-style dressing gown of silk, belted at the waist. Her legs and feet were bare. "I should hope so," she said. "Are you going to shoot me, Darling?"

"Only if I have to."

Her face changed, grew harder. "All right. Who do you think I am?"

"You're a hired killer from New York. You call yourself 'Charon' after the ferryman of Hades from Greek myth. And you've come here to kill Marcus Daly."

"My goodness! All that?"

"All that and more," I said. "You made a deal with a man named Hardesty back in April in a Helena church. You agreed to kill Daly for ten thousand dollars—five thousand payable that night and five thousand more when the job was done. How am I doin' so far?"

"Fascinating," Karen said. "Pray continue."

"Except there would never be a second five thousand. Hardesty made his deal without his employer's knowledge or approval. When his boss found out, he refused to have anything to do with the scheme and fired Hardesty.

"Meanwhile, Marcus Daly and his wife befriended you. They took you in as their guest and gave you their hospitality and their trust. You betrayed that trust, and arranged to murder your host with poison."

The suite's sitting room was furnished with a round table, an overstuffed chair and divan, and plush drapery that framed the window. Beyond, through the open door that led into the bedroom, I saw an elaborate bathtub. Karen sat down on the divan and crossed her legs. "Ungrateful of me," she said. "How exactly did I do that?"

"You gave him a bottle of fine Irish whiskey and urged Malachi to prepare him a hot drink for his cold. Trouble is the whiskey was laced with aconite."

Karen's eyes changed from blue to deep purple as I watched. "So ," she said. "You interrupted my bath to accuse me of murder. Is our friend Mark dead then?"

"No, he's alive. I managed to get to your 'gift' just in time."

The dressing gown fell away from Karen's legs. She made no move to cover them. "Let me get this straight," she said. "You've kicked in the door of my room and threatened me with a gun for a murder I didn't do?"

"I figure you'll try again. From what I hear, when 'Charon' takes a job she finishes it—no matter what."

Karen's face held no expression at all. She might have been playing a statue in a stage play. She turned her head and looked into my eyes.

"Did this gentleman you mentioned—Mr. Hardesty—tell you all this?"

"Some of it," I said. "Hardesty got worried I was comin' for him, and tried to kill me. We traded shots and a mountain fell on him."

Karen smiled a cold smile. "Some people will do anything to get out of paying a debt."

"I learned about 'Charon' from a Pinkerton agent in Chicago. The same agent filled me in on the life and times of Karen Killgallen, actress."

"Including, I'm sure, the stories and rumors about my childhood. You seem to have gathered information from a variety of sources."

"You could say that," I said. "I learned some of it from observation. You claimed to know nothing about guns, and yet when I let you hold my .44 the first thing you did was open the loading gate and check the cylinder. Only someone who knew about guns would have done that.

"'Charon' spoke with a lisp. *You* speak with a lisp at times. You have a vocal range that makes it possible for you to impersonate women, men, children—anyone."

"All right," Karen said. "Where do we go from here?"

"To jail. I'm arresting you for the attempted murder of Marcus Daly. And there must be other warrants out around the country for 'Charon.'"

"I suppose there are. But it does seem to me there are a few problems with your plan. First, you can't prove I attempted to murder anyone. A bottle of whiskey laced with poison might have come from anywhere. And you certainly can't prove I'm this—what did you say his name is again—this 'Charon' person."

"However," she went on. "If I *were* 'Charon' I'd be a very formidable individual. Such a person would be heartless and cold, determined and clever, and skilled in the use of every kind of weapon."

Karen stood up. Her eyes shining and her lips parted, she began to move slowly toward me. "You know I'm neither heartless nor cold, don't you, Darling? Remember our day at the meadow? Remember 'catch me if you can'?"

She was crowding me, moving into my space and into my mind. I took a step back. "I remember," I said, "and I *have* caught you. Now you'd best stay right where you are."

She smiled. "Surely you aren't afraid of me," she said. "I have no gun, no weapon . . ."

Don't trust her, said the warning voice in my mind, *not for a minute! Remember Marshal Ridgeway's rule—¡Cuidado! Take care!*

"It's no good, Karen," I said. "I'm taking you in. You might want to put some clothes on."

Karen's smile was wistful. Loosening the belt of her dressing gown, she turned away toward the bedroom. "All right," she said. "Avert your eyes."

As I turned my back to her, I realized my mistake. Karen threw the full weight of her body against me from behind, her left arm tightening around my neck. Falling backward, we crashed to the floor. I tried to bring my pistol to bear, but felt it slip through my fingers and fall away. Karen's right hand pressed hard against the back of my head, and I struggled to free myself as her grip tightened. I brought my arms up, trying to break her hold, but the pressure on my neck only seemed to increase.

Fighting for breath, I remembered wrestling matches back in Dry Creek when I was a kid. Those had been contests of strength with the other boys for fun, but the steady tightening of Karen's grip told me *this* match was deadly serious.

Her lips brushed my ear. "One last embrace," she whispered. "An ancient Japanese chokehold called the Naked Strangle. You'll be unconscious in less than five seconds."

My strength was fading. I began to shake; I wanted to cry out, but could not. I thought my head might explode. A blood-red haze broke behind my eyes.

"Goodnight, sweet prince," Karen whispered, and darkness fell.

Regaining my senses was nearly as unpleasant as losing them. I opened my eyes to find my head pounding like a trip hammer, and it was touch and go whether I would air my paunch. My tongue was dry, and big as a cow's. I had a ringing in my ears that put me in mind of a cicada convention. Everything hurt.

I rolled over and sat up. The window of the sitting room was open, its curtains blowing in the wind. The door stood ajar, the jamb broken by my kick. I am not especially quick-witted in the best of times, but right then my mind seemed to be working even more slowly than usual. Karen was a professional assassin. She had taken me out with some kind of sleeper hold. Why hadn't she killed me outright?

The answer was six feet away, on the carpet. Weighted down by my revolver, a sheet of hotel stationery lay next to my hat. Holstering the gun, I picked up the paper. Written in purple ink in a woman's flowing script was a brief message.

"Merlin," the note read. "I owed you a life. The debt is now paid in full. Yours, Karen."

There was no doubt about it; Karen Killgallen was gone, skedaddled, vanished without a trace. She had paid her bill at the hotel in advance, and neither Freckles the bellhop nor the bushy-browed manager had seen her leave. I figured she most likely left by way of the fire escape outside her window so she would *not* be seen. I paid for the damage I'd done to the door and went over her suite with a fine-tooth comb, but I found nothing.

Karen had vamoosed pure and simple, and that was that.

Curiously, even though no one in Butte City knew where she'd gone, that didn't stop them from having their own ideas. Marcus and Margaret Daly were sure she'd returned to her home in New York. Doctor and Mrs. Lambert believed she was visiting friends near Denver. And John Maguire, impresario of the Grand Opera House and Lyceum Theater, was certain she was preparing to embark on a European tour of her one-woman show.

Furthermore, there was no evidence as to *how* she'd gone. Everyone assumed she took the train, but no one had seen her at the depot, nor did anyone remember selling her a ticket. Fat Jack opined that she might have taken the stage to Helena and caught a train from there. But the truth was nobody knew, including—and especially—me.

Back at my hotel, I telephoned Marshal Ridgeway and filled him in on the key points of the case. I told him about the attempt on Daly's life and related what I'd learned about Karen from Abby Bannister. Recounting how I arrested Karen and how she gave me the slip was not easy to do, but I told him that too. Ridgeway set a high standard for his deputies, but it was well known that he stood by them even when they made mistakes.

"You will no doubt slip up at times," he said once. "You will make itty-bitty missteps and huge boneheaded blunders, and I expect you to learn from them all. However, committin' the same mistake twice will be a source of considerable aggravation to me.

"In addition, I require that you do not attempt to hide your mistakes or cover up any scat you may have left behind you in the trail. Instead, I ask that you admit your shortcomin's so we can deal with the damage. To err is human, as they say, and to forgive ain't near as easy, but if you *mess* up I expect you to *'fess* up."

The circumstances surrounding the attempt on Marcus Daly's life blew over like a storm cloud on a summer's day. As far as Daly was concerned, a person or persons unknown tried to poison him by tampering with a gift bottle of whiskey given him by his houseguest, the celebrated Karen Killgallen. An alert deputy U.S. marshal (that would be me) thought the bottle appeared to have been tampered with and took it away to be tested by Doc Whitford.

Marcus Daly himself was relatively unconcerned. Occasional encounters with crackpots and disgruntled employees were all in a day's work for a copper king. As far as he was concerned the attempted poisoning had been thwarted, no further threats had manifested themselves, and it was time to get back to his usual routine. There was copper to mine, horses to breed and race, and an old enemy to bedevil and harass. Life was good, and much too short to worry about the occasional malcontent.

Had he been told Karen Killgallen was a professional assassin, hired by mistake on behalf of his principal rival to kill him, chances were good Daly wouldn't have believed it anyway. So I accepted his gratitude for intercepting the whiskey and simply told Oodles O'Brian, his bodyguard, to continue to keep an eye out. His feelings still tender from not having been there to rescue his employer himself, O'Brian said he certainly would, that he was *always* on the job, and that I should commit an impossible act upon myself.

A coroner's jury was convened in the case of Cecil Hardesty's death. His body—or what was left of it—was found by Jim Murray's miners in the rock and rubble of the ore dump at the Alice May. I recounted the events that led to the shooting and Chief McGinnis said he saw no reason not to believe me. He said I was a bona fide lawman and Cecil was pretty much a no-account son of a bitch. Since Cecil wasn't there to say otherwise the jury ruled I'd probably gunned him down in the line of duty and in self-defense and they acquitted me on a writ of good riddance.

Afterward, I bought beer for one and all at the Blue Frog Saloon. Jim Murray said his miners had

371

sifted through the rubble in an attempt to find Cecil's Colt's Dragoon and my .44 Peacemaker and Remington derringer, but without success.

I told him I understood, but that I sure hated to lose the Peacemaker. The gun had sentimental value, I said. My friend Orville Mooney left it to me after he pulled it too slow on a horse thief and died with it in his hand. It had been an excellent weapon, I said, fine-tuned and fancy, with ivory grips and engraving on the cylinder and frame.

"Please tell your men much obliged for lookin' for it," I said, "and tell whoever *didn't* find it the sight is off and it shoots about a half-inch high at fifty yards."

TWENTY-FIVE

THE EYES OF THE HEART

Molly O'Dhoul sat primly on an upholstered divan in the lobby of my hotel as I came back from the Blue Frog. As ever, Molly was a delight to the eye with her auburn hair and green-checked dress, but on that day she looked as though she carried all the cares of the world on her shoulders.

Her eyes were red from weeping but she managed a shaky smile when she saw me. I answered her smile and crossed the lobby to where she sat.

"Molly!" I said. "Have you come here to see me?"

"That I have," she said. "Sure and you must think I'm a shameless hussy entirely, callin' on you here at your hotel—but I don't know where else to turn."

I laughed. "Believe me," I said, "I've known a few shameless hussies in my time, and you don't qualify. Now what's the matter, and how can I help?"

Her smile faded. Tears welled in her eyes. "Ah," she said. "My brother is breakin' my heart. Eileen O'Grady has come here at last, but Scrapper won't see her or allow me to."

"Eileen is here? I thought Scrapper told her not to come."

"He did, the prideful fool! He wrote the poor thing a letter sayin' he's changed his mind and tellin' her not to come here. She can keep the passage money, he says, but he no longer wishes to marry her.

"The trouble is Eileen never saw the letter! She was already on board the ship, bound for America! And now she's come to Butte City on the train with no one to meet her. Ah, well—at least I know where she's stayin'. I received a note by messenger this mornin'—she's taken a room at Mary O'Leary's boarding house."

Molly's eyes blazed blue fire. Indignation rode her with its spurs on. "Someone has to tell her Scrapper has changed his mind," she said. "*I* can't because Scrapper forbids it. I know it's a lot to ask, but could you . . ."

I took a step backward. "Me? Wait a minute, Molly—I don't even know the lady! I'm a total stranger to her!"

"That's true," Molly said, "but you're a decent, caring man—Eileen will see that. You'll break the news to her gently, with respect for her dignity."

"I . . . I just can't do it, Molly—I'm headin' out this afternoon and goin' to Helena. I have a train to catch . . ."

Molly stood up. Her shoulders slumped. "You're right," she said. "Forget that I asked. Sure and I had no right at all. Go on now, love—catch your train."

Kissing me on the cheek, Molly turned to walk away. I stuck to my guns until she had nearly crossed the lobby.

"Wait, Molly," I said. "I . . . I suppose I can take a later train. There's no real hurry . . ."

Molly flew into my arms with a happy squeal. This time she kissed me full on the mouth.

"Oh, *thank* you, Merlin," she said. "You're a true friend, and a grand man for certain!"

As Molly strode through the big double doors to the street, I couldn't help but compare our moods. Now *she* was happy and *I* was miserable.

O'Leary's Boarding House turned out to be a Queen Anne–style dwelling over on West Park

Street. Equipped with a gabled roof, a turret, and a wraparound porch, the house was painted in five different colors and sported a sign that advertised ROOM AND BOARD FOR LADIES AND GENTLEMEN.

When first I reached the corner on which it stood I just ambled around in circles for awhile, like a dog looking for a place to lie down. When I finally convinced myself the house wasn't going to do me harm and that I was truly stuck with my promise to Molly, I walked up the front steps and gave the doorbell a twist.

A moment later, the door opened and a silver-haired woman maybe five feet tall looked up at me. "Yes?" she said.

I doffed my hat and smiled. "Afternoon, Ma'am," I said. "Is Miss Eileen O'Grady at home?"

"She is that," said the woman. "And who might you be?"

"My name's Fanshaw, Ma'am. Merlin Fanshaw. I'm a friend of Scrapper and Molly O'Dhoul."

The silver-haired lady squinted against the afternoon sunlight. Behind her, in the shadows of the vestibule, I saw movement. Another woman, this one wearing a dark suit and veil, said, "Let the gentleman in, Mary. I'll speak to him."

The woman at the door looked me over as if to say she still had her doubts, but she opened the door wide and stepped aside. I ducked my head and walked in.

"I'm Eileen O'Grady," the veiled woman said. "You said you're a friend of the O'Dhouls?"

"Yes," I said. "Molly asked me to come and talk with you. Is there someplace . . ."

"Surely. We can use the parlor."

Eileen led me through the entrance hall to the parlor and took a seat with her back to the window. She gestured at a nearby chair and I sat down facing her. With the window at her back and the dark veil covering her hair and face, I couldn't see her features clearly. I remember thinking: *If this is the beautiful woman Scrapper described, why is she hiding her face?*

I went straight to the point. "Miss O'Grady," I said, "I know you and Scrapper have waited a long time to be together. That's why what I have to tell you is more difficult than I can say."

I paused and took a deep breath. "Scrapper wrote you a letter a while back asking you not to come here, but I don't reckon you saw it. By the time his letter reached Ireland you were already on your way here. I'm just as sorry as I can be, but the fact is Scrapper has changed his mind about marrying you."

I don't know what I expected. I thought she might break down and bawl, throw a hissy fit, or maybe just die of a broken heart. I was braced for most anything, but in my experience a woman seldom does what a man expects.

Eileen paused for a moment. Then she said, "I'm sorry if telling me has caused you distress, Mr. Fanshaw. The truth is I've *also* changed my mind. *I* no longer desire to marry *Scrapper.*"

She sat perfectly straight on the edge of her chair with her hands together in her lap. "It's strange," she said. "I have loved Scrapper O'Dhoul nearly all of my life. I can't even imagine loving another man. But I suppose I'd rather have my memories and dreams of Scrapper than to marry him."

"Excuse me, Miss," I said, "but I don't understand."

"I'm sure you don't, for how could you? Perhaps it's just that for both Scrapper and me the time for marriage has passed."

I strained to read her expression, but with the sunlight behind her and the veil hiding her face I could not. Again, I wondered why the woman Scrapper had kept in his heart for so long would hide her face behind a veil. And then, somewhere on the edges of my consciousness, awareness began to dawn.

"Miss O'Grady," I said, "When Scrapper speaks of you he always mentions your beauty. Could it be you no longer believe you're the beautiful girl he remembers?"

I heard a sharp intake of breath. Eileen's hands clenched, and then trembled as they reached up to grasp the edges of her veil. "You're a very perceptive young man," she said. "My beauty, as you call it, has changed indeed."

Raising the veil, Eileen turned her face to the light. It was my turn to catch my breath. A masklike scar nearly covered the left side of her face. The scar was bright pink in color and gave her mouth a twisted appearance. "A kerosene stove exploded," she said. "My face happened to be in the way."

Truth burst above the horizon of my mind and scattered gloom and darkness.

"Miss O'Grady," I said. "As hard as it might be for you to believe, this may yet prove to be the best day of your life."

When Molly opened her front door and saw Eileen O'Grady standing at my side she nearly fainted. She stared blankly, the color draining from her face, as if she couldn't believe her eyes. "Molly," I said, "You remember Eileen, don't you?"

Bewildered, Molly glanced from Eileen to me and back again. "I . . . What . . ." she stammered. "That is, *Fáilte* . . . welcome, Eileen!"

Molly didn't wait for an explanation, but greeted her guest with an openhearted embrace. *"Céad mile fáilte romhat,"* she said in the Irish, "a hundred *thousand* welcomes!"

Beyond the women, I saw Scrapper standing in the kitchen. His face was turned toward the

commotion, confusion stamped on his face. "Who
. . . who is that, Molly?" he asked. "Who's there?"

"It's Eileen," Molly said. "It's your Eileen, all
the way from Cork. Merlin brought her."

"*Merlin* did!" Scrapper said. "Damn ye for a
false friend, Merlin Fanshaw! Did I not make me
wishes *known* to ye? And still ye . . ."

Eileen's voice was soft. "Have you nothing to
say to me, Scrapper O'Dhoul? Nothing, after all
this time?"

"Eileen?" Scrapper said. "Is that really
yourself? I told Molly I didn't want to see ye . . ."

Eileen took a step toward Scrapper. "Sure and
that isn't the first lie you ever told. You love me
still."

"I'll not deny it," Scrapper said, "but it changes
nothing. We cannot marry. We will not."

"And why is that? Because of your eyes?"

"So . . . That traitor Merlin told you that, too.
All right, yes—because of me eyes. I'll not
saddle ye with me blindness, Eileen. I'll not have
ye as me nurse and caretaker. That's not what we
planned."

"Life changes everyone's plans," Eileen said.
"You were a strong young man back then, with the
eyes of an eagle. And I was a beautiful girl, or so
you said."

Scrapper and Eileen stood face to face, an arm's
length apart, but neither made a move to touch the
other. Scrapper's voice sounded strained as he

said, "Aye, ye were. I gloried in your beauty, and I never tired of lookin' at you. Now I can see your beauty no longer. Yet 'tis still there. I feel it— ye've not changed."

Eileen reached out and took Scrapper's calloused hand in hers. "Ah, but I have," she said. "Touch me. Touch me now."

I caught my breath. As she did at the boarding house, Eileen drew aside her veil. She was weeping now, guiding Scrapper's hand. Hesitantly, his fingers touched her scarred face, and for a moment the world seemed to stop turning.

Then they were in each other's arms and Scrapper was kissing her cheeks, her eyes, her mouth. "I will see ye again, me darlin' girl," he said. "I'll see ye every day with the eyes of me heart."

Caught up in a world of their own, Scrapper and Eileen sat together on the parlor divan, sharing thoughts and feelings too long unspoken. Molly looked on, basking in the warmth of their reunion.

I was happy for them, too. Scrapper was a good friend, and he had a hard row to hoe. I was glad to see some happiness come into his life. But as I stood there I began to feel like some kind of Peeping Tom, as if I shouldn't be watching a moment so personal and so private. Quietly, I stepped back into the entry area, opened the door, and slipped out into the early evening.

Molly's soft voice called me back. "Leavin' so soon?" she asked.

I turned. Molly stood outside on her porch, watching me. Quickly, she came down the steps and into my arms. Softly, she said, "You're somethin' of a wonder, Merlin Fanshaw."

The admiration I heard in her voice made me feel awkward. I grinned, trying to lighten the moment. "And you," I said, "are full of blarney, Molly O'Dhoul."

"Blarney, is it? You brought us the truth about Digby's death, and you saved his troubled spirit from wanderin' lost and lonesome over the earth. You heed to bring Scrapper and Eileen together in spite of their fear and their foolish pride. Because you did those things you've set me free as well. We owe you much."

"Friends don't talk of owing," I said. "I was in the right place at the right time, that's all." Pushing Molly back, I looked into her eyes. "There is one thing more," I said. "I don't rightly know how to bring it up, but reckon I have to.

"I value the hours we've spent together—our buggy ride, our picnic at Elk Park, the evenings with you and Scrapper here at your house. But . . . well, I guess what I'm tryin' to say is my feeling for you is one of friendship. I hope I didn't lead you to think it somethin' more."

Molly gave me a quizzical look. Then her smile widened and she laughed aloud. "Lord love you, Merlin," she said, "you've not led me anywhere! I have a sweetheart of my own, young Tommy Fitzgerald!

"Tommy works for Mr. Joseph Chauvin at Northwestern Furniture over on Broadway—he's just been promoted to assistant manager! When I said you've set me free I meant now that Scrapper and Eileen are together *I'll* be free to marry *Tommy!* See what a wonder you are?"

The train to Helena was already moving when Fat Jack dropped me off at the station. With my valise in hand I made a run for it, darting and dodging past the people walking on the platform. As the train began to pick up speed I caught the handrail of a passenger car and swung aboard. It was then I noticed a man running alongside the train carrying a package wrapped in paper. Looking directly at me, he called out, "Hey, Fanshaw! For you!"

The man looked to be a copper miner, one of the hard-rock boys. He wore a cloth cap and a ragged wool jacket, and he held the package aloft like a torch. "From the Alice May!" he shouted. "For what you done for Scrapper's brother!"

Coming abreast of the car, he handed the package off to me and dropped away, back into the crowd.

Holding the handrail, I leaned out and called back, "Much obliged!"

In the vestibule of the passenger car I unwrapped the package. There, in my hand, laid the lost revolver from my showdown with Hardesty—my Colt's .44 Peacemaker!

Center Point Publishing
600 Brooks Road ● PO Box 1
Thorndike ME 04986-0001 USA

(207) 568-3717

US & Canada:
1 800 929-9108
www.centerpointlargeprint.com